Playing **CUSTER**

Playing CUSTER

a novel

BY **GERALD DUFF**

TCU
PRESS

Library of Congress Cataloging-in-Publication Data

Duff, Gerald, author.
Playing Custer : a novel / by Gerald Duff.
     pages cm
ISBN 978-0-87565-606-9 (alk. paper)
1. Custer, George A. (George Armstrong), 1839-1876—Fiction. 2. Crazy Horse, approximately
1842-1877--Fiction. 3. Little Bighorn, Battle of the, Mont., 1876—Fiction. 4. Historical
reenactments—
Montana—Little Bighorn Battlefield—Fiction. I. Title.
PS3554.U3177D57 2015
813'.54—dc23
                                    2015000681

TCU Press
TCU Box 298300
Fort Worth, Texas 76129
817.257.7822
www.prs.tcu.edu

To order books: 1.800.826.8911

Cover design by Rebecca A. Allen
Text design by Preston Thomas

Front cover image by Mads Madsen
Back cover image ©User: Belissarius/Wikimedia Commons/CC-BY-SA-3.0

THIS BOOK IS DEDICATED TO THE MEMORY OF MY
FATHER
WILLIE ELLIS DUFF
THE FIRST TO TEACH ME THAT HISTORY IS FICTION

Thou of the tawny flowing hair in battle …
Bearing a bright sword in thy hand,
Desperate and glorious, aye in defeat most desperate, most glorious
…
Leaving behind thee a memory sweet to soldiers,
Thou yieldest up thyself.

"From Far Dakota's Canyons"
("A Death Sonnet for Custer")

WALT WHITMAN

I regard Custer's massacre as a sacrifice of troops, brought on by
Custer himself, that was wholly unnecessary.

ULYSSES S. GRANT

The West does not need to explore its myths much further; it has
already relied on them too long.

WALLACE STEGNER

Waymon Needler
NEAR SHERIDAN, WYOMING

June 17, 2001

W<small>E PULLED INTO THE PARKING LOT OF THE</small> G<small>OLDEN</small> W<small>EST</small> M<small>OTEL</small> on the edge of town just as the shadows were falling in earnest, and I was glad to be doing that, having been driving the Highlander all day. I had gotten used to the fact that the closer each year we got to the site of General Custer's final battle, the less Mirabeau would agree to share some of the driving duties.

The farther west Mirabeau Lamar Sylestine got, the more he worked at turning himself into what he considered to be a real red man. He was a full-blooded Native American all right, but he was an Alabama-Coushatta from East Texas, and that nagged at him the further he got into the Great Plains where the Sioux and Cheyennes had once reigned. I had learned to count on his transfiguration process getting more intense and detailed each year, though I didn't mention my observation to my faithful Indian companion, knowing how upset he'd get with me, how much he'd either want to argue the point or worse than that, how he'd do what my father used to call "sulling up." That meant not saying a word on any topic and never deigning to acknowledge a comment by me or even to look in my direction.

He felt like he had to do that, working to shed all his white-man ways each year as he sank as steadily as he could into the self of Eagle Beak, a

1

Sioux warrior of the Dog Clan of the Hunkpapa. By the time we got in range of the valley of the Little Bighorn, or the Greasy Grass as Mirabeau as Eagle Beak insisted on calling it, he'd hardly even lower himself to use a knife and fork when we stopped somewhere to eat our last twenty-first-century meal, if you could call food served in a diner in roadside Wyoming that. He had dedicated himself to putting away the ways of the white man as he sought to reestablish his red man identity, and it was an exhausting ordeal Mirabeau had to go through in his annual cleansing process. The purification wasn't up to the standards of the Sun Dance yet, but I was growing increasingly afraid that ritual would pop up some year as the next step Mirabeau would undertake to spiritualize himself for the ceremony of reenactment to come.

I shuddered to think of a computer software specialist hanging by rawhide ropes attached to pieces of bone cut into his chest muscles while he chants words he's memorized from the Sioux language. I confess that I know authenticity is at the core of any true enactment of a historical event, but still you've got to draw the line somewhere. We are living in the twenty-first century, after all, hate it though we do at times. We don't wall up cats to scare off witches these days, or dance around a totem tree with ropes hooked into our flesh until we tear loose and pass out bleeding. I certainly don't, at least, but I knew never to bring up the topic to Mirabeau Lamar Sylestine, a.k.a. Eagle Beak, for fear he'd take it as a challenge. He'd be working himself up into that mode if he ever thought of subjecting his body to the Sun Dance.

So as I pulled into the parking lot of the Golden West, the motel we'd finally settled on a couple of years back as being the cleanest one we'd run into yet on our yearly expedition, I decided to say to Mirabeau something like this: "Well, here's our last time to lie down on a real mattress for a week. We better relish it while we can. It'll be hard ground and short rations the next thing we know." So I did that in as innocent a tone as I could muster.

Mirabeau didn't answer, and I hadn't expected him to. If he had, I'd have thought he needed to have his temperature taken, since he certainly wouldn't have been acting normal. Normal to a true enactor of a historical moment is exactly the opposite of what normal is in the untranscended world. What's up is down, and what's down is in the stratosphere as far as the true translated enactor is concerned. So when Mirabeau—Eagle Beak, that is—had no verbal response to me, I knew we were moving into the state of mind needful and most fervently sought by us. Like always, it gave me a warm feeling, and I felt tears sting my eyes at that moment. I didn't let that show, of course. I was transforming into a trooper of the Seventh Cavalry, and as such I had no time for sentimental display, much less blubbering about how I felt.

A soldier under the command of brevet General George Armstrong Custer didn't congratulate himself for being what he was to the point where he'd have to shed tears over it. The tear shedding was left up for Iron Butt himself to do, if he chose to go public with his feelings. (That's what the ordinary enlisted trooper called the commanding officer back in the day, Iron Butt, and that's a part of the tradition we carried on, using the labels of the past and giving them life again, no matter how insulting to the modern sensibility they might now be.) The way I see it, a man who's already proved himself to be bold under pressure, to always ride toward the sound of guns, and to live with his nerves stretched to the breaking point, he can cry in public all he wants to. Who's going to have sand enough to take note of that behavior or judge it? Let Custer be Custer. As if he could be anything else. He never reenacted a thing. He was what he was, and we mere mortals of today are the ones who yearn to escape our ordinary selves.

No, the trooper who has to keep up a bold front and not ever let anybody see him express any emotion other than the drive to kill the enemies of his country, he's the one that can't afford to show what he's really feeling. General Custer and some of his lieutenants, say Myles Keogh and his like, he can reveal depths of character. The average man can't chance that, thin as he is in himself. Who can trust himself to meet any demand these days? Today we have choices. Not in 1876, though.

Like me, for example, back in Annette, Texas, as a teacher of secondary school home economics, I can't ever show my emotional side in public, for fear of being called worse things than what I am ordinarily. I've got to act horny as a billy goat every minute I'm on public display, for example. If I don't, people are eager to feel their suspicions confirmed. I can imagine what my colleague Truman Greenglade would say if he saw a tear glisten in my eye. He'd go way beyond calling me light in my loafers.

There's no telling what he'd accuse me of. One thing I do know, though, he could never keep up with me on the plains of western Montana as I ride into battle, a trooper of the Seventh Cavalry. And I could call my commanding officer Iron Butt just like his men did back in that golden time when the guidons fluttered in the western breeze and all enemies before us we were trained, ready, and eager to kill. It wasn't an insult, that label of Iron Butt, but a sign of affection and respect. Ha, I say, to any and all mockers. Ha to you.

"Are you ready to get something to eat?" I asked my faithful Indian companion, adding the name Eagle Beak to the question. "Or do you want to rest up a little before we eat our last meal for the next few days here in the twenty-first century?"

"You go on ahead, Major," Eagle Beak said. "I've got enough pemmican made up to let me start my proper diet tonight. I don't have to wait until tomorrow to leave the white man's food alone. I can do it now."

"So could I if I wanted to do," I said, a little snappish because of the implied put-down of my seriousness about the process of devolvement we were entering on. And more than that, Eagle Beak's calling me Major was a conscious attempt to remind me that I had never got higher in rank after six years of reenactment than assuming the character of Major Marcus Reno, the least efficient and valorous officer of the Seventh Cavalry back in the summer of 1876. But the most drunken, beyond question. He excelled in that activity. And I'd got promoted to that character at the last minute to fill in when Dr. Daniel Mayfield had come down with a bug and had to flee to a hospital in Bozeman, leaving Reno's contingent leaderless. There's never anybody sicker than an ailing oral surgeon. He knows what to fear, and he fears it. "But I don't need to congratulate myself by passing up a nice steak dinner before we even get within a hundred miles of the Little Bighorn," I went on to say to Eagle Beak. "I'm resting easy in my mind about that."

"The Greasy Grass," Eagle Beak said. "It's the Greasy Grass, not the Little Bighorn." He was trying to get back at me by making that red man correction, but I could tell by the way he walked over to his bed in room 128 of the Golden West that I had stung him a little by my remark. He'd felt it, so I could relax. Lay off, I said to myself. You're bigger than that. Let the would-be Sioux warrior have the last word this time.

"I'm going to go over to the Golden West dining room and see if I can rustle me up some grub," I said, knowing Eagle Beak wouldn't answer me, but letting him see I was steadily leaving Waymon Needler behind as I eased from my present self into the identity of a true man of the nineteenth century, a trooper who never thought twice and never would about such things as the calorie count and fat content of what he was eating. When he was hungry, he fed, just like his horse did. Just like a natural man with an honest appetite. Eats was eats to him. Grub was grub. "Don't worry. I won't wake you up when I come back to the room."

"I don't need to be told that," Eagle Beak said. "My sleep is always healthy and deep, but the slightest sound will bring me to full consciousness, battle ready and fully alert on a hair trigger."

"That's a real clunker of a word to use," I said as I opened the motel room door, "and you a warrior of the Dog Clan of the Hunkpapa."

"What?" Eagle Beak said, as I knew he would. "What word?"

"Consciousness," I said without looking back at my faithful Indian companion. "That's the one that doesn't ring historically true."

"I used it so you could approximate where I was in my mind," he said. "You wouldn't understand the Sioux word for that state. I had to dumb it way down to get a little smidgen of the meaning across."

"Smidgen," I said and left to get my supper. "Smidgen. Another dud. See you later, Red Man."

Chew on that, I thought to myself as I headed across the parking lot toward the eating area of the Golden West Motel. See can you worry it down. That phrasing was a true signal that I was sinking deeper and deeper into my Seventh Cavalry trooperhood as I marched, feeling the hide and bone and mind of Waymon Needler, Master of Arts in Home Economics from Stephen F. Austin State University, slipping steadily away from me. Thinking that, I started whistling *Garry Owen* as I proceeded toward my appointment with a big slab of beefsteak, matching my every step in the parking lot to the rhythm of that theme song of the Seventh Cavalry, brevet General George Armstrong Custer's personal selection, an anthem particular to the 1876 roster of that proud name.

Patrick Bruce
PRIVATE, COMPANY F, SEVENTH CAVALRY

JUNE 24, 1876

A NYBODY IN THIS COUNTRY WHEN HE FIGURES OUT YOU'RE FROM Cork or Dublin or anywhere else in Ireland, well he figures he knows just how to judge you and treat you and size you up one way and another, since you're Irish, you understand. It's like wearing a sign.

See, you like to get drunk, and you like to fight, and you're piss-ignorant about most things, and you don't ever look ahead further than the next meal you're likely to run into or the next drink of the water of life you're liable to encounter. You're an Irishman, understand, and you're flannel-mouthed, and you care naught for most things. And the things you do care about, you do love beyond what a sane man would allow himself to feel. You're always too much or too little. Never just the right amount.

But all that's easy to live with, I've discovered from the experience of looking about me and listening to others talk about a way of living while actually living a life different from the one they announce. They like to brag and talk things up here in this big land they wander back and forth across, and there's nothing about bragging and boasting and patting himself on the back that an Irishman needs to seek instruction in. That's bred into him. It's sweet honey to him.

Getting to the Montana territory with the Seventh Cavalry is where the story begins for me, I reckon, more than getting from Cork to America would be. Lots of Irishmen have made that voyage and there's nothing new to tell about that trip. Water everywhere you look and most of it moving up and down, and a lot of time spent below decks in the dark sweating and listening to other folks moaning. Like I said, not a lot to tell about that would interest a soul.

The real tale begins after I'd landed in that most southern of all cities in America, the one close to where the big river empties out into the Gulf of Mexico. How I left New Orleans and where I headed then is what led to me riding on a gray horse in Company F of the Seventh Cavalry in the Montana territory looking for Indians along with General George Armstrong Custer in the year of our Lord 1876 and of the United States of America its hundredth birthday.

I worked my way north up the great river as quick as I could, leaving New Orleans in the dark of night and wishing it had been darker. Dark enough it proved to be, though, and I ended up in a few days in Memphis, Tennessee. It was my luck they was in the middle of yellow fever kill-off among citizens rich and poor, white and black, big and little. In no time at all some soldiers there arrested me and every other able-bodied man and put us to work digging holes, taking dead folks out of houses and ditches and wherever else they'd fallen down to meet their Maker, and then putting them in the holes and covering them up. I did that until the two fellows guarding me and some other lads, black and white, made the mistake of not looking close late in the day, and we acted like sane men will.

Well, of course, being left unguarded, me and Willie and Ferguson threw down our shovels and walked off, and I didn't watch to see what the darkies did, but I expect they acted like ordinary men, though they didn't talk like men do, and walked off. They may have turned south and got on along down toward Beale Street where that lot of dark-skinned folks wanted always to go, but I myself headed for the river down at the bottom of the bluff on which all those buildings of Memphis was standing empty in the yellow fever panic, and Willie and Ferguson came along, just humping it down to where the boats and rafts would be lined up for dealings with business in that city. That would have been true ordinarily, but with all them people dying by the wagonload each and every day in the city, all we saw as we drew near the wharves was only three vessels with just two of them looking seaworthy, that is to say with no visible holes to let the river inside the boat. The other one had the hole in its side open to the world, and it hadn't gone anywhere in a good long while and likely never would again.

"I'm heading upriver to another Catholic city I've heard tell of, boys," I said to anyone who wanted to hear. "Like New Orleans it is. It's called St. Louis, and with that kind of name it must be blessed."

With that, I proceeded to the gangplank of the larger of the steamboats resting at the foot of Poplar Avenue in Memphis, knocked mud off my boots as best I could, and called out to a fellow doing something to a coil of rope near the bow of the boat, a vessel named the *Tennessee Belle*, according to the letters painted a time ago on a plank at the bow. I say a long time ago, since what I was reading was chipped and faded, and by that I knew the crew had to be shorthanded. And I would have bet all I had at the time, which was nothing but my boots and the clothes I stood in, that the *Tennessee Belle* was short a fireman or two.

The worst job on the below-deck crew is that one, the fireman's duty. Hot, backbreaking, short of air to breathe, and the work post of the men most liable to be blown to Hell by a boiler exploding. And if you worked long at that job, you'd finally see a boiler or two jump up in the air and leave the ship unannounced at the most inconvenient time, taking everything with them. They have a habit of that. That's the job they gave me, and off we went north up the Mississippi River.

Here's how it was when the *Tennessee Belle* docked in St. Louis, and I was able to step off board and come into a new city, a thing that always got me to feeling fired up. The trip up from Tennessee had been an easy one. All the needful stacks of cut wood had been located where they were supposed to be when we'd stopped to pick them up, not much of the fuel stolen yet, and the rain had let off on us. The two darky fellows that worked with me to keep the boiler fired didn't have much to say shoveling alongside, and they did their jobs, and one of them even gave me an extra shirt he wasn't using, seeing as he did that I had nothing to wear other than what I had on when I shook the dust of Memphis, the Fever City, from my heels.

"A blessing on you in Heaven," I told him when he did that. "I had to leave where I was in Memphis without looking around to see if I'd forgot and left something I'd be wanting."

"That'll happen to a man in Memphis," the one named Catullus said. "More times than not. Almost every time, a man will leave Memphis just the way he come into town. Moving fast and looking around to see if it's anybody noticing him."

"The difference between a man looking around Memphis when he first get there and the time when he leaving," said Tommy, the other darky working that furnace down below decks, "is he wanting folks to notice him good when he come in, and he ain't wanting nobody to see him when he leaving out."

"And double damn them," Catullus said. "When a man come into town, ain't hardly nobody take a look at him. Now when he leave, it's always somebody wanting to see him real bad. They got their eyes peeled for him for sure."

⊠

I spent most of my time in St. Louis in a part of the place they called Dogtown, and I did that for more than one reason. First, that's what I was told about by a young lad in the first place I walked into looking for a drink of the water of life. It went like this, the way he told me. If you're looking for the Irish, seek Dogtown and you're sure to run across some folks from the Old Sod.

"That's where they live, most of them," the boy had told me. "The micks. No offense now, you understand, me calling them that. That's what they call themselves."

"I don't hold that against you," I said. "I know you just let that slip out, not thinking. For if I was to call you a wormy little peckerwood, see, that would be just an accidental way of speaking with no harmful intent going along with it. Understand me, lad?"

"Yessir," he said. "Dogtown, that's the place you're likely looking for. I don't mean nothing by that or by nothing else I might say."

"And what do the Irish people do in Dogtown, here in St. Louis?"

He didn't know what to say to that, so he buried his nose in the mug of beer he had sitting on the bar in front of him, afraid to say anything back to me and more afraid not to answer when addressed. I left him alone, though, since some of what I'd said about accidental ways of speaking was probably true, and it wasn't until the times I was feeling stirred up and restless that I'd look for a reason to get my feelings hurt. If I felt that need, I could always do one of the three things that made an Irishman what he was, particularly a Corker such as myself. One was to drink, one was to pick up a shovel and commence to move some dirt or coal or something around with it, and the other was to fight. I chose that day just at sunset in a snuggery on the bank of the Mississippi River in St. Louis, new to the city as I was with five dollars to spend, to do the first of those. I drank. And I found folks to talk to, and I ended up wandering sometime around midnight into Dogtown to take a sniff of what there might be to do for a young fellow eager to succeed in America in that part of this great country.

I ended up in a couple of weeks working for a man named Jimmy Sandlin who'd seen me in a bit of a scuffle in a drinking establishment in Dogtown. I's laid out a fellow who took exception to some words I'd said, and I did it with a good strong right to the side of the head. I don't know how it was I had insulted the man, but I'm glad I did since that bit of smashing around led to me setting up as a fighter in Dogtown with Mr. Sandlin as manager and arranger of who it was I fought. I must confess all this activity involved betting sums of money, along with the drinking and bloodletting.

The bouts I went through weren't all like the first easy ones. Some of them I was damn glad to have behind me, a few I don't remember well, either right after they were over or days and weeks later when I would be asked a question by someone who'd witnessed one and wanted a clarification or a comment about a point of pugilism so displayed, and some I couldn't have commented on at all. That last type came into being because I'd had my head scrambled early on and was fighting on instinct and not coldly reasoned plan through the course of that tussle.

But taken together, all went well there for my six-month career as pugilist in Old St. Louis on the Southside, well enough in fact that after the first three or four bouts I'd played a part in, I was given a name. And here it is, one of the times I was called by a label because of something I'd done, not simply because of the way I looked or how that look fit in someone's expectation of the way an Irishman ought to be regarded. Here was me then. The Dogtown Boyo. That was the name that got slapped on me after I'd put four or five lads flat on their backs with their eyes rolled back in their heads.

"I like the sound of that moniker," Jimmy Sandlin told me the first times I heard it yelled at me. "The Dogtown Boyo, here he comes, yonder he goes, there lies his latest victim on his back as peacefully asleep as if he was napping in his own bed after a hard day's work. The Dogtown Boyo has struck again."

A true boxer is somebody that doesn't expect things to be reasonable and ordinary and civilized. He's like a soldier in that way, meaning a real soldier, not just somebody wearing a uniform and drawing pay for doing that. No, a real boxer is like a soldier who'll think it's sensible behavior for another man he doesn't know and hasn't ever met before to try to kill him. To be willing to stop his own particular personal heart from beating, his brain from working, and to render him just so much dead meat that'll start rotting and stinking as soon as the last breath is drawed by the man who used to live in that carcass.

So, the real soldier will say to that way of thinking, you're surprised? And like the true soldier, the real boxer will go along with that. This fellow in front of me means me harm. Naturally. What's remarkable about that? I mean to lay him down, too. Watch this lick I hit him.

That's the lesson I learned in St. Louis, particularly in the part of the city called Dogtown. And that's part of why I left the city after six months or so, a step or two ahead of some people Jimmy Sandlin had promised a result which I was to produce and didn't. It involved betting, of course, not true boxing and putting the other fellow on his back with his eyes rolled up, but taking a fall not justified by blows delivered. It was making me sick to take such punishment and to lose the good name of the Dogtown Boyo, so one famous night I turned the tables on Jimmy Sandlin and those he promised what he didn't deliver.

When I left that great city on the Mississippi, my fighting career over and me having gone contrary to the deal that Jimmy Sandlin had set up, I departed in great haste under cover of darkness, as the writing fellows say in the stories they make up about misdeeds and mischief.

West I'd go and west I went, up the Missouri toward the Dakota territory where I'd heard and been reading in the St. Louis papers about how an army general, an officer named Custer, had led an expedition into the Black Hills that found gold—and it open to all who'd brave the trip to harvest it. That's where the real money was, and I was sick of making Jimmy Sandlin's days easy for him. I would change bosses, and be my own director of fortune seeking.

No more fighting, I told myself, not for the Boyo. The work's too hard and the wages are too little, and the knots them other boys put on my head hurt too much. Let me go into the wilderness and pick up nuggets of gold from the earth itself. The Indians ain't using it, and I know just how to employ it to benefit me.

There's the life I want and need, and I'll pursue it into the plains and wilderness alongside them who know where to go, how to get there, and how to handle any red Indian who dares to say me no. So up the Missouri I would go and I'd end up living in the open air with gold in my hands and in my pockets, ready for whatever could come next. It's the Missouri River, it's the gold, and it's following where General George Armstrong Custer had set the path for a man bold enough to take it.

And my deciding on that course and following it is what has brought me to where I am today, a private in Company F of the Seventh Cavalry, riding my own horse, a gray, a thing I'd never done before less than two months ago. But I'm here, staying on Wild Rover like I was born to ride a horse in this hot empty country of the Montana Territory, not a speck of gold in my possession despite all that digging that's ruined my hands for good, and I've got me a job which does pay a little, feeds me, and gives me a blanket to throw on the ground to lie upon. Temporary, you understand, but it's better than trying to make it alone out here so far from any street in any town, not even to mention the great cities of New Orleans or St. Louis.

And what's rousing about me being where I've ended up at this time in my life is that all us lads in the Seventh Cavalry are getting to chase red Indians, the Sioux and the Cheyenne and the Arikara and the rest of them tribes, and the way things are looking now, we'll be closing in on a big lot of that heathen bunch tomorrow. Then it'll be the Devil take the hindmost, and I'll be in my first real action as a soldier in the cavalry of this great nation I've come to find myself in. Let the fun begin. The Boyo is here.

Johann Vetter
LIEUTENANT, COMPANY L, SEVENTH CAVALRY

JUNE 24, 1876

THE WHOLE REGIMENT IS LAGGING, SCATTERED FROM FRONT OF column to rear, from scouts to mule train and all in between— each and every company of men, their officers, the commanding officer himself, his three mounts and his seven dogs, any and all parts of this moving mass in this desolate country—all elements considered as part of the whole and the whole itself, all a random scatter as in a body of water drying up for lack of flow. Here is a pool, there is a mudhole, a few gasping fish in the shallows nearing death, and no promise of rain to come. All withers away, and nothing moves with direction and purpose.

What that lack of integrity means to the part of the command for which I am responsible is clear. No matter how dedicated to the regularity of order which I demand that my men be, they are infected by the slackness around them. They loiter, they slouch, they speak out of turn, they maintain no vigilance, and they stumble on with as little self-regard as though they were students leaving a bierstube in Heidelberg at the end of a long night of carouse.

There is a time for departure from strict attention to duties and obligation, I admit. Relaxation must be allowed at periods, lest undue and unnecessary strain builds and swells until control vanishes in a bursting forth of energy. I think of my own past behavior at times. I remember the hours and weeks and months of devotion to books and laboratories and hard study at the University in Heidelberg, the late midnight sessions of poring over preparation for examinations in the classrooms, the eyes of Herr Professors Ernst Stutzen and Larst Beismueller and the others resting upon us students, gauging our worthiness and commitment.

And the releasing of attention afterwards, the examinations met and overcome, approbation won from our professor, *unser dichter,* and our fleeing to the stube down the steep ascent below the promontory on which the university stands, the beer and wine and city girls by the river below, the songs we sang, the stories we told, the challenges we delivered, and over all these brief periods out of the discipline of the classrooms loomed the other testing we endured in the drinking clubs and in the societies of the saber. These tests came from us and were delivered to each other.

My men here in this American military organization, as bold and adventurous as a cavalry regiment can be at times, though not consistently, I see these men noting the scars on my cheeks, and in particular the diagonal mark left through my left eyebrow by a slash from the saber of Hans Weiler, himself son of a baron and the best swordsman in his time of attendance at Heidelberg. They see these marks of testing and endurance and courage, and now and again one will ask me their origin and meaning. I can tell that they wonder and gossip and make up stories about my dueling scars. I value them in a way they never could, these marks of valor and endurance. I have been blooded, and I know the truth of armed combat.

Passing now on my bay mount back toward the rear of my command as I check their posture and deportment on horseback and—most important of all—the look in each set of eyes as we move nearer to the enemy we must face soon, I see Clifford Probst gazing straight ahead as he maintains a proper distance between himself and the man before him.

"Private Probst," I say, "adjust that headwear a bit. It's not properly set."

"Yes, sir," he says, tapping the brim of the straw hat he's wearing. That deviation from uniform I do not approve, those civilian straw hats, but our commander has allowed them, foolish for adornment as he is, and I speak to Probst only as an excuse to recognize him. The headgear is set as well on his head as it can be, given its nature, and only Probst's innate Germanic strain causes him to attend to my comment. I'm not concerned about him and his ridiculous straw hat in particular.

Like all things in this country, questions of where men and manners and morals come from historically are of little interest to Americans, such as Private Probst's national background and origin. When I remarked to Clifford Probst that his surname was one I had met before, he informed me that it was Irish and that his father had told him that. An ignorant old fool of a father he must have been to think that Probst was Irish, and I soon disabused the private of his mistaken notion about his background, he showing little interest in the correction. So I'm not Irish, he undoubtedly thought, but German instead. Who cares about that?

Think what he does about his background and his name, Probst is nevertheless an acceptable soldier of cavalry. His Germanic origin does show itself, no matter how unacknowledged it may be. The red Indians we'll be facing soon will see no difference between troopers such as Clifford Probst of Deutschland heritage and those from Italy and Scotland and Ireland. All my men and all in the Seventh are simply white eyes to the Indians. And my task is not to seek difference but to enforce similarity. The men for whom I am responsible will perform in a soldierly manner as a unit or I shall know the reason why. And I will amend that accordingly. And they will obey and will meet the enemy and destroy him.

"Lieutenant Vetter," Sergeant Davis said, as I turned my mount to trot back to the head of Company L, my small inspection tour completed, "I'd like to speak with you a little, if you've got time."

"After I've spoken to the Captain," I told him, not really needing to wait until after I'd spoken to my superior, but letting Davis know I would set the schedule, not he. He understood that and the reason for it, so when we did ride a little later at the head of Company L, I continued the pattern of command by being the first to speak.

"You said you wanted to make an inquiry, Sergeant," I said. "What would that be?" And then allowing myself a lighter reference, I went on to let him know I had knowledge of his past. "Do you feel about this coming encounter with the Indian Nation as you did before Gettysburg?"

"Well, Lieutenant," Sergeant Henry Harrison Davis, late of the Fifth Alabama of Longstreet's command, said, "I didn't realize you knew I'd worn a different uniform."

"Not only do I know that, I have been told that by the time you ended your career in the Army of Northern Virginia, you had reached the rank of major."

"By the time we stacked arms, it was so few left in General Lee's command that everybody was getting promoted," Davis said and laughed a little. "They had run so short of men to call major and colonel and sir. Every man that could still walk around got bumped up, like it or not. We had more officers than men, the way it seemed."

"I can't believe those who were promoted didn't deserve the recognition," I said. "And the increase in salary."

"Now you're trying to make me laugh. The last money I drew from the government bursar was in September of 1863, and that was in Confederate currency not worth what it cost to print it. Just pictures of Jeff Davis and Alex Stephens you could nail on the wall for decoration."

"But you stayed on to the end, Sergeant Davis," I said. "Salary or not."

"I was younger, and didn't have a lick of sense. I couldn't muster up the will to quit. It was easier to hang on, rather than to let loose."

"I understand not having the sense to attend to personal matters," I said. "I could be back in Deutschland, in Hesse, married to a nice hausfrau, if I'd had a fair share of good sense. But here I am in the Montana Territory helping General Custer look for wild Indians instead."

"I do believe he's going to find some directly, if we keep moving in the direction we're going now. A lot more of them than we ever saw together before in one place, I expect."

"You must have heard about the troopers who went back to retrieve the boxes of provision which'd been lost off one of the mules, I think."

"Yes, I did. From Company M. Indians had already found the boxes and were breaking into them with an ax when the troopers rode up."

"How many hostiles were there, I wonder," I said. "I've heard there were only three or four who ran when they saw the troopers."

"That depends, Lieutenant, on who you ask and when. By night time when we get word to stop the regiment, I predict we'll learn it was in excess of four hundred Indians hacking open those boxes of hardtack."

"Or more," I said and laughed a little to show Sergeant Davis I was agreeable. "And it took only two troopers of the Seventh to chase all the red men off."

"Right, they'll be saying that. And you just asked me if this felt like right before Little Round Top that July afternoon, that day the Fifth Alabama was sent up that pile of rocks to take it one way, come what may."

"Well, does it?" I said. "Were you confident you'd be able to take that objective back?"

"Like every charge I was in, all I was worried about was whether the men would head the direction I'd pointed them. It didn't cross my mind to think about whether we'd do what they told us we were supposed to. So when we dressed ranks and took off up that hill I was glad to see most of us pointing toward the same thing. That's all I was thinking about."

"You don't worry about the troopers in the Seventh Cavalry carrying out orders, do you, Sergeant?" I said. "They won't be facing troops prepared to receive a charge the way it was for you and the Fifth Alabama. The Sioux don't fight as one from what I've been told. A determined phalanx of troops will scatter them like a handful of wheat."

"Yes sir, I have heard that," the former major said, looking off toward the long line of the horizon to the south where a plume of dust was hanging in the air, "I expect you might be right. I hope so."

And then Davis said something which I've been thinking over ever since hearing it. "I hope that bunch of Indians will try to fight like white troops, and not just swarm like a bunch of yellow jackets when you stir up their nest."

"Yellow jackets?" I said. "What do you mean by that?"

"Wasps," Davis said. "Stinging wasps all coming at you in a wad so you can't tell one from another. The kind of swarm I used to see back in Virginia when I was a young boy looking to get into mischief, poking at something I didn't have enough sense to be scared of. They couldn't hurt me, I figured. I can outrun a swarm of wasps if I have to."

"We're all mounted here in the Seventh Cavalry," I said. "And we're trained to fight as a unit. We're stronger together than a mere count of numbers would indicate. We are the fingers of a hand, clenched to make one strong instrument with which to strike. A fist. Wasps would see us and scatter, and so will the Sioux and Cheyennes. And you know why, Major Davis?"

"I'm just a sergeant now, and I reckon you know a lot more about striking than I do, Lieutenant Vetter. Anything I thought I knew about battle before was either wrong or I've forgotten it. So please tell me why you think that way about the course we're headed on."

"The Indians lack the one crucial thing we possess in abundance, Sergeant Davis. That's why. And that characteristic they want is discipline. That's what makes the Seventh Cavalry soldiers. These tribes range independently, and that freedom is what will betray them. Lack of organization is what dooms them. Discipline is what saves and defines us."

"Well, sir," he said, "I hope that's true, and I hope that bunch of independent warriors will prove to be easy to cut right through."

"Mark my word," I said. "You'll see my opinion proved."

As experienced militarily as he was, Davis had been ruined by the defeats he had suffered in that war in the East; the reversals he'd encountered had cost him his confidence as a soldier. Whether he knew it or not, Sergeant Davis had fallen a grievous distance since his time as a major in the Army of Northern Virginia. He feared defeat now, and he gave off an odor of trepidation with every opinion he voiced. Predominant in his thinking was not the true aim of the successful soldier—to seek out his country's enemies and kill them—but the selfish desire to survive and not be wounded. When a soldier's mind is set on maintaining his physical being, he loses that faith in the successful carrying out of the orders under which he operates. As he thinks of saving himself, he loses sight of the proper aim of the true soldier. He fears death, rather than relishing the dealing of it to his enemies.

"The Fifth Alabama fought well in all the engagements it undertook," I said to Sergeant Davis. "From what I've heard and read. Is that not so?"

"Oh, they fought well all right," Sergeant Harrison Davis said. "You have to give them that. Yes, they fought like soldiers are trained to do, and they did that right up to the time when eight out of ten of them lay dead on the field."

"That kind of disaster can't be the fate of mounted cavalry up against the rabble we'll be facing, Sergeant," I said. "Such losses as the Fifth Alabama endured came from artillery, from grape shot and sustained volleys from repeating rifles, not from arrows and clubs and muzzle-loaders."

"Point taken, Lieutenant Vetter," the former officer in the Army of Northern Virginia said, touching his hand to his hat brim in salute, "I appreciate the stand you express. You're probably closer to the truth than I am."

"Wasps may swarm," I said, "but all you must do is bear their first attack and then bat them out of the way."

"Bat them?"

"Bat them," I repeated to the soldier who'd suffered such defeats as to set up a permanent hesitation in his outlook. I could not help but feel a little sympathy for him. "Knock them out of the way, find their nest, and then destroy that. The battle is over. Das Ende."

"I'll keep that thought foremost in my mind, Lieutenant," Davis said, turning his mount to trot off. As I watched him head for his place in the Company L cohort, I felt as though I had done a fairly good job of bolstering his confidence. That duty of an officer is as crucial as that of leading men directly into armed conflict. You inspire soldiers to follow and do their duty not simply by command but by mental encouragement and example. You do not flinch, nor turn away. You face the saber and earn the scars to prove what you've done.

Tomorrow we'll encounter the Sioux and Cheyenne Nations, and we'll show them what a small number of disciplined troops can accomplish against a great mob of savages covered in paint, feathers, and animal skins. It will be a lesson to the Indians, to the troops of the Seventh Cavalry, to Generals Terry and Sherman, and to the country at large. History will bear that out.

Isaiah Dorman
SCOUT AND INTERPRETER, SEVENTH CAVALRY

JUNE 24, 1876

✕

E LIKES TO STAY OUT IN FRONT, ALWAYS, NOT JUST PART OF the time, but whenever it looks like folks might be noticing him up there on that big brown horse he calls Victory. I'm not just talking about when there ain't the possibility of no hostiles anywhere around, now. I don't mean when he's thinking of letting off some steam by riding ahead at a good gallop while the rest of us are going along at a steady gait just to get us to where we're supposed to be at day's end.

Or say he's just feeling restless or feisty, tired of just slogging along at the same pace as the rest of us in the Seventh Cavalry, whether we're a real soldier, all enlisted with our names wrote down and fixed up so we draw our wages every month just as regular as the snow comes to the Montana Territory in the wintertime, or not. It could be somebody like me, just a scout who knows enough of the Sioux way of talking to get by. He'll even want to see somebody like me, a black man that used to be a slave even, look up to watch him helling off on his mount toward a empty prairie. Any audience he's got, he'll play to, because that's all he's got at that time. He'll make it do.

He needs to move, see, and he likes for people to be looking at him picking up speed and getting ahead of everybody else. So he'll put the spur to his mount, and maybe say to one of the officers riding along beside him, "My horse needs a change of pace. See if you can keep up." Or maybe it'll be close enough to the end of day for him to want to pull out that big pistol and bang away at a rabbit or a grouse or an antelope, or if he's lucky, to take a shot at a buffalo bull hauling across the prairie. Then he'll whoop and holler.

"Come on, Tom," he'll yell at that brother of his, a grin on his face big enough to show all them white teeth, looking just as happy as a trooper walking into a tavern with money in his pocket. "I'll get there before you do, no matter how hard you flog that poor old mare to stay with me." Then off he'll go, that yellow hair just a-flying in the wind, his hat either punched down tight on his head or hanging from a rawhide string around his neck so it can flop up and down in the wind. There he goes, while everybody watches him. George Armstrong Custer, brevet general at full gallop, chasing something he's wanting to kill and doing a damn good job of gaining on it, be it quail or pheasant, rabbit or deer, coyote or wolf, buffalo or Indian, woman or man, with Tom whipping his mount and trying to catch up.

While he's running off and getting ahead so far in front you can't even see his dust, the rest of us in the Seventh Cavalry are plodding along headed for where we're supposed to be by nightfall in that big country. He's happy, and we're all looking at him getting littler as he goes, and that part a good many of us is glad to see. The more Iron Butt is out of sight, the more chance we have to let down a little and act like folks and not have to go along looking like we're ready to jump in any direction he shows us without taking a minute to think.

We can draw a breath, without worrying about whether we'll have time to draw another one, or be able to do that after the next possible thing to happen does happen. That's what I'm talking about. Something is always liable to happen when he's at the head of the column, or riding beside it, or in it, or behind looking at how we're dressing our lines, as if that made any difference out in the Montana Territory. This ain't Washington, DC, with a big parade down one of them streets going on. You'd think he'd know that.

But I've heard him say more than once, and that to his staff officers where they're all together making plans about finding Sioux and Cheyennes to kill or just riding along in the middle of the day, something like this. And he's said it lots of times and more times on this campaign than any others I've been on. This expedition is the big one for the general. It's going to make or break Iron Butt. "Gentlemen," he's said, "if you want to ride slow on a good mount in a dress procession up Constitution Avenue in the capital, wearing your best dress uniform and all your decorations on display, you've got first of all to ride like Hell itself on an empty prairie. You must have your reins in your teeth, pistol in hand and blood all over your outfit as you chase and kill the enemy. The nastier you look and the more damage you do in the territories, the more chance you'll get to dress up, meet pretty women, draw good compensation, and ride around New York City in a fine carriage."

"You get to eat well, too," I heard one major say back. "And drink good whisky and fine wine."

"You get to eat whatever you want to," the general said. "There is no limit to the enjoyments earned by the successful warrior. To the victor belong the spoils."

He could sound like the happiest man in creation, the general could, times like these when we was on the move and thinking ourselves ready to catch the red man napping and not knowing what was about to come down on him like the wrath of God. But the things he made happen for the Seventh Cavalry could change as quick as the weather will in the West. Sun will be shining, a little breeze maybe touching you, and then a bolt of lightning will strike out of a clear sky. Boom. Here it's come, and nobody ready for it or have time even to dread it. First thing you knew was that a big noise had happened, and a man was down and down for good. And his clothes was burnt and smoking, and his eyes was wide open more than they'd ever been before. But they wasn't seeing a thing and never would again.

Like what happened just two days out from Fort Lincoln, when the general let loose a bolt from the blue on me. It came out of a thing next to nothing. It was just one word from the Sioux language, one that can mean different things at different times, not the same all the time. English ain't usually like that, or at least the kind of English I learned growing up on the McClain Plantation in Panola County ain't like that. Maybe it could be if it's wrote down in a book now, and I ain't going to argue about that, since I don't know a blessed thing about what's put down in a book. I have held books in my hands, now, and I have even tried to piece out a page or two. Don't get me wrong. I ain't ignorant.

But I never got any good out of it, and I left it alone after the one time I tried it, just in the way a man who's picked up a hot horseshoe in a blacksmith shop will never do that again barehanded. But that's words wrote down, and that wasn't where my strength with ways of talking out loud happens to lay. Saying words out loud and listening to different folks talking about the same thing but doing it with sounds different from the first ones. I could always do that, from the time I was crawling around the cabin floor in the slave quarters. It was easy then back down South, and it was just as easy after I'd walked off the McClain holdings and come west.

By the time I'd run into White Deer Woman of the Oglala and took up with her, it wasn't more than two moons passed that I was speaking her people's language as good as most of them did. And I could still speak English and understand what folks said to me in that tongue, and that's the very thing the United States Cavalry gave me a job to do. I didn't want to go off for long from White Deer Woman at first, but after she started in to foaling every year, it got to where I would rather be riding around with white men in uniforms, eating their rations, drinking their whisky, and telling them in English what an Indian might be saying in the ways the Sioux and Cheyennes and Crows talk. I'd rather do that than sit around the camp full of Indians wondering when and where we was going next and what was left to eat.

It was easy for me to do that, the white man's business, and a lot better than having to hear the Oglalas call me Black White Man and Buffalo Hair and Walking Midnight and whatever else they could come up with. They did always want to remind me I wasn't a real white man and not one of them, no matter how many babies I might have got on my wife, a woman of their people. Being a translator, as the army called it, and guiding the Seventh Cavalry to where things was, as a scout—both them things took little effort and they paid good enough. And best of all, when I was with the Seventh Cavalry, I didn't have to listen to all the bragging about coups taken, scalps lifted, and cowardly acts of the white man which made up most of the subjects the Indians liked to talk about.

So what happened with General Custer getting sideways with me came out of the thing I did best, talking like a Sioux and knowing what they were saying when they talked to me, and being able to put all that together in English good enough for a white man from east of the Mississippi River to understand. Here's what caused the thing to happen which I ain't got over yet, and I don't reckon I will, no matter how I might try. A black man ain't like a white man in that way. From the time he's crawling around on the dirt floor of a cabin, if there happens to be a cabin, to the time he closes his eyes for the last time and they throw him in a hole, your black man has got to be able to be talked to like he ain't nothing but a piece of trash and not no real part of a man compared to the white man. He has to learn to just take that treatment, not fight against it in the open where the man can see you do it, and then later on not let himself worry about not acting the part of a man. It makes for two minds in the same man.

I can just see how General George Custer, old Iron Butt himself, would conduct himself if he'd been treated the way he treated me that time I called a Sioux word wrong and give it a meaning it didn't have in the eyes of somebody raised talking in that tongue. He'd have had to swing his fists at the least, if not pick up a knife or pull trigger on the man who'd just talked to him the way he talked to me.

The word that started it all up was one the Sioux used to tell how long a trip on foot or horseback would last. It would be so many *lagu* long, see, if a Sioux was telling you. But now if a Cheyenne said that same word to you, he'd mean something different altogether, so that would change the meaning. "Isaiah," Iron Butt had said to me, "if we left here in the morning around three o'clock and put in a full day, how much longer would we have before we came up on the branch feeding into the Little Bighorn? Ask this Indian that looks like he's been sucking a lemon for the last hour."

I did that, putting the question to an Indian his bunch called Pine Standing Still, him being Cheyenne. He said something back to me that I got most of, I figured, since who was going to catch me if I didn't. Surely not Pine Standing Still, since he didn't know but one or two words of English. One was whisky and the other one I don't remember. So I told the general what I thought I'd heard, and it come to be the fact that we didn't get to that little branch feeding into the Little Bighorn until about five or six hours after I'd told Iron Butt we would. He had a couple of the Crow scouts come get me where I was sleeping well after midnight, and bring me back to his tent to answer some questions. I could tell by the way the two of them was eying me that something was up.

"Ho, brothers," I said. "What does Yellow Hair want from me in the dark?" I knew neither one of them scouts would answer, even if they wanted to, but I knew another thing, too. If they wouldn't even act like I'd said a word to them, that would tell me all I needed to know. If you'd dug your own hole, you'd have to crawl in it by yourself, they'd be saying without a word. They wasn't about to play a part in what was liable to be coming next. A Crow will watch out for himself first every time the chance to do that comes up. That's why so many of the white man's army used them as scouts. Crows will look ahead to what's coming, no matter how bad the news about it may be. If a storm's showed it's coming, the Crow will be the first to start looking for a cave to crawl into. If a fight's brewing, the Crow will be either ready to hit the first lick or run before the first lick gets hit. And that's what the white man was bringing most of the time, bad weather and hard licks and all that goes with it.

So when I asked the Crow scouts about why Yellow Hair wanted me to come see him, one of them said to the other, "I hear from far off something I've heard before."

"What is that, White Man Runs Him? Buffalo? I think I hear it, too."

"No, it's not the buffalo," the other one said. "It's not like thunder, the thing I hear. It's like reeds rattling when the wind blows."

"You mean when it's not rained for a long time? When the reed is dry and the pods sound like beans shaking in a gourd?"

"Yes," White Man Runs Him said, sounding satisfied. "That's the sound I mean. You said it right."

When I heard that, how interested both of them was in some rattling noise that nobody else could hear, I knew all I needed to understand why Iron Butt was wanting me at his tent. He didn't like something I'd done or not done, and he was about to let me know just what it was that had got his blood up. "When you get that sound figured out," I said to the Crow scouts, "be sure to remember just what it was you was hearing. I would like to know what you decide. That's a big thing to worry about." Neither one of them, White Man Runs Him or Too Many Arrows, showed any sign I'd said a word. From looking at them, you couldn't have told that I was even anywhere around. That was the worst thing, feeling like they wasn't even seeing me.

And that was just how I felt as I started walking toward the tent where General Custer was waiting on me to ease his mind about something. I was feeling like I wasn't even there, like a wind was blowing through me and not slowing down a hair as it pushed me to get out of the way. I couldn't even see straight as I headed toward where I didn't want to go, so much so that I put one hand up to cover one eye and let the other look for where I had to step, not trusting both to agree.

Don't let me see too much too quick, I said inside. Don't let it come all at once like a herd of buffalo topping a hill. Let it be gradual. Let it warn me.

There was a light in the general's tent, like there generally was out in the field, since he was always writing something down or reading what somebody else had wrote down or rubbing grease into the hide of something he'd killed and was fixing to stuff so it would look like it was still alive. A beaver, maybe, or a bobcat or a fox or some bird he hadn't seen before. The light from the oil lantern was stronger than it would have been if it was coming from a candle, and it made a big shadow of the general on the tent where he was, copying every move he was making at his table no matter how little. He'd had his hair cut short a couple of days before, instead of keeping it long, which made the shadow of his head look like it was just his skull outlined there without no flesh on it. It looked to me like I could see the bones of his head beneath the skin and hair covering them. What was usually covered about the general was showing itself. Seeing that, it came to me to say Oh, Lord, Iron Butt is just waiting to get at me from the inside out.

I tried to make a noise to let him know I had come, and I did that by hitting my knuckles on the wood stake holding up the canvas of the tent, but he didn't show no sign of hearing that. So I cleared my throat and said, "General Custer, Sir, I just heard you wanted to talk to me."

"Get in here, Dorman," he said without looking up from the folding table. "I'll tend to you directly, translator."

"Yes sir," I said, sticking my head in but not stepping inside yet because if I did I'd be close enough to Iron Butt to almost be touching where he was sitting writing on something. Even then, it felt tight to me where I was, and I started drawing short breaths not wanting to learn what General George A. Custer might smell like at close quarters. I'd never thought of that before, and I wondered why I was worrying now about not wanting to suck in air that might have already touched the commanding officer of the Seventh Cavalry. I couldn't figure out the reason for my notion, but it gave me something to think about while I waited for him to take full notice. And that was a little comfort and rest to my mind. It didn't last long, though.

"People've told me, and you told me yourself that you could accurately translate from not only the language of the Sioux and the Cheyennes but the dialect spoken by the Crows," he said, straightening up and turning them blue eyes on me. "Isn't that true, Dorman? Isn't that what you claimed the first time I let you talk to me?"

His eyes was blue, like I said, but they didn't look lighter than brown eyes would have done that time of night. You could tell they was blue, and usually blue eyes will look kind of empty like there's not as much color in them as would be in brown or black. Custer's eyes didn't look empty then, though, there in the tent around midnight close onto where Sitting Bull and Crazy Horse and the rest of them chiefs was camped with their people. No, Custer's blue eyes looked plumb filled up all the way to the bottom.

Stop looking at them, I told myself. Don't let them eyes spook you. He can't tell what's inside your head, no matter how much them eyes with no bottom to them says he can. Look at the tip of that sharp nose of his, and think about how different a white man's muzzle looks from yours and what that might mean. Old Granny said the white man's nose is made sharp so he can easy poke it into a colored man's business and see which way he might try to jump next. That's the hawk in him. Think about what Granny said. A black man's nose is like the turtle's. Broad, but strong, and able to take a hard lick and still let air get through to where it has to go.

"Are you listening to me, Dorman?" the general said. "Did you hear what I just said? Are you paying attention to your commanding officer, Scout?"

"Yes sir," I said. "I was just waiting until you finished before I said anything back. I didn't want to break into what you was saying before you got through saying it. That's why I ain't been talking."

"I believe you might be trying to play me for a fool, Dorman. And I think you might believe you can get away with not doing your job. I think you might consider yourself to be a civilian working for the Seventh Cavalry on a contract basis. I'm beginning to think you believe you're not a soldier. You might believe you're not subject to military discipline."

When General Custer was saying that, he was slowing down a little with every word he said, so that the last thing he said about military discipline seemed to take two minutes getting out of his mouth. I knew what that meant, that slowing down that General George A. Custer lapsed into when he was talking to somebody who'd come up short, somebody that wasn't paying close enough attention to what carrying out orders meant. Them last two words he said to me there in that tent and the way he said the words made them come out like two heavy taps on a drum. Real slow and final sounding. Bump and then bump again.

"Oh, General Custer, no sir," I said, my legs giving out as I was looking in the direction of them blue eyes so deep you couldn't see no bottom to them. "I don't think nothing like that. I know where I am and what that means. I ain't just a civilian now. I understand what it means to be on a military campaign. I know I got my duty to do what I'm told to do." My legs kept losing hold of where they ought to been, and by the time I'd finished saying them words in English to let the general know I wasn't thinking a single wrong thing about my place, I had sunk all the way to my knees. Where was they going to stop, my legs? Am I going to fall on my face in front of the general with every muscle as slack as a loose rope? Am I going to end up with my face shoved into the dirt here in the middle of Indian country?

"I know who I be working for, and I'm glad to be right where I am with the Seventh Cavalry. I'm sorry I misheard that Indian word and said wrong about it. I wouldn't have said something I didn't think was right. It was only just a mistake."

"A mistake," General Custer said. "A mistake, you say. All that's happened to delay me is a mistake, and our getting here five hours after I planned to arrive in range of the Sioux and Cheyenne camps should be of no consequence. That's what you're saying, Isaiah Dorman. Is that right?"

"Oh, no sir, General Custer, sir. The last thing I want is to provide you wrong words. I'm sorry for what I did. It grieves me to my heart."

"You know what I'm inclined to think, Dorman," the general said, looking down at me like I was stinking buffalo dung that had ruined the shine of his high boots. "I'll tell you my thoughts. I believe you might have lived with the Oglala so long with your squaw woman that you're suffering from divided loyalties. I think you are not committed to advancing the success of my campaign against the tribes aligned against me. I suspect you've deliberately delayed my troops. You've done that to give that bunch of savages an opportunity to escape from the trap I've been laying."

"No, sir, General Custer, no, sir," I said. "When I left the Oglala, I left for good. I ain't no kind of Indian. I never was. I just lived with them for a little while. Found myself hooked up with a squaw, and got sorry for it. I'm the same as a white man now. After leaving them Sioux, I ain't never looked back."

"You're not trying to claim you're a white man, are you?" General Custer said, the way he was talking letting me know he wasn't about to laugh at what I'd said, but that at least he found what I'd said to be wrong, to be crazy, to be so strange as to be funny. It was like a joke that didn't work, but it was something worth poking at.

"Not on the outside," I said, feeling the muscles of my legs starting to tremble as I was kneeling there in the dirt, "no, sir. I ain't claiming that color. But on the inside I'm just as white as any trooper in the Seventh. I'm white inside, General Custer, and that's what I'm proud to be."

"White men don't grovel when being disciplined," the general said. "They take their punishment like a man, not like a beast."

I knowed that was wrong. It was just something General George A. Custer wanted to believe, not something he'd come to think after seeing it proved out in this world. And I knew what he said was wrong because I'd seen troopers flogged for going to sleep on sentry duty or stealing something to eat when it wasn't time for everybody to draw rations. And when them fellows got caught and then tied to a wagon wheel so they couldn't get away while the strap was put to their backs by the company blacksmith, they didn't bend over and take their whipping with a smile on their faces and tell the smithy to lay it on them.

No sir, they squalled and cried with every lick that was hit, and they didn't sound a damn bit different from the way a yearling child will when it's being whipped for wrongdoing. They begged and cried, and they bled and pissed themselves, and sometimes they passed out. And that was the lucky ones that did that, and the hard part was coming to again and having to get over what had happened.

The other thing I knew about what happened to men who got caught for what the officers called an infraction and was whipped for it like dogs was what you wouldn't expect. A man who'd endured that kind of punishment you would think wouldn't be likely to commit another dereliction, but you'd be wrong. A man who gets punished won't learn not to never do again what had got him in trouble in the first place. No, he will not swear off such behavior forever. It generally turns out he's the one most likely to do it again.

Here's what I have come to learn from being born as a slave in Virginia on a tobacco plantation and sold down into Mississippi and living that life, and then after the war coming out west and throwing in with the Oglala first and then with the Seventh Cavalry next, just trying to make a living and get by. If you ever get known to the white man for being a troublemaker, you might as well have a brand burned on your forehead and it saying "I'm the one did it." When they look around for somebody to blame, they will look to the one who's been found guilty before. He's the safe one to grab up, tie to a wagon wheel, and beat the living hell out of with a wide leather strap. Or if what's gone wrong is bad enough, he's the man to be stood up with his hands tied behind his back and shot dead by folks he used to be one of. But he's not one no more. He's become just a lesson to other folks now. He ain't a man.

That's why I knew I had to let General Custer know I wasn't going to argue with him. If I could make him believe I had faced up to where I'd let down, then I might have a chance of not being labeled as one of them men that was always at fault, white or black, real American or some off-breed Irish or German or something else foreign like so many of them soldiers in the Seventh. If I had to, I was ready to start eating mouthfuls of the dirt at the bottom of that tent belonging to the commanding officer. I'd do that and like it. I would eat it like hard candy.

And it didn't take me no time to start blubbering and crying in front of Iron Butt as he stood over me with them blue eyes with no bottom to them blazing up like a prairie fire. I didn't have to make it up, neither, my crying of real tears that rolled down my face like I was a titty baby. I squalled like I meant it, and I did. I begged that white man who was my commanding officer to believe me and give me another chance not to fail. Let me have a chance to do my duty, I was begging him. But that wasn't the main thing I wanted. What I really was after was not being bent over a wagon wheel, tied to it with ropes and my shirt pulled off, and whipped on my back until the blood run down like water.

It wasn't that I couldn't stand to be hurt. I'd been whipped before, man and child, like every black man is if he lives long enough. Not wanting a whipping was part of it, sure, but the main reason I was crying and squalling and scrabbling around in the dirt didn't come from being afraid to be whipped like I'd been caught stealing sugar from a supply wagon or sneaking tobacco out of somebody's pocket. No, what was in my head as I shook it back and forth until the tears splashed down like a bucket of water come from something different.

Here it was, then. I'd been a slave, and the war got me loose from that way of living. And I'd got to go west of my own choosing. Then I'd lived as a free man with a bunch of Indians who might have took me to be part buffalo and told me so to my face but didn't hold that against me. I'd been judged able to have one of their women as a wife, and they'd never called me a nigger like what had been done every day back East, and that made me know they took me for just nothing but a man. I wasn't a thing else, part buffalo though they judged me. Hell, them Indians love the buffalo. Ain't nothing wrong with being confused with a buffalo.

And that had got good to me, and leaving that life there to be an army scout and a man who could figure out and tell what other folks might mean while talking a different tongue, that put me up in the judgment white men made of me. I might have been a nigger to them officers and men, but they didn't mean when they called me that that I couldn't do the job. I had something they didn't have, and it meant to me I had a piece of the world that belonged to me alone. I didn't want to chance any losing of that. If I would've been whipped like a dog in front of men in the Seventh, I'd have lost what belonged to me, and I knew that. So I was fully satisfied to kneel in the dirt, looking at the boots of General George A. Custer as I cried, and I would have licked them shiny boots if I had to, if that would have let me off without a whipping for all to see.

Turned out I didn't have to do that, after all. What I'd showed that commanding officer about the way I'd felt about my dereliction of duty, as officers will call it, worked to my benefit. My tears was real, and he believed them to be coming from a source he approved of, so when he turned away from looking at me and went back to his field desk, he said only one thing. But it was the sole thing I was looking for, and hearing it I felt myself ready to do all I could to guide Iron Butt to a place where he could kill as many Indians as he wanted to. What he said wasn't much, but it was golden to my ears.

"Isaiah Dorman," he said, not looking at me now, "I expect you to do your duty and guide this regiment to where the Sioux and Cheyenne are located. You're dismissed."

"I will do that, General Custer, sir," I said, scrambling up off my knees. "I promise you to find them savages by morning. And I know you'll make them sorry I did."

Leaving that tent, I could feel the night air cool on me as I headed toward where they had the horses tethered, and every tear was dried for good by the time I got to where my mount was waiting.

Bloody Knife SCOUT

JUNE 24, 1876

✕

*W*HEN IT FIRST COME TO ME TO KNOW IT WAS TRUE DIDN'T HAPPEN when the Seventh Cavalry left Fort Lincoln, me along as the General's head scout. It wasn't when we saw the big boat in the river, all full of packs to tie on the mules, all them people standing on the deck hollering at the horse soldiers and making the kind of noise white men like to hear when they call it singing. They had their bugles and drums to beat on, too, and the other whistles that made different sounds, and the band that Yellow Hair usually had with him was there this time. They was going to go along with the rest of the horse soldiers looking for Sitting Bull and all the other ones with him, chiefs and warriors and old men and women and children.

I had heard all that noise and moving around start up before in them times General Custer and his Seventh had gone out looking for Indians to capture or kill and sometimes both. So I wasn't surprised by all the racket we was making as we got ready to leave the river where the steam boat was and start up our journey toward the Greasy Grass where Sitting Bull and Crazy Horse and all them Sioux and Cheyennes was got together in that valley the white men called the Little Bighorn. There'd be another chief and his bunch there, too, I was thinking as I loped off on my horse ahead of all the soldiers General Custer was getting ready to lead to where they could catch some Indians, if everything went right. That chief was

Gall. He'd be there with the Hunkpapa, the ones I thought at one time I kind of halfway belonged with. Gall would be there.

They showed me I was wrong in thinking that, though, not just the one time, neither, but twice. I knew that, but I was the one counting, and if you're the one counting up whether you're at a place you belong or not, you got the count right. Numbers writ in blood don't wash out, no matter how much water flows over them and how many years they get behind you. They don't get behind you, that's the point I'm making. The years may lag back a little, like a young boy will when he gets tired trying to stay up with the grown men on a buffalo hunt. But he catches up finally if he keeps the ones he's chasing in sight. They get tired, too, and finally he's the one with the strength and heart to stay with them.

So I counted the numbers right, the number of times I tried to be one of the Hunkpapas, my father's people, and I had them fixed on my heart the way you can make a mark on a rock with a piece of steel from a knife. It stays for good, that mark does, and you'll be able to read it as long as you have eyes to see.

Gall would be there, I told myself again. That was another time for me to count, and it would be another chance for me to kill him. And I'd do it for sure and certain this time, and he wouldn't be able to crawl off holding his guts in with his hands like he'd done at the white man's fort on the Missouri River. That was the night I'd put a soldier's bayonet into him six times. An ordinary warrior would have died from the six stabs of that bayonet, but I knew at the time it'd take more killing than that to finish off Gall. That's why, after I'd put the bayonet to work, I swung that shotgun around to the front of my body from where I had it hanging by a string behind my back.

And if I'd been able to put that load of shot into his chest or his head or his throat, Gall would have had to die like a natural man. But that soldier standing there, a white man, knocked the muzzle of the shotgun to the side just as I pulled on the trigger, and the load went into the ground just beside Gall's head where he was laying after I'd put that bayonet into him all them six counts.

"Damn you, Bloody Knife," that soldier said, twisting the gun out of my hand after it'd gone off and missed Gall. "How many times you want to kill this man? How many times do you think a man needs to die?"

"He ain't dead," I told the soldier. His name was Brailow, I remember. Sergeant David Brailow. "Gall ain't dead yet."

"Well, if he ain't dead this minute, he will be the next one, and there ain't no reason to shoot a dying man again. Look at all the blood and guts coming out of him."

"He ain't dead," I told that soldier. "Gall ain't about dead. Just let me shoot him one time, and then we can forget all about him. We can go get something to eat, and maybe drink some coffee and take a smoke. We can sit down and tell stories to each other. You like to hear the way Indians think, don't you? You told me one time you did. I got plenty of stories to tell you."

"That ain't got nothing to do with me letting you shoot this man, this Chief Gall. He's either dead already or about to be, and I want you to come with me to see the officer of the day about what you just did. We got to fix it so nothing gets held against me. And held against you, too, if the officer will believe it."

"The white men ought to give me a medal for trying to kill Gall," I said, letting go of where I'd grabbed at the shotgun the soldier had pulled out of my hand. The heat in my blood was going down by then, and I knew enough talking had happened so that I couldn't finish up the job on Gall. If I did, they'd for sure put me in one of them cabins with no windows and maybe even hang me if they got to talking to each other about how I'd killed Gall of the Hunkpapas. The white men never did like for Indians to be killed by other Indians. They figured that was their business to tend to, I reckon, and if they let an Indian kill another one, especially one who was a chief like Gall, they was afraid that it might stir a bunch of the other ones up. That's the last thing the white men wanted, a bunch of Indians fighting among themselves, getting all worked up, and maybe blaming the soldiers for them killing each other.

"If you'd have let me put that load of shot into Gall, it would've saved all of you a lot of trouble later on when you're going to have to do it yourself. I had him down, bleeding all over himself, and all the time it would have took would have been one more heart beat to finish him off."

"Stop talking that way and come on with me, and let's go see the officer of the day. I promise you we'll come on back after that and you can look at Gall and see how dead he already is from that bayonet you used on him."

"He won't be here," I said to Brailow, "and it won't be because his women took him off dead to get ready to cry about him. No, it won't be that reason. He won't be here because he'll crawl off if we leave him still breathing, and by the time we get back he'll be laying up somewhere healing like a year-old child with a sore toe. Then you'll have it to do all over again, kill Gall, and if you ever get that thing done it won't be until after he's put a bunch more horse soldiers in the ground."

We did that, left Gall bloody on the ground in front of the jail cabin, and the man called the officer of the day listened to most of what we had to say. Then he judged that what I'd done as an Indian policeman to Gall when he'd got to roaring around drunk saying what he was going to do to every white man and woman and child in every fort in the Sioux lands as soon as Sitting Bull and Crazy Horse and the rest of the chiefs decided to let him do it was exactly the right thing for me to do to Gall. Now the officer of the day wasn't too worried, but he finally said, "A few of these hang-around-the-fort warriors will talk big about getting even, but that won't do a thing to bring Gall to life or get the rest of the Sioux able to do a thing about one more dead Indian. Don't worry about them planning ahead for any damn general movement. It's not in their nature to carry through on anything."

I didn't like hearing that kind of talk from a horse soldier, not because it scared me or I believed the way he described the Sioux, but because I could feel something beginning to stir in my head. Where it was located in my skull was far back behind my eyes, so I couldn't see what shape it had yet, but I could hear a mumbling sound, the way you can pick up on people talking a long way off. You know they're telling each other something, but you can't hear them clear enough to understand.

And if you tried to sneak up close enough to hear them better, they'd see you and stop talking. So all you had to help you understand was what you could imagine. And that's always worse than what really is true. Most of the time, that is. I've seen it the other way, too. Something that took place you never could have thought up. You can get surprised out in the Sioux lands.

Here's what was true when me and the horse soldier Brailow got back to where I'd put that bayonet into Gall six times in places where a man ought to die from having that done. Gall was gone. The spot on the ground where he'd laid bleeding with his eyes closed was empty. He wasn't there, and there wasn't any women standing around crying about the man who'd been killed. Why? Here's why. Gall hadn't died, but had crawled off like a snake with its head cut off. He was still moving, and he wasn't thinking just like the snake ain't, but he was carrying a full load of poison with him everywhere he went.

I didn't say a word to the soldier who said that Gall would be dead when we got back to that cabin where they'd had him locked up when he got on the rampage, but I thought one true thing. The next time I saw Gall he would kill me if I didn't kill him first. And I already missed my best chance to beat him to it.

Gall had commenced killing me a long time ago, back when we was both too young to call ourselves men yet. Here's where that long time of Gall working on killing me got started. It was with the Hunkpapas, where I was living with my father and mother back even before much was going on with the white men in the Montana Territory. A few of them was there, but they wasn't pushing much on us yet.

My father wasn't the reason Gall and the rest of that bunch of Hunkpapa Sioux young folks got turned around wrong on me. How could he have been, my father, named Stands Where He's Put? He was as full-blooded as any of the rest of that bunch, a Hunkpapa Sioux, one of the freest men that can be found in any of the Indian Nations. What set my father apart and what led me to never being considered or treated like I was one of the people I had born into, grown up with, hunted with, and looked and smelled like, all that came not from my father but from the woman he'd married.

That was my mother, and she was Arikara, but the Sioux all called her a Ree, and that label was what put me in trouble just soon as I was born. Where my father run into her first, I never asked about. It would have been like asking the sun why it always showed up only in the day-time and never at night. It just did, and it does, and that's something you'd be a fool to worry about. The sun is the sun, and the moon is the moon, and they live different. Same with my mother and the man who'd married her.

He saw her somewhere, living with the Rees as she would have been at that time, born into them as she'd been, and he knew just as soon as he saw her that she was the one he wanted out of the rest of all women. She wasn't Hunkpapa, she wasn't any kind of Sioux, she was a Ree. But he took her and brought her to a Hunkpapa village and they put up their tent, tethered their horses, and started having a bunch of young ones, all of them not pure Sioux and for sure not pure Ree. They was living with the Hunkpapas, after all, not with my mother's people, so how they could have been anything, my brothers and sisters and me, but half this and half that and whole nothing?

That's what set Gall and the rest of them against me, when they first began looking outside themselves, like will happen to a jay showing up in a bunch of crows and trying to fit in with them. The crows notice that, because that bird ain't just like them. The jay couldn't be what he wasn't, that bird, and every crow could see he wasn't one of them, and so they decided let's all go take a peck at him and see how he handles that treatment. Will he notice? Will he fight back? Will he run and hide?

So they came at me, that full-blooded bunch of Hunkpapa Sioux, me the jaybird in that flock of crows, from the time they could first see that I wasn't exactly like them. Young ones don't ever notice what is the same among them, whether it's their color of hide or the way their noses all look pretty much the same or the way they talk and whistle and sing and tell the same stories about ancestors counting coup and killing enemies and bragging about it. No, what they notice is not all the big ways they're alike, the ones easy to see. They notice instead the little ways they're different, and the little ways become the reasons for the way they act toward one another, how they treat somebody not themselves.

My mother was the one that was the first to teach me to talk, so what I sounded like from the start was a young one who could call lots of things more than one name. A rock wasn't just what a rock is named by the Sioux. It's that, yeah, but it's the name the Rees give to it, too. She told me what things was called by the Rees, and my father knew what they happened to be called by the Sioux. I'd look at an ax, say, or a tentpole, and when I did, I could bring up two things to call it.

I learned quick not to call a thing by its Ree name in front of the purebred Hunkpapa Sioux young ones, though, if I didn't want to have an argument about it and maybe a fight or least a tussle. I couldn't stop myself from knowing what I knew, and that made for a little war inside my own head. I didn't want to think that things could be called more than one name, and I sure didn't want to believe that what a thing was named didn't mean much. It wasn't supposed to be a matter of choice what a thing was, but if you could call it two names and both of them be right, what was true about the world you lived in? The sky, the water in the rivers and streams, the food you ate, the people who were your mother and father, the Nation you were part of, the Nations outside the one you lived in, a human being here and one yonder, and the white men everywhere? If all that and more was just whatever you wanted to call it, what that meant to me was that I was all by myself and couldn't depend on anything to stay fixed and not move around on me. Nothing had to be what you thought it was and was told it was. Everything could be just a lie. How could you tell when it was and when it wasn't?

So when the young ones of the Hunkpapa Sioux pointed me out as jaybird rather than crow and when they challenged me to fight them because I must not be truly one of them because of that double way I was made up, it pushed me farther away from everybody outside of me, want to or not. I came to believe not what I'd been told, but what I saw.

Gall was the one all of the rest of them looked up to, and anybody seeing the way he carried himself and how he acted could tell he'd be a chief when he got his growth. He was a little bigger than anybody else, he was always sure that whatever he said and believed was true, and he never was of two minds. When he looked at me, he couldn't tell what he was seeing, so he let the rest of them know that. He led them to act on that, too. So most every day I was trying to stay with that bunch of purebred Hunkpapa Sioux, I ended up having to try to prove what I was. That gets old quick, living like that, and it got harder every morning to get up from where I'd been sleeping, to get me something to eat, and to go outside the tent, and then have to be battling in a little while, again, to show other ones better off than me that I was worth having around.

My mother saw that in me, the way I was living, and in the rest of my brothers and sisters, and finally when I was up a little in age, she left my father for a while and took us to live with her people in the land of the Arikaras, the Rees. And at first I was ready for that move, and it made me think I'd be able now to be more of a match for the ones I was put among, my mother's bunch. There wouldn't be any Gall to lead the rest of the young ones around in a war to show me I didn't belong with the Hunkpapa Sioux.

And that seemed true to me at first, being there with the Rees and my brothers and sisters and my mother, a woman everybody in that place liked and never believed she looked funny and who called her sister and daughter and showed in every way they all thought she'd come back to her true home.

That worked for a while, like I said, and then it didn't any more, and here's the way I learned I was a jaybird among the crows again. It happened to me when one of the Rees about a year or two younger than me, a crippled boy named Pine Tree Bent Over, came up to me when I was playing with a bow I'd made to hunt rabbits and squirrels and whatever birds I could find.

"What you got there, Bloody Knife?" Pine Tree Bent Over said. "Will you hunt now?"

"That's what you do with a bow and the arrows to shoot from it," I said, figuring he was not really wondering about what I was holding there late in a summer day. He knew that and was just making talk. And what I said back to him wouldn't have been of any interest at all to Pine Tree Bent Over, if I'd called the bow what he did. I didn't do that, though, and I didn't even know when I'd said that name for what I had in my hand that I used the Sioux word. That name for bow was so hard fixed in my head that I couldn't have told anybody where that word had just come from.

Pine Tree Bent Over could tell, though, and he looked hard at me and then yelled out without turning his eyes away from my face something that every young Ree in hearing could know from what he'd just said. "You think that's what a bow's called, Bloody Knife?" he said in a loud voice. "It's not. That's what the Sioux call it when they're about to let loose some arrows on a Ree."

Everybody that heard him say that came running as soon as they did, and it wasn't no time until I was in a tussle with a bunch of young Rees about me being a Sioux instead of Arikara. That's the way it was going to be, I knew, as I tried to keep from getting throwed down on the ground and stepped on and kicked at by the boys I wanted to think was my brothers. I did the best I could, but it was too many of them, and I ended up not going hunting with my new bow, but stumbling back to the tent where my mother was, my bow left behind and broke into pieces.

When I was with the Sioux too many of them named me a Ree, and the same held true when I was with my mother's people. Rees called me Sioux. I was not going to be living at home wherever I was, no matter how hard I tried to make myself be what other Indians expected. I made one last try at that, leaving the Rees when I was a full-grown man, and going back to my father's people, the Hunkpapa Sioux, to try to live with them again. It didn't do for me that time, neither.

When I got back there what I was dreading proved to be true. Gall was now bigger, stronger, better spoken, and convinced more than ever that I wasn't one of the people he was meant to lead. So they didn't tussle with me this time, or roll around in the dirt wrestling, or slap me without their fists clenched up. No, it was worse than that, though it hurt less than when it happened the first time. And that's when I found out that the way you feel inside yourself can make you suffer a lot more pain than the body you walk around in. What you're afraid of has got a lot more room for pain than any hurt that can come to your flesh and bones.

So when they threw little clods of dirt at me, called me names, spit on me, touched me with the ends of willow limbs calling those little switches plenty big enough to whip me like I deserved, me being so weak that a grapevine could break my neck, that's what told me I'd made my last try at being one of the Hunkpapa Sioux or even the Arikara. I was nothing pure, not a being truly itself. So I took what I thought was the only way left to me.

I went to work for the white man, for the bluecoats, the horse soldiers, for General George A. Custer, the chief of the Seventh Cavalry. And here's what was the two comforts for me in doing that. First of all, it made no difference to that bunch of white men, soldiers or officers, what kind of Indian I was. I could be Hunkpapa or any kind of Sioux or Cheyenne or Arikara or Crow or any other people, and all I would be to that bunch was just another Indian, no different from any other one from any other Nation. And I had come to the point where that name Indian suited me fine all by itself.

The other comfort, and it was a special one for me, was the chance to kill Gall and every man, woman, and child he thought belonged to him in particular. I got my first go at making that dream come true at Fort Lincoln, but Gall got to crawl off before I could finish the job I'd started with that bayonet and would have settled up with a shotgun if that soldier hadn't stopped me.

But that's not going to be the only chance I'll have to kill Gall, and do it so he knows that I'm the one doing it, me the misfit that doesn't belong nowhere. We'll catch up to him and his bunch tomorrow, and that'll be because I'm the Indian scout that Yellow Hair likes the most, so much he lets me tell him the truth, even when he doesn't like it, a thing he won't allow the Crow scouts to do. And Yellow Hair likes only his truth and nobody else's. He will lie to himself and to every man around him, fixing the world the way he wants it to be whenever he feels the need. But I will use a different truth, which belongs to me only, as my guide. My truth will let me lead the Seventh Cavalry to where its location will put me in killing range, no matter what words from what Nation you use to name the thing I'll do to Gall, chief of the Hunkpapa Sioux. The kind of tongue I speak will not matter.

I will kill Gall, and he will kill me, and at last we'll be truly the same in this land. Why do you think I've put the paint on my face that says I'll be in another world by the time the sun sinks tomorrow? I know what's going to happen on the Greasy Grass, and all I want is for that to be a surprise to Gall.

Sitting Bull
CHIEF OF THE HUNKPAPA SIOUX

June 24, 1876

THE COTTONWOOD POLE WAS TALL, A TREE'S BODY THAT SEEMED to reach almost to where the Old Man lives. The young men hunted for a long time to find this one, and when I asked who had picked it out for the Sun Dance, they told me they all had known it when they saw it. It was the pole waiting for them to cut down with their axes. Long Bear, Little Man Jumps, Gives Away Meat, and Last Badger, all these Hunkpapa warriors had pointed to the tree by lifting their chins toward it as soon as they spotted it on the riverbank. Not one had to speak aloud.

Then they lopped off the branches and dragged it to the center. The women painted it, with blue and green and yellow and red, and they had to use more paint to show the colors of the earth's directions than ever before with any pole for a Sun Dance. When the hole for its home was dug, it was made deep and straight into the world's body, and the string hung within it with a stone fastened as a weight did not move, and it did not quiver as the old men measured it. It pointed straight down then and would forever, letting any man see that the heart of the world lay beneath where the pole pointed as it had been laid out by Abba Mikko when all was first made.

The rawhide straps cut from buffalo hides were tied together by the old men who practiced fastening things of this land together so that they would hold forever. The knots, no matter when the strap might break, were truly solid, soaked in water taken from the Greasy Grass and dried in the sun until hard as bull buffalo horn. It was a good pole for the Sun Dance. So good in itself and in its colors and its foundation and the straps depending on it that every young man begged to be first to dance.

"My father," they called out to me as I sat in the circle made with red and yellow flower petals, the pole at its true center, the sun climbing high so the shadow of the pole fell only at the foot of the tree of color, "my true elder, chief among us, let me be first to dance."

I made no sign of hearing their calls, unless it be misunderstood what I would do as the shadow of the pole began to creep toward the east, the red direction of the world. But I nodded once, allowing myself a show of the pride I felt in hearing the young warriors of the Hunkpapa declare their desire for pain and suffering and understanding in preparation for battle with the men who would drive us from the Black Hills and the wide plains. When the shadow of the pole touched the spot within the circle of flowers at the place I had marked to begin the cutting, I raised my hand to hush the calls of the young men and then I walked to the center of the design and sank to the ground to sit with my back against the painted cottonwood.

Then came my brother with the awl and his best knife, sharpened now so that a hair could be cut by a touch of the blade. His shirt was new and worked with porcupine quills in the shape of the sun and moon. "Are you prepared to accept fifty cuts for each arm, my brother?" he asked me. "Has your mind listened to your heart?"

I nodded, but did not speak, and he sat down beside me, the awl in his left hand and the blade with the edge burning silver in the other. As was proper, he started at the tip of my left shoulder, seizing a pinch of skin with the awl and drawing it out so that the knife would have room to work. A small pain came as he snipped the first part of myself I would give to the Sun Dance, and after that no other sensation reached my heart and my head as my brother worked his way with the awl and blade down the left arm to its wrist, taking what he cut away and placing it in a bowl, counting it piece by piece. When the left was complete, he began the right arm at the wrist and began to work up toward the shoulder, as was proper, and at the first cut I began to sing the song that came to me on that day of heat and blood.

And the song was of battle, not wanted or planned, but coming like the rain when the sky is clear and the sun is shining and no water should fall from the sky. But it does, though the sun shines and no clouds hide what a man may see. The rain does not listen to what men tell it to do or not to do, or when they complain and shake their arrows at it and lift their clubs as though to hit it. It is the rain. It comes when it will. And so the battle comes to the people. Here in the night or here in the morning when the sun comes again to give light for living or at the end of day when shadows creep from the hills and winds rise in the valleys and sweep down upon the people, telling them to seek shelter from the storm that is promised. Then the battle comes when it will, and men make it happen in the world though they are outside it. They are not the battle. When it comes, the battle is them.

The song given me by the cutting came to me new and never known before in my hearing or inside my head where no man may know it but me. But it came, and I sang it, and I did that without knowing it, yet every word came as true and solid as the Sun Dance tree I leaned against. I was the mouth of that song that day, not the maker but the speaker only. And each word of the song was a polished stone with no flaw. And when the song was finished with me, coming three times from my mouth before letting me know it was done and I now had a task to perform, I rose up from my place at the base of the cottonwood of many colors. And I did not feel the wounds of my arms, but I saw their lips and how they spit my blood.

"Here," I said to my brother, standing still within the circle where the Sun Dance would be, the bowl of my flesh new and bloody in his hands, "come to me with your knife and cut the place to fix the bones into my body. It is time to dance."

And he did that, slicing into the muscles of my chest and forcing the bones tied to the rawhide ropes through the openings he had made, and only the first cut made me feel it. And I was glad of that first pain, for without pain nothing comes to any good in this world.

"Dance, Sitting Bull," my kinsman said as he pulled once on each rope tied to the bones fixed in my chest, "be my brother. Be our chief. Tell us what will come and what we must do when it does."

And I danced for two days and nights around the cottonwood tree made into a pole painted with the colors of the earth's directions, and the rawhide ropes were strong and did not break and the bones thrust through the muscles of my chest did not tear loose from the flesh. And

I drank no water and ate no food. All that made time for the dream to come, and as I sang the song Abba Mikko gave me to know without having to learn it, I could feel the dream building inside my chest and my legs and arms, and finally as I sank down on the morning of the third day, the dream was complete in the way a picture made with colored sand is done when the artist feels it come all the way into itself. I knew what I had dreamed and as the muscles of my chest at last gave way and tore loose from the bones my brother had cut into my body, I sank to the ground inside the circle of the sun dance pole, and I left the world for a time and my dream came then and it was given not only shape but a meaning which I knew and could speak. I tell it now.

In the dream, all was light, and I could see what belonged to the vision I beheld. I was in a place in my lodge inside the circle of the Hunkpapa dwellings, and the women and children were there, and I was eating the liver of a buffalo, red with blood and sweet and rich to the taste. And as I ate, I began to hear a sound, a deep beating as of a heart at night when all others around are asleep and leaving only one awake to listen. The sound grew as I harked to it, and it became the hoofbeats of many horses, all coming toward the village where I sat eating the liver of my brother the buffalo. I knew the sound because I had heard it before enough times to know it was not the hoofbeats of the ponies ridden by the people and could not be. No. The sound had steel in it, which struck the stones of the earth and if it had been nighttime sparks of fire would have flared up at each hoof strike and lasted no longer than does the light from a bolt of lightning in a summer storm. But the man in the dark would have seen that fire, quick as it was.

It was white men riding, and the white men were soldiers, and I knew that because the sound was made up of many small parts but all these came together as though not a company of horses were running toward the village of the Hunkpapas but one only and that was a great horse so large its eyes were like moons and its teeth like the stones in the mountains of the Black Hills. The sound came, and the soldiers leaned forward to tell their horses to run faster, and now in my dream the many soldiers were crossing on their mounts into the circle of the Hunkpapa village. And the sound was thunder now.

But something happened in the dream which cannot come when men are awake and watching. As the soldiers dressed in their blue clothes and carrying their big knives and their long guns crossed into the circle of the village they were changed in a way I'd never seen before, and they were no longer riding horses with hooves covered with steel that dug into the earth. Not now. All the soldiers were in the air, falling from their mounts, and the horses were in the air, too, and they were turned upside down, like the ones that had been riding them, and they were falling into the Hunkpapa village with the men that rode them. As the soldiers fell, many had their heads come loose from their bodies and fall to the earth. And the heads had been scalped, and the skulls were white. Blood came from long tears in the blue cloth of their clothes, and these tears came from knives, and arrows were stuck in the bodies of many, and arms were cut off and legs were slashed so that the white bones of the soldiers shone through their bleeding flesh, and smoke from rifles and small guns blossomed around them like clouds. As they fell upside down, they lay still, all these soldiers in blue clothes, and they spoke no words ever again, for they were sightless and dead as they touched the ground.

"The blue soldiers will come to us," I said aloud in my dream, "and the people will win a great victory in the battle." And as I spoke to the ones who listen to a dream, I awoke to see all of the humans awake and standing around me, the ones at the Sun Dance, the Hunkpapas and the Lakotas and the Minneconjus, and there were other warriors there to listen to my dream made by the Sun Dance. All the Sioux nations, and the Cheyennes, as well, and they listened to the message I had been given while dancing for three days about the pole with the bones in my chest and the ropes fastened to the top of the pole to hold me in place for the dream to take me.

"They will come, the soldiers who ride with Yellow Hair, the one some call Son of the Morning Star," I said to them to let them know the vision I had been given. "They will come in tomorrow's light after the sun rises again, and they will fall upside down into our camp, and they will die for having come against us with the long knives and the rifles and their little guns. This I have been granted to know for the truth it is. A great victory will come to the People, and we will thank Abba Mikko for it."

Then the warriors who had watched the others in the Sun Dance and me, Sitting Bull, chief of the Hunkpapas, these warriors gave voice to their satisfaction about the dream I had earned. And they sang and laughed and were glad, and I was glad as well, but inside my mind was deeply set another vision, and this one was not ripe to tell yet. But I knew it would be a sad story to voice when the harvest of truth came, but I told myself not to think of that until this next day had come, the day of soldiers falling into our camp, bleeding and dead as they came to earth, their skulls white and burning where the scalps of men had once been.

Monahsetah
WOMAN OF THE CHEYENNES

WHEN THEY HAD COME UPON THE PEOPLE AT THE WASHITA THAT winter, the blue troopers with Yellow Hair on a big roan horse leading them, it was so early in the frozen day those years ago that none but an old man, whose name I did not know, saw them before they reached the village. He tried to run to tell the Cheyennes what was falling upon them, but one of the blue soldiers spurred his horse and ran the old man down. He was broken and could not rise, though he shouted a little. The soldiers had not been playing their music yet with the big whistles and horns and drums, so all people in the village, save the one old man, were still in their beds of buffalo hide and deerskin and a few blankets traded from the white men at the forts. Some may have been awake by then, not wanting to leave where they lay, but I was not one of those.

What woke me at first I do not remember, and maybe I never knew, but the sound of the rifles and little guns and the music from their whistles and horns and drums all mixed together with the way women were screaming and children crying and men yelling and asking each other what was happening and who was it running horses through the village, all that pulled me from the sleep where I was dreaming. All became real then, not a dream, though it looked like one, the kind of dream that says you cannot move and you are in danger and that suffering will come upon you even before you can cry out. But that dream is one you can leave, and be glad you are not really there where you thought you were, but outside it instead, in the world where you can rise from the coverings of your bed and think of eating the food you are now hungry for or think what will the new day bring.

No, the dream I woke to there in the Cheyenne village our chief Black Kettle had told us would be safe on the Washita River since we had a flag of the white men lifted high on a pole to let all who would see it know we wanted no fight, but only to live through the winter until the warm weather came again, that dream was as bad as any I had wanted to wake from in the past. That dream that came on the Washita to all the Cheyennes of Chief Black Kettle did not end. It went on for a long time, starting then those years ago, and still happening now in my heart and in the minds and hearts of all those who lived through that time and could not escape it. It will not cease.

That dream that happened on the Washita and that has no end had in it many sounds. The gunshots from the rifles of the blue soldiers and from their little guns in their hands. Their big horses running through the village, tearing through the lodges, the sounds of the women screaming and calling the names of children, the children crying and speaking words to answer their mothers that they could not find, the men of the Cheyennes shouting to each other, some running toward the blue soldiers, and some away, and the cries of those hit by the bullets and cut by the long knives of the soldiers who used those, and the noise fire makes when it begins to eat the skins and poles of tipis and lodges, and above and behind and under all these sounds of killing and crying and screaming and cursing was the music that the soldiers with horns and whistles and drums made. It has not stopped, that music. They always play it.

That part of the dream I was living on the Washita did end after a time, a long time which seemed short, and then the Cheyenne warriors and the old men unable to fight and the young boys too small to fight, all these were dead or dying or had run away and hidden under the riverbank and behind the boles of the willows and the brush across the stream, and some of the women and children were dead or dying, too, and these made no cries any longer. They lay on their backs and their sides and their bellies, and all were as different as they had been in life, but all had one thing they did together. They lifted their hands before them with the palms open, and after a time their raised arms were frozen in that way and they could not be straightened to pull them down ever again. They were all alike, and they have stayed that way. Ice does that, and death does that.

Most women were not killed, though, or wounded so they could not stand. And I had hidden during the killing under a buffalo robe in the lodge of my father, Chief Little Rock, and I was one of these who lived, and after the killing was finished and the blue soldiers had no reason left to shoot their guns or swing their great knives against the warriors of the Cheyennes or gallop their horses through the lodges of the People, some of the chiefs of the soldiers began to tell all us women and children, the ones able to walk, to move together in a great crowd which became a circle of us all made on the edge of where the village of Black Kettle's people had stood.

As we stood together, the moaning of the women and their cries and screams and those of the children who had not been separated or lost, and the voices of the blue soldiers and their chiefs telling them what to do next, rose around me like a smoke going up into the sky from a great fire on which wet wood has been tossed, so wet it makes all dark around where it burns. Such smoke hurts the eyes and the mouth, and it works its way inside the bodies of anyone it touches. And they cannot breathe, and they must cough and gag to draw air into themselves or they die.

Think of the smoke, I said to myself inside without speaking to be heard by anyone. Think of it only and how you must find a way to breathe so you may live. Do not think of the blue soldiers with their guns and long blades riding through the village to kill those who live in it. Do not let the music they make with their beating drums enter your ears so that it can be truly heard inside your head. Let it flow over you as does a small wind so meager you can hardly feel it. Make yourself solely the victim of the smoke from the wet wood on a great fire, not of anything else. Not men, not soldiers, not the music they play to kill by.

That thought became precious to me, like water is when you have not drunk it for a long time. Only it will do. Only it will satisfy. It occupies your entire mind and will tolerate nothing but itself to abide. Be only Monahsetah inside you, I told myself. Nothing is in this world but you alone. Nothing can ever again put out its hand to touch you.

It was then I heard the ponies, the horses of the Cheyennes, beginning to cry in the brush enclosure where the men drove them together at night when the time for rest came to all in the village. The ponies were screaming because many of the blue soldiers had been told to gather around the pony enclosure and to shoot every one of them as they milled about in circles, great and small. No one could ride them now as they screamed and died. No warrior will have a mount to help him fight the blue soldiers with all the ponies dead in the snow. Only in the sky now will these ponies carry ghost warriors higher and higher until only the clouds can see them. Think only of them, I said inside my head, only the dead ponies with their dead riders looking to fight the dead enemy in the clouds above.

Then some of the blue soldiers came toward the circle of women and children in the snow, and they were laughing and showing their teeth as they came toward us. Walking before the white men in blue clothes were Crow and Ree warriors, and these the blue soldiers called scouts. I had seen one of them before, a man as old as my father, and he was a Crow named Spotted Dog. Maybe he'll know me from the time he came to my father's lodge, I thought, my heart leaping, and he will remember that one of my father's wives fed him as he talked to my father Little Rock about the white men at the fort where they wanted the Cheyennes to come stay with some Lakota Sioux. Spotted Dog will think back to when he saw me bring him berries to eat along with the buffalo heart he was chewing, and he will help me now as my father listened in silence to him talk. He may remember my father's wife, not my mother but another woman, Holds the Sun, as good to me as my own mother had been until she died, as she gave him food to eat in that lodge.

And he was looking at me, Spotted Dog was, as I stood behind an older woman and her two children in the circle of Cheyennes the blue soldiers had pushed together in a great clump like winter berries in a basket held together since they were the same thing in a bunch, though each was itself, too, alone.

"Ahh," Spotted Dog said, lifting his chin to point at me, "here is one I know. I have marked seeing her before. I do not forget her."

"Spotted Dog," I called out, not as I should have done if I had been in my father's lodge and the Crows had come inside to talk and smoke with the second chief of Black Kettle's people. I spoke his name instantly without thinking whether it was proper to do that, but because I knew him and hoped he would know me and help me leave the circle of crying women and children and be safe in the world again. "I am Monahsetah, daughter of Little Rock. I saw you once in my father's lodge."

"Look at this one," Spotted Dog said, turning to face one of the blue soldiers behind him, a man who must have been a chief by the way his clothes looked with the silver buttons upon his coat. "What do you think of her? What will he say about this one, huh?"

"Did you not hear me, Spotted Dog?" I said, wanting him to talk to me or in my direction, not toward the blue soldier chief just behind him. The chief was not he who had spoken to the Crow. I had. Spotted Dog should answer me, Monahsetah, daughter of Little Rock, a second chief of the Cheyennes. "Do you remember the meal you ate which my father's wife prepared? Do you not still remember the sweet berries I brought you?"

The blue soldier chief said something to Spotted Dog in the white man's language, and Spotted Dog said something back, and then all the soldiers who had heard it laughed, all looking at me with their mouths open and their teeth showing still.

"Little Sister," Spotted Dog said to me in words I could understand, this time looking at me but glancing back at the little blue chief, "any man who sees you does not forget. Your face burns in his head."

The little blue chief spoke words in my direction I could understand then, not in English but in the language of the people. "It will not be only his head that will burn when he sees you, Sweet Black Berry."

All the soldiers there laughed again, some not knowing what was said but laughing anyway, and others looking at me the way the young men of the Cheyennes had always done when I walked alone in the village without my father near, their eyes poking at me.

"She first," the little blue chief said, pointing at me not with his chin but with the fingers of his right hand, the fingers he used to feed himself food and to shoot his rifle and cut flesh with his long knife, and then pointed to other women both near and away from where I stood in the circle left alive after the fighting and burning and killing at the Washita. "That one, her, that one and that one," he said to Spotted Dog, who spoke to each one pointed out, calling one woman after another to come outside the circle and follow him. Most did that quickly, but some refused, looking down at the ground or turning their backs and trying to go in another direction.

Then the crying and screaming got louder again as the other blue soldiers pushed into the crowd of women, pulling at the robes of those that were wanted outside the circle, jerking them around to face outside and forcing them in the direction the blue soldiers chose.

"You, Monahsetah," Spotted Dog said to me, reaching for my hand, "come now with me, and we'll go where you must be seen. Do not hold back. Do not fight me."

I let him take my hand and pull me out of the crowd, and I did that not because I wanted to do what he wanted, but because I was the daughter of a chief of the Cheyennes, and I would not fight with a Crow named Spotted Dog who scouts for the white man. Who sees me next will know who and what I am, I told myself, and that person will not treat the daughter of Little Rock as I'm being handled now. Spotted Dog will see the mistake he made when he laid hands on Monahsetah, and he will be punished by the chief he brings me before. He will have a surprise waiting for him, surely. So I walked beside this Crow who had eaten in my father's lodge, and I did not hang my head, and I did not cry aloud or show tears to him or those white men who watched me go by them, making noises with their mouths and tongues and gestures with their hands.

I will not see them, I told myself. None can make me show I'm afraid.

✷ ✷

Up ahead of where Spotted Dog led me past a place where I could tell there had been hard fighting between the blue soldiers and some men of the Cheyennes stood a tent that had been put up after all the shooting had ended. As I passed the bodies, I tried not to look down at the Cheyenne warriors lying in the snow, its white stained red in big splotches as though after a buffalo hunt, and I wanted to tell myself in words I could believe that they were only resting there, maybe asleep and maybe not. That was foolish, I knew. The men were dead, and to see these warriors was to know that as soon as my eyes let light come into my head.

I knew two of them we passed, and one was my kinsman, the son of my mother's brother, but I did not know him by his face. That was gone, but for one eye, and the blood and bone left was like a mask made for a dance after a good hunt of buffalo. That mask was meant to be happy, its wearer surrounded by drums and singing and much meat to eat. But all was quiet now.

No, I could not tell Runs Faster Than You by his face, but by the shirt he wore which had shells worked into the shape of a bird across its front. Runs Faster Than You had traded for the shells from an Indian who brought them from near the big water in the south, and he was proud of the way his mother had made the shells become a bird on his chest.

After seeing him asleep in the snow, as I told myself he was, I did not look at any other of the Cheyennes now still forever, but kept my eyes fixed on the flag blowing in the breeze above the tent the blue soldiers had put up so soon after the fighting. The flag was not like the one Black Kettle had tied to a pole and put up at the heart of the Cheyenne village on the Washita, the one which was of the country of the white men with stars and red stripes like blood across it. That flag was the one the white chief had said would tell the blue soldiers that the Cheyennes of Black Kettle and of my father Little Rock were friends and would not fight with the soldiers. It would save us, Black Kettle had said. It did not work. Nothing did.

The flag on the top of the tent was pointed, not shaped like a blanket, but more like a knife blade pointing. It is only cloth, I told myself as Spotted Dog led me toward the flap of the tent. It is not a knife, and it cannot cut nor make me bleed. Like all things made by the white men, it means only itself and nothing else.

I have learned what's true about the pointed flag of the blue soldiers. A piece of cloth shaped like a knife blade can cut more deeply and let more blood flow than any blade made of steel. The cut it makes is not in the flesh, but in the heart. And the cut does not heal, like that from a true cold sharp blade of steel, but its wound stays open, and it swells and it bleeds and its odor can be smelled for a long time.

"Stand here, Monahsetah," Spotted Dog said to me when we came near the tent. "If you run, I will catch you and hit your face with my hand. Do not move."

"I will not move," I said. "But I stay because I choose to stay, not because I fear your Crow hand hitting me. You may hit me so hard I bleed, but you will never touch me, you well-named Dog."

"Your mouth is poison," Spotted Dog said. "But the chief you will meet now is poison-proof."

I did not answer this poor excuse for a dog, much less a man, telling myself that I had spoken the last word I would ever offer to Spotted Dog, this Crow who had eaten in my father's lodge and returned that hospitality by leading blue soldiers to wipe out Black Kettle's people on the banks of the Washita. It had been a long time between the meal Spotted Dog had taken in Little Rock's lodge and the killers he had guided to our village. He would see, though, as would the white soldiers, that a daughter of the Cheyennes has a strong memory which will wait as long as need be to repay those who have wounded the People.

"Come inside this tent, Black Berry girl," Spotted Dog was saying as I stood with my eyes fixed on the pointed flag moving in the cold wind, the sound it made causing me to think of the darkness of shed blood against the whiteness of snow. "Yellow Hair will look at you."

Remembering my vow never to speak to Spotted Dog, the scout, again in this world, I did not correct his calling me by a name not mine but one he had made up to cause laughter in the blue soldiers. When I bent over to step inside the tent, I stayed as far from the Crow as I could, looking down to avoid touching him or his garment as I did, so that I didn't see who else was in the tent until a voice spoke.

"How are you called?" the voice said in the language of the People, and then changing to the English of the white man, the voice spoke again. "You're a pretty woman, and that's plain for any man to see."

I did not answer the voice of the man who had spoken, and for a little space I thought I should keep looking down at the dirt inside the tent as though I had not heard anyone address words to me. Then I thought if I did that, I would be behaving as a young woman of the Cheyennes is taught she must do when a young man shows an interest in her. If the white man who had spoken to me about how I appeared to him were to know how a Cheyenne woman should conduct herself before a man, he might think I was considering him with the interest an unmarried woman has in a man. I lifted my head and looked straight into the face of the man who had called me such a name. Let him not be mistaken, I told myself. I am playing no part of a game.

I knew him when I saw him that first time. It was the man the Cheyenne and Sioux called Yellow Hair, even those years ago when he brought the killing to the Washita. It was long, his hair, like that of a warrior of the people, no matter which nation the warrior comes from, but it was not black or even reddish as that of some few Indians can be. It was golden in color, like the sun early in the day before the clouds come to cover it, and the hair on his face was a darker shade of the same color. I looked away from it, but I didn't drop my eyes from his face. He was wearing the blue clothes of the soldiers, but he had no coat on, as cold as it was that day on the Washita, so cold the blood froze as it left the bodies of the dead.

"She doesn't speak any English, does she?" the yellow-haired chief of the blue soldiers said to Spotted Dog, still looking at me as he spoke.

"She speaks some," Spotted Dog said. "But she will not let anyone know that. She is hard to deal with, this one. See how she stands so straight up, and you can tell from that how well she likes herself."

"What's this little sweetheart's name?" Yellow Hair said, still looking directly into my face and now beginning to show his teeth as the white men do when they want to look like friends. "Did she tell you that?"

"I know her name from before. She is Monahsetah, and she is the daughter of Little Rock, the second chief of Black Kettle's Cheyennes. She has not been raised as a girl child should be. She has a sharp tongue and is too proud for any woman."

"I like them proud like that now and then," Yellow Hair said. "Who wants to ride a horse that's been broken so long it won't even buck in the morning? Something that wakes you up, that's what you want, scout. Am I right?"

"You're always the man who's right, my chief. But this one here, she's not a broke horse. I would not like to turn my back on her. You cannot trust her."

At that, the chief of the blue soldiers laughed and waved a hand at his scout, motioning for him to leave. "I won't turn my back on her," he said as Spotted Dog bent to step under the canvas flap and leave the tent. "I can swear to that. But I'll tell you this about wild stock, scout. The quicker you break them, the better they end up liking to bear the saddle with you in it."

"Do you want me to come get her later?" Spotted Dog said. "So we can put them all together, these women, until tomorrow, as we do always?"

"No, I don't think so," Yellow Hair said. "It might be a long night for her, and we're moving out of here before daylight. No reason to put her with the others yet. I'll let you know when I'm finished with her."

After Spotted Dog had left, the chief of the blue soldiers looked back at me and began to show his teeth again. "Do you know what it means when I say turn around?" he said. "Or are you going to keep acting like you don't know what I'm saying?"

"I know a little of your white man talk," I said, speaking slowly to let me remember the words I had heard in the forts where the Cheyennes had spent the last two winters and also those words the Black White Man had used when he spent his time with Black Kettle's people, several seasons in all. "Not the words turn around. What that says, I don't know."

"Here, Monahsetah," he said, reaching out to put his hand on my shoulder and then pushing me a little. "I'll show you what to do and how to turn. Just do what I say."

I did not move in the direction he pushed me, and he stepped back and put his head to one side as he looked hard into my face. "Don't you want to let me see you?"

"You see me now," I said. "And I see you. I see all that is around me. I see all I want to see."

"Do you know behind?" Yellow Hair said. "If I say I want to see you from behind, do you hear that?"

I did not answer that, though I knew what he meant. Why should he know what I knew, I said to myself. The more you give away of what is yours alone, the less of you is left. Let him wonder what I know and what I do not. I know enough to let me know what he wants. All that is left to me about that matter is to wonder how far he will go to get what he wants when he looks at me, Monahsetah, daughter of a chief of the Cheyennes.

"I want to see how you look from every side," he said, not showing his teeth this time, letting me know he now was serious in a way he wasn't at first. "I want to turn you around like I'd turn around a grouse I'd shot, one I wanted to keep for later. Do you know what I mean by that? Have you seen a dead bird look like a living one? I can make that happen."

I did not let my eyes drop as though I did not understand Yellow Hair or worse than that, was afraid of him. He might do with me what he finally wanted, but it would not be because I surrendered to him. I would not give up what I was. If I had had time to prepare myself when the blue soldiers came riding into the village with guns and fire and their music, I would have hidden a knife under my garment. That would have put me in a good place to make a surprise for the chief of the soldiers. How would he have looked then out of his pale blue eyes as he turned me to study the side of me he could not see now? Would he have wanted to see me turn around to show what other woman I was from behind if I had a knife to pull from under my clothing and plunge into him as soon as he drew near enough?

I could think of that, see my hand reach beneath my garment to the place where a belt of deerskin held the blade warm against my side, watch it spring from the darkness where it was hiding into the light of the tent, observe the shining edge where a stone had sharpened it, and appreciate the track it made as it leapt to bury itself in the body of the man who had brought soldiers into the village of Black Kettle in a camp on the Washita— I could believe all that as if it had happened if I had had the time to ready myself for what was to come. And it would have been my comfort, for me alone. But I had not time. I could only dream now of the flash of a blade to save me from Yellow Hair and what he wanted to do to me. It was not real, that knife shining along its sharpened edge, but only a thing you see in sleep when the world that is not seems to be the world that is.

So when Yellow Hair put his hand on me again, this time not softly to turn me around so as to see my body from another side, but a touch made to mean strongly so that I would feel his power and drop my head and weep tears as he would push me down on the bed near the wall of the tent, I had no blade to prevent him. But I had teeth, and when I grabbed his hand and brought it toward me and let my face bend toward it, he must have considered that I was yielding to go in the direction he wanted. He must have thought I would beg and pour water from my eyes on the fingers and palm of the hand with which he intended to guide me to lie down where he wanted.

He did not resist my pulling his hand toward my face, and I heard him make a sound with his mouth the way a man will do when he is hungry and begins to take the first bite of a meal a woman has cooked. "Ahh," Yellow Hair said deep in his throat as I brought his hand and my mouth toward each other.

But he made a different sound when I sank my teeth as hard as my jaw would let me into the flesh of his palm. Then he yelled and tried to jerk his hand away from my mouth, but I held on with my teeth as long as I could do that, feeling the blood coming into my mouth and not letting go until he had hit the side of my head with the other hand, hard enough that it did not hurt but made a great sound behind my eyes and throughout my body and a bright light blossomed as though lightning had struck a tree before me. But the light it made did not vanish as it does in a thunderstorm but faded out like a burning ember when it falls away from the fire.

In my head I felt myself leave the tent where Yellow Hair was yelling and a soldier was running to stick his head inside the opening, and then it was dark and I was asleep, but I did not dream. And that was what I wanted, not to dream but to sleep without knowing where I was and who I happened to be. I wanted the dark, and it alone, and I wanted there to be nothing but that where I was. Nothing.

✩ ✩

When I came back into myself where my body lived and breathed air and where I knew the name I was given and believed I was that woman who others saw and said Monahsetah to call me, it was a little time before I knew where I was. I could see that it was beneath a thing above me that hid the sky. It was not buffalo hide or deerskin, and I wondered why the cloth of the white man was above my head, not letting the sky be seen or rain come. Then I knew where I was when I saw something move at the edge of where my eyes could see, and turning my head to look directly at whatever it was, I could see a white man looking downward at something before him. It was his hand. It had a piece of cloth wrapped around it, and a spot of blood showed upon its surface, showing the reason for its being there.

It was then, seeing the blood my teeth had drawn from the hand of the soldier chief called Yellow Hair, that I thought to slide my fingers down my belly which was bare and to let them touch between my legs, finding what I knew I would. But I would not let the tears gather in my eyes and I would not cry out or give any sign of mourning what had happened to me in the white man's tent.

I was not there, I told myself, when it took place, that act Yellow Hair had performed upon the thing I lived in, my body. My head was asleep when it happened, so it was as though it didn't take place in my knowing, and that was a comfort to me. I had been like the grouse he had talked of, the one he killed and then made look as though it were alive again, its eyes open and its head cocked to one side as it perched upon a branch of a tree low to the ground. It would seem to those who did not know the truth that the grouse had never died, that the shot which hit it had no power to take its life from it, and that the white man who had pulled the trigger on its living in this world of prairie and sky had the power to turn back time to an earlier day. He would seem to have power over death itself. He could bring it forth and then take it away.

But I knew he did not have that strength, and though the grouse knew nothing now, being a dead thing of feathers and beak only, its eyes showed it had left this life forever and was not subject to the power which the white man claimed. The eyes were only buttons of glass and had never seen light. It was a lie, though the bird did not know it said what was not true. The only animal that can lie is a man.

I had been alive when Yellow Hair, chief of the blue soldiers, had tried to make me cry and beg, but I had not yielded to that. So when I bit his hand and his blow made me leave this world for a space, I was not killed, no matter what he did to me when I was not myself and not truly there in the tent on the bed raised up from the dirt floor. He had not taken me from myself, but only what was left of me when I had departed this world where I was daughter of a chief of the Cheyennes, where I was the woman Monahsetah. When I returned to this body, both parts of me were united into one again, but the part of me that lived outside my skin and blood had not been touched. It could not be reached, since it had not been there.

When Yellow Hair looked up from his bitten and still-bleeding hand, and said to me, "How are you now, Black Berry?" I was not ashamed and I had no reason to be. I was able to look directly at his pale eyes and answer.

"I am as I always have been," I said. "Why should I be anything but that? I am not a dead bird you have killed and brought back to life. I am Monahsetah, a woman of the Cheyennes. And I am here."

★ ★

He took me with him when he led the soldiers away from the killing they had done on the Washita, that time when the weather was so cold that the dead bodies of the Cheyennes of Black Kettle and Little Rock became ice and did not bleed much. That would come later when the sun warmed the earth enough to let blood flow and smells rise for the buzzards and coyotes to know there was new meat to be eaten.

I was put on a horse of the blue soldiers, and I was made to ride behind where the white men went on the way back to the fort, at the rear with the other women of the Cheyennes that had been chosen to stay for the journey with the little chiefs and big chiefs. At night after all had stopped to put up cloth tents and build fires and cook food, the women were led to the tents where they would stay with the blue soldiers until morning. At first some fought against the soldiers who came to untie the rawhide strings from their hands so they could be led away. But that did not last past two nights, the struggles of the Cheyenne women to stay away from where they would have to lie with the white men. As soon as they all came to know what was going to happen to them would happen and could not be stopped, they went along. They all lay down where they were put.

I never fought when the soldier came to untie my hands and lead me to the tent of Yellow Hair, and some women wondered at that, even believing that I wanted to have happen between the chief of the blue soldiers and me what took place each night. A young woman named Night Bird asked me about the way I conducted myself when the time came at end of day to go to the tent and lie down with a man not a husband and not of my people.

"Do you want to do what they make us do, Monahsetah?" she said, rubbing her wrists where the rawhide had chafed them during the day's journey. "You see how other women of the Cheyennes cry out and weep and fall to their knees when the blue soldiers come to get them. Why don't you do that?"

"Because I am not touched by Yellow Hair," I said. "I will not weep and mourn when I am not touched."

"Not touched? He does not take you? Is he one who loves other men, then, this great chief of the blue soldiers?"

"I am not touched inside," I told her. "I do not know if he touches my body, because I do not let myself feel that. Do you feel every breeze that touches your face or your hair? Do you know each time the sun warms what it sees of you? I do not. And I am not touched by Yellow Hair, no matter how much he may try to make me show that I am."

"Does he know he does not touch you when he thinks he is doing so?"

"Does the wind know I do not feel every whisper of its breath? Ask the wind. I do not care how it answers. It is a fool, the wind."

That went on each night, the Cheyenne women led into the tents and let out in the morning light. Some were taken to different tents and made to lie with a man other than the first one. Some had to be with more than one man in the same night. And some made noises and cried out in the darkness. I was made to do none of that. Instead, each night after all was quiet but for the sound of horses cropping grass and coyotes howling somewhere far off, Yellow Hair had me brought to his tent, and during each time I would not let my mind know what my body endured.

In seven days and six nights, we came with the blue soldiers and their chiefs, large and small, back to the fort where they lived when they were not riding in the land of the people. It was then that Yellow Hair tried to talk to me on that last night before we were to reach the end of the journey back from the Washita to the fort. "Black Berry," he said as he lay on his back after a long time of trying to touch me while I thought of the way words and drums made up together a song of the Cheyennes, even making the song come alive aloud as I remembered more of what it was while Yellow Hair worked to touch me. "Are you singing to me? Are you glad to be here with me? Is that what you mean by your song?"

I said nothing, but stopped my song and closed my eyes to think of how it felt at end of day in Black Kettle's village when the men of the Cheyennes had made a good hunt and brought home plenty of buffalo or antelope or deer, and the women had all come together to cut up what there was to cook and share. They would all sing then, even many of the men, and make each other laugh by the stories they told.

"You know we will reach the fort tomorrow," Yellow Hair said, "and I will not see you again when we do. I have my wife there, and I will not be able to do this with you again."

"Who is married to you?" I said. "Is she a human being?"

"Of course, she's a human being. She's a beautiful white lady, and we have been together for a long time. She will not want to know I have lain with you, though. We are husband and wife."

"You didn't," I said. "Not one time did you lie with me, and you never will. If the woodchuck who is your wife asks you, tell her that. It is the truth."

"The woodchuck who is my wife? The truth? What do you know about truth? What woodchuck? You people never make any real sense," he said and reached his hand toward me, open and turned upward. But I was ready for that, and I did not let the Monahsetah inside myself know my body was being touched. What my body did those times when it was touched by Yellow Hair I do not know. It lives its life, and I live mine.

✯ ✯

Before we were to reach the fort the next day, I told the blue soldier riding beside us women that morning that I needed to get off the horse they had tied my hands to and go behind some bushes. He was older than many of the other soldiers, and he would talk at times to one or more of the Cheyenne women without seeming to want to lie with us. He had much gray hair on the side of his face. He took a long look at me, then back toward the front of the line of blue soldiers, and finally let me stop the horse while he loosened the rawhide strings on my wrists. "Don't take too long," he said. "Every one of you little sweethearts will start asking to piss if you do. We ain't got time to let all that happen."

I did not speak to him after he said that, but I looked directly into his face after I had slipped off the horse and before I turned to head for a gully leading toward a creek not far from the line of horses and blue soldiers and Cheyenne women with their hands tied in front of them. The soldier looked back at me, and I could tell he wanted to let me know he was being friendly, so I nodded my head twice at him. I did not smile, though. I would not let any blue soldier or other white man see me open my mouth to them.

The gully was not deep, so after I jumped down into it I had to bend over as I stayed close to one wall of red clay that crumbled as I touched it, and I began to work my way down the gully toward the creek itself. I wanted to keep from being seen by anyone in the bunch of soldiers on horseback as I began to put more room between me and them, and I thought I would have some time to hide myself before they knew I was not planning to come back. They would think for a time that they couldn't see me because I was hiding while I did what the older man thought I was doing, squatting down to let my water go.

I was all the way to the creek bank and had turned to run in the direction the stream was taking when I saw not far ahead of me a beaver lodge sticking up above the pool made by the animals to give them a place to live. I did not think what I might do, but knew as I saw the lodge that I had been given it by Abba Mikko to help me. I walked into the pool, lowered myself beneath the water and held my breath until I had found the way into the lodge the beavers had made for themselves to enter their home. It seemed to take a long time to go through it, a time all dark at first, and I was afraid my breath would give out before I found air to breathe and light to see as I worked my way toward where I hoped the living chamber of the beavers would be. Abba Mikko helped me again, and I came to an open space where I was able to raise my head above water with air coming into my body and into my eyes a little light reaching from openings in the branches the beavers had cut and used to make their home.

I heard a rustling sound and a splash of water, and that was all except for the sound of water moving slowly in the pool the beavers had made. I lay on a mat of leaves and branches and closed my eyes and let myself believe I was back in the home of my father Little Rock, second chief of the Cheyennes, and I came close to sleep, so close that time passed without my knowing it and enough darkness came outside to hide all light in the beavers' home in the creek.

When I came back to myself fully awake, I returned the way I had come through the passage that went underwater and led to the world outside. No creature was there, and no sounds came from where the blue soldiers of Yellow Hair and all their horses and the Cheyenne women bound with rawhide had been when I left the world where men lived and fought to find myself a bed where I could rest with animals.

There was little moon that night, but enough to see water in the creek, and I followed that path until light began to come in the sky after a long time. I crawled into a thicket and lay down beneath a low bush and let myself sleep again, not waking until the sound of something crying broke into a dream I was having about eating with my brothers and sisters as we sat together by a fire, reaching into the same bowl together, our bellies becoming full and satisfied.

The crying seemed to be coming from a small child lost from its mother, hungry and alone and afraid, but when I crept out from beneath the bush I saw that it was not from a human but from an antelope, one too young to be alone away from a herd of its kind. "Hola," I said, "where are your people, little beast? Have you wandered away and gone where you should not?"

It did not answer me, the crying antelope, but moved away a little distance from where I lay on the earth, and then turned to take a step away from the creek, stopping after that and looking back at me as though to ask if I were coming, too.

"Wait, little one," I called. "Yes, I will go where you lead me. Let us begin."

And so we did, and I followed the lost antelope for two settings and risings of the sun, and on the third day, I was back at the Washita with those who were left of the Cheyenne village of Black Kettle, the chief who had lifted a flag of the white men over his lodge, a piece of cloth which he believed would protect the People from harm, since he had been told that.

When I saw the lodges of the people raised again before me, fewer now and no flag up and the marks of a dead fire still all around, I turned to the little antelope to tell him that we had come to the place where I wanted to go, but he was gone. I was not surprised by that or worried about him, though, knowing he was safe to return to the thicket there on the banks of the creek where the beaver had given me a place to hide from the blue soldiers and their chief Yellow Hair.

So I lived with the Cheyennes again and when the moon grew and waned and grew again and enough time had passed, and it came to be that a baby entered the world from my body, his hair was yellow, too, and his eyes were not the color of mine but lighter in shade and different in shape. He was my son, mine alone, belonging to no father, and I gave him a secret name, and that name was Antelope.

✶ ✶

My husband of three winters is named Steps on the Mountain, and he and my son the people call Yellow Bird and I and the sister of my child with the yellow hair are a family of the Cheyennes. We were for a time on the reservation of the fort that the white men told us they had made for us, and when there was no buffalo in the winter of last year, we stayed there together with the people because of the meat the white men gave to eat. Now the buffalo have come back to us, as they are intended by Abba Mikko to do, and we have left the reservation to be with the Sioux, and the Cheyenne camp is at the edge of the village as it is always meant to be when we are together with that Nation.

The young men who ride each day in all directions to see what is around us, all things such as beasts and men and weather, say the blue soldiers are coming to us again, just as Sitting Bull said they would do, and what they intend for us is what Yellow Hair wants to have happen. He thinks to make us return to the place the white men have made for a reservation, and if we do not, he will do what he has done before.

The blue soldiers who make their music with whistles and horns and drums and singing will do that again, and the music will make them want to ride faster and braver against us with their rifles and little guns and long knives. They will come with fire and steel and bullets against the People, Sioux and Cheyennes, and all who will stand with us, and they will try to drive us as our hunters drive the buffalo off the high rocks to fall and die on the ground below.

This time, though, Sitting Bull has said the buffalo will turn and lower their heads and use their horns to break the horses and the hunters riding them, and the warriors of our people will turn in the same fashion and cause the blue soldiers to fall upside down into the heart of our great village on the Greasy Grass. The world will be not what it was before, but what it needs to be to protect us, men and women, old and young, and children, those dark and those light, both with hair the color of the night sky and those with hair yellow like the sun.

And our chiefs, Sitting Bull and Crazy Horse and Gall and the others, they all know why the blue soldiers come on us with Yellow Hair, the Son of the Morning Star, leading them, but I know a thing the chiefs do not. And that thing is secret, and it is thus stronger. And it tells me why Crow scouts were sent in peace to the Cheyennes more than once in the years since that killing took place at the village of Black Kettle on the Washita, sent with open hands from Yellow Hair to ask about Monahsetah. Is she still with the Cheyennes, the Crow scout for the white men, the one named Bloody Knife asked. Does she yet live? Will she come to the reservation at Fort Lincoln as she should? And then he asked the question which I never wanted to be answered. "Does Monahsetah have a child?" Bloody Knife said. "And if she does, is he a light-skinned one, and does his hair show not only darkness but a shade of the sun?"

And I was never there when the Crow scout asked these questions sent from another man, but I was told of them by others who had heard them put to the chiefs of the Cheyennes. And no answer was ever given Bloody Knife, the scout for the blue soldiers, but still he returned each year to ask them again, and he carried the questions as one who would carry a sick and dying child. With care, slowly, and with downcast eyes and a soft voice, and a concern not to upset any of those who love the child and mourn the darkness that is coming as surely as the cold rain falls in the dead of winter.

Yellow Hair is coming to the Cheyennes again, and in force and in this summer season, and that will be on the rising of the sun tomorrow, but his coming will not be as it was before. The buffalo will not be driven off the high rocks again. This time the buffalo will offer his horn.

This time Monahsetah will not be asleep in her father's lodge, not knowing where to turn or where to run or who can protect her from the blue soldiers with their music and weapons. She is awake now and has prepared. She has not had a full sleep for over five winters, but she is not tired, nor drowsy. Her eyes see where all things are and where they are not. And she is able now to allow herself to suffer the world and all that's in it. She has given up fear, and it hides from her, fear itself afraid.

Libbie Custer
FORT ABRAHAM LINCOLN, DAKOTA TERRITORY

June 24, 1876

I AM THE WIFE OF A SOLDIER. THAT DO I PROUDLY PROCLAIM. I, BORN Elizabeth Bacon in Michigan and now accompanying my husband at this stage of his military career in the uncivilized wilds of the West, claim that distinction. As wife of a soldier, as I tell the new brides of young officers, I am privileged to be truly married to a warrior, for in that role, as minor as it is compared to my husband's, I am making history. I am the wife of a soldier, and oh what a soldier my Autie happens to be.

Before we married and began our journey through life bound as joyously together as are the moon to the earth and the stars to the heavens, my Autie, my cavalier, paid court to me as a prince must to a princess. My father, an august and respected man and judge and a pillar of our community, had his doubts about the life a wife of a soldier must lead with the long separations, the constant travel from one barren and dangerous assignment to another, and all the uncertainties of life with a man whose dedication to his country and his duty is all consuming. But such existence is noble, as well, and a wife and helpmate's role pays tribute to the strength of character and will which reside in the bosom of a true patriot and warrior.

George Armstrong Custer, upon my first sight of him in the dusty street of my home in Michigan, seized my imagination and my admiration thrillingly. And in due time he seized my heart. As our love progressed and flourished, my father realized finally the deep truth of Autie's dedication to me and me to him, and he yielded as a tree swept with a hurricane wind must bend or finally break. He gave his permission for continuing courtship and his blessing for its culmination, and I was married in a simple and truly beautiful ceremony marking the blending of two souls into one.

I wanted to defy convention and wear a light green gown on my wedding day, in a testimony to the life which comes to the fields in the spring after the long, cold, dispossessing winter and as an emblem of our new and maturing love. Autie in his sweet and glowing nature would have allowed me to wear sackcloth and ashes, should I have wished them for some strange reason, but at the last moment, the final day before the ceremony, he sent word to me in a letter which I immediately treasured as I have all his writings I have received, great or small, and he declared therein his willingness to approve of any and all plans marking our union I would have executed, and then in syllables which I have written on my heart for all time, he said these glowing words to me.

> Dearest Libbie, possessor of my heart, my mind, and my soul, could you see it possible in your decision about what gown you will adorn in your wearing of it at our nuptial ceremony to think more kindly of a traditional all-white garment that you would come to my arms in situ? I ask this favor of you so that to the eyes of all witnesses you demonstrate in symbol the fact of your exquisite and utter purity of heart and being. Let no man or woman who may be blessed to be granted a glimpse of you on that magical day doubt the statement of purity and perfection made of the truth within your bosom by the gown you choose to wear.

I wore the white gown my Autie asked of me. And I have never regretted that yielding to convention which such garment represented. As I said in a letter sent only a few days ago to him in the saddle as he takes his beloved Seventh Cavalry in pursuit of the benighted savages it is his task to subdue in the service of his nation and to the good of civilization itself, "Dear Autie, better are we to die together than die divided."

I meant by such statement to request his allowance to accompany him on this great venture into the wilds of the Montana Territory, knowing he would not allow such event to transpire, but wanting to render unequivocal my dedication to him, my husband, my cavalier, and this nation's hope as we enter the second hundred years of the existence of these United States. His response, my dear Autie's answer to me, was wonderfully couched and succinctly written, yet so dearly expressed and tender that tears come unbidden when I think of that precious letter.

> Would I die without you, my love, my life, my Libbie? I answer
> that as a cavalryman would if questioned about his conduct before
> engagement with the enemy. What will I do when my reason for
> existence, the soul of duty, calls me? As always, I will ride to the
> sound of the guns. So to you, my dear slice of heaven, my morsel of
> sheer goodness and beauty, I say this. Without you I am nothing,
> and to die in your absence would be to live in hope of reunion.

So when that day came not two weeks ago when the Seventh Cavalry prepared for departure from Fort Lincoln, properly loaded with the materials and the stout souls to perform its duty and to discover the hiding place of the red Indians of the Sioux and the Cheyennes and the others and bring them to proper order and due obedience, I began my preparations as wife to the commander of the regiment, knowing my duty and as determined to fulfill its requirements as my Autie was to measure up fully to the demands placed upon him by responsibilities he so gladly shouldered.

As was my obligation as wife of the commander of the Seventh Cavalry, I called together all the wives of officers in that sterling group of stout men and spoke thusly to them. "Ladies of the Seventh, dear hearts and beloved wives of the leaders of that wondrous regiment, I want to speak to you upon a topic I know is as familiar to you as are the dear faces of your husbands and your hostages to fortune, your children, if you and your soul mates are so blessed. And my message is this."

At this point, early in the day, all the mists from the river not yet dispelled by the heat of the sun so new in the heavens at this moment of morning, I chose to lift my gaze from the faces of those women as devoted as I to the men who would move into the dangers of their mission in the land of the savage tribes and directed my attention to the flag so proudly displayed at the center of the parade ground of the fort. Not yet moved by a breeze, this emblem of what our men had dedicated their lives to defend, this bit of colored cloth, hung limply. But oh it spoke so eloquently of our reasons, one and all, soldiers and wives, for being where we found ourselves answering duty's call in the western wilderness of our nation. I pointed that out to the wives at some length, and then I said this to them in conclusion.

"Women of the Seventh, because you are in your feminine way as much a part of this regiment led by General George A. Custer as any soldier in its number, here is your duty assignment for this mission of hazard and hope. Support your husband in all he does to advance the cause upon which my husband leads them. Love him, do not question him, be a silent but rock-steady presence behind him as he goes, and should he not return, do not grieve overmuch. For surely, our heavenly Father will grant you and him reunion and joyous eternal existence as the ages roll."

The women responded well to my words, paltry and weak as they were, coming from a woman such as myself, but I was surprised to discover that only a few in that group of officers' wives chose to applaud upon the completion of my remarks. I expected more response than I received, but I remembered that the heat of the day was beginning to build and, more to the point, many of these wives had not had the advantage of education and breeding I had enjoyed in my wonderful upbringing in Michigan. Nor had they traveled extensively in the East and enjoyed its cultural advantages as I had done with Autie.

Remember, I said to myself as the wives moved away to line the parade ground through which the men of the Seventh Cavalry would soon pass in formal procession as they moved to begin their assigned mission, remember what Autie says to you when you complain about instances of a want of sophistication and understanding in the women you must lead and to whom you serve as example. These girls, old and young, he would remind me, are not your equivalent, just as a flock of crows in their loud cawing never measure up to the eagle who flies above them, silent and steady in the deep blue of heaven.

In due time, the opening peal of the bugle resounded across the open space of the parade ground of Fort Lincoln, announcing a call to order of officers and men, and the procession of the Seventh Cavalry toward the gates began in true and thrilling earnest. At that moment, I expected the usual lift in my breast to occur at such auditory messaging, the sense of a great event about to commence stirring in my vitals, but instead a completely different sensation arose within me, seeming to start in the calves of my legs hidden beneath my skirts and beginning to creep upward through each succeeding part of my body as the head of the procession of uniformed mounted men and Indian scouts and mule drovers came into view.

Autie, I thought, Autie, feeling the name welling up so that I would speak it, and then it came to me as a great dryness grew in my throat that I wanted to shout out to him, to say words which would cause him to pause and reign in his beautiful roan stallion, words which would halt the entire procession of his regiment and freeze in place all motions of all creatures a part of it, men and horses and mules, and Autie's great pack of dogs trotting along beside him as he rode his horse, resplendent in his buckskins and white hat, a great flowing neckerchief in the deep color of blood gathered at his throat.

"Autie," I would say if I allowed myself that moment of weakness springing so powerfully from devotion to have its utterance, "turn away, dear heart, from the bloody field which lies before you. Hazard not your sublime life and being in this task of danger and peril. Remain with me, your meekly devoted helpmate and wife. You have sacrificed enough for your nation and its ungrateful leaders. Stay, my love, stay with me."

Should I have weakened and spoken such words aloud, my Autie would have heard them no matter how distant from me and understood what they represented, but he would never have heeded the call to retreat before a task of duty and danger, however threatening it might be. No, he would never have turned away from the lonely responsibility facing him. Not George Armstrong Custer, Commander of the Seventh Cavalry, hero not long hence of the Battle of Gettysburg, and cavalier par excellence. Instead he would have been shamed by my outburst, by my revelation of a scared and timid soul within, and he would have proceeded on his way, undeterred, but disheartened by weak words said by a woman so blessed to be called his own.

Knowing this fact in every fiber of my being, I drew in a deep breath and directed my gaze not at the sight of my brave and noble husband leading his gallant band of strong men and willing Indian scouts and mule drovers out of the safety of Fort Lincoln and into the open and treacherous wilds of the savage Montana, but instead I looked up at the clouds of mist above the great military procession. Let me steel myself,

I spoke to the trembling woman within, hiding behind the strong and resolute façade I fought to preserve and present, let me appear as strong as he, weak though I truly am.

As I did that, my eyes fastened not upon the solidly real parade of animals and men upon the packed earth below but instead upon the mists which hung above it all in billows and clouds, just now being touched and highlighted by the beams of the glorious morning sun. What I saw there in the heavens struck my bosom with an emotional blow so severe that I must confess I staggered for a moment beneath its force.

Suspended above the procession of the Seventh Cavalry and all that combined to make up its being was a vision in the clouds of mist, a vision composed of an exact copy of all beneath it, exact though hideously reversed so it appeared to the eye to be upside down. By a meteorological freak, the officers and men and horses and conveyances appeared by some optical illusion to be hanging from their heels as though suspended in air, held by a force which robbed them of true direction and strength and presented an image of frustration and complete indirection, as though a bitter foretaste mocking their endeavor was being provided in and by the heavens.

"Look," one of the young wives of a junior officer exclaimed, "look at the image in the sky. Isn't that droll and amusing how all below is reversed and upended?"

Some few women standing with me tittered and laughed in agreement, seemingly entertained by the ocular vision before us as our men proceeded away from us, the heavens above commenting on the futility of their endeavor and intention as shown in reversal. "Please," I said aloud to all women assembled there, "let us not be frivolous at this moment. The Seventh Cavalry under the leadership of brevet General George Armstrong Custer is moving away from us on its mission. Be reverent, be silent, and be proud of their brave dedication."

"I hope," I heard one of the young women mutter to one near her, "they get turned right side up before they get to where they're going." Her name was Rosalie, and she was often childlike in her utterances. She was married to a second lieutenant whose name I could not recall at the moment, and that fact in itself was comment enough on the frivolity of her comment without my speaking a word in rebuke. No name, no weight.

"Autie," I said to myself, "will I see you again soon?" No answer came from within or without to that trembling inner query, and it was several minutes before the reversed image of the procession painted by nature in the clouds above vanished before us. When I looked away from that false vision finally as it faded, and as I sought a last glimpse of the true band of men, I could discover nothing of the real Seventh Cavalry still evident. And as I realized all view of them was gone, something moved far off and difficult for me to make out, a living speck vanishing as quickly as it had made itself visible for an instant. Could it have been a prairie wolf? Or was it one of Autie's hunting dogs? Let it be Grip, I said within; let it be that one beast he loves so much. If I cannot be granted one last image of my brave husband, let me have seen a true heart wholly his, animal though it may be. Let some living blind beast loyal to my cavalier be the signal granted me. Oh, Autie, my splendid warrior chief!

Crazy Horse
—OGLALA WAR CHIEF, VILLAGE ON THE GREASY GRASS

JUNE 24, 1876

THEY WILL COME TOMORROW, THE BLUE SOLDIERS WITH YELLOW Hair riding before them, and I know that for good reason, but not because of the accounts of the Sun Dance where Sitting Bull danced for two days. He had a vision, he told the council as we all sat together in his lodge, and the council took his word to all of the People in this village, the Sioux of each Nation and the Cheyennes and any other who would listen. I go where I am needed, so I was there when he told the council what had been granted him to see after he had sung and danced around the Sun Dance pole until the polished buffalo bones pushed beneath his flesh finally tore loose and let him fall.

Then it was, Sitting Bull said, that he saw inside himself the blue soldiers falling into our camp with their heads pointed down and their feet up in the air instead of in the stirrups of their horses, and the horses were upside down, too, and they were falling like the riders. Many soldiers had no heads or arms or legs, since all these had been cut away from their bodies, and much blood flowed like the water in the stream of the Greasy Grass in the spring. The council liked the dream Sitting Bull claimed he had earned by suffering and singing and dancing for two days and nights and for not crying out in pain as the rawhide bonds pulled at the bones beneath the cuts that had been made into the flesh of his chest and sides to hold them fast.

The chiefs of the council said "Howhn, howhn, howhn," and they leaned forward where they sat, and some stood because they could not sit still any more. They drank from the gourds and they smoked much tobacco, that of the white man and also that taken from the Black Hills where it grows for the Indians to use. They shouted, and some sang, and many gave thanks to the Old Man who lives in the clouds, and others told about what they would do to the white soldiers in blue clothes and hats all alike when they came close to the camp on the Greasy Grass. They spoke of their sons and their grandsons and the young men married to their daughters, and they praised what these young men would do with their arrows and rifles and stone clubs and little axes and sharp knives and the long knives which came from the blue soldiers first and now belonged to the Sioux and Cheyenne warriors who had taken them in other battles from the still hands of blue soldiers now dead. More will join these dead, the council said, so many the women in the lodges of the white men will weep until the snow flies. And the men of the council shook their hands in the air before them, and they said "Howhn, howhn" again many times.

It was not that, though, what the council said as they told about Sitting Bull's vision in the Sun Dance, that told me the blue soldiers were coming. And when Bear Standing by Himself said to me, "Crazy Horse, what will you say about this vision of the blue soldiers falling into our camp upside down with their guts hanging out and their hands cut off and their legs missing and bloody? Have you a word to say as war chief of the Oglala?" here was my answer. It was not in words, laid out in the air to please the mind of any who wants to listen. I did not boast of what the warriors of the Oglala would do to any blue soldier who came toward us with a weapon at ready. I did not mention what I had done before, either as a man or as a boy wanting to be a man. I did not speak of deeds done and now dead. Here is what I did, without words, to answer the question Bear Standing by Himself put to me.

I held out my open hand to the council member sitting beside me in the circle—his name was Snow Storm in Summer—and after he looked at me, he took his knife from a scabbard at his side and gave it to me. I tested it with my finger and found it duly sharp with its edge gleaming like the eyes of a wolf in the light of a fire at night. Turning one hand up, I held the knife in the other and drew its edge across my palm, watching a line of blood leap up as though I had called it to do that and it was ready to answer.

"Hownh," Snow Storm in Summer said when he saw the true line of blood called forth by the blade, and then all others in the council joined him in speaking and calling my name. I said nothing. Then I licked the line of blood from my hand, watching a new one replace in my hand the one now on my tongue, the one which tasted first like iron in the mouth and then like honeysuckle blossoms which children eat when the world turns green again after the darkness of winter. All strong, all brave, all sweet.

Then I left the meeting. After I departed the lodge where Sitting Bull stayed in his place to talk further with the council about what he had seen after his dance at the Sun Pole and about what he saw would happen in the new day to come, I did not see the others all around me, Sioux or Cheyennes, women or men, children or dogs and horses, but I knew they were there in the village on the Greasy Grass. A man does not need to test all he encounters by noting it and counting it and asking it if it sees him. The world will be there, seen and not seen, heard and not heard, tasted and not touched, whether he wants it or would not have it. It is outside him. He is outside it. It stands as he does. Alone.

When I reached my lodge, I saw no one inside, and I was glad I would not have to refuse to look at my wife, Black Robe, or her sister tending to the work that was there to do. Black Robe would not have wanted me to speak to her, if I gave sign I wanted to remain silent, but her sister would have spoken and when I did not answer it would have meant something to her. I did not care what she thought of my ways, but I did not want to have to think about not thinking about it. I wanted my head empty of all but one path. I had another thing to consider, so I went to the place where I slept in the lodge, found the small basket holding the stones I needed, and I scattered them over my bed of buffalo robes so that I could not lie down without feeling the stones and pebbles pushing into my flesh. The hard things of the earth would not let me sleep or rest in comfort while I lay upon my bed and considered what would come tomorrow when the blue soldiers rode against us. A pebble will not forget to do what it does always. It will keep you awake. That is a true thing you can trust.

By the time night would come fully and most people were asleep in the village on the Greasy Grass, I would have thought of what I must do in the day to come, how I must prepare myself for the battle which Yellow Hair would bring to the Sioux and the Cheyennes, and how the day would come in all its parts, the beginning of the sounds and the great motions of the men and horses, and the flying of arrows and the raising of smoke from the guns and flashing of the sharpened edges of blades. Then would come the close work after many blue soldiers had fallen, the swinging of the little axes by the boys and women and the lifting and falling of the clubs, the way the knives would be used to discover and show to all what lies beneath the skin of a man, and what is inside his head where he truly lives alone and with no others until all is over and he is not there inside himself anymore and never again will be. Always it will be the same: something is not there any longer, but what it was can never be seen. To see it is only to see where it was, not where it is now.

First, though, must come the stretching of my body on the bed of stones, the considerations within my head of what I owe to others and how I must pay it, and how I must prepare myself so that when my people see me ride on the next day they will know who I am and what is meant by the way I present myself to the world outside. And the blue soldiers will know me, as well, when they see me come with the warriors of the Oglala against them.

And here is what I learned in the vision I saw, when I was a boy hoping for instruction on how to become a man, and it was a vision I had alone and not while I was fastened to bones stuck into my flesh so that all could witness me spinning about a great pole for days until I dropped free as did Sitting Bull as he danced before all who wished to see him and admire what he did.

My instruction came to me when I walked out into the Black Hills alone, when I ate nothing and I drank no water, and I saw no other man or woman, and when I walked until my legs would move no more. And I walked not toward a thing, but away from another thing. And I fell down into a hole I could not cross because I had made myself weak, and it was night and there was no moon and the stars were so far away they could not give me light to see, even if I had wanted it. I did not want it.

I wanted a dream that would tell me who I was and how to live with that man I would become after I was a child no longer. And I was granted that dream by the Old One, and here is what I saw, and here is what I learned I must do as a man in the time to come when I would live my time in the world. And then be lost to time forever.

In my dream, there was another dream, and that dream had in it me watching another man prepare himself for battle against those who would come against the People. I knew that man was the man I would become if I learned to put aside what I was as a boy and not take the path that could be easy and open to me. That path would be filled with others, men who would be my companions as true and brotherly as they could be, and women who would lie with me and love me and be my wives if I wanted them. And the women would do all that wives must do, and they would make it their tasks to make my time in the lodge peaceful with all I needed of food and drink and talk and listening, and I would have many children, boys and girls both, to grow and become Oglala men and women. I would see all that.

That path would be easy, and having taken it I would live until the Old Ones called me to lie down and breathe and be no more. And I would be in the earth, a part of it, and there would not be a man who would be called my name ever again, and I would never be remembered by those who came after me. I would be of earth only.

As I lay in the hole where I had fallen, in my dream inside a dream, I felt warm and easy as I saw what could lie before me, there for the taking and the having, there in the way ripe blackberries hang before a child in summer, ready and sweet for the eating as much as a stomach can bear to hold. But once begun, that feast is hard to turn from, and always one more handful waits there to fill the mouth, so sweet and with such juice abundant that you eat until the body sickens and vomits all you have eaten outside yourself again. Yet still you want the blackberries, sick as you have become, and you can never find the satisfaction of being full enough.

Then I saw a man in the dream who would be me in my time to come in the world, if I would study how he conducted himself as he prepared for a battle alone, the struggle only he would face and that unaided. He did not speak to me, and he did not look at me, but I could tell he knew I watched him to see what path he would take different from the one that ended in the sweet glut of blackberries in the summer and the peace of wives and children and comrades in warm lodges, waiting to vanish and turn into scattered and nameless dirt when came the final day to lie down and die.

The dream man was dressed only in one garment, that of buckskin, about his waist and loins. He wore no other clothes, and his hair hung down his back undressed with ornaments of shell or beads and showing no sign of bear grease to make it shine and stay put in a pattern. He lifted his hand to one ear and placed behind it a small polished stone which, when he dropped his hand, I could see had been tied there with a string.

I spoke then, asking him what it was that he had done with the stone, and he said, "I put it to my ear before battle, so I may hear what is needful and no more."

Then as he turned away from speaking to me, thunder came from the sky, but I did not see the flash of lightning that always comes before. I put my hands to my ears to stifle that great noise so loud it was painful, and when I looked back at the man before me he was covered with white spots on his body which meant the marks of hail, and he had a lightning bolt painted on his face from forehead to chin.

"Are you the thunder man?" I said, for in the dream I was allowed to ask that.

"No, not just a thunder man," he said, pointing to his head, where now perched a red hawk, its talons sunk into the undecorated hair of the man. "With hail and lightning painted on me and a red hawk on my head and a stone behind my ear, I am what you will be if you live as you must until you are the war chief of the Oglala. If you present yourself to the enemies of the People as I show you yourself now, and if you paint hail stones on your horse before battle, and if you do one other thing, arrows and bullets can never harm you. You will live forever as you lead your warriors into battle."

"I will do all that," I said. "I will live that life, and I will serve my People in the way you show me. But what is the other thing I must do?"

"It is to refrain from an action. You must never take a scalp of the enemy," the warrior in the dream, the man I would become, said. "Whether the enemy is the Crow or the Arikara or the white man, you must not seek such a trophy. Shun decoration. Live this way, put aside all boasting, all regarding of yourself, and you will become what the Old Ones mean you to be."

"Who will I be?"

"Crazy Horse, war chief of the Oglala, who can never die, if he lives as he should."

Then the warrior in the dream inside the dream was on his horse, and he had no weapon in either hand, but I knew he was armed. I could feel myself slipping deeper into a great weakness I could not overcome as I lay in the rocky bottom of the hole where I had fallen before I dreamed, and I feared becoming asleep before I would be able to speak further with the warrior I might become. But I could not keep my eyes open and my mind alert, and when I woke all I could find as evidence that the warrior had been there was the stone he had placed behind his ear. That I still have, and that I have always worn into battle, and I will wear it the next time the sun rises as I lead the People against Yellow Hair and the blue soldiers. Tomorrow I will hear only what I need to hear as the stone reminds me to do, and I will feel the thunder in my bones and see the lightning in the eyes behind my eyes. And my body will bear the marks of hail stones, and my horse will do that, too, and a red hawk will perch upon my head as I ride before the warriors.

And I will think on what I always must as I go against the enemies of the People. I will remember the time I did not heed the words of the dream man I would become, that day when I in my pride as a young man in his first battle took the scalp of an enemy I had killed, an Arapaho warrior. I was punished for that by the Old Ones who allowed a wound to come to my leg. I will say again to myself that I must take no scalp and make no boast. And I will remember again my daughter who died in a time when I was not in my lodge where I should have been, and I will think how I lay beside her body for three days, hoping she would speak to me one last time. She never did, and I had to leave her dead in that place. I will say to the blue soldiers tomorrow and to Son of the Morning Star who leads them these words I always offer before battle.

Do not touch me. I am Crazy Horse.

Captain Myles Keogh
COMMANDING OFFICER, I COMPANY, SEVENTH CAVALRY

JUNE 24, 1876

*T*HE CROW SCOUTS ASSIGNED TO ME SPEAK BETTER ENGLISH THAN two thirds of the troopers in my company. And I'm not even talking about the Irish enlistees now, not a bit of it. I can understand each and every grunt and swear word and bit of slang these boyos offer up, myself being from that cursed isle, though a long time it's been since I've seen the place. But not nearly as long as I want it to be, my absence from the place of my birth and upbringing. I might someday go back, but I'm not going back alive, as the comedian says.

When I say there's a language problem in the Seventh Cavalry, it's not because of Irish lads who've come to America and joined up in the US Army for nothing better to do and them looking just to be joined to a thing that'll furnish the necessaries of food and a place to sleep and enough clothes to wear to be considered decent enough to go out among people. And there's no problem with me as their captain giving orders in English and having them disobeyed by the ones of I Company born and bred in this nation so newly stitched back together after the Southern rebels tried to tear it apart. That bunch of born Americans understands what I and the lieutenants and sergeants say to them all right, the ones whose granny and gramps came here years ago from whatever Godforsaken outhouse of a country they hailed from across the big water, looking for a square meal and a roof to shelter under.

Here's the real problem for sure that keeps me and the men I'm responsible for always in hope a given order's been comprehended if not carried out. I've got a whole third of my men in I Company who've arrived in America in the last few years from Italy. I've got another chunk of them from Germany, here in the land of these United States, not speaking more than forty words among them of English, even as bastard a version of that noble language as the American version is. And I've even got some funny buggers from places I can't even call the names of. Lithuania. Malta. The list grows.

Let me say this as the commander of I Company. It makes for confusion, bad feelings, and a general sense that you can never tell what any man will think you've said to him, and it's damn sure certain you can't tell as an officer or non-commissioned sergeant with any certainty what any of these foreign yahoos means when he gets to jabbering his native tongue or tries to put his smidgen of English to work in the hope of successful communication.

I must confess, though, that my years of service on behalf of the Papal Defense force in Italy does serve me in good stead, though each day those encounters when we fought on behalf of Mother Church and the Papacy against the Piedmontese and the rest of that Italian rebel bunch get farther and farther away from me. The less you gabble in a foreign tongue the more you forget the wrongheaded way you've got to speak it, so there's that problem to contend with. Any Italian I picked up is fairly well gone and forgotten nowadays. These days in the Montana and in the Black Hills, I find myself more at home talking to a Crow or Ree scout at times than to a speaker of any of the civilized tongues I've had to struggle with.

So tomorrow, if that's the day we get the deed done, as our commanding officer King Georgie, as I call him behind his back, claims it's going to be, I'll be thinking half the time not about rounding up and killing Indians but being sure my order to my subalterns and my men are at least halfway understood before there's an effort to put them into execution. I do have to watch myself, though, speaking of what words one uses in naming things and people, and I sure don't want to slip up and say just plain George or any variation of that first name when I'm talking to his nibs himself, brevet General George Armstrong Custer.

I may now be just a captain of one company of the Seventh myself, the I Corp or as some of the enlisted men call it, the Idiot Company, but I should by rights of past history be called a brevet Major in light of my service to the Union Army in the Civil War, so dear and departed that conflict now feels to me. There was some real soldiering done back then, and I was in the thick of it, as Custer well knows, and though I don't talk about it even at night when the bottles are going around and the officers in the Seventh are singing songs and recalling their days of glory back in that time when we were fighting Bobby Lee all over Virginia and Maryland and Pennsylvania, I earned decorations for valor and performance there, too, to add to the ones I got from His Holiness himself in the Vatican. I know that's the medal George really envies me for, though he'd never admit it. He may have been breveted as the youngest general yet in the American army, but he's never been decorated by the Pope for defense of Holy Mother Church.

That decoration and distinction he'll never have, and the way I know he's always in a bother about it when he sees me is the fact he'll always think to bring up some slighting statement of opinion about foreign wars and tin badges being given away by the bushel across the sea in those small countries. He cannot leave alone trying to talk down all that has distinguished my military service. "Great Britain is small," I once said back to him when he'd let off on that nation. "It's tinier than the state of Virginia, it is, but I don't think folks judge its military by the size of the acreage they defend."

That burned George Armstrong Custer, that truth did, when I said it, but it didn't rankle him near as much as his lovely little wife Libbie fingering my Agnus Dei medal I was wearing at an evening at the home of the beautiful duo of Custers back at Fort Lincoln. That little charmer wife of his had been into the wine pretty deep that night, what with the dinner served to the officers and their wives and to the officers without wives, such as me, Captain Myles Keogh, the lonely lad of I Company, and she just couldn't seem to keep her neat little white fingers off my medal and the chest it was resting on.

"And what was it in particular you did to merit having the Pope pin this medal on your uniform?" she asked, lifting it up from where it lay suspended by a ribbon and turning it so the light of the lamps hit it better for viewing. When she did that, it would have felt to a lesser fellow that she was sneaking in a caress to his broad and manly chest. Myself, I didn't note, being used to ladies clawing at my chest, even and perhaps especially married ones. If you believe that, the notion that I wasn't aware of what was going on in that laying on of hands by a dainty and delicate little creature like Libbie Custer, why then I've got a horse I'd like to sell you at a good price. Blooded he is, and not over three years old.

But to the point, Georgie noted what was going on in the mutual admiration between his most seasoned and accomplished company commander and his dear little wife with the tiny curls hanging so sweetly down her forehead and over her little pink ears, and he bestirred himself, as I remember, from where he was standing near the bowl full of punch being solicited for attention by Major Reno, and began to move toward the window seat where Libbie was studying my Papal decoration so closely. Reno was constitutionally drunk already, and past that stage as early as it was in the course of the evening, so it was easy enough for George to slip away from that particular underling with no one thinking the less of him.

Libbie didn't see George coming toward the two of us there by the window, so deep was she in poking at the Agnus Dei medal that had taken her full attention so strongly, and I knew she wouldn't be looking up at her husband with a pearly smile and a twinkling eye to greet him. She wouldn't, that is, unless I gave her indication of his impending arrival. So I didn't, hoping Custer's lovely little dove would be still at work poking at my medal and hitting my chest in the middle of that business. That's what happened, exactly, and my commanding officer, brevet General Custer, came into view just as Libbie turned her attention from the medal she'd been so taken with and was turning her gaze up at me, with her special little smile and twinkle directed not at her Autie but at Myles instead.

I straightened as George came within a couple of steps of where his wife and I stood in converse, and I did that for two reasons, one George would acknowledge and another he would not, since that second one stung a bit. He'd be at his ease and in full acceptance of the fact that a captain of one of the companies of the Seventh would come to a semi-straighten-up when he as commanding officer was spotted coming into range, but he'd not like the fact that when I did put myself at full upright length, I was at least two inches taller than he was. And that was a rankle to Georgie, my being a larger and, may I say without fear of successful argument against the point, my being a better-looking man than he. At least in the opinion of women who'd remarked upon that fact at times over the year, indirectly for the most part, but at times saying such things as "Oh, Myles, when I see you and General Custer standing together, I find myself thinking you look more like the head of the Seventh Cavalry than he does."

"Oh my, no," I'd had occasion more than once to respond. "Only those who truly don't know General Custer would harbor such wrong-headed notions. I'm naught but a junior officer of small accomplishment, compared to the wonderful deeds of my commanding officer." And then I'd smile and look off to one side, bringing my profile into good prominence for better viewing by any and all interested.

"Libbie," George said, stepping into the cozy little space his wife and I had established by the window and not acknowledging I was there at all as he did, "I'd like you to come say hello to the new young wife of Lieutenant Sturgis. She's been asking about you."

"Oh, Autie, I certainly will," Libbie said, taking her fingers away from the medals on my chest as though she had reached for an item on top of a stove and discovered it to be too hot to pick up. "I've been remiss, but I have a good excuse. I had asked Myles about the beautiful gold medal he's wearing on his uniform coat, and he was taking great pains to answer all my silly little questions about its origin and what it means."

"I warrant Captain Keogh was," George said, now giving me a glance as he put a hand out to draw his wife in the direction he wanted. "He's always ready to talk about his medals."

"I do wish people would leave me alone about them, General," I said. "I know they're just being kind to ask about such an outlandish-looking set of decorations. I guess that's due to their scarcity in the States."

I felt good enough about the way that whole event and exchange had gone to allow myself more drink than I should have that night, though I'm sure I didn't match the amount that Major Reno got down that thirsty throat of his. I know I wouldn't be spoken to by Libbie again that evening, and in fact I caught her looking at me only a couple of more times during the rest of that gay gathering at the home of the Custers.

★ ★

I must confess I had some section of that little episode of Libbie and the Agnus Dei medal in mind as I stood in a conference circle of company commanders in Custer's tent at the end of another long day of trailing the pesky red man across that desolate landscape of the Montana. But now we were close onto the bunch of them, according to all signs and all reports from the Crow and Ree scouts working on behalf of the Seventh. The drag marks of travois, the great gouges of unshod hooves, the fresh piles of manure from both horses and Indians, and near the end of day the fact that a small cadre of troopers had happened on a group of Sioux breaking into a bread box that had fallen off the load of one of our pack mules, all these indications said to us we were hoving into range of the whole bunch of Sioux and Cheyennes we'd been assigned to find and whip into shape for the good of one and all.

Major Reno was up and talking at great length, as always, and Custer was staring down at the ground as he generally did when the old dark-faced boyo who liked his whisky so much began to orate. It would be only a matter of a couple of minutes at most that Georgie would allow Reno's rant to go on, and all the rest of us were already beginning to feel the climate build there in the commander's tent, and the longer Custer delayed cutting Reno off in mid-career the more we knew it'd likely be a big boom of an event when it happened. The feeling I got when I caught the eye of Captain Cooke for half a tick, before we both looked off so as not to be suspected of judging any damn thing which might be going on, was akin to the way a storm coming on in that western country would always feel before it got there in full force with all guns firing.

What you'd know out here in the Montana and the Black Hills about weather was that a great spell of it was coming long before it finally arrived. The sky is so big here, so big you can see a disturbance in the elements building a long way off and a good space of time before you can actually feel the effects of the storm. You get plenty of warning in the West when a big bad spasm of ill wind and portent is preparing to come your way and do its damage. You can see it, and you can hear it, and you can know there's no way to outrun it, to hide away, to get good shelter from the bad time coming or to delay its getting to wherever it wants to go. Lads, it's coming and it'll get here and it'll boom and it'll blow and it'll do you what it wants, and there's not a damn thing you can try to slow it down or make it stop. Nothing avails against a big blow in the West.

That's the way it began to feel in Custer's tent on the night before the day we expected to catch up to the Indians we'd been seeking to find and to give a good solid spanking to. A storm was building, one that promised to be longer and stronger than any we'd had to endure before, and Reno's jabbering on about what he should be allowed to do with his division of troopers and how he should and should not be judged in his handling of the task that would be set him by brevet General Custer was naught but a little wind way ahead of the big blow that was going to come. And when that one got here, it would be moving sagebrush and small trees and bits of earth and rock, and all of us within reach of the storm Custer would stir up would have to just lower our heads and suffer the damage until all was calm again.

But a new thing occurred at the end of Reno's yammering on, as it began to lose steam and to sputter and die, and that in itself was a strange and wondrous moment, for I'd not seen Reno allowed to talk until he quit of his own accord before. Up until then I'd seen nothing bring Reno to a standstill but Custer's shutting him up like slamming a door to a room you'd finished being in for a long time to come. No, no, that time it wasn't the way it went. There in Custer's tent, that trailing off of Reno's rant fell silent of its own weight.

"Well," Georgie said, "thank you for your expression about the work ahead of us, Major Reno. Now is there anything else anyone wants to add to that before I lay out what we'll be doing the rest of the night here and on the morrow to come?"

Strange doings, said I to myself, keeping my head down so as not to risk looking around me and getting caught viewing another man with a question in my eyes, George Custer being one who never let a questioning look by another pass without a killing look of his own if not the expression of a strong challenge to such behavior.

After a pause of fully half a minute, though it felt like a week to me, Captain Benteen cleared his throat and prepared to launch a salvo or two. I fully expected that fusillade to take place, having seen such firing occur before whenever Benteen and Custer were in the same location, so I tried to let my mind wander. Generally, my mind thanks me for such allowance, but that meeting of officers that night in the commander's tent was so out of the ordinary as to force me to listen more to what Benteen was giving voice to than I ordinarily wanted. It would be naught but his quibbling over some details of assignment made him by Custer, I figured, but after the first sentence or two, it came to me that more serious disagreement than usual was being brandished about. Not only did Captain Benteen find fault with what his commanding officer was telling him to do with the troops assigned to him, but he was threatening some physical violence if Custer did not withdraw some assertion he had made about some matter earlier in the conversation.

Damn me, I thought, I should have been listening to all that was said for a change rather than dreading being in a conference so long I'd feel like busting out the side of the tent and running off into the dark where the Indians lived. I'll have to ask Cooke later on why Benteen is so exercised and why Custer is backing off what he's supposed to have said or implied about Benteen's performance.

"If any man," Captain Benteen was saying, "chooses to call into question an action or statement of mine that's been supposed to have occurred or been uttered, I stand ready to settle the account so offered by any means amenable to both the accuser and myself."

"You misunderstand me, Captain Benteen," Custer said in a mild and placatory tone, so unlike his usual dash and volume that this time I could not resist seeking the eye of William Cooke for confirmation of what I thought I was hearing. He wouldn't look at me. That told me all I needed to know. "Please accept my regret at misstating in such a fashion as to confuse your understanding," Custer was saying. Benteen glared and grunted, saying naught else, and in less than five minutes we were all dismissed after being told to have our companies ready to move in two hours, with full weaponry in the dead of night so as to get the jump on the hostiles. We'd be in place for action early in the next day, it seemed. I'll be ready for that, I said to myself, thinking I'd repeat the statement to Cooke when I got the chance. I'll take that option, given a choice between facing the Sioux and Cheyennes or being in the same boxing ring with Benteen and Custer.

A drink or two from my next-to-last bottle of whisky, and an inquiry of Cooke as to his supply remaining of the liquid in question, and then off to issue orders to my sergeants. When the sun begins to rise on the morrow, the twenty-fifth of June, we'll have laid eyes on the village we've been seeking and then we'll see where we go from there. Then my questions to put to Cooke. And just what is up with the boy general? And why has he cut off what's left of his hair? And stuck a straw hat on his head where the golden locks used to be? Damned if I would so violate my appearance, but then of course I've got a lot of manly tresses to spare, and what you've got a lot of, hair or Papal decorations for valor or the admiration of sweet little women or whatever the possession might be, you leave it all in place for later use and display, if need ever be. Then or now, it's time to get ready to mount up.

I was ready for a good stiff ride horseback and a chance to chase the wily red man across the plain now that we'd have him and his fellows all rounded up in one place easy to get at. A fine airing out it would be for the Seventh Cavalry, and I'd make sure my part of it, my little I Company of men, did their part in such a way as it showed to best advantage. A nice little United States of America medal would match up pretty as a picture next to the old Agnus Dei, and won't that please the ladies?

JOURNALIST AND REPORTER FOR THE BISMARCK TRIBUNE, DAKOTA TERRITORY, ON ASSIGNMENT WITH THE SEVENTH CAVALRY

JUNE 24, 1876

RESPLENDENT IS THE WORD I WANT TO USE IN DESCRIBING THE appearance of George A. Custer, Commander of the Seventh Cavalry, when the fighting is over and the outcome of the battle is settled for good for that collection of Indian tribes gathered together on the Little Bighorn. I sense the final curtain poised for closing on that bloody drama that has been played out for so long by those savage nations. That word, resplendent, in its meaning and in sound and appearance, whispers like the prairie wind come to announce the impending storm which gathers. That word, I claim, though standing alone with no others to support it, seems highly apt to what I want to express of the sense of bravery, gallantry, and commitment to duty I'll be conveying in print to the public of Dakota as emblematic of the action the Seventh will see tomorrow and the crucial role its leader will play in achieving the victory. That victory will mark the end of major resistance by the Sioux and Cheyenne nations to the spread of civilization, commerce, trade, and governmental justice in the West. Long have we waited for the day of deliverance, and that day promises to dawn tomorrow.

What then will stand between America and the fulfillment of its destiny, now that the Civil War is further behind us and all that impedes the growth of peace and prosperity to the rest of our share of this continent are the unschooled and unruly savages? That crowd of heathen primitives shall have had their day. They shall fade into the sunset of history, forgotten and unmourned.

What is fated to come out of this joyous opportunity for me personally is difficult to set reasonable limit to, I must tell myself. But I must restrain my enthusiasm, keep tight rein on my assiduous note taking and my writing of copy, and stay as calm professionally as I can force myself to be. Given the size of the accomplishment brevet General Custer will achieve tomorrow, my sole account of how it plays out in battle, complete with eyewitness detail and the vigor of personal participation by this observer in this great action, and the hunger of the Eastern press for news of the final clearing out of the Indian and what obstacles to progress he represents—all this will give my work such prominence and attractiveness that my name overnight will be a watchword in all the newspapers of American cities of all descriptions.

I may be writing on simple assignment for a small news journal in Dakota, but the telegraph will spread what I report to the papers of New York, Philadelphia, Baltimore, Boston, St. Louis, and all others hungry for word about the great work of the Seventh Cavalry on expedition in the Montana Territory. As a result of my reporting and of my written words, I'll be called to what new assignment and what new city I know not at present. But it will not be located in a small town in the raw West. This coup will propel me to heights unimagined.

So, resplendent. That is the word. That label will begin the story I will write, and the adjective that will end it will be triumphant. My little motherless daughters back with my sister in Minnesota will have nothing to say of me but praise. Their futures will be assured. My editors—past, present, and to come—will seek me, and I will pick and choose from their offerings. My poor wife, were she yet alive, would praise the day she settled for marriage to a mere scribbler of words, a journalist with dim prospects at best initially, and I will be able to announce to the West, to the nation, and to the world at large this simple declaration.

I go with Custer and will be at the death of the red devils.

Waymon Needler
ON THE LITTLE BIGHORN, EARLY MORNING

JUNE 25, 2001

I WAS RELATIVELY WELL MOUNTED, MY HORSE ONE OF THE USUAL bunch from Rent-A-Real-Ride in Bozeman, the horse supplier to the Last Stand Reenactors for the last five years, if not longer. When I first looked at the markings on the gelding I was to mount a week ago, I even suspected I might have ridden this animal one time before, a couple of years back when I was filling the part of an Irish émigré, a private in the brigade that had been totally wiped out with Custer himself on what's now called Last Stand Hill. I hadn't really had to do much riding then as the young trooper, since to be historically accurate—and that's what we strive for in every detail, as much as we can achieve it—the fighting that took place at the end on the hill was mostly on foot, and I had been killed by the terrible wounds of two arrows in the chest, finished off by a stone club wielded by a young guy calling himself Red Bird Flies Up. Not to worry: the arrows were inserted in a device worn beneath the cavalry shirt and the club was made of foam rubber. It looked wonderfully real, though, in the video and in the still photo.

I hadn't minded not getting to ride much back then when I was playing Patrick Bruce, the raw recruit lately from Ireland, not because I had a problem with my horsemanship—I didn't, having had plenty of instruction back in Texas and lots of practice there and in Montana on an annual basis—but because as Patrick Bruce at least I was a full participant in the last major action of the reenactment, and I did die on the hill with General Custer himself. I wasn't stuck off with Reno and Benteen's divisions away from the dramatic heart of things. I admit I didn't stand out, being a brand new rookie private only enlisted in the Seventh Cavalry for a little over a month when I was slaughtered, but there was a great photo taken of me, by chance selected for publication in promo material and appearing on the front page of several newspapers—small ones, sure, but still in the public eye—and that photo shows me with the arrows protruding from my chest and me falling down with my Springfield single-shot just tumbling from my grip.

It was very dramatic, that shot, even Eagle Beak admits that, and I've had it blown up and hung in the room we call the study at home, the place where we put up diplomas and certificates and recognitions of achievement and family pictures and curios and whatnot. Marie wouldn't let me display it in the living area, where I wanted to put it above the fireplace, since according to her it didn't match the décor well enough. Don't get me wrong. She is most supportive and endures my ongoing involvement with the Last Stand Reenactors, and never complains about the time it takes to do it right or the money I spend on equipment and travel. She even went with me once to the reenactment but got bored since she wasn't directly involved. I really think you have to occupy a position in the Seventh to really feel a part of the whole ethos of the historical tribute. It's an emotional thing. But she's a real trooper, my wife, and when I use that term to praise Marie, it means something. Let me tell you, speaking as a member of the Seventh Cavalry, the rank of trooper is as serious as a heart attack.

But on the occasion of the 125th anniversary of the Last Stand on the Little Bighorn, or as Eagle Beak a.k.a. Mirabeau Sylestine adamantly prefers to call it, the Greasy Grass, I am well mounted on a horse given by its corporate owner in Bozeman the pedestrian tag of Big Brown, but called by me Cheyenne Thunder when I'm in the saddle, and I'm gratified by that since I've got a lot of riding to do in my role of Major Marcus Reno, what with the charge toward Sitting Bull's village, the encounter with that swarm of warriors, and the retreat across the Little Bighorn and the defense at the top of the ridge. Or as it's been called for well over a century now, Reno's Hill.

And back to the name of the horse I'm riding: a horse doesn't care what it's called, especially a professional animal. They're really dumb, actually. Not like pigs.

I know, going into my impersonation of the major, that Reno is not a sympathetic character, of course. I stay well up on the history of that military expedition, on new developments in research and altered interpretations of events and fact, and I understand Reno's reputation will never be rehabilitated. I know he was a drunk, that he was slugging down whisky during the battle, that he abandoned his command in combat and ran for his life, that he called his abject flight a charge, hoping to forestall criticism of his cowardice even as he was displaying it. All the well-founded reasons to hold Reno in contempt I understand and join in. I was the first to laugh this past practice week when the Benteen reenactor called Reno a drunk cowardly fool and pointed at me in full uniform as we were having lunch at the caterer's wagon, saying something like "He's the reason Custer died, that man standing right there with a mouthful of Philly cheesesteak."

I learned a long time ago when I was the subject of bullying in my school days that the best response is not to get emotional or fight back, but to join in the laughter. That hurts inside, and I know it, but at least you don't get your butt kicked physically if you join in ridicule of yourself. Usually, that is. What I'm getting at is this, and it's something Eagle Beak knows well for a couple of good reasons. Here it is. Reenacting Reno, taking on his persona, and channeling his thoughts and historically accurate statements is not an end in itself to me. All of that is a bridge to another shore.

And on that shore stands the figure of Yellow Hair or Long Hair or Son of the Morning Star or whatever label of the many assigned him back then and over the years you may want to choose. I mean the man himself. I'm talking about brevet General George Armstrong Custer, who perished with his entire command on the hill where the visitor's center maintained by the National Park Service now stands. As I perform Marcus Reno truly and well to the best of my ability, my eye is on the prize. With each expression of ineptitude and drunkenness and cowardice I successfully generate in my portrayal of Reno, I work my way closer to the selfhood of GAC.

When I say that, I know that Larry L. Lamont has been Custer for donkey's years. And for good reason. I know he inhabits that personality

24-7, twelve months out of the year in DuBois, Wyoming, where he moved from Huntsville, Alabama, as soon as he assumed the persona of Custer the first time he was allowed that, giving up a most lucrative insurance agency to take up the task of having to develop another one in a tiny, less prosperous locale. I know his wife, born Myrtice Williford in Hazel Green, Alabama, now calls herself Libbie Custer and dresses the part most of the time. I've never seen her in shorts and flipflops and a casual hairdo or dresses from Walmart. I know the couple is childless, just as were the Custers. They keep dogs, blooded wolfhounds, as did GAC. They eat authentic foods from the nineteenth century, or at least as true to the recipes and ingredients that Myrtice continually seeks for her arsenal of materials to reproduce an authentic diet for her and the general. Here's the clincher as far as I'm concerned. I have never seen either one of them eat a single morsel from the caterer's truck during a reenactment week, and let me tell you, Bozeman's Best Beef, Barbecue, and Beverage turns out some toothsome fare that would tempt anyone. The Custer couple nevertheless does not partake. I tip my hat to Larry L. Lamont and Myrtice as GAC and Libbie.

One thing I will not do, by the way, however, is to call her Libbie outside the dramatic confines of the reenactment itself, no matter how she might insist we all do. And oh does she do that. She won't even acknowledge her real name when it's yelled in her ear.

I understand all these facts, and I take them into myself. I consume them as though they were edible fare. I face them, just as GAC faced Crazy Horse and Gall and Sitting Bull and over four thousand Sioux and Cheyenne warriors on June 25, 1876. But as he did not quail, neither shall I. I shall suffer inhabiting the selfhood of Marcus Reno in durance vile, and I shall wait and I shall work and I shall live in darkness. And eventually at some magically-charged moment I shall reenact that moment of defeat and perseverance and glory over 125 years ago on the Little Bighorn yet again as I do this year, with one change. That change shall be an acceptance of fate, destiny, and circumstance. It will come when and as it is meet to do so. I shall accept it. And on that day to come, I shall assume the burden and responsibility of my role as George Armstrong Custer himself. I he, and he me.

At this point so early in the morning, most of us full of a sturdy breakfast and refreshed by a good night's rest, we were milling about on our mounts, those of us who have horse assignments, while the foot cavalry, as we laughingly call them, scurried from spot to spot dealing with issues of uniform adjustments and repairs, questions from old hands about departures in procedure from earlier reenactments, and all the last-minute demands which arise with any dramatic production. At this point in the day, were General Custer or any other officer or enlisted man from 1876 transported from that time 125 years ago to spyglass hill where he could look down on the great clump of us below, I knew what that time traveler would be likely to say.

"Eagle Beak," I said to Mirabeau in a voice he could hear but not one so loud it might look strange to a disinterested observer watching Major Marcus Reno speaking to a painted and befeathered Sioux warrior, "what do you think one of the old boys in the original bunch might say if he was looking at all of us today waiting to kick off the action of June 25, 1876? Indian or trooper, either one."

As I suspected he might do, Mirabeau responded to me with a couple of words in the Alabama language, an associated tongue of the Creek tribes of the eastern forest, but I wasn't ready to let him get away with that so early in the morning, particularly since he'd been trying it every day during practice week. "All I heard you say was some curse word found only on the reservation of the Alabama-Coushatta back in East Texas, Mirabeau," I said. "If you can't speak Sioux, stick with English so folks can know what you're trying to convey."

"All I said," Eagle Beak said finally after drawing a long breath and letting it out as though it pained him, "was that anybody from the original bunch would be saying where is everybody? No matter if it was a white man or an Indian, he wouldn't know what to think about seeing less than a hundred Indians and a little over that of whites standing around while they arranged themselves to fight."

"Well, it's a dramatic reenactment, Eagle Beak," I said. "It's not the thing itself. What matters is the idea of the thing, not the thing itself."

"That's the way you white men live. Not with the truth, but with an imitation of it, and that satisfies you right down to the ground."

I didn't try to argue the point with Mirabeau, having heard the same thing said by him for several years now. At first I was bothered by that attitude, and I even asked him why he came from East Texas all the way to Montana each June to take part in an event he thought to be a living lie. It took me a while to understand what motivated him, but when I finally did it all made sense, and I could feel relaxed about my faithful red companion. Here's what came to me about the third time Mirabeau and I had traveled from home to Montana to take symbolic part in the bloody event on the banks of that river.

During that evocation of the Last Stand, I was playing the part of an Italian-born soldier, late from New York City and on the run because of a legal problem back in the Bronx, and Mirabeau was a brave in the Hunkpapa branch of the Sioux, nothing more than the Indian equivalent of a foot soldier of no real prominence or history. He was all nicely painted up, though, armed with a bow and a quiver full of arrows and a stone club with a sheaf of buzzard feathers attached to it. Mirabeau was wearing his real hair long then, and the computer place where he was employed was run by a gaggle of young guys from California who didn't care how they or their code writers or even their clients looked to the world at large. All that mattered to them was rooting for West Coast college football teams on the weekend and raking in greenback dollars the rest of the time. Long hair was cool with them, if they even noticed it.

So, given the good costume and the weapons and the paint pony he'd been assigned and especially the long hair flying in the wind with feathers and beads worked all through it, Mirabeau Lamar Sylestine looked about as real an Indian as one weighing no more than 125 pounds with all teeth intact and in excellent repair could look.

"Mirabeau," I said, being jocular, "you are looking so good, my fine young warrior. Give me a high five." At that, he turned and gave me a look that had about it more authenticity than any other bit of acting business I had ever seen on the banks of the Little Bighorn up until then and since that day. It said, that look of intense concentration did, not "I'm about to kill you, white man," or "Just keep standing there until I get my stone club unlimbered," but instead it asked a simple question: are you a human being? Are you and I of the same species of mammal, or am I being talked to by a porcupine suffering from brain damage?

Mirabeau, or as I should say, in his present manifestation, Eagle Beak, was clearly seeing before him not a member of his reenactment group from Annette, Texas, and not a fellow inhabitant of Coushatta County in a different country. No, he was in the presence of maybe a talking raccoon, or a possum that stood on its hind legs and walked around like a man, or it could be a coyote that wore eyeglasses. He was in the Indian equivalent of purgatory. Or maybe the main dining room of a giant Chuck E. Cheese.

What I'm saying is that Mirabeau Lamar Sylestine in his transformed state was truly not himself but another being. Understanding the fact of what had happened to my faithful Indian companion, when he donned the proper covering and picked up the appropriate weapons designed to obliterate another being from life itself, had let me know I'd never be able to achieve what he had done and would be able to do again at will. He had become what he had imagined, and for good or for ill, I'd never be able to become any being other than Waymon Needler, teacher of home economics in the public high school of Annette, Texas, no matter what strange garb I donned or makeup and fake beard I put upon my face. I was who I was, and imagine though I might until I passed out and wet my pants in a fit, I'd still wake up knowing that.

I never told Mirabeau what I had realized on that day those several years ago, there on the Montana prairie. Nor have I ceased to attempt to imagine a self for me other than my once and present and future one as I seek each June to escape the bounds which hold me. He didn't need to know what an advantage he held over me, and I was certainly not going to admit to being a lesser creature than he, real or imagined. To let him know that would be to admit that what he thought about the nature of the Native American had at least some truth to it. They were different, I told myself, in strange ways, and that's why we had had as a race to wipe them out and find ways to keep the remainder under close control. What else could we do as a people?

The reenactment we create each year on the Little Bighorn is not only entertaining and historically relevant, it's also necessary. It's as potent in meaning and as crucial to ongoing life for the white man as the Sun Dance was for Sitting Bull, chief of the Oglala Sioux. We have to do the reenactment to keep the very nature of time in order and the structure of reality securely in place, but we can't let the Indians know why we're doing it. What we provide in support of our ongoing culture here in the twenty-first century supplies the same function as the whisky and the smallpox we began giving the red man on a steady basis hundreds of years ago. It was him or us, and we knew it. We had to poison him like we did if we intended to prevail.

"What are you talking about?" Eagle Beak had finally asked me at that moment when I stood staring into his eyes as I realized why I knew what I had to do on behalf of my race. "What do you mean, Waymon?"

"Nothing," I said. "I'm just messing with you." Little did he know how true that was and how true it will remain. Just messing then, messing now, and messing in time to come. Here, little red fellow, take a bite of this sweet thing we fixed just especially for you. Come on, open up, you'll love its lasting taste. But first let me cut your hair, get rid of those hideous garments, and teach you to speak English and write words down on paper. Learn to communicate, for goodness sake.

That was then, though, when that realization took place, and the present moment was in the year of our Lord 2001 and thus the 125th anniversary of the Last Stand, and sounds of crucial announcements were being teed up by bullhorn. Alec Murray was about to speak, and when that happens, all other occasions of public address pale in comparison.

"Here it comes," I said to Eagle Beak, "the marching orders for the day delivered from on high. Get ready to genuflect." That little attempt to humor on the early morning of June twenty-fifth had no effect on my faithful Indian companion, and I didn't expect it to. What it indicated, unfortunately, is a truth about my habit of behavior in the face of any tense moment that I may find myself facing. Rather than quieting down and trying to vanish into the woodwork, as most shy people do at such times, instead I start trying to find ways to lighten the mood. That typically involves not-so-funny asides at too many points, and on too many occasions loudly stated opinions which are intended to dampen down anxiety. The danger is that they often end up annoying others.

An example, one I'm a little hesitant to express, but I'm among friends, right? See what I mean? I'm doing it right now, even as I'm trying to reveal a truth and by such revelation ameliorate its downside. But I'm too deep into the river to turn back now, as members of Major Reno's command must have been realizing as they struggled to get back across the Little Bighorn to where there were not so many Sioux and Cheyenne warriors putting arrows and chunks of lead into the air and swinging clubs at their heads as they stumbled through the chest-deep water, pursued by what they must have thought to be imps of Satan himself.

Here's the example, then, I was about to offer but had to leave off until I had calmed my nerves enough to start babbling about it. It has to do with one of those ordinarily private moments between a man and a woman, in my case me as husband and Marie as wife, those episodes of total closeness, if you get my drift. Too many times that I hate to even admit, I'll be at the moment of truth during a romantic encounter with my mate, not to put too fine a point on it, when all is coming to a conclusion devoutly to be wished (that's a statement from Shakespeare, I think), and just as I'm achieving what Marie at that moment so desires that she's showing evidence of that fact and thus making me too aware to be able to bear the stress, it'll come into my silly head to make a comment to break the tension. To give a specific, I remember saying something on one of these occasions that so outraged my dear lovemate that she not only banished me from the marital bed but kept me at arm's length for fully a month after.

Here's what I said to her, a thing that just burst out of my mouth. And I said it with a measured rhythm, even including sound effects of steam escaping a boiler under great pressure. "Here comes the choo choo down the track, rocking and whistling. I can hear you huffing and puffing. Better jump back."

She took that wrong, thinking I was trying for a cheap laugh when laughter was the furthest thing from her mind. She said my attitude was flippant, and it revealed how shallow I was and how little a romantic moment with her meant to me. I must admit I made things worse by what I said next, and again it just popped out as an expression in support of a need I had to try to return to a calmer state. It would soothe, my nutty brain suggested to me. "Well," I said, lying there beside my wife so ill-used, "I understand you're not in the mood any more, but could you find it in your heart to give me a little reach-around in the meantime?"

I'd just recently seen some gruff character say that in a movie, thought it inappropriate in an artistic production, but in the moment of stress in which I found myself there in the dark with my wife smoldering beside me as she felt around for her pajama bottoms, that's what jumped into my crazy head. She took it wrong, but I was never able to get her to see where she had misinterpreted my intention.

So, there on the early morning of June twenty-fifth, fully uniformed in an outfit designed to be as much as possible like one Major Marcus Reno would have been wearing that hot day back in 1876, sitting on a horse with the emblem of the Seventh Cavalry worked into its saddle blanket, Eagle Beak beside me resplendent as a Sioux warrior in full war paint, when I heard the voice of Alec Murray begin to come out of a really high-quality and powerful bullhorn, I had two choices. One was I could have stayed quiet and thus been unable to contain myself and Lord knows what my body might have done: vomited? Passed out? Pissed itself? Or I could have made a little joke out loud for the benefit of Eagle Beak. The choice was obvious.

"His master's voice," I went on to say, nodding my head toward where Alec's voice had its origin and even leaning toward Eagle Beak. "Hark, hark, the lark."

"Shut the fuck up," the undersized brave beside me said from his pony. "If you start up, Waymon, I swear to God I'll brain you."

"You're speaking to Major Marcus Reno, you little savage," I heard myself say. "And I need a drink."

"I'm not . . ." Eagle Beak said, breaking off in the middle of his utterance, and I knew why he did that. It would just encourage me to keep chattering in my moment of stress. Instead, he pulled rein, and his pony took a step away from my mount off to the side in response.

"If you had a stirrup on that rig . . . " I started to say, wanting to comment on the disadvantage Native Americans on horseback typically had in comparison to the white man's stirrup, but I was able to stop in the middle of that, since Alec Murray had just said something that seized my attention and that of all other reenactors listening, whites and Indians alike.

"Let me repeat, so that all members of this dramatic company can be certain they heard what I just said. Larry Leland Lamont has been taken ill, I repeat, and by that I mean severely. Let me assure you that Triple L is not in any drastically serious state or situation, the doctor says. He will be fit for duty, but not for the next forty-eight hours or so. Myrtice has kept me posted since about three a.m. when she first called to let me know the news." Alec spoke these words in the usual timbre he assumed when tasked with addressing a public group, but I could not but detect another layer of meaning just below the surface of his beautifully articulated words. That layer bordered not on the hysteric, I must say, but it was touched with a tone ordinarily associated with a state near panic. Alec Murray was communicating clearly, but he was revealing, despite his professionalism and his need to inform clearly, something else as well.

Let me put it this way, since I may speak with some validity as a teacher, one who uses the verbal to inform, instruct, and above all to control the hearers of the message. Suppose I in my role as instructor of home economics were to note a disaster in the making in a class devoted to baking a casserole, say. Suppose further that I detect a young student about to add an ingredient or adjust improperly some setting on a range oven, and I realize if I don't speak clearly and to the point instantaneously all will go for naught. The hour of instruction will have failed. Perhaps some student will have been burned badly enough to require medical attention, or someone's clothing will burst into flames. Or at least the casserole will be ruined. If I do not communicate effectively, a disaster looms. My voice must be controlled, but there will be emotional pressure behind what I say.

That's what was happening with Alec Murray. "It appears at this point, my fellow dramaturges, that we may not have brevet General George Armstrong Custer ready to lead the Seventh Cavalry into its annual disaster on this historic day. The 125th anniversary of the Last Stand of the Seventh on the banks of the Little Bighorn at this point threatens to be leaderless."

Cries arose immediately from the troopers and warriors, but all had in common one theme: deep fear and doom. "No," I shouted, pleased to be able to release the tension I had been feeling build in me. "No, not that." I felt better immediately after the relief of speaking. I shouted again, but not words this time, just a simple outcry of heartfelt alarm.

"It's the Greasy Grass," Eagle Beak said beside me. "Did you hear that? Alec just called the river by its government name. That river was called the Greasy Grass long before any white man named it."

"Focus, Mirabeau," I said. "Focus. It's not important what anything's called if Custer's taken so sick he can't lead the Seventh."

"Alec," someone was shouting—Jimmy Proudfoot, a present-day Sioux subchief who yelled, it sounded like to me. "Can't you step in for Larry? You've done Custer years ago, right?"

"No, no," Alec said, his voice now showing less dismay and a lot more zip now that his past days as an reenactor had been mentioned. He'd been okay handling the role of Custer, people told me, back in the day, but the first time he begged off and let Larry L. Lamont step in for what was supposed to be a one-time shot, the reenactment had found its true Custer.

Alec had truly suffered his last stand. He was never asked to impersonate the Son of the Morning Star again. "Folks, first of all I can't compare to the performance Larry puts on," he went on to say manfully. "I know that and as a professional I applaud what Larry can do. He is Custer, people, and we all recognize that. And we love and admire him for his talent. And I haven't had occasion to think about the part for years, that's the first thing, and the second has to do with my health."

"Oh, no, no," came the cries, to which Alec raised both hands, palms out, in a graceful gesture conveying regret and finality.

"The medicos say no stress physically for yours truly any longer. None. I'm warned not even to perform as announcer these days, but I'm not yet ready to relinquish that yet."

"Perish the thought," one of the Cheyenne warriors shouted, shaking his turtle rattle back and forth and moving his feet as though he were about to break into a mourning dance. "No one could do it better than you, Alec."

"Thank you so much, Duck Killer," Alec Murray said, "for those kind words. But I'm out of the equation. Things being what they are now with Larry Leland Lamont, what can we do to meet the challenge before us? That's the vexing question."

"God, he does love that bullhorn, doesn't he?" Eagle Beak said. I didn't respond to that, not wanting to miss a word, and naturally not wanting to encourage such off-the-point carping. Who cares about bullhorn usage at such a moment?

"Could we just postpone for the next two days?" White Man Runs Him said in his high-pitched voice. "You know, just wait until Larry gets well enough to take on the mantle." Terence Leaping Deer as White Man Runs Him does a great Crow scout bit in the annual reenactment, State Farm Insurance agent in Bozeman though he is, and he's highly regarded professionally in little theatre circles as a character actor. He doesn't much physically resemble what a Crow scout would have looked like, and you can tell that by studying some of the old photographs of the historic White Man Runs Him. That's because Terence is actually of Japanese heritage. His parents were imprisoned in a camp in California during World War II, despite being native-born Americans—part of the embarrassment of that nasty little episode of the treatment of minority groups in periods of peril. We too often fall short as a nation, alas.

But put Terence Leaping Deer in full costume as White Man Runs Him and pose him beside Larry L. Lamont in Custer's white buckskin uniform and the long locks and the red kerchief at the throat, it'll never cross your mind that you're looking at a man of Japanese genetic heritage who can sell insurance well enough to have been recognized as one of the top State Farm agents in Montana. And let me tell you, accident and weather-related losses in the mountain state are per capita among the highest in this nation. It's always been rough to live in the Montana territory and try to make a living fighting off disasters while keeping your scalp firmly attached to your skull.

But when Terence Leaping Deer (how he assumed that surname I won't go into) mentioned the possibility of postponing the reenactment on the 125th anniversary of that event so crucial to the mythic history of the United States, the roar of disapproval and rejection that arose from the uniformed troopers of the Seventh Cavalry, the mule handlers, and the Native Americans in fully authenticated costume was so loud I was put in mind of the sounds of battle that must have erupted on that hot afternoon of June twenty-fifth in 1876 when Crazy Horse's bunch broke through the line of the troopers with Custer on that sacred hill.

I'll confess that my throat suffered sharp pain as my scream of defiance to such a proposal joined the others around me. Even Eagle Beak, deep into the cool phase of his impersonation of an Oglala Sioux warrior, joined the rest of us in shouting down the idea of a postponement of our reason for being where we were. "Now is the time," Eagle Beak was shouting as I just simply voiced the word *NO* over and over again.

"Now is the time," Eagle Beak said again and again, following that statement with another. "All correspondences are in place, all are in place."

"What does that mean, Mirabeau?" I said as the uproar died down a bit and as White Man Runs Him repeated his own phrase, which seemed to have a calming effect.

"I was just saying," Terence Leaping Deer said as himself and not as White Man Runs Him. "Not to worry, folks. Please."

"I was just saying," Eagle Beak said to me, picking up on the disclaimer. "I was just stating the obvious fact about correspondences. And resonance." He said this last word to me as though daring me to raise an objection. So I said the word as though asking a question.

"Resonance?" I said up.

"Resonance," Eagle Beak said down.

"Say no more," Alec Murray was shouting into his bullhorn. "Say no more," and the way he said that with a humorous twist broke the spell enough for most folks to quiet their noise. I repeated my question to Eagle Beak about what he meant by resonance, and he turned a dead eye on me as though looking at a simple-minded child who'd asked something like, "What makes the wind blow and then stop and not blow anymore?"

"If you have to ask about what correspondences and resonance are in the event we're working to recreate," he said, "I don't know what to say to you, Major Reno. Read Mircea Eliade, dip into Northrop Frye, look into your own dreams and try to understand. God!"

Not only was Mirabeau Lamar Sylestine heavily into writing code for a living, he also took courses at night at the community college in Annette. He subscribed to magazines that never had a single photograph or a reference to a commonly known person anywhere in them. What else can you do for self-entertainment if you weigh less than 125 pounds, don't date women, and aren't gay? Because of his reading of such specialized material, he does not consider me as possessor of an intellect equivalent to his, but I put it to you this way. Who has a master's degree and who has only a bachelor's? I'll say no more.

"I know what correspondences are, Mirabeau, and that other term you used, too," I said with a little heat, given how stressed I was by our sudden situation as a reenactment corps. What we faced on the morning of June 25, 2001, was a gastro-intestinally stricken Custer on our hands, a general so disabled by some lower bowel condition that he couldn't leave his motel room, much less make all the mistakes again as he'd done in his first manifestation as commanding officer of the Seventh Cavalry in June of 1876. I'm talking primarily about his decision to divide his force into three groups and how he distributed them. Why, oh why, did he send Benteen so far away from where the real action started up? And Reno chosen to attack the village? What? Huh?

"I know correspondences," I went on to say to Eagle Beak, "and I know they aren't limited to old-fashioned personal letters sent by the post office. Do give me a little credit, please."

Eagle Beak said nothing in response, and I wasn't surprised by his refusal to engage further, as deep into his Siouxness as he had descended by the morning of June 25. I wouldn't have taken it as strange if he had broken into a death song of the Oglala at that point, given his dedication to seceding from all that was twenty-first century and white-culture related. But I'd made my point, and he'd had nothing to counter it, so I was feeling a little justified in leaning back in my saddle and relaxing a bit. My beard was itching a little, given the fact that it was cosmetic and not real, due to my not being able to grow a decently full Reno facial adornment, even if I had been allowed to do that as a teacher in a public high school in Texas. Put it this way. There were no official restrictions against neatly maintained facial hair for teachers in our school district, but Sam Olson—we called him Sam the Sham behind his back—as principal of Annette High would make evident his displeasure with any departure by one of his teachers from a conventional look. Not only would he withhold favors, he would find ways to cost you money.

So I was scratching at a particularly itchy section of my cosmetic Major Reno beard, just in the neck part where the facial hair properly begins on a male, and I was concentrating when doing that, not wanting to get a peeling-off effect started. I had suffered that before at a reenactment, and it had itched constantly and worse of all it had looked fake and caused some laughter among spectators watching me struggle in hand-to-hand battle with Tommy Prejean, who was playing a Cheyenne warrior and as part of the program was about to bash me on the head with a foam rubber club—it looked perfectly real. Don't get me wrong—and some wit among the group watching yelled out these words. I've not been able to forget them. "When you go to scalp him, Indian, why not just peel off his beard and save you some trouble?"

There are many things wrong with that idiot shouting out such a thing, but I won't detail them all. Let's just say the main effect you want to avoid as a reenactor of an historical event is any action that will look funny. That ruins everything, an anachronism does. Timing is all.

So since that episode, which still haunts me, I've spent the bucks necessary to get the best cosmetic facial hair available and have that attached by an expert in working with real actors who make a living in the industry. That means, if I happen to have the responsibility of the part of a bearded trooper or officer of the Seventh, that I must wear the facial adornment for the whole course of the full reenactment. It will sweat, it will become hot, and most of all, it will itch. I call that a small price to pay for authenticity, however. The men of the original Seventh suffered physical discomfort, Lord knows. I can do that myself.

But given my history with cosmetically attached facial hair, I was focusing on the problem of gently scratching my neck to get some relief while not disturbing the security of the attachment of the beard, and in so doing I was not paying full attention to the words from Alec Murray's bullhorn. They came, as always with Alec whenever he hit his stride, as steady and mellow as a mountain stream. Until, that is, I found myself being punched on the upper arm by Eagle Beak, who was not only leaning forward on his pony's back to reach me but urging the little beast to move nearer so he could get my full attention.

"Waymon," he was saying, "Waymon," in this suddenly intense kind tone, and that alone set me into a puzzled state, not even to mention the most significant fact about what he was saying. Mirabeau, a.k.a. Eagle Beak, by calling out my legally real name—notice I'm not saying my emotionally real name—was breaking the illusion of reality which he ordinarily was one of the most reliable maintainers of among any and all reenactors.

"Waymon," he said again, using the computer-geek tone and voice he always employed back home in Annette when living in the twenty-first century, even though he claimed full-blooded identity as an Alabama-Coushatta in East Texas. "Waymon, didn't you hear what Alec just said?"

"Not exactly, Mirabeau," I said, gigging him a little by using his back-home name instead of the Montana label. "I was thinking about what Marcus Reno would have been considering early in the morning of June 25, 1876. So I missed something Alec said, I guess."

Everybody was looking at me, troopers on the big American rental horses, Sioux and Cheyenne warriors on their much smaller ponies, and the Crow and Ree scouts working for the Seventh Cavalry. In particular the Crow scout White Man Runs Him had spun around so far on his mount that he was almost facing me directly. "What's wrong?" I said to Eagle Beak, putting my hand up to my beard as I spoke and patting at it. "Is my beard coming off? So what if it is. I'll get it glued down right just as soon as Alec turns us loose. It's not that funny."

A couple of the Sioux warriors near me started laughing when I said that, throwing back their heads to get room for a full guffaw, and one of them, a fellow from Wyoming with the real name of Jerry something—

he owned a Burger King franchise in Dubois—and the reenactment label of Bear Eating Fish, after he finished his chortling, said, "You might as well take off that Reno beard right now and save yourself some trouble."

Everybody seemed to think that was just hilarious, and I gave the facial hair a good tug, expecting to reveal by its peeling away from my face the reason for all the giggling at my expense. It was still solidly attached, though, and about then Alec Murray chuckled through his bullhorn. "Waymon Needler," Alec was saying, and then correcting himself, "Major Marcus Reno, I should say, to be perfectly correct for the present time and before anything about that changes, I was just telling the troopers of the Seventh and the warriors of the Sioux and Cheyenne that in light of the misfortune that's befallen Larry Lamont in his role as General Custer, I held a meeting before good daylight this morning with the executive council. And to a man, and to a lady, not to exclude Moving Robe Woman, they all agreed that we should approach you about stepping into the boots of our commanding officer in this emergency."

"You mean," I said, then stopped speaking before naming the name. "You mean," I began again, causing a few polite chuckles to well up again, this time not so numerous and a lot more serious. "You mean the council wants me to step into Larry's shoes because he's sick?"

"I said boots, not shoes," Alec said with one of his big grins pasted on his face like a movie poster. "Cavalry boots, to quote myself correctly, and I hope we can continue our conversation about what we need to do over there in the general's tent. Let me just say one more thing, though, and it's at the heart of the task before us. Who else knows more about the Last Stand at the Little Bighorn, and who has studied more deeply over the years the character and actions of GAC on that day than the man from Texas, Waymon Needler? I ask you all that question, as you behold him on his mount."

They all started yelling then, the troopers giving a hearty shout all together much like the sound of an organized cheer at a Texas A&M football game, and the Sioux and Cheyenne warriors voicing that high pitched chant they'd use on going into battle, and I swear I could even hear some trills from eagle-bone whistles the Dog Clan of the Oglala liked to use. That sound is blood chilling, even today. Think about how it must have rung in the hearing of troopers on those hills in 1876. Mirabeau was pounding me on the back and yelling something I couldn't understand with all the noise going on, but I didn't worry about that. I knew what my faithful Indian companion meant, and as I leaned forward on my horse and felt it begin to move in the direction I had the beast headed, I began to peel the Reno beard away from my face, starting at the neckline where it had begun to itch so badly. I couldn't feel a thing now as I pulled away at the fake facial hair, though. No pain, no discomfort, nothing physical. To tell the truth, I was too caught up in trying to recall exactly what configuration of upper-lip beard George Armstrong Custer had been wearing when he led the Seventh on that day a century and a quarter behind us. Not to worry, I told myself. I'll get that mustache right. They'll all help me. We'll all get it right today, and make it be just the way it was, here on the banks of the Little Bighorn where we meet once more to turn back time.

Meanwhile, listen to them yelling at me now, I thought, troopers and Sioux and Cheyenne warriors and Ree and Crow scouts, all joined together to let me know they'll do their part to make it right, if I'll join in and do mine. I will, I said inside my head where no one but the general himself could have heard me, already feeling the personality of Marcus Reno beginning to slip away from me as I rode my great bay horse at a measured walk toward the headquarters tent where I knew the spirit of brevet General George Armstrong Custer was waiting to infuse my sense of self with his essence. I could feel the slovenly slouch of Reno with his paunch becoming faint and growing into the proud upright posture of the commanding officer of the Seventh as I rode, my shoulders thrown back, my chest lifted, my breath coming in a strong deep measure.

My horse knew what had happened, as horses will do in their sense of a shift in the human world that controls them once they leave the state of nature. There is no thought process taking place in the brain of the horse, as there ordinarily is even in the most limited of humans. But beneath me as I leaned in the direction I wished my mount to take, I could sense the animal's gathering his force into himself, and I knew in a physical way that the horse I was riding, a mere rental for any with the coin to claim him, was sensing that he would not be carrying Major Marcus Reno in a timid charge. He would not be in support of that most lamentable segment of that dark day. The beast I was bestriding would not suffer the ignominy of the sudden undisciplined retreat back across the river, Sioux warriors all around with clubs and arrows and bullets picking off troopers of the Seventh Cavalry as they fled leaderless through the stream, up the steep bank, and into the cleared area where they'd be hostage to fortune until the carnage was complete. The horse I rode would not carry a burden of shame.

Instead, the beast I had mounted in my role as Major Reno, coward and failure as an officer that he was, would be transformed into the bay ridden by the Son of the Morning Star himself. At end of day, the intended mount of an inconsequential officer who'd failed his responsibility as leader would be supporting instead the man at the focus point of the Last Stand of the Last Great Cavalier, George Armstrong Custer. I could feel the muscle knowledge entering the movement of the bay beneath me, and I joined the beast in completing the core unit of a cavalry commander. The fighting unit of horse and rider. I was becoming one with the beast I commanded, and I would rise to the occasion of the new task before me.

"Take off that headgear," a trooper yelled. "That slouch hat don't suit you, General."

I lifted my hand, took off the hat authenticated as to type of what Marcus Reno wore in all surviving photographs of him in headgear, and hung it with an air of dismissal on my saddle horn. Everybody cheered at that, even Mirabeau Lamar Sylestine, caught up himself so much in the moment that he had allowed his horse to trot along close behind me. I waved my right hand briskly to one side and then extended it ahead in a gesture mentioned by all biographers and commentators on Custer as his habitual signal to those he led, whether in a marching formation or in a full-scale saber charge into the face of the enemy. The sound that arose at my gesture from the troopers I would soon command in battle was so loud that ravens flew up from a patch of cottonwoods near the Park Center buildings, adding their caws to the tumult.

I restrained myself from speaking a single word, even to myself in silence. Later, I told myself, later. Wait to give voice as Custer until you're properly uniformed for your duties as commander of the Seventh. Be patient as the mantle descends.

Mirabeau Lamar Sylestine
ON THE GREASY GRASS

June 25, 2001

*I*LIKE ALWAYS TO CONTROL MY EXTERNAL APPEARANCE, NO MATTER how I might be feeling inside. That's an ingrained habit, that attention to detail, some might say, one earned by constant repetition of an action, or in this case, an inaction. Put this way, such explanation implies that all choices are no more than the result of an animal need to avoid pain and achieve comfort. So as I've learned to act certain ways while becoming acclimated to the world in which I've been forced by happenstance and genetic makeup to inhabit, I do some things and avoid others. I admit that limitation. We can't all be perfected in manner and appearance at every moment.

In other words, in my growing years when I was treated by white folks in Annette as an Indian, weak in the head and desperate for alcohol, and not good for much but playing basketball and pounding on a tom-tom in the dances done for tourists to the reservation, I learned how to be an Alabama-Coushatta the same way a squirrel learns how to act like a rodent. By avoiding plan and depending on sheer instinct. By not saying, but by doing. By playing the red man, to put it another way.

Wrong! That's not all there is to me. And I show anyone who believes different how wrong they are by my being one of the best information techno-geeks in three counties. And I have a college degree, and it's not in education and certainly not in Native American Studies, though that's now offered in most Texas institutions of higher learning. No, my degree is technical, scientific, and utterly ahistorical. I don't need to be taught about Indians and their mystical ways by people who depend on theory.

So that's the way I handle all misidentifications of me and my direct proclivities. And yet, and yet, I must confess. I do think of myself as an Indian, and I have traveled for each June of the last eight years from the logged-out thickets of East Texas toward the open spaces of the American Great Plains. All right, I'll go ahead and say it. I make that journey to play Indian. And I play Indian with a bunch of white people who end up like me on the twenty-fifth day of that month in a great melee on the banks of the Greasy Grass. Yes, I play Indian, and I dress up and apply paint to my body and put feathers and rocks and other pieces of trash in my hair, and I try to use as few words of English as possible, hard as that is when you're trying to make purchases at any business establishment. Finally, you just point and nod.

But I do all that, and I do it not because of an intellectual drive to be more in touch with the realities of history, but because of an emotional debt which I find it impossible to pay up for good. If you want to be able to function within the limits of the self you're born into through no choice of your own, you have to make concessions, take half a cake and be satisfied with it, and play the cards you're dealt. I understand how to say all that stuff and even how to live by it. I know all those mixed metaphors are at verbal war with each other, but that's business as usual for a Native American in the twenty-first century. It's been that way ever since the first idiot Indians in the West Indies didn't pick up a rock and kill every white man that landed with Columbus off those three little boats they had us memorize the names of in school in Annette, Texas. The Niña, the Pinta, and the Santa Maria. See?

That to me is the crucial fact of American history, one that doesn't get much, if any, show in books and movies and other treatments of the red man native to these shores. To put it another way, the problems the Native American people have had on this continent since 1492 don't have a thing to do with all those wars and battles, big and small, which took place during all that time. No, it's not because of hostilities between Native Americans and all those latecomer immigrants black and white and yellow. The problems of civilization and peace making and keeping didn't come from ongoing conflict. We didn't make the mistake of trying to use violence to keep our land and our way of life. We made the mistake of not killing every white-eye we saw as soon as we saw them, one by one by one. That would have taken care of the problem. Well, for a while at least, a year or two.

I know that's not practical, and I don't really believe it when I'm using the tools of educational improvement and understanding I've gathered over the years from study and diligence and attention to completing tasks. Acting white, in other words. If you don't believe me and think I'm just bragging, just call me at work or e-mail me or text me or follow me on social media, do it blindfolded as to my appearance, and then tell me true if you can detect any Indian-ness in me or my character or my work habits and products. Let me tell you, hoss, right now, and save you some trouble. You can't.

But let me take it a step further and admit my dwelling on the dark side at strategic points. We're back at the beginning when I touch that topic, that being my annual submergence into the character and selfhood of a Sioux or Cheyenne warrior of the late nineteenth century in what the white men called the Montana Territory and what the Indians called the Black Hills. Back in that state, and I say back for several reasons. Chief among these is the notion of backness as meaning a retreat in time and an introduction to a state not real but imagined and therefore a lot more satisfying than the real could ever be. Back in that state there is a magic moment for me. It is the instant I feel most real and most genuine and most alive. It is when I'm bashing the brains out of a white man wearing a beard and dressed in blue clothes with metal buttons on the jacket bearing the likeness of an eagle on them. A bad likeness, I'd like to add. White men can't do eagles. Indians can.

Don't get me wrong. When I'm bashing those brains out, watching the gore fly up, and seeing the bone beneath the skin beginning to creep out, what I'm using as a weapon is a rubber-foam war club looking real enough to cause the spectators to look away from the carnage, fake as it is. And the blood and gore and exposed wounds on the Greasy Grass are all accomplished with theatrical makeup and an endless supply of rubber foam and a special red jelly that clings and drips just like the real thing it's aping. The brain matter? A plastic powder that looks like scrambled eggs when you mix it with water.

And when the battle's over and the white troopers of Custer's Command, the ones of them I've killed that day, and I get together, the beer in Ed's and Millie's Tavern in Crystal City is cold, tastes great, and helps the beefsteak slide right on down. And some of the jokes, depending on who's telling them, are funny enough that all the troopers and Sioux and Cheyenne warriors and the Crow and Ree scouts are laughing like hyenas on an African plain, slapping each other on the back, pointing out stupidities and mistakes made by each and all in this year's battle, and swearing allegiance to each other and to coming back next year to do it all again. Pals to the end in a common enterprise.

Just fun for the boys, eh? A break from the old ordinary day-by-day workweek and the tedium of life with the wife and the kids and the bills and the everyday, everyday, everyday getting up in the morning and doing it all again for a paycheck never big enough. But that life away from the battlefield is home, back in Texas, or Nebraska, or New Jersey, or Mississippi, and that's where we all end up returning to at the end of the day, dragging our trailers and RVs behind us.

True, that, all of it. But the thing that makes me come back again year after year is not the release from the ordinary, not the being with a bunch of men not having to be conscious of needing to please some woman who controls the climate of the home cave, not simply all that break in routine. No. What it is that drags me back is that one moment that takes place somewhere along the way, when the dream becomes so strong it fades into the real. And I know it's hard to believe it could be possible.

But it's true in the way what's real to Indians is true, and all I can do is not explain but to testify. The art of explanation is not strongly developed in my folks, fake it though we sometimes do so well. To the white man, the real may become a dream and thus vanish. To us, those who lost this land that we didn't even know we had until it was gone, the dream becomes the real.

As I sat on my little pinto pony watching Waymon Needler, formerly a.k.a. Major Marcus Reno, start to begin his transformation into the blood and brain of brevet General George Armstrong Custer, it came to me to wonder about what one moment does to change all that's before and open up all that might be coming, seen rightly and imagined so well it becomes true. Waymon is changing into Custer, I said to myself, as I watched him trot off on his big American nag toward that meeting where the ceremony of transference from one man to another will take place.

He is changing from the man he's prepared to believe himself to be and becoming another altogether. Waymon Needler is eager and able to think himself into being the commander of the Seventh Cavalry, at least for a few hours here in Montana.

Is he crazy, I asked myself, and I knew as I was forming the question that calling him deranged was to question my own sanity. No, trying to explain the nature of the moment on the Greasy Grass when I become not an Alabama-Coushatta Indian, with enough education in a white man's school to be able to make a practical living in this century, but an imaginary Sioux long dead—this leads me to admit that Waymon is not nuts as he trots toward a state of believing he is George Custer. If he's nuts, then what am I? Not one bit saner than that home economics teacher from East Texas with the false beard and the dazed look in his eyes.

Here's how it works practically with me, I was thinking as I joined everybody else, white and Indian, in cheering for Waymon as he rode to meet his date with destiny. Somewhere along the way every year when I come to stand on the banks of the Greasy Grass, I stop being who I am back in Texas, and I can't go into what that state of mind and body happens to be, exactly. That's the whole point of being a reenactor at the Last Stand of George Armstrong Custer, whether you're playing red man or white. Appearances to the contrary, you don't know what you are back home—wherever that might be   during a successful reenactment on the site of the Last Stand. I won't list all the locations all my fellow reenactors come from. Let's just say their homes are demographically diverse, to use a damned good white man phrase. But every last one of them at home is no realer in his life there than the people he watches on TV or likes on Facebook or follows on Twitter.

What's real and can fill you up to the brim so that you don't need to worry at least for a little while about who you might happen to be—that condition happens in flashes and fits and starts, the way your head feels completely satisfied when you get off a sneeze you've been delaying, or to bring it down to a different level, the way you lose all you are for just a second or two when in a sex act you ejaculate all those little halves of people you grow inside you without ever having to think about it. Could any man ever be able to answer the question "Who are you and what's your name?" when he's seized up in the throes of orgasm? He's most real then as a creature in the world and unaware of that fact at the same time. Are you ever real when you're pondering the question of whether you're real? If you can get outside of it enough to think about it, how can you know it well enough to consider it?

No, I said to myself then, as I watched Waymon in the process of becoming Custer, a man dead for over a hundred years, you can't know who you are at the moment you are most yourself. And that's why I come each June to Montana to be my true self somewhere along the way, even if it's only as long as an orgasm lasts. That instant of reaching where I will be who I truly am has come in some years on the Greasy Grass when I am swinging my rubber-foam club up against the head of an enactor doing an Irish-born trooper or a farm boy from Illinois come west to escape the girl he's knocked up in New Salem, or a captain, a graduate of West Point and a veteran of service in the military forces of the Confederate States of America, who's left his home in Georgia to lose himself in the wastelands of the West since Georgia's not there anymore and promises never to return.

One time the moment I became my true self occurred when my pony leaped a depression in a draw reaching up from the river, allowing me to touch the back of a fleeing trooper with my coup stick, harming him not at all but confirming my courage and skill as a warrior of the Hunkpapa Sioux and causing a cry to burst forth from my lips in a language I had never spoken before. Or since. But that cry was real enough to cause a living twentieth-century Sioux to look at me funny.

And thinking of that moment coming unannounced as it did in the midst of some action I was taking as a warrior of the Hunkpapa on the banks of the Greasy Grass as I helped to realize the truth of Sitting Bull's dream of blue soldiers falling headfirst dead into our village, I knew what I had to have on that 125th anniversary of the great victory of the Sioux and Cheyennes over Long Hair, the Son of the Morning Star, and his blue soldiers. If Waymon Needler could become Custer, I could in this year of great moment commemorated as the white men count time on a calendar become who I truly was in the dream, that vision more true than any part of my life back home where I ate and slept and went to work every morning. I would be in this year the warrior at the heart of the dream I had sought. I would be Crazy Horse, war chief of the Sioux.

"Hoka hey," I yelled, Crazy Horse welling up in my head in full battle dress, seeing Waymon near the tent from which he would emerge as Custer ready for the fate which he'd spent all his days pursuing. "Hoka hey. It is a good day to die."

Major Marcus Reno
ON THE SOUTH BANK OF THE LITTLE BIGHORN

JUNE 25, 1876

I MADE A LITTLE JOKE ABOUT THE CANTEENS, BOTH OF THEM, TO Schulz, after we had gotten confirmation of what Custer wanted me to do with the companies he'd assigned me to take across the river and to the southeast of the big village.

"Sergeant," I said, "it's likely to be hot work later today, so I've got a double ration of what I'll be needing. I hope you've provided for yourself."

"Oh, sir," he said, "I never take myself out of range of what will satisfy my thirst. And you can swear by that." He patted the canteen on the pommel of his saddle, and I did the same to my supply, laughing a little to let him know he and I were seeing eye to eye and there'd be no need to say another word. I had, naturally, in addition to the canteens a great jug of water itself, and I fully intended to take that along, given the heat of the day and the experience I'd had before when facing enemy fire. It always seemed to me that I never got hungry during a campaign, as much as I enjoy my victuals when I'm not in the field, but the instant I heard firing, no matter how far off in the distance or who it might be coming from, I felt a thirst kick up that lasted until all action was over, no matter how long that might take and how much I might drink to assuage it.

After the second skirmish I'd suffered back in the war against the rebels, one in which I'd not thought ahead well enough to provision myself with sufficient drink, I made a pledge to never let such happen again. The first and last thing I made sure of when taking the field was to assure myself that I had water and as close to an equivalent amount of whisky safely provided and close. Strong drink taken in moderation does sharpen the thought processes, make one more alert to possible dangers and miscalculations, and enables a quicker coming to conclusion about points of strategy and performance. A commander of men in the way of hazard in battle owes it to his troops to take every advantage of any aid that may help him carry out his duties with greater dispatch.

Enlisted men who're well trained will expose themselves to fire and danger and hazard as part of their obligation as soldiers. They are owed the best judgment and most alert attentions of their commander in return for their enduring the possibilities of injury and death which attend military operations. A judicious use by the commander of every aid he can muster in carrying out his responsibilities is paramount. It has always been my practice to put first the accomplishment of the mission I've been assigned by my superior officers and then to maintain diligent attention to the welfare of the men I command. If whisky in strategic moderation is called for, it is my duty to accept its aid.

Be damned, I've always said, to those who mouth platitudes about Dutch courage and the possible deadening effects of strong drink taken beyond reasonable limits of consumption. Let he who has not heard the whistle of lead and endured the sight of bare steel pontificate all he wishes about the evils of alcohol. Let us test his principles on the subject when he might be faced with a rain of Sioux arrows or a hail of lead from the muzzles of rifles. Tell me then how you feel about abstention, my dear buttermilk soldier.

Suffice it to say that when General Custer sent me with but 180 or so able-bodied soldiers to move against the southern end of Sitting Bull's village of many thousands of Sioux and Cheyennes, a full four thousand of them experienced and bloodthirsty warriors, I had in my possession a sufficient amount of whisky to serve the good purposes a commander in battle might need. As we forded the Little Bighorn, choosing a crossing that presented no problem for horses and men, I chose that moment to fortify myself with a sip or two from the canteen of whisky I had tied to my pommel. The other larger bottle was contained in a saddle bag, wrapped carefully in a length of cloth to protect it from possible damage or loss, and the second canteen I tied to the other side of the horn where it would be available for ready access.

A couple of our Crow scouts had come back from riding ahead, and they were in some haste, letting me know through Bloody Knife that they had spotted several Indian women and children digging prairie turnips not far ahead, and not far from that bunch, an old man and a half-grown boy fishing in the river.

"If they see us coming," Bloody Knife said, "and if we get much closer, they will see us. They'll be able to let Sitting Bull and Gall and Crazy Horse know we're here. They'll be ready for us by the time we reach the village."

"Do what you have to do to stop that from happening," I said to Bloody Knife. "We need to surprise them, if we can. If you can take that bunch prisoner without any one of them getting a chance to go back to the village, do that."

"Officer with the Dark Face," Bloody Knife said, addressing me as many of the Crow scouts did because of my beard, I suppose. Certainly my skin color couldn't have looked dark to an Indian as black in the face as most of them are. "I reckon you know we can't take a chance on getting all of them without one getting away and warning the village. That man and the boy, they saw us, and they are on the move already."

"I understand. Just do what you have to do. And do it quick enough to make it work."

With that, Bloody Knife wheeled his horse around and made a motion to the other scouts who'd been waiting to be told that they could do what they wanted to do. A couple of them yipped a little, and all of the bunch began seeing to their weapons as they hurried to get back to the spot where they'd found the turnip-diggers at work.

Too often we see the red man as being of one breed, one opposed altogether to the progress which civilization is bringing to the remainder of the nation the lands of which they roam, doing nothing of consequence to it or for it, ever. But the fact is that the tribes have warred against each other since time began, and they continue to do so in the most barbaric fashion. The Crow scouts worked for the Seventh Cavalry for reasons more than simply to draw a wage and accumulate goods. All that was to their benefit, as they saw it, but high on the list of excuses for working for the white man was the opportunity to kill Sioux and Cheyennes, their age-old enemies. Any occasion they could find an excuse to make war on the people they considered their foes, they did so with relish.

And they didn't care whether their victims were old or young, men or women, children or warriors. The Crows and Rees descended with knife and club and gun on one and all of the Sioux and Cheyennes, and to be fully honest about it the same behavior was true of the other side. These savages that some bleeding hearts back in the East consider to be noble red men relished dealing death and destruction to anyone they took to be their enemy. And if they were asked why members of other tribes were always considered fair game for violence, any representatives of any so-called Nation of Indians had nothing to offer except to comment on a difference in ornamentation or food eaten or manner of building shelters or a lighter or darker shade of skin color. They never made sense, the noble red man, and that's why they had to be crushed to earth so that civilization can advance. The Seventh Cavalry and the rest of the military of this nation have ridden against these savage heathens with just cause.

By the time Bloody Knife returned to report where matters stood with the turnip diggers and the father and son on the river bank, I had given orders for preparation for the movement of my battalion against the village up ahead, which was still hidden by a bend in the Little Big-horn. The troopers had made their weapons ready, had counted off who would be involved in direct action and which men would be horse hold-ers in the event of dismount, and the lieutenants and sergeants had seen to their individual commands. That left them to issue the essential cav-alry command: find your foe and leave him dead on the field.

Immediate opportunity to partake of a bit of fortifying whisky was present for me about then, and would soon vanish in the process of our move against the village, so I seized the chance to prepare myself for the hot work to come. "Captain," I said to Myles Moylan, "while there's still time and supply, would you like to join me in a brief salute to the work which we are about to direct?"

"I would," Moylan said, waiting to reach for the canteen I lifted in his direction until I had taken the first sip, "and I hope to be able to join you in a more leisurely consumption of the water of life after we've given Sitting Bull the good whipping he's been begging for."

"To a speedy accomplishment of our duty," I said, taking the can-teen from which Moylan had just drunk and then, thinking ahead of the mission, taking one more good strong mouthful before replacing the stopper. "Give orders for our advance at a trot toward the objective General Custer's given us."

As the captain carried out my order, I noted that Bloody Knife was approaching along with two others of the Crow scouts, Half-Yellow Face and Left Hand, their mounts sweated up enough that the dust was making muddy streaks not only on the animals but on the riders' garments. "What news?" I said. "What happened with that bunch you were after?"

"Dead," Bloody Knife said, "wiped out, all but the old man."

"You couldn't catch up to every one of them, then? Did any get back to the village?"

Bloody Knife didn't respond to my query, but looked off toward the south and then down at the pistol hanging around his neck by a length of rawhide. I knew what that meant. Failure. "The old man got back to the village, I suppose," I said. "He's told the Hunkpapa at this end of the camp we're coming."

"Who can tell?" Bloody Knife said, casting his voice into the tone Indians use when they're trying to avoid the truth. "Old men vanish in the dust like squirrels hiding in a bunch of cottonwoods. You never see them again, but you can hear them chatter. Where the old man got to, and where he is, I cannot know. No man could."

"We're on the move, then. We'll have to step up the pace. Go back up toward the village and tell me what you see. We'll be right behind you."

"I already know what I'll see," Bloody Knife said, "because I already know what I've seen this morning of my last day in this world."

"Why do you say those words? Did you see how many warriors Sitting Bull may have? Do you know how many men are still in the village and how many of the ones fit for battle are out on a hunt too far away to fight us?"

"I don't know how many Sioux and Cheyennes may be hunting buffalo or where the buffalo may be today, but I know one thing," Bloody Knife said. "And I know it well. Another thing, too, I know."

"Tell me what you know already."

"There are as many warriors on the Greasy Grass as there are leaves on the trees in the spring or ants on a hill that's been stirred up by boys to watch them run. So many they look like earthworms working on the ground after a hard rain."

"And Sitting Bull's people know we're coming?" I said. "The old man you didn't finish off has told them, you think?"

"Do you have to tell the geese it's time to fly south because the snow has come?"

"All right," I said, looking directly into Bloody Knife's face, a thing he didn't like to have done, like all Indians, but I wanted to let him know that I knew he had not done his job when he let the old man not end up the way the boy did. How hard was it to make sure one old man didn't get a chance to tell what he'd seen? "Go ahead and see what's true now. Maybe there won't be as many warriors as you think."

"I do think this one thing," Bloody Knife said. "I know it. We killed the two women and all their children as they ran from us from digging the turnips. I saw their faces. And I know who they belonged to."

"Who?" I said. "How do you know?"

"They were the wives of Gall, and the children were his. I knew them as we killed them. It will be a long day today, but when it is over, all the days will be done. Then I can rest in a new land."

He turned his horse and loped off ahead with the other Crows, already starting to sing something, the words of which I didn't know and had no interest in learning. The tune of his chant was one I had heard before, those times at night when the Crow scouts were singing before lying down to sleep. I shook my head to rid the drone out of my thinking about it, but the singing in my mind didn't stop until I'd had one more drink from my first canteen, the one that was by then almost empty. The big jug was still there, fastened to my saddle, though, and I put my hand on it to make sure. It was as solid as a pistol grip, hanging there wrapped in a double thickness of cloth, full enough not to slosh much.

"Moylan," I called out, "give the troopers orders to begin a trot toward that bend in the river."

Gall
WAR CHIEF OF THE HUNKPAPAS, VILLAGE ON THE GREASY GRASS

June 25, 1876

*T*HE GUNSHOTS CAME FROM BEYOND WHERE THE PEOPLE WERE camped on the bank of the Greasy Grass, the first three or four close enough together it was hard to count how many there were, and then one after the other spaced out like the shooters were taking their time to make every bullet count. That would be the way you would shoot buffalo if you had the white man's rifles to do it and didn't have to depend on putting enough arrows into an animal to make it fall down finally and let its eyes go sightless and its tongue hang out of its mouth like it was trying to taste what it wanted to eat but had lost the desire to feed and forgot to tell its tongue that thing. I am dead, the tongue is saying, but I don't know that yet.

No hunters from the village were anywhere near where the women and children were after turnips in the place where they grow in the summer beside the Greasy Grass. There's enough water there most of the hot time for the roots to take hold and stay alive until the women gather them for cooking. It couldn't be hunters. No hunters would be close to the village since game would stay far away from us, and any boys trying to kill birds or muskrats or rabbits would be using bows and arrows for that. They would make no noise like gunpowder does. It was white men, I could tell as soon as I heard the guns go off, and if not blue soldiers it would be the Crow or Ree scouts working for them.

We knew the white men were coming, and we had known that before they got close enough to shoot guns. So I was not surprised to know they were here, the blue soldiers with Long Hair leading them and the Indian scouts telling them where the Sioux and Cheyennes were staying and how many of us they guessed there were. The shooting starting up quick without any talk first was a thing I had not expected, though. Surely Long Hair would want to sit down with the chiefs in Sitting Bull's lodge first. He would like to smoke with us and make promises and tell us what would happen to the People if we didn't go back to the reservation forts and eat the beef there. Long Hair liked to talk to the chiefs. He liked to smoke with us, and he liked to stick his legs out before him where he sat on a buffalo hide on the ground so that any man who wanted to look could see his long boots and their bottoms and admire the white buckskins he wore as clothes. They could study his hat and his long yellow hair and listen to him trying to use Lakota words to talk to us, but ending up always finally speaking with his hands and showing his teeth as he did that, looking like a man who'd heard a funny thing and wanted to show that to others watching him. We could see all that as he met with the council.

But that was not the way it was going to be this time, I could tell, as soon as I heard the gunshots coming from the place of the turnips that my oldest wife Tall Crane Woman had said she had a taste for this day. Long Hair would not be sitting in the lodge, smoking the pipe as it moved around the circle, and he would not see ashes dropped by someone upon his boots and not know what that told us when it happened. Not this time. I let myself remember that time before the Washita, the place where Long Hair's blue soldiers had killed not just the People but the ponies, too, by the hundreds. That was later, when all the water was frozen and the wind blew so hard that lodges could not stand, and there wasn't enough to eat anywhere in that country.

The time before the Washita I thought about was when Long Hair had told us what bad things would happen if we didn't get out of the white men's way, sitting the way he always did in a council lodge with his legs stretched out before him on a buffalo robe and his black boots shining where they'd had grease rubbed on them. When he finished telling us what bad things would happen to the People if we didn't do what the white men said, one of the little Oglala chiefs had emptied the ashes from the pipe we'd all been smoking right onto Long Hair's boots. It made a sound like a handful of sand sifting onto rocky ground, soft but steady. Every Indian there made a cough in the back of his throat when that happened, but Long Hair acted like he didn't even see it when it took place. He didn't look down or up, and he didn't change the way he was showing his teeth as he looked about him. We knew from that he didn't know what those ashes on his boots meant. We did know the meaning, though, all of us there. We saw what was coming.

This time, Washita already behind, Long Hair had not come to the village on the Greasy Grass to tell us what bad things would happen if we kept on trying to live as we had always done. Instead, he would be asking us to understand what he would have to do if we did not take his advice and change the way we looked at the land around us and the animals on it and the weather above it, the clouds and the wind and the rain and sun and snow, changing each season and returning again each year to stay for a time and then to change again as it had always done and would always do if left alone. It was time for the weather to change forever and for good, he would say to us. Thunder and lightning and rain and snow were not to be predicted, not to be expected, not to occur as before. Everything in the sky and in the wind and under the sun was going to have to be different.

No, Long Hair had not come to talk and to pretend to listen. Not today. Not any longer. He had come not to tell, but to show us that his stories about the bad things to come if we did not change our ways were not just words laid out in the air to admire. He would not speak again with the common breath that comes from inside a man's body and goes forth in language that ends up into the ears of another and says words inside his head. Long Hair, Yellow Hair, the Son of the Morning Star, this man would talk now with the rifles of his blue soldiers. He would speak with their big knives, with their big horses, maybe with their bigger guns, the ones they called cannons, and he would not listen to words from the chiefs of the People any longer. Now all he could hear from us was what we had left as a means to talk back to him. Our guns, our knives, our clubs, our arrows so many they look like geese against the clouds—all these would talk the language that Long Hair would have to hear and be lessoned by. He did not know that yet, and we had to tell him that truth.

I heard the new conversation between Long Hair's soldiers and scouts and our People begin in the middle of that day in the hot sun of noon, and it barked like a rifle, moaned like a coyote, and it howled like a wolf. It was a thing with its foot caught in a trap, too high up on the leg to be chewed off. All that talk had come to grief, and now it would stay that way.

Listening to the gunfire on the Greasy Grass, by the time I was able to pick up my rifle, a new one that shot more than one time without having to put new bullets in its side, and my knife that I kept sharp, and my stone club, my oldest daughter had already caught my horse and was sitting up on her pony ready to leave for where the sound of shooting came from.

"Come on, my father," she said, "if you are ready to go now. I will paint my face all one color in due time, and that will be red. But that will have to wait. Now we go to where my mother and your other wife and my sisters and brothers have been digging the turnips."

"They will not be there any more, I'm afraid," I said, mounting my horse, a strong pony bigger than most and marked with white feet and a white face against the color black. "I think they may all be dead now, all those we know, there in the place of the turnips."

"Maybe so, or maybe not. Maybe some are only bloody and are not all the way dead. Let us hurry, my father. If we get there soon enough, maybe there'll be some soldiers we can kill."

She was wrong, my daughter Red Bird Flies Up, about part of what she had said. The part she was right about had to do with blood and where it would be, and we saw it all over my wives, my older one Tall Crane Woman and the younger one Brown Robe, coming from holes where bullets had punched their sides and backs and arms, and it was on the faces of the children and on their heads where they had been hit with clubs until the bones showed.

"Crows," I said, "and Rees," knowing that was the part she was wrong about. There were no blue soldiers to kill, even if they had been there, since they had not wiped out my wives and children, my sons and daughters, the sisters and brothers of Red Bird Flies Up. The scouts for the blues soldiers had done it, and what told me that was the way the children had been hit with clubs. "It was not the blue soldiers that did the bloody work here where the turnips grow each year. It was other Indians, the ones who belong to the white men."

"Do you forgive the white man, then?" my daughter said. She was cutting away at the hair on the back of her head where it grew long and she looked at me with her eyes so dark all I could see was black, using a long knife to saw away at her loose hair, without being able to see what she was doing or where she was cutting. She was throwing it on the ground hard as if it was something she hated and wished to see no more. "Since our family has not died at their hands? Will you not blame Yellow Hair? Is that what you think, my father?"

"I think nothing," I said, pulling my knife from where I kept it tied to a string hanging from my shoulder and testing its blade with my thumb. A line of blood sprang up where I had touched the edge. "I think nothing about who did this, or why he did it, or what he did it with. I cannot think now, and I may never think again. I feel only my heart now. And my heart is bad."

"As is my heart," Red Bird Flies Up said. "As it always will be from this day. And it is good to me not to think. All I must do now is paint over all parts of my face with the color red, and I must gather my weapons and ride into the face of our enemies."

"Do not let them kill you, my daughter," I said, feeling something start to move deep within my belly, a pain as though from a bee stinging a tender part of my flesh, a place where I could not touch to rub it. "You kill them first. Get there before they do. Wipe out all of them you can reach."

"I will find a way to make my heart get better, and that will come through blood. I will not stop my war against the blue soldiers and the Indians they own until my belly is so full of blood I must lie down to rest or vomit it all up."

"Hoka hey," I said. "Listen for the sound of their horses and their rifles. Find where they are. Then go to them like a hummingbird to a flower. Feed deep on that sweet nectar. Hoka hey, my daughter, my girl. Help my sick heart find blood.

AS MAJOR RENO ON THE LITTLE BIGHORN

JUNE 25, 2001

HERE I WAS, THE SUN PLAYING ON THE BRASS BUTTONS OF MY uniform, as I sat mounted on a black stallion named Frisco in the middle of the first rank of troopers, looking to my right and left, checking off with the captain and the lieutenants and sergeants of Major Marcus Reno's command their readiness to lead men into battle against the largest collection of Native American warriors ever gathered in one location. Speaking to my inner self without giving sign one of hesitation or an overactive imagination, I sent a stern internal reminder to the creature inside me who acts instantaneously and doesn't think first before leaping.

"Listen," I was saying to that self within myself, the one that gets me into trouble much too frequently for me not to maintain a vigilant guard and pay due attention to what that inner Donald Ray Peeples might say or do at any moment, "stay low. Stay quiet, and whatever you do, don't call the enemies we're facing today anything but Indians or Sioux or Cheyennes, as the case may be. Don't go all anachronistic and label them Native Americans or First Nation Peoples, as the wuss Canadians do. They're Indians, they're savages, they're untrustworthy, and no matter how you've been conditioned to think of them as noble and dispossessed in historical terms, this is the nineteenth century. It is not the year 2001, and the entire concept of political correctness does not exist and won't for years to come. No one here has ever seen an automobile or television or a cell phone or heard of any invention more complex than a freight train." Thus was my inner counsel, and it calmed me.

"Don," Lieutenant Varnum, a.k.a. Larry Gentry of Mount Vernon, Illinois, said, "How does it feel to be promoted so quick?"

I didn't answer, naturally, and gave no sign of having even heard what the lieutenant of one of my companies had just uttered, letting him know by my silence that if he didn't immerse himself into his role, he didn't exist as far as I was concerned. He was 125 years off the point.

"Hey, don't you feel a little strange, I mean, being moved from the role of a company captain to playing Reno? I mean it's all happened in less than three hours. A man's got to feel shellshocked, right? Who am I? He's got to ask that. What am I doing here? How do I spell my name? Is my beard right?"

I saw that my silence would not silence Larry Gentry's eternal need to chatter, especially right before a dramatic action was about to begin. I'd have to speak to him to get him to shut up and move himself back into the time over 125 years in the past, but I was not about to respond in the persona of Donald Ray Peeples, all dressed up in the uniform of a major in General George A. Custer's Seventh Cavalry, thank you very much. I would address him as what it was my dramaturgical and historical responsibility to assume: the role and personality of Major Marcus Reno about to lead his three companies directly into battle against the tremendous village on the bank of the Little Bighorn on that fateful afternoon.

"Lieutenant Varnum," I began, "have you seen to your troopers? Are they in place for the advance and the charge to follow? Have you counted off to establish the fourth-man horse holder?"

"Uh, yessir," Gentry as Varnum responded, dropping his head a little and correcting his posture enough to give at least the semblance of the proper appearance of a junior officer. "They're ready to go, all eighteen of them."

"All what in total? How many?"

"Was it a hundred in that company? I've forgot if I ever knew the count of that company Varnum was attached to. Call it fifty, I guess, give or take."

"It is over a hundred," I said in a firm tone. "The word *was* doesn't apply here, and I require you to remember the accurate statistics for the task we are assigned to accomplish."

"All right, Jeez, then," the lieutenant said. "I get it. But look at the few we got mounted up this year. It's hard to pretend there's a bunch when we got only eighteen mounted and the hostiles have got only thirty or so total. But I get it."

"I get it?" I said with a little fire in my voice. "Did you say get it?"

"I comprehend, sir," Varnum said, and I felt a small glow rise in my face through my whiskers, genuine and authentic for 1876, and actually the prime reason for my being promoted to the role of Major Reno when Waymon Needler had to vacate the post to assume that of the Son of the Morning Star himself. I always grow real whiskers and they look truly great, I have to say in all modesty, and I avoided the razor that year even longer than I usually did before June. I did not feel myself ready for such a promotion, though, to the role of Major Marcus Reno, even when it had been offered, but I would never have given public notice of that. A man feels within himself who he is and when he is that persona. He will know when he becomes truly able to shift from one self to another with authenticity. If duty calls, the trooper answers.

"Lieutenant Varnum," I said, feeling I should reveal a more congenial side, as I imagined Reno would have done, from my knowledge of his personality among Custer's total command. I stay on top of that study, reading all I can find as soon as any new opinion appears. Reno, if nothing else, warts and all, did socialize with his junior officers and at times with enlisted troopers, so I felt justified in paying homage to a known fact about Reno's behavior that day when he faced the task of delivering the first blow against that huge encampment of Sioux and Cheyennes. "Would you like a little whisky before we begin the advance?" I went on, smiling in a comradely way.

"You got real whisky in that canteen, Don?" my lieutenant said, instantly betraying his obligation to stay in character and reverting to the personality of a staid burgher in a Midwestern town in the twenty-first century. "Sure, give me a swig."

I handed him one of the canteens fastened to my saddle, and when he took in a healthy dollop, he jerked back and almost spewed the liquid out. He did get it down, though, not as Lieutenant Varnum, but as the good Rotarian he was back home in the Prairie State. "Iced tea," he said. "I should have known. Shit, Don."

"This is theater, Lieutenant Varnum, despite how we work to make it look real," I said. "Did you really expect me to fill two canteens and a stoneware jug with hundred-proof whisky? Actors never partake of mind-altering drugs in performance. Keep that in mind, if you please."

"What about Peter O'Toole?" Varnum said, back in his Larry Gentry voice. "He was famous for drinking the real stuff and smoking the true weed on stage and in film shoots. You can tell he's stoned half the time in *Lawrence of Arabia*. His eyes are rolled back in his head."

"Correction, please. O'Toole was famous for appearing to be doing that. He was an actor, for Pete's sake, and his job was to fool you into thinking what you were witnessing was truly taking place. Just as we've got the obligation to perform today."

"I won't argue when you're talking like that," Larry Gentry said. "But things are not always what they seem, Don."

"Precisely," I shot back. "Precisely. Now dress the lines of the troopers, and let's go see what's in that valley and how many. Remember how uninformed we all were at this point on the day."

"Ho," Lieutenant Varnum intoned as he swung around to check the line of mounted troopers, and I took a good long sip of iced tea from one of my canteens. Ah, whisky, I said to myself, and then out loud. "At a trot, advance battalion."

Our eighteen troopers, though not an eighth of the total force Major Reno had in that charge toward the Hunkpapa encampment at the edge of Sitting Bull's village, began doing their bit to put on a good show. When they did, the light playing on the metal of their weapons and uniforms and the bits and bridles and saddles of their mounts and the sounds of a troop of cavalry beginning its rhythmic beat of hooves at gallop, cheers of appreciation began to arise from the spectators ranked up on both sides of our location. I did not let myself look around at the cheering, not wanting to break the illusion of reality we'd established. I wanted always never to break the frame of dramatic distancing and thus the spell, but I could sense from the corners of my eyes that my troopers were proceeding as the originals must have done over a century ago. I was heartened.

Those originals in 1876 would have been apprehensive, their emotions screwed to the sticking point, and their nerves wound tight enough to vibrate, and my men were matching their appearance as best I could judge.

"Come on, Seventh," I found myself shouting, "let them see what you do," and as I allowed myself that outburst, a cheer arose from the eighteen actors, representing well over a hundred troopers willing to hazard their lives back then.

"Could I have a little more of a drink from your canteen, Major Reno?" Lieutenant Varnum shouted. He was in the moment now, I was relieved to know, and he was back to that point when it had appeared to Major Reno and the Sioux themselves that another successful charge by the Seventh Cavalry was well underway. Confident, the troopers advanced toward Sitting Bull's village, their pace picking up now as their mounts sensed the desire to close with the enemy. At this point, all was optimism and abandon, and the reality of what was to come later of Major Reno's charge lay still ahead, like a hidden rattlesnake.

"Here you go, Lieutenant Varnum," I said, the canteen in my hand, "have one last drink before we reach full gallop. It'll taste like heaven."

Up ahead a cloud of dust was building, and the first yips and shouts of warriors were coming from the area where the lodges were located, only a dozen or so this year and all built of synthetic materials, but their colors were showing up well. The spectators will be impressed, I told myself, if they'll just narrow their focus. All I've got to do now is give a good account before we have to break and run for the ford across the Little Bighorn. That's always the hard part for the man doing Reno, the time when he has to demonstrate that emotional reverse and start that wild retreat. I've always thought it was easier for the original Marcus Reno to get fully into manifesting that weak side of his character back in 1876 than it is for a reenactor to persuade the audience it's all believable.

Why? It's simple. It was easier for Reno to change persona so drastically, but not just because the event was utterly real at that point—all those arrows, the repeating rifles the Sioux had, the clubs they swung and the knives they wielded, the brains dashed out and the blood flying and the screams and cries of the savages and of the men being slaughtered, the whole catastrophe—but because Major Reno was drunk. He'd consumed almost two canteens of whisky, and the alcohol let him do what all drunks do well. They show what they really think, and they do it unconsciously.

Tell an actor to do just that, show what's really inside his head and heart, but he must do it stone cold sober. If he can achieve that illusion, unaided by being in a mindless state, he's Brando, he's Newman, he's Meryl Streep, he's Maggie Smith, and he's a top-drawer historical reenactor. When you're watching yourself, you can't forget who you are. All the shortages within will show their ugly heads no matter. To know yourself is to know your weakness. The only way to show your strengths as an actor or as historical re-creator is to find a way to forget and rise above that diminished sense of who you happen to be in this dark time.

Some reenactors must rely on strong drink or drugs, some must be so limited intellectually that they believe they are what they'd like to be, and some fortunate few, like brevet General George Armstrong Custer on that last day of his life, are truly at ease with the creature they believe themselves to be. They don't question themselves or their own motives, and they never feel a need to reexamine anything. They are at ease with who they are. That's why they aren't actors or reenactors.

I told myself as I rode in full charge toward that cloud of dust kicked up by the hostiles that showing uncertainty and second-guessing is just what historical reenactment is supposed to do. That was the fatal flaw of Major Marcus Reno, his inability to lose himself in the moment. Use your weakness, I told myself, as I neared the point in the charge where as Reno I had to fall prey to paralysis and second thoughts about what I was doing and where I was leading these troopers.

My personal weakness makes me real and able to capture most fully the truth of Reno's doomed charge because of that failure of nerve. Go with it, Marcus Reno, I told myself as I reached closer and closer to the moment of quailing failure. Be wrong, and be damned one more time.

"Sound a halt," I told the bugler riding beside me, an Italian émigré in 1876 named Tolio Da'Onot, barely able to speak English, newly enlisted, as portrayed by Allen Flanders, who in the current century is a floor supervisor for Walmart in Nashville, Tennessee. Al also claimed to have played trumpet in the Nashville Symphony at one point but had to leave because of professional jealousies in the horn section. That I didn't buy, though I know horn sections are notorious for being contentious—it must have something to do with all that pressure on the brain that blowing through a metal mouthpiece requires—but Al did know all the nineteenth-century bugle commands in use when the Last Stand took place, and he did have a good lip. That's what he said anyway, and I never saw any reason to quarrel with his accounts of his triumphs and bad treatment as a result of those. If you stick your head up, somebody will try to knock it off. I know that to be true.

He tootled several notes into his bugle, troopers began reining in their mounts, all but one whose job was to portray the ride on the famous horse that ran wildly in circles during the whole attack and retreat by Reno's battalion, and that horse was urged on by the reenactor astride him to do what the original horse did so well back in the day. The current horse didn't want to do that, and after a brief fight with him, the trooper gave up and dismounted with the rest of the eighteen who I commanded to form a skirmish line.

"Didn't Reno drink some more whisky as soon as the line was established?" Lieutenant Varnum said.

"By all accounts, yes," I said. "But we don't need to mimic every little action that somebody claimed to have remembered. What you should be doing is limbering up that long-range Sharps rifle someone had. You need to try to pick off a Sioux or two while we're setting up here."

"Right," my lieutenant said, sounding interested. "Didn't a marksman hit a couple of warriors at real long range? Broke some young kid's legs? I think I remember that."

"That depends on who you read. But you better hurry. Those Sioux are working themselves up into a charge, and they'll be here in a minute or two. They will not wait nearly as long as they should."

"Why's that, I wonder? They've been rehearsed."

"Every year in the postmortem authenticity assessment meeting they always claim it's because the Hunkpapa got their blood up because our Crow scouts killed Gall's family in the turnip patch. But I've stopped buying that story. They just want to get more action going sooner. That's what it comes down to. These Indians, God bless them, will not subject themselves to accepted historical facts about details of June twenty-fifth. They want to rewrite history. They really don't respect it."

"Well, they did win the day back then," Varnum said. "You got to give them credit for that. And that fact makes these current-day guys want part of that action, too. Hell, they haven't won a damn thing in over a hundred years. As a people I mean."

"Please, Lieutenant Varnum," I said. "Get into character. Now is not now. Now is then. Speak like you're speaking then. Is that too much to ask?"

"Yes sir," my lieutenant said, and I was pleased to hear him defer to his superior officer. That allowed me to think about the real matter at hand, marshaling my command into a skirmish line that could try to do something to meet the response of the Oglalas. I had my hands full, and so did Major Marcus Reno at this point in 1876. Along with everything else, he was faced with not knowing whether to have the troopers function as dismounted infantry or stay aboard their horses.

"Dismount," I ordered, "See to your weapons," and I said these words with as much enthusiasm as I could muster, knowing what happened next and what I was next faced with as commanding officer of the battalion. But that's always the burden of the historical reenactor. He has the task to emulate what truly happened, while knowing what losses he must endure if he's to remain true to historical fact. And that he must do, above all things.

Yet, I thought as I took a long slug of liquid from one of my canteens, remaining true to all accounts of Reno's resort to alcohol on that day, yet I must convince the spectators on the hills and especially the historical intelligence within me which impels and judges, that what's happening now is what happened then. No one knew at the time what the outcomes would be. We know now, and that's our burden. We have to conduct ourselves as though then does not exist now. It's a bitch, though I'd never say that out loud.

It makes for double thinking, self-criticism, and it opens every action to the judgment of Monday-morning quarterbacks, to use a current phrase. Here's what I know, I told myself within as I watched my troopers beginning to bang away at the clumps of approaching Sioux and Cheyennes, painted and befeathered and armed with newer and more efficient rifles than my poor lads with their single-shot issues. I know that I must in a few minutes tell my command to mount up, to dismount, and then to mount up again. I must take a deep drink of my fake whisky, I must tell my troopers that to save themselves every man is on his own, I must break for the river and cross to the other side as the sound of savages killing my men with guns, knives, clubs, arrows, and bare hands swells behind me. Then I must make my way to the top of that hill which from this day forward will bear the name of Marcus Reno, Major, Seventh Cavalry. And, I told myself as I attended to the canteen now emptied of the last dregs of fake whisky, that hill's name will live on through history as an emblem of shame and cowardice. Reno's Hill.

"Mount up," I yelled to my lieutenant, Varnam relaying the command to the troopers. "To horse," I screamed, and then after a delay of only a few seconds, "Dismount. Prepare to receive a charge."

I'll be having them break and run, I instructed myself, as survivors of that battalion all testified later that Reno did as he watched things go wrong, his panic growing all the while. I did not have to tell myself to act flustered and out of control and afraid. I was all that on June 25, 2001, on the low bank of the Little Bighorn. I was experiencing all those emotions and more, lost in the character of my man and in the heat of a moment over a century old. To feel that way is not reasonable, and that unreason is the glory of the reenactor. We hunger and live for the unreasonable.

"Mount up," I screamed, my voice sounding desperate, so much so that Lieutenant Varnum looked at me in horror. Bravo for you, Varnum, I said within, for showing you're becoming the character you're trying to be, and then I sealed my historical fate and spoke the shameful words that define Major Marcus Reno for all time. "Any of you men who wish to make your escape, follow me."

And then I broke for the river, my head scout Bloody Knife racing alongside on his mount, warriors yipping and swinging clubs and shooting arrows close behind. No spectators on the hills cheered as we broke and ran, and that let me know my reenactment was a success. I wanted to hang my head and weep. The only bit of historically accurate event missing was what happened when a rifle shot smashed into Bloody Knife's head and left a spray from his brains all over Reno's face and uniform. Well, I thought, you can't have everything.

To the hill top in full gallop, in panic and horror and disgrace and abject fear, fulfilling in full my obligation to history's stern principle: let then be here now. Given how enthusiastically the Indian reenactors were swinging their rubber mallets and popping away with blank rifle and pistol rounds, I wondered how much louder and disorganized Reno's retreat could have been back on the original day. I'm almost convinced I'm there, I told myself, and I could tell that the Indians from the Sioux reservation were in the same state of mind. I hope it looks right to the spectators today, because it feels frighteningly real enough, no matter how few troops I actually have in my command. Here's to my eighteen men, playing the part of over a hundred survivors of the battle, I thought, as I looked to my left into the dark eyes of a Cheyenne warrior pounding along beside me on his pony.

I could tell how much that hostile wanted to knock my brains out with his fake foam club, but being the well-trained impersonator he was, he refrained from violating history's dictate by doing so. Major Reno had survived the battle on the Little Bighorn.

"Some fun, huh, Donald?" he said as he shook his club in my face. "Hoka hey, honky white man, hoka hey."

"Stay real," I said, having to break the illusion right before I was to reach the top of the hill where we'd make a successful stand. "Do what you're supposed to do, warrior, if it's not too much to ask. Keep in character, please."

So many of the contemporary Native Americans just don't get it. Too often they take part in the annual reenactment for the wrong reasons, and that's simply to get a chance to dress up and ride horses and bash white men with foam rubber clubs and shoot blanks at them as they retreat. And then party every night back at the motel for a week with free booze and eats. But you can't operate without the Sioux and Cheyennes and Crows and have the authenticity you must always strive for. They're the only people with the perfect look, and you have to take the bad along with the good. And on top of that, if you critique them in ways they don't appreciate, they get worse in creating the proper look and behavior. They will sulk like spoiled children.

Indians, I told myself as I crested the hill and began to swing my horse around. You can't live with the red man, and you can't live without him.

The Sioux and Cheyenne reenactors had begun to fall back by then, gathering to work up a full-scale assault against the blue soldiers on top of the hill, and we all began to prepare ourselves to telescope over eighteen hours of real-time action back in 1876 into a little over thirty minutes of here and now. Focus, I told myself, don't let down now. This is no time to ease up. Stay the course now, and you won't lose any spectators to the action that's set to kick off on Custer's Hill in a little less than an hour.

I had witnessed in years past too many times a wholesale departure of spectators from the siege on Reno's Hill to the area where General Custer's Last Stand was performed, people eager to get seats with good views, and I wanted to put on a show which might stem some of that retreat. If it's not one matter of strategy and action, it's another for the commander of a cavalry division, then or now. Adapt or die.

Put it this way: you cannot trust summertime viewers of a historical reenactment not to slink off from a crucial moment to seek something they think may be more graphically violent. The steady decline in serious representations of historical events in movies and on television has simply jaded the ordinary viewer. I swear that sometimes I expect us to have to introduce space aliens into our production of the Last Stand in order to keep the attention of the average ordinary spectator. Everything is becoming more dumbed down.

"Hurry it up, Lieutenant," I shouted at Varnum, "we can't let down now. We have only about two minutes to get going before the crowd gets restless."

"Dismount," Varnum was yelling to his company, "form a skirmish line. Keep your heads down."

A nice touch, the lieutenant's last bit of advice to his men, I considered. It sounds almost real, though I wish the Indians waiting to attack would stop standing around and talking to each other so much. I'm sure back in the original day they didn't just chat after they'd chased Reno's battalion across the river, up the hill, and into a flat space where they couldn't escape. Why can't the Native Americans ever wait to socialize? I swear they lose focus and get so primitive at times.

People, please be serious.

Captain Frederick Benteen
ON THE LITTLE BIGHORN

JUNE 25, 1876

When the trumpeter from the companies with Custer's battalion came pounding up, his horse in a lather and favoring a rear leg as it was brought to a stop by John Martin near where I was standing by a little creek, I already knew what was going on. Not specifically, now, am I claiming that I could tell the full state of affairs back across the river. Custer didn't want me in at the kill, and I'd known that before the Seventh left Fort Lincoln. He was hoping that by the time I'd reconnoitered all that empty area he'd have finished up the main business all by himself. So when I arrived on the scene, he'd be able to look at me with that little half smile he liked to display when he figured he'd put something over on somebody, especially a soldier experienced in leading men and getting a job done with the least casualties and the best result. I've done it again, that smirk would be saying. George Armstrong Custer has ridden successfully to the sound of the guns.

But something he hadn't planned on, or something he'd misjudged badly, had taken place, and now he had to turn to me to see if I could pull his chestnuts out of the fire. Proof of that was standing bang in front of me, half-winded with his eyes popped wide open, his horse bleeding from what looked like a gunshot high up on its left hindquarter, and his mind racing as he tried to think of the right words in English to say to an officer.

"Trooper Martin," I said, looking not directly at him as I spoke but at Captain Weir who gave me a nod that showed he was thinking what

I was. "What have you got for me from the general?" My saying that let the Italian trumpeter off the hook of having to explain in spoken English what his message was, and he looked grateful as he leaned forward and handed me a small scrap of paper. "From General Custer," he said. "Put on the paper by Lieutenant Cooke. He wrote for me that."

So then I read for the first time that message that has become so famous since I first got handed it by John Martin, Italian trumpeter of the Seventh Cavalry. It's been read by many a thousand since then, God knows. At that first view, it was so smudged from being carried by Martin and so ill written, showing in what haste Cooke had been when he scribbled the words on that page torn from a notebook, that soon after that whole business and disaster had occurred on the Little Bighorn I copied the message in a fair hand on the top portion of that same document. I knew as soon as I saw what Martin had brought me that I'd want to save the original for later perusal by all those having business in knowing what was said, what was written, what was conveyed by the message, and how the directions on the scrap of paper were carried out. That was hard evidence. After reading it, I folded it and put it in a small pocket on my uniform, where it safely survived the day and the ones to come. They tell me it's at West Point now, behind a big sheet of glass.

"Benteen, Come on, Big Village. Be quick, bring packs. W.W. Cooke P.S. Bring pacs" That's all that was said, and the brevity and the misspelling Cooke made of the word packs when he repeated it let me know more than the words stated. Here's what that was, in brief. Custer was in a state of surprise, and that surprise had to do with the number of warriors he discovered he was facing. He was afraid, not for himself necessarily, but for the success of the mission undertaken by the Seventh Cavalry, thus the request for more ammunition packs. On top of that, he was regretful that he had broken the Seventh into three divisions, sending two of them away from where he thought the significant action would be taking place, action where he alone could claim credit for the victory over Sitting Bull and Crazy Horse he fully expected to enjoy.

The last unspoken message the scribble by Cooke said to me was that Custer had now realized his fate was in my hands and that he had to implore me to save him from this display of arrogance, the latest among many during his military career. Benteen, come on, indeed! Be quick, indeed! Bring packs, indeed! I was not fooled, and I did not get flustered.

Now it was clear that brevet General George A. Custer had been forced by events and by his poor planning and prideful ignoring of reality to call upon me for aid. We would see what would come of all this.

"Where's the general now?" I asked John Martin. "And what's wrong with your horse?"

"The Indians are skedaddling," Martin said, surprising me with using that word, his command of English being as weak as it was, "and the general has already charged through the heart of the Indian village. The hostiles are on the run."

I knew better than that, but I resolved to take Custer at his words so carefully relayed by his Italian trumpeter. I could imagine him saying just this to Martin, "Be sure to tell Captain Benteen that the hostiles are skedaddling, but let him know he is not to delay in bringing the packs to me. Impress that upon him, both parts of this message." And then, of course, his adjutant Cooke, being a prudent and careful man, would have insisted on writing the message down for me to read, lest there be confusion sowed by the oral report of an Italian speaker new to this country.

I was not confused. I was not uncertain about what I should do next, and I was not to be buffaloed into leading my companies into a situation untenable and doomed. "Let's look at your horse," I said to Martin. "I think he's been hit by a shot." We did that, taking full time to do so, enough to convince the trumpeter of the Seventh Cavalry that a bloody hole in horse-flesh doesn't just appear for no reason, and then I gave orders to move.

As we moved out at a good trot in the direction of where the general was said to be, I could see a good distance ahead of us a rising pall of smoke, and by the time we reached a rise which let us see into the valley of the Little Bighorn, I caught sight of what I took to be no more than a dozen or so dismounted soldiers being ridden down and shot by over eight or nine hundred Indian warriors. All was happening quickly, but it seemed to the eye to drag itself out in slow time, like a picture you could look at and study. Those soldiers were as good as dead, and they knew it. But they were maintaining fire in the face of the Lakotas and Cheyennes.

"That's not Custer's companies," Captain Weir said. "Who are those troopers?"

"That's some of Reno's bunch, what's left of it," I said. "Where's that village Custer's supposed to have already ridden through?" I know I must have sounded surprised and flummoxed to Weir, and I thought I'd let him think that for as long as he could, figuring he'd function better as a line officer the longer he didn't know what I had realized: how terrible and how wrong all before us was going. That part of the campaign was already over for those soldiers and the dead ones in the valley, and now I had to find a way to save the rest of us, if possible.

It wasn't a quarter of a mile farther on, my command now at a fast trot with me a good distance ahead of the rest, that I recognized in a bunch of troopers coming toward us at a gallop the red bandana that Major Reno habitually wore tied on his head beneath his hat, said hat not now in evidence—lost probably in the breeze of his full gallop—and the wearer was holding his right hand high over his head. The man was winded, and his countenance, generally so ruddy that the Crow scouts called him the "officer of the dark face," was a pale color with splotches of red covering his cheeks. He appeared to be about to burst.

"Benteen," he started yelling before he got within range to speak in a normal tone, "For God's sake, halt your command and help me. I've lost half my men."

"Where is Custer?" was the thing I said back to him, thinking I'd be damned in hell with my back broke before I let myself show any part of the outdone attitude Reno was broadcasting in front of officers and men. "Have you heard from him?"

"I don't know where he is now," Reno said, pushing close up to me but still yelling as though he was yet forty yards away. "Some of the men say they saw him across the river waving his hat at us the first time we dismounted to receive an attack. I didn't see him doing that, though, busy as I was."

Busy knocking back a gill or two of whisky, I told myself, if I know Reno and his habitual resort to Dutch courage. "How many men do you have headed for that hilltop?" I said. "And how many Sioux and Cheyennes do you believe you might be facing?"

"It's thousands of them, Benteen. They're swarming. You've got to join forces with me or we'll all be wiped out in no time at all. I told Custer he didn't assign enough men to me for that sweep through the valley. He wouldn't listen to me, Benteen. He just looked at me and grinned a little bit and never said a word back."

"Be thankful that's all he did," I said. "We have to get to that hill and set up a skirmish line across its brow. This time I believe we might have bitten off quite as much as we will be able to well chew."

"There are so many warriors gathering at the base of the hill where we're trying to rally that they look like grasshoppers swarming," Reno said. "But we made a charge up that hill. It was not a rout, and it was not a retreat. It was a strategic movement of men."

His face was beginning to assume its usual dark tint, and he was well into justifying his actions and the situation he found himself and his troopers in, so I could tell that the presence of me and my companies was having a salutary effect on him. Reno was ever a man who felt better and more secure when someone else of equal or superior rank was present to give him the means to shift blame and assume injury and find ways to justify what he had or hadn't done in the situation he'd just found himself sliding into. Give Reno a slight to resent, and he'd perk up in spirits almost immediately no matter how many enemies were close enough to smell the whisky on his breath. He'd rather be arguing the merits of his point of view than finding a way to fight back against those people dying to dash out his brains and cut the throats of all his troopers. Every man finds his way to navigate in this world, willy-nilly, I suppose, and Reno had found his. Don't deal with reality. Argue against it. Try to explain it away.

Not his route for me, though. I'd rather pick up my own club and break open the head of the one trying to do me harm than worry about whether I was right in some judgment and whether I'd been wronged in reputation by a maligner like George Armstrong Custer. But to each man his own poison and his own remedy. I know what I can live with, and I projected I'd discover in due time what I could die with. But not just now, not here on this rocky hill with Reno lamenting his fate and mistreatment and hundreds of red-skinned murdering savages at the base of this pile of rocks and brush launching arrows and shooting bullets and aching to put knives into white men's bellies and rip the scalps from their heads.

"I'm going to stick this company guidon up in this rise of rocks," I said to Reno, grabbing said signal flag and moving to cram it into a crack in the stone summit of the hill. "Its flapping might attract attention from Custer, and if it does, he'll see he needs to bring his companies here to our rescue. In the meantime, I got to say that this is a hell of a place to fight Indians."

"That's a good idea, the signal notion," Reno said. "Now if we can just hunker down, maybe a good bunch of us will survive this disaster."

"Not if we just let Sitting Bull set the schedule of events," I said, waving my hand to Weir and my lieutenants. "We are not going to retreat in a rout from this hill. We will work and fight our way back to that location where there's some cover."

I knew Reno would resent that notion, preferring either to run pellmell away from the hostiles or hunker down and hide his head in the sagebrush, but I was determined not to let my movement of troopers disintegrate into a mad dash. We'd back up because we had to do that, but we'd have our faces turned in the right direction and we'd be fighting back every step of the way. Not only that, but I hadn't slept in over twenty-four hours, and I had to find a way to lay my head down for a spell if I was going to be alert enough in the long run to be able to keep men moving, listening to orders, and doing their best to carry them out. I know it sounds strange that I was thinking of ways to get a nap at a time like that, but the body knows what it knows, no matter what the mind might be saying.

It was all of a piece that hot day in June 1876. One battalion commander drunk and fearful to the point of madness in the middle of a battle, more Lakotas and Cheyennes in one location with weapons and their blood up than had ever happened before, the commanding officer of the Seventh Cavalry nowhere to be found, not a sound of "Garry Owen" being played by the band as the Seventh charged the enemy, and me, Captain Frederick Benteen, dying for a little sleep as arrows and lead and stone clubs flew about my head.

Isaiah Dorman
SCOUT AND INTERPRETER, ON THE GREASY GRASS

June 25, 1876

I'D GOT SENT OFF WITH HERENDEEN AND GERARD TO SCOUT FOR Major Reno when General Custer decided to divide up the Seventh Cavalry into three battalions on that day before we got to the Greasy Grass. So I wouldn't be with the general's bunch like I usually was, and when I first heard from the lieutenant that I was to ride with Reno's battalion I was glad of it. Anybody that had been with the general's bunch when some kind of fight was about to start knew he'd have to count on being led right into the middle of the worst action of the day. Now if things went right, and the Indians broke and ran, and the main thing you were doing was chasing down squaws and young ones and setting fire to lodges and picking out what you could get away with from the goods lying around, why then it was good to be with the main bunch.

We have got to where we call that battalion, the one directly led by Iron Butt, the hammer, since that was the part of the tool that would hit hardest and do all the damage. Generally, the ones with Major Reno or Captain Benteen, they wouldn't get to be right in the front of the main part of that hammer. They supported the head of the hammer, held it up and made it able to hit its hardest. They came in last, that's what I'm saying, and most of the hard hitting that took place first had done been took care of, and General Custer and his battalion could take the credit for that, get first chance at the goods and picking through the women for the best ones, and hear all the cheering for them for being the ones that took the day and earned the victory.

But on the morning of yesterday's hot day in June, after we had got a late start at getting to where the general had wanted to be already, when they told us scouts which battalion we'd be guiding, I got a feeling different from the one I had at the Washita. Back then I was part of the ones in the battalion that was the hammer, like it was called, the one that let down hardest once the other ones had set the nails and got them ready for pounding home. That was good to me.

But I'd been hearing things all that day and night before as we worked our way into the Montana country toward where Sitting Bull had all the Lakota tribes and the Cheyennes joined up together on the Greasy Grass. It was too many of them, the Crow scouts and the Rees was saying, all them Lakota Sioux and Cheyennes emptying themselves from so many reservations where they'd walked off and didn't want to go back to. Here's the way White Man Runs Him put it when I asked him why he was sitting flat on the ground singing a little song to himself in the middle of the night, so low you could hardly hear it, but I did hear it. And I knew what it was.

"You sing of seeing a new country," I said to White Man Runs Him, speaking in his tongue. "You tell of going to a place you've never been before and of eating a meal at a strange place, a kind you've never tasted before."

"This is true, Half-Buffalo," he said, then using my white man name, he went on. "Dorman, I rode ahead this day, way beyond where the general told me to go. I climbed that rock where you can see far from. You've been in that place, I know. Every scout's gone there sometime." I nodded yes, but said nothing that might slow him down.

"I could see the horses of the people of the Lakotas and the Cheyennes, and I could count the smokes from the fires made for the cooking by the women. Let me tell you what it looked like, Dorman."

"Tell me. What did you see?"

"There were so many ponies, all brought together in one spot, that when they moved it looked to me where I was sitting so high up, it looked like worms after a long and hard rain."

"Worms?" I said.

"Like worms upon the ground, and them all working as far as you can see. So many you don't try to count, since the number is too big to wait for the end of the job of counting to come. You can't never count all the worms."

"And the cook fires?" I said. "Were they many as well?"

"The smoke from them all came together, and it made a cloud covering the sky like a storm was coming so hard and long and big that all who are caught in it will drown."

"Were you afraid to see these things?"

"Not just afraid, truly. But sorry was the way I felt. I am sorry to have to leave this world I know and go into the new one that's unknown to me. I don't like to eat strange food for the first time."

Then White Man Runs Him looked away from me and began to sing his song again, and I left to find a place to rest for the hard work coming on the next day. I hoped I would sleep.

So the next morning, still full dark when we made ready to ride ahead of the troopers and I was told by Herendeen that I would be riding not with Custer as part of the hammer, but with Major Reno as guide to his battalion which would begin the first attack on the village, I was more glad than sorry. But I was both.

Maybe me being with Reno's bunch would keep me from getting a chance to gather up my share of the goods left over after Custer had killed all the ones he could get to and run off the rest of them, but if things didn't go right like they ought to do for Iron Butt I'd not be in the bunch that had to pay the price. He did always seem to get what he wanted when he went after something, though, whether it was burning a village and killing a bunch of the ones trying to stop him or it was picking through the women after the fighting was over and taking the prime one of the bunch. He always won the day, General Custer did. I got to say that. But the way the scouts were carrying on, and that thing that had happened with the dead chief three days back, all that had made me have a funny feeling.

Lies had been told about me, too, and what I've found out about lies, time and again, whether they happen to be about you when you're a slave belonging to a white man back in Virginia or Louisiana or a freed man in the Black Hills scouting for the Seventh Cavalry, it all comes to this. People will believe a lie long before they'll believe the truth. Why that is, I don't understand, but what I've got figured about lies, I ain't never seen to fail to work out. Folks like a lie a lot better than the flat truth. Lies taste richer, like the marrow you dig out of a bone you've roasted in a fire. Better than the real meat.

When we come up on the grove of cottonwoods three days back, we could see plain before us where they'd put it up. The old chief was dead, and he was trussed up in a buffalo hide and up on a scaffold of tree limbs tied together. And he had his medicine bags all around him, and them tied down, too. If nobody disturbed where the Sioux had put him ready to go on off into the country where they figure to go after they ain't alive anymore, everything would have been fine for him and the body he used to live in. If a bear had tore down what was left of him and rooted around where his body was or if buzzards and possums and ants and bugs had worked their way underneath the coverings around him, any of that would not have bothered the people who put him there. That's what happens, they'd say, and they'd lay it off on Abba Mikko.

But now if blue-coat soldiers had even touched the platform where the old chief's body was waiting for the varmints to get at it, much less tore off the buffalo hide and took the medicine bags or the arrows or the knives and axes or the cook pots stuck up in there for the dead man to take with him to the next world if he decided to do that, then it would be hell to pay. And I wasn't the one that did that, put a hand on a single thing there, or started any of that. I don't mess with dead folks.

White soldiers did it, tore up the platform and cut open that buffalo hide and took what they wanted of the stuff there that was meant to be used in the next world where Sioux go when they're dead. White folks did that—one of them the brother of General Custer himself, the one named Tom—and then they threw the old dead chief down on the ground and one of them even shot the dead man in the face just to see what a hunk of lead will do to a skull up close.

Here's what I did after they got through poking and playing. I took the old man's body by the legs and drug it off to the bank of the little river there and dropped it in to let it float off or sink, whatever it wanted to do. I was figuring by throwing it in the stream I was doing the dead man a favor and honoring the Lakota people at the same time. I've lived with them folks for years, and I married me a wife from the Santee, and I speak the language they do. I wasn't doing nothing against the People when I did that with the old man's body.

But that was the truth, and the truth doesn't stand a chance against a lie, like I done said. What got told about me after I'd thrown the dead man into the river and watched him sink real fast—it seemed like it didn't take no time for all sign of that dead body to be gone—was not that I was getting the dead chief out of the reach of any other white soldier that wanted to play with the body like it was a child's toy, but instead this notion here. And it didn't take any time for the lie to be told, I think by a Ree scout or maybe a soldier in F Company, an Irishman I believe he was, and less time than that for everybody to hear it and believe it no matter how much I told the truth about what I meant by doing that. That Ree or that Irishman said I had dragged the old chief's dead body over to the river and used it for bait to try to catch some fish.

That is a lie, but nobody but me chooses to know that. I say *chooses* rather than *knows* because they have decided to believe what they want to believe rather than what's true. Why? I figure it this way. It makes a better story to tell and to believe, a story that I used a dead man, a Lakota chief, for fish bait. And folks in the Seventh Cavalry want a good story more than anything else. Just look at General George Custer himself. There ain't nothing he likes better to do, other than leading a charge against some enemy, but to sit around with the officers and scouts of an evening and sing songs and talk about what's been done and what will be done tomorrow. And that's no matter which tomorrow we're talking about. Whatever happens tomorrow will be subject to retelling to make it better for the next day's storytelling. For lots of folks, talking about a thing is better than doing the thing itself.

That story told about what I used for fish bait was not true, but I knew I was going to have to pay for that body in the water one way or another no matter how much I knew that was a debt I didn't owe.

✯ ✯

A late start this morning for all three battalions, except for the scouts. All of us had been ahead of the bunch led by Major Reno since the middle of the night when the general gave the order for the Seventh to strike camp and head for where Sitting Bull had set up his village. The scouts was me and Herendeen in front of the bunch and eight or nine Rees along with a couple of Crows. I couldn't ever get a good count of that bunch with us since one and sometimes two or three would wander off along the way while the rest of us were trying to read sign in the dark and then the stragglers would show up again later. Not that it was hard to find sign of where Sitting Bull's people had come and gone. It had been so many travois and ponies come through the country we were traveling that it was like following a broad road back in a white man's town somewhere. The only thing you had to worry about on that wide trail was that you might get off your horse before good daylight and put your feet in a pile of dung left by all the ponies.

By the middle of the day, Reno's bunch was working its way across the river to come in on the side of where the village was set up. Me and the rest of the scouts had got well ahead of that movement and had slipped up on a bunch of Lakota women and some young ones digging away beside the stream at a place where you can always find wild prairie turnips growing at the right time of year. I'd eat turnips dug from that same place many a time back when I was living with the Lakotas. The stream was loud enough, and the women and kids were paying close enough attention to what they were after, that we were able to get close to the bunch before the first one to look up spotted us. It was a yearling boy, him having good hearing at that age and not so interested in digging up roots.

He turned to a woman bent over there working away with a deer antler for a tool as she dug for turnips, said something to her, and after what seemed like a longer time than it really was, she turned around to look at us. She commenced to yelling, saying the soldiers were coming, and then she began scrambling around looking for her young ones, like the other women had started to do. Seeing the way one of the littlest children reached for her mother and grabbed ahold of her dress made something inside my belly seem to move and tighten up, and I pulled up on my horse's reins and stopped him dead still.

The rest of the scouts I was with, especially the Crows who whipped up their mounts to get to where the women and young ones were standing by the little piles of wild turnips they had dug up, didn't do what I had done. They charged ahead, giving voice to some yells and chants that tribe will use when going into battle, and it didn't take long for it to be all over. Most of the young ones took off running, except for them closest to baby age who had scrambled to cling to their mothers when all the yelling and shooting started, but the women didn't break and run before the charge against them. Like the Sioux always do, men or women, they stood their ground and faced up pretty good to what was coming down on them, knowing what that was going to be. But they didn't want to give the enemies, Crows and Rees in this case, the opportunity to chase them down and strike from behind.

Some of the women even tried to fight back, one standing up against the Ree coming at her with the stone club in his hand, and her swinging the antler she'd been using to dig turnips like it was a weapon. It didn't do her no good, nor her little girl child, neither, but the mother hadn't run. After I saw her do that, I turned my mount and rode back out of there toward where Major Reno's battalion was forming up beyond a bend in the river you couldn't see around. I didn't want to look at any more of what was going on in the place where turnips come up in the spring beside the Greasy Grass, sweet and new in that month of the year. One other thing about what I'd noticed when we come up on that bunch had bothered me enough that I knew it'd stick in my head as long as I had a head.

The woman who first spotted us coming up, the one who the boy had spoken to first when he heard the hooves of our horses, she was somebody I knew I had seen before at the Standing Rock reservation a couple of years back. It was that second wife of Gall, the younger of the two wives he had married, and by that I knew one of the other women there to dig turnips was probably the older one of the two wives to Gall. Both of his wives was going to be killed by the scouts, along with some of his children, too, I expected. I didn't want to be there for any part of that, not because I knew what Gall would want to do when he learned what the Crow and Ree scouts had made happen, though. That wasn't no hard puzzle to figure out, predicting that outcome.

It was me having seen who one of the women was, that was what made me not want to be around to witness what went on in among them piles of turnips and the muddy holes in the ground they'd come out of. I knew her and had talked to her a few times back on the reservation, just in greeting or nodding at her as we passed by each other. She had spoke back to me. She wasn't just another Sioux woman caught by some scouts for the white man without no warriors around to take care of her and her young one. She seemed more real to me, since I knew who she was. I felt a little bit off in my belly, like I said, and I wanted to get back to the main bunch of Seventh Cavalry troopers, where there was noise going on and a lot of movement taking place. Horses would be all nerved up and restless, and soldiers would be seeing to their weapons and equipment, and the officers would be hollering and giving orders. And all that would fill my mind up, and maybe make me stop thinking about them piles of turnips and that little girl hanging onto her mother's dress, about to cry as she looked up at me on my Army horse.

☆ ☆

When Major Reno gave the order to advance to the lieutenants and they passed it on to the sergeants and by way of them to the troopers, I was in a position on the far right of the line and about thirty yards ahead of the main body of men, where scouts ordinarily put themselves at the start of a situation that's about to become a charge into the enemy. To my left was a Ree, a young man named Eagle Finder, who'd never worked for General Custer's Seventh Cavalry before, and he was looking straight at me as we waited to be told to lead the advance of Reno's battalion.

"Black White Man," he said, reaching down into a deerskin pouch fastened to a string around his neck, "here's something for you. I think you missed getting a taste back there when you left early."

"Call me Dorman," I told him. "Only the Lakotas use that name Black White Man for me. What you got in that bag?"

"I thought the Oglalas call you Teat," he said, twisting his face into what he meant to be a friendly expression, I supposed. "Like the she buffalo. Why do they name you thus, a bag that calves suck?"

"Some do that. Or they used to. Why, you ask me. Think of this. What color is the teat of a cow buffalo?"

"Black," Eagle Finder said. "Like the middle of the night when the moon has been eaten up by the sun."

"Look at my face. See the color? It's an easy reason to call me Teat. But let me tell you, they didn't call me that, the Sioux when I lived with them, because they thought it meant I was like a woman. That's not what the name meant to them."

"No?"

"It was the color black, not my nature, which qualified me to be known as Teat. But you don't call me that, Eagle Finder. If you do it one more time, I'll be like a he buffalo you ain't able to get out of the way of. You see what I mean?"

"Oh, yes," he said, looking at me out of the corner of his eye. "I meant no offense to you, Dorman. Here, do you want a turnip?"

"No, I don't eat turnips from now on. Never again will I do that."

"It is sweet," Eagle Finder said, rummaging around in his deerskin bag. "Taste but one, and you'll want another."

"That turnip you relish now," I said, "will make your stomach sour before this day is gone. Mark the word I say. You will see that turnip again. So will we all. Come, let's proceed. The trumpeter will blow his big whistle now."

And he did that, and the line of troopers began what the officers called a fast trot, and the other scouts and I urged our horses forward to stay ahead of the blue soldiers who'd be following us as the rest of the day began to unfold like a picture made with colors on the white skin of a month-old deer just killed. Somebody was drawing lines on that skin that would show what took place and who made it happen in just that way. They would have to color the picture in later, when all the fighting and killing was over, and by then the drawer of all that happened would be able to take his time and get it right. The color he'd start with, and end with, and use most of would be red. It would be all over each thing any man touched that day.

I knew that, so I was not surprised when Major Reno's companies of troopers had met as yet no Sioux or Cheyenne warriors trying to stop them from moving toward Sitting Bull's big village on the Greasy Grass. That was at first, a thing put off until later, and we went along easy and fast for a while, and the officers riding alongside the major had time to laugh and talk to each other as they rode in front of their men at a fast trot and as they passed around bottles of whisky to put to their mouths for a good strong drink before things got too busy.

It wasn't until a big cloud of dust began to rise up in front of us far enough off that we couldn't see what was causing that to happen that Major Reno and the rest of the officers got quiet and started asking each other questions you couldn't hear unless you were right on top of the ones talking. I knew what was causing all that dust to start hanging in the air, though, and so did the Ree and Crow scouts riding along with me up in front of the main bunch of blue soldiers. Two of the Crows began to sing a song that I had heard about before but had never witnessed being said out loud.

"What's that, Dorman Buffalo?" the young Ree scout Eagle Finder said. "What tune are the Crows singing? What story is it they're telling?"

"You know what it is," I said. "I don't have to tell the words for it in a different language from the one it's in when the Crows sing it. That song don't need to be explained or talked about. It's easy enough to understand."

"Do you think they're right to be singing it, then? Do they know things I don't?"

"Don't ask me what you don't know. I ain't got time to list all them things right now that you don't know while we're waiting for Sitting Bull and Crazy Horse and the rest of them to come busting out of that cloud of dirt in front of us."

"They're coming then, the Sioux and Cheyennes?" Eagle Finder said, beginning to touch his free hand to the rifle he had hanging around his neck and shoulder on a rawhide string and then to the long knife stuck under his belt. "That's why the Crows are singing about dying. They're thinking about the ones coming to try to kill them."

"They're not singing about dying," I told him right before I began to lean forward on my horse to pick up the pace. "They're singing about how to die the right way. We're way on beyond worrying about whether it's going to happen or not. He's done decided that's going to happen."

"Who? Who said it's going to happen?"

"Call him whatever name you want to. We're all talking about the same one, no matter what name we put on him. He does what he does. He doesn't need nobody to give him a name."

"Dismount," I heard Major Reno hollering to the officers and them starting to repeat what he'd just said. "Dismount and form a skirmish line. Horse holders, head for that patch of woods by the river." That's when everything started happening at once, the troopers pulling up on the bits in their horses' mouths, enlisted men all piling off and handing their reins to the horse holders before they threw themselves on the ground to begin sighting in their single-shot army-issue rifles, the officers staying mounted and yelling orders at the men in their companies, the sounds now of the Sioux and Cheyennes getting closer in front and singing songs about coming up close to an enemy and what they were about to do there, shots going off and arrows arching high in the air and beginning to land far enough in front of the battalion's position not to matter yet, and me doing my part by scrambling off my horse and fetching my repeating sporting rifle along with me as I flopped down near where I tied my horse's reins to a steel rod I'd run into the ground.

It didn't take long for us to be able to make out different warriors in the big cloud of dust they'd whipped up with their ponies, them being close enough now for us to see the figures of ponies and riders moving in little and big circles as they advanced toward us, puffs of smoke coming out of their rifle muzzles and arrows starting to climb up into the sky and come down. Reno's troopers were getting off volleys by then, and I knew that in a few minutes, hot as it was in the middle of the day in late June, that the rifles would heat up enough for the cartridges to start swelling and jamming in the firing chambers, causing the volleys to peter out as the soldiers had to work to prise out the stuck shells before they could get other ones put in to shoot.

It came to me to think that my repeating sporting rifle was more of a curse than a blessing while the rest of Reno's Seventh Cavalry battalion had only the single-shot weapon and it jamming and becoming unable to fire fast, if at all. All I got from being able to use a good weapon that wouldn't fail me in a shooting battle was not an advantage but me being noticed, instead. I could already tell that the Sioux and Cheyennes were starting to pay attention to the steady fire coming at them from my part of the battlefield. Before long, somebody was either going to decide to do more to kill me than ordinary or that he wanted to get ahold of the weapon doing such a good job of keeping up a steady fire. That would mean killing me, too, I told myself, so I thought to say something out loud that the overseer of us slaves back on the plantation in Virginia had many a time applied to a situation one of us had got ourselves into. You're damned if you do, and damned if you don't, Toller or Flora or Hamish, he'd say to one or other of the slaves he was running. You don't know whether to shit or get off the pot, do you?

Thinking of Jim D'Orsay saying that to me, grinning the way he did when he said it, like he was admiring himself for being so smart a man, that made me smile a little myself, even as lying flat on the ground behind a little bush I got off a shot which knocked a Cheyenne off his horse. Too bad for that warrior, I thought to myself, but damn if I want some other Indian to believe he just has to have the rifle that just did that job so nice and neat, while its owner is still able to shoot at another man before the first one has even hit the ground yet.

I got off two more shots before I had to reload the magazine of my rifle, such a pretty thing it was with its walnut stock and blued steel barrel, and by the time I got that almost done as I lay as flat and close to the ground as I could manage in behind that bush, things had got so hot and close with all the warriors swarming in and around and against Major Reno's skirmish line that he'd decided to give the order to mount up and move. I didn't do that as soon as I heard the lieutenants screaming that order out to the troopers on the ground, since I was wanting to finish loading my rifle to full capacity, but most everybody else was reaching for the bridles of the horses the holders had waiting for them and swinging aboard. They were glad to do that, too, those that weren't too shot up to mount up again, though not every man had a horse waiting to carry him off. Some mounts had been turned loose by the trooper supposed to be holding onto four horses at the same time while trying to stay out of the way of Indians wanting to knock his brains out or slit his throat or put a bullet through his chest or belly or head. Some horses had been shot to death or wounded so bad they couldn't carry themselves away from where all the killing was going on, and some had busted loose from the man trying to hold four of them together at once and had lit out for anyplace somewhere else.

My horse had stayed tied to the steel rod I had stuck into the ground close to where I'd been roosting behind my bush and banging away at any Sioux or Cheyenne I could draw a good bead on, and not only that, he was chewing away at the weeds and bushes in range of where he was tethered, looking as calm and interested in eating as if he was all alone on an open prairie with not a man in sight. I mounted up, holding my rifle in my right hand as I pulled on the bridle to turn my horse toward the river and the hills on the far bank, and by the time I'd kicked the roan in the ribs twice we were moving into a full gallop away from where the majority of Reno's battalion was fighting to get mounted and get going while Sioux and Cheyennes pushed their ponies right up into the middle of things, looking to do all the damage they could.

We hadn't gone more than fifty yards toward the Greasy Grass, me and my calm Seventh Cavalry mount, when he stepped into a prairie dog hole, one of lots of them on that flat side of the river, and tumbled down in a heap. I was thrown clear over his head, and he missed falling on top of me, but that was the last and only good thing that happened to me on that scalding hot June day. When he tried to get to his feet, my roan horse was just able to do that, but only three of his four legs was working, the one he'd stuck in the prairie dog hole broke so bad I could see bone showing. That horse never made a sound, though, as he hobbled off to one side of where I was checking my rifle to see if it still worked—it did, and I started looking around for somebody to shoot, figuring I'd get the first bullet fired at the next man coming at me—and the roan still didn't let loose with a holler like most horses will do when they're hurt or scared. He was hurt, but he didn't act scared, and he never made a sound other than a long grunt when a Sioux warrior who looked not to be over fourteen or fifteen years old rode up close, held a cavalry pistol to my horse's head, and blew his brains out.

The roan went down like all his strings had been cut, just the way a man does when he's head-shot and just like that young Sioux with the yellow paint all over his face did when I used one of my last rounds to shoot him just above where he had a stuffed bird tied into the hair on the left side of his head, the round knocking a feather loose from the dead bird and doing a lot more than that to the boy's skull. I told myself to stop thinking about how that horse would likely have got me across the Greasy Grass in a calm gallop if it hadn't been for the prairie dog digging a hole in just the right spot to get me knocked to the ground and ready to be killed. What I needed to do then, I knew, though my heart wasn't really in it anymore since there wasn't going to be any chance of me getting through this fight on the wrong side of the Greasy Grass, was to shoot as many Indians as I could before they got me hemmed up to where I couldn't do another thing but die. It wasn't a lot I had left I could do, but as long as my sporting rifle still functioned and I had bullets to spend, I had a thing remaining for me to handle. It was why I was there. That's what I was raised to do, and I figured I'd do it until I went down like the roan and the young Sioux who'd killed him.

I took good, slow, and careful aim using up the cartridges I had left, and at the time I reached a count that told me I had probably three shots left in my good rifle, though I couldn't be dead sure about that since I knew I might have lost count when my horse hit the prairie dog hole, a bullet hit me high up on the left side of my chest. It didn't hurt exactly, feeling more like somebody had thumped me hard there with a balled-up fist, and I figured it hadn't hit my heart since I didn't keel over and pass out.

I kept on shooting at the right kind of people, feeling my chest getting wet from the blood coming from the hole the bullet had made and still nothing hurting much yet. By the right kind of people, I didn't mean just any Sioux or Cheyenne warrior I saw in range, but the ones that seemed to be noticing me. That's who'll kill you, speaking generally. The ones narrowing their eyes and drawing a good bead, that's who I mean when I talk about the right kind of people. The ones taking their time. I hit two more of them, and watched them stumble and fall, both of them already dismounted from their ponies to do some close work on some trooper they had done knocked down, I reckon. They had given sign of having noticed me already, though, so I figured I'd slowed things down a little by putting that two to rest.

Then my rifle clicked on a spent shell, and I knew that was probably going to be it for me there in that damn hot June day on the bank of the Greasy Grass. Maybe I should have shot myself in the head, I was thinking, when I still had a shell left. But that came to me too late, and I probably couldn't have made myself do it, anyway. I'd spent my whole life trying to stay alive and get an advantage, and it was hard to change that way of thinking right when it looked like I was coming to the end of it. I thought I might pull out the knife I kept fastened to my belt in a scabbard my wife had put some quill decorations on to pretty it up back when I was living with her at the Standing Rock agency, but after second thought I decided not to try to get all mixed up in hand-to-hand work. I would lose that fast, and it might make them madder than usual if I put a blade into somebody who was going to be the one to do the killing. They were probably going to take their time anyway, and the more they got worked up beforehand the longer they might take to string things out.

I was thinking that, feeling the blood coming down my chest and now into the pants I was wearing and being glad nothing was hurting much yet, when the first one came up on me that I didn't have the chance or means to shoot at. It was somebody that looked familiar, but I couldn't think of his name until after he'd spoken to me.

"Black White Man," he said. "Teat, I didn't know I'd be seeing you with these blue soldiers. How long you been working for them?"

"A couple of years, off and on, Blue Bird Sees Him. Not regular all the time, but when I needed something to do."

I could tell he was pleased I remembered his name, and he was about to say something else when one of the troopers came thundering by on his horse, the reins loose and flying and the mount out of any kind of control. "Good bye, Rutten," I said as I recognized him, even as popped wide open as his eyes were, giving him an appearance and an expression I'd never seen on him before.

"He is a scared blue soldier, isn't he?" Blue Bird Sees Him said. "You think he might suspect there's people here who want to kill him and cut his scalp off?"

We both smiled a little at that, him more than me, and Blue Bird Sees Him then stood up from where he'd been squatting beside me and pointed to my rifle. "That was you," he said, "who's been doing all that good and fast shooting with that pretty rifle."

"Yes, that's been me all right. But I run out of ammunition and didn't get to shoot at you when you come up. You better take that rifle while you can. Somebody's going to want to have that fine piece of equipment."

"Maybe I will," Blue Bird Sees Him said. "But I've got to get back in the fight, and it looks like you've made your choice, Teat. I'm not going to be the one that kills you. I'll leave that to somebody else. But I am going to fix it so you can't use your legs to walk off any more and leave your wife and young ones in the lodge while you work for Long Hair. I can't just leave without letting you know what that choice has cost you."

"You can't let me give you this rifle and then you put a bullet in my head?" I said. "Could you see your way clear to doing that?"

"I'd like to, but I can't help you out with that," Blue Bird Sees Him said and pointed his weapon at my shins. It was a shotgun, and I was surprised I hadn't noticed that before. When he fired it, that did hurt in a way the bullet through my upper chest and out my back didn't. My legs felt like fire had been set to them. And the blood and pieces of bone just jumped out like they had been dying to leave where they belonged.

"So long, Teat," Blue Bird Sees Him said. "I'd like to do more for you, but I got to go help get this deal all wound up."

"Do you think somebody will finish me off before the women get here at the end of things?" I asked, and not being able to stop myself, groaned out loud about the way my legs felt.

"If I don't get wiped out on that hill," he said, pointing across the Greasy Grass to a gulch filled with Seventh Cavalry blue soldiers scrambling up it with Indians all over them, swinging clubs and counting coup and shooting arrows and banging away with carbines, "I'll come back by here and make sure you're dead as soon as I see you. I can't promise you anything about the women now."

"I understand that," I said, the pain in my shins now so strong that I was hoping the blood coming from my chest wound would hurry up and leak enough out to put me to sleep. "I hope you don't get wiped out, Blue Bird Sees Him." He waved his hand, lifted a bone whistle to his mouth, blew a breath through it, and was gone. Not the women, I thought, watching a riderless Seventh Cavalry horse pound by me, headed for the river. Not the women. Let it not be the women.

But the next one to stop the horse she was riding and take a long look at me was just that, a woman of the Sioux, a Hunkpapa I judged from seeing the bone beads worked into the sleeves of the shirt or blouse she was wearing. I was pretty sure that was the people she was coming from, and I could have been certain if her hair hadn't been let all down the way it was. It didn't have any pattern to the way it was braided or put together with a rawhide string, since it wasn't really fixed any way in particular but allowed to be loose to blow in the wind whichever way it wanted. She had done that on purpose, I knew, since she had chosen to mount up on a pony to fight like a man with the rest of the warriors of the Hunkpapa Sioux, and one way she showed that was to let her hair be free to do whatever it wanted.

The other thing she'd done to let anybody that looked at her know what she meant her work to be now was to paint her face red. And the paint began at her neck and went all the way to her forehead where the hair started and from one ear to the other, covering up all the skin you'd ordinarily see revealed on the face and head of a woman of the Sioux.

She wasn't a woman anymore. That's what she was saying. She was a warrior of the Sioux, and she would kill the enemy until every last one was gone or until she was wiped out herself. The men who saw her riding with them as a warrior would be heartened by that vision of her, and they would be challenged to show what they could do to let this warrior woman know they were up to the job of killing anybody and anything in the way of the Sioux.

"Hola, Teat," she said, hopping down from her pony and coming close enough to me to be able to squat down and look directly into my face. She was carrying a cavalry pistol that looked long enough to serve as a crutch if she had pointed it at the ground. "I thought you'd probably be with these blue soldiers, but I didn't know if I'd see you or not. And here you are."

"I didn't know you until you got close to me," I said to Moving Robe Woman. "I guess it was all that red covering your face up that kept you hid."

"I'm not hid, Teat," she said, laying the cavalry pistol across one knee as she squatted before me. "This is who I am today, a warrior of the People. I'm who I am, and nothing else. They already killed my little brother today, and now it's my turn."

"Deeds is dead, huh?" I said. "He was just a baby last time I saw him. Too bad he's gone. But let me ask you something, Moving Robe Woman, something I'd like you to do for me. "

"Your pants are all wet," she said. "Don't tell me you've pissed yourself just because you got shot."

"I didn't know I was doing that if I did it. I think my clothes are wet with blood instead of piss, though. See, I got a hole up here on my chest, and it's been leaking for a while."

"Oh, well, that's probably what it is. Tell me something else, though. Why'd you start working with these blue soldiers? Why'd you join up with Long Hair? I wouldn't have thought you'd leave your wife and throw in with this bunch."

"Oh, I don't know," I said, looking at the cavalry pistol laying across Moving Robe Woman's knee. It appeared to me like something good to eat looks to a hungry man. "I didn't have any real reason for it. I just wanted to get some money from the white men, and I can talk their language. You know that."

"You could do a lot of things, Teat," she said. "You could marry a Santee Sioux woman, get children with her, talk to Sioux and Cheyennes and Rees and Crows and white folks and them all understand you. You could act like a buffalo. Look like one, too. All that. And now look at you."

"Well, yeah. I can't argue with you about that. But let me ask you what I want you to do for me. Can you listen to me?" Moving Robe Woman looked off at the swarm of Indians chasing the troopers across the river, up the ravine, and into the brush, yipping and yelling and banging away, and then back at me with the kind of expression on her face that somebody in a hurry has when you ask them to wait on you for a little while. She would not wait long.

"I was wanting to ask you not to kill me. That was it at first when I saw who you truly were beneath all that red color on your face. But now, I know I'm going to be dead in a little while here, one way or another. I don't want me getting dead to be that other way."

"If you didn't want to be killed, why didn't you stay home where you belong with your wife and children and not come to attack me?"

"I didn't come to attack you, Moving Robe Woman. I got nothing against you."

"When you bring the blue soldiers and talk for them, you attack me, Teat. You stab me and shoot me and cut off my hair, Dorman. That's what I call you now. Dorman."

"Won't you just shoot me with that pistol you're carrying? That's what I want now. I want you to kill me quick. Before they get here, the women."

"They will be angry with me, Dorman," Moving Robe Woman said. "You know how women can get. Especially the Hunkpapa women. Look at me, the way I'm dressed and what I'm doing, if you want to know that truth for certain. Do you know how many blue soldiers I've killed today?"

"I expect it's been several, Moving Robe Woman. It's my turn. Will you shoot me now?" I said. "Before they come here to me. There'll be plenty of white men left for them to work on without having to work on me."

"That's true, and I'm glad you know that. But they will work on you dead or alive. You know that. That's what they do."

"If you kill me, I don't care what they do to my body."

"They'll want to draw blood out into a cup and look at it and taste it to see if blood from a black white man is different. If it's good, they'll all drink it down, swallow by swallow. They'll want to cut off your man parts because you left your Santee wife and took away from her what you used to be as a man to her."

"They will do all that, yes," I said. "And I understand that, for it is their way. But I want to be dead when all they must do is being done. I tell you this. Some lies have been told about me. I did not fish with the corpse of a dead Sioux taken from his burial place. I did not use his flesh for bait. I was not that kind of man. My body was wrong in many ways, and my mind was wrong along with it. But I did not do that thing. Please make me die now."

"Who knows where you'll go after you die, if you ask to be killed?"

"Moving Robe Woman, I'll take my chances on that. I'm not a true Sioux. I'm a black man from a place called Virginia, and I want you to kill me now. Maybe I'll go back there when I'm dead."

"All right," she said. "I'll do it for you. Go to Virginia by yourself, all alone with no wife and no children and no more home in the Black Hills. See how you like it then."

The muzzle touched my forehead, the steel a little cold as hot as it was that day. The first time Moving Robe Woman pulled trigger on the pistol, it misfired and nothing happened but a click. We both smiled when that happened, and I said my last word in this world. "Don't play with me, woman of the Hunkpapas. Send me back to Virginia."

The next time the trigger pulled true, and a bright light opened there before me as far away as I was from Virginia late in the day in the Montana Territory on the bank of a river the Sioux call the Greasy Grass.

Billy Kills His Horses

AS GALL, WAR CHIEF, HUNKPAPA LAKOTA, ON THE GREASY GRASS

JUNE 25, 2001

*T*ALK ABOUT YOUR MISMATCHES. HERE'S A CLASH BETWEEN appearance and reality. And it's a major one, me playing the part of Gall at this year's reenactment of Custer's Last Stand. Gall, the one who used, among other instruments of destruction, a club to smash Seventh Cavalry soldiers. Oh, I understand why I was chosen for that role, despite my most earnest protestations and my almost blanket refusal to stand in for a war chief, for grief's sake, and him married to at least two women simultaneously at last count. Both of that duo were killed in the prelude to Custer's big scene on Last Stand Hill, we all know, but still, you understand. A war chief with two wives, and him known for ferocity and implacable hostility to anything in the least bit subject to more than one interpretation. A man who never saw ambiguity in a single thing he ever encountered his life long.

But look at me. I admit it. I understand the reason I popped into the director's mind when he considered the crucial role of Gall and how best to fill it. Here I stand, well over two hundred pounds in weight and not quite six feet in height, which adds to the burliness of my affect, and me a contemporary Hunkpapa Sioux, born and raised on the res and still unable to this day to be able to achieve full and lasting escape velocity from that spot of desolate Montana. And my name, so fitting for a "brave" (excuse the double entendre) fixed upon me at birth, being what it is. Billy Kills His Horses.

Well, that label grew to be good for laughs when I was a student at Montana State, majoring in fine arts with an emphasis in drama, but that bit of humor doesn't occur to people who behold me for the first time. To the casual and immediate observer, what I am, plain to see and appreciate at first glance, is a big, brooding Indian, large featured and most likely heavily into alcohol and ready to brawl at the slightest provocation by some paleface who's not careful to watch what he's saying, or how he's saying it, or how he looks when he's giving voice to some insult to this hulking red man before him.

That's what Alec Murray saw when he first glimpsed me a year ago, the day I deigned to show up at tryouts for the annual ritual of reenactment at the historic site of the Last Stand. I hadn't been anywhere in the vicinity of any of these yearly events for years, of course, not since I'd gotten wise enough to recognize what they were meant to represent and to celebrate. And to profit from. And let me tell you, none of that profit redounded to the benefit of the red brothers and sisters descending from that bunch who gave General Custer and his boys such a rough reception all those years ago. As a child, I had shown up each year at the reenactments between my sixth and my fourteenth birthdays, I think it was, but I did it for nothing but the free-lunch goodies they gave us and the chance to ride horses and run around wearing breechclouts and war paint, pretending to be wild children of the plain.

When it came to me, aided by the interpretation of the annual reenactment told me by my teacher of English at Bozeman High School, that the reenactment of Custer's Last Stand of 1876 was simply a rip-off of history and an occasion for white folks to play Indian and feel noble and titillated, it was then I withdrew from the lists and didn't show up again. Not until this year, I must hasten to add, and there's a story attached to that decision. It's short, and I hope it'll be sweet.

Word is and rumor has it that scouts for a major motion picture, yet another attempt devoted to the Last Stand and to be produced and directed by Spielberg or Clement Dohlan, will be in attendance at the 125th anniversary reenactment, and they will be looking for talent. I, needless to say, have been and continue to be looking for a way off the res and out of Montana until I find it, and here may be a chance for me. That's why, to put it in a few words, I showed up to audition for a role in this year's big whoop-de-do, knowing and dreading all the while that I'd be selected to play some brutish red-man character from those dear, dead days of yore. But, hey, you take your chances, right? You can play only the cards you're dealt, show up and stay up, and all the rest of those clichés one mouths to justify becoming engaged in some activity that demeans and diminishes one's sense of self.

But I showed up to display myself to Mr. Alec Murray, artistic director of the reenactment of Custer's Last Stand and himself at one point an actor of minimal notice, enough to get him parts in several films, not blockbusters but ones from major studios that did make the nut in their time, as my old drama teacher, A. A. Abernethy at Montana State, informed me.

"Do not stick your nose up in the air at this chance, Bill," he'd said to me. "Don't get it out of joint, either, when I tell you that at times you must lower your sights if you want to bag a big one."

"I do not hunt wild animals, A. A.," I said, "as you know, and I do not fish, either. I attempt to bag nothing but the truth. And thus I reject your chase metaphor."

"To the pure, all things are pure," he said to me, and I must admit that truth hit me like a thunderbolt. Didn't every actor begin at the bottom, dwelling with the lowlife creatures and dismal situations found at that depth? Didn't every one of them lower himself to participate at whatever level he thought might prove promising? Is there any thespian with perfectly clean hands? I don't think so.

"Shall I wear my Caliban costume?" I asked A. A. at that point, letting him know he had me leaning. "Remember how the audience gasped at first sight of that getup at every performance? It wrung them out to dry. It simply made that production of the *Tempest*. And I am not just boasting."

"Granted, but I don't think you should don the Caliban garb, Bill," he said. "Let Alec Murray see you not as a would-be professional lusting for the bright lights, but as a contemporary young man right off the reservation. He should not be thinking Shakespeare, Bill, when he sees you. He should be saying to himself—my God here's an Indian whose last name is Kills His Horses. What authenticity!"

That name, oh my, my Native American name. It has been my burden lifelong, but as the bard said about the rose, any other label wouldn't affect the quality of the scent. He said it better than that, of course, so don't misunderstand me. I can quote lines from Shakespeare if I want to. I know how. I do, I do.

Growing up on the res with that moniker was mostly no big deal, and not one of the People as they call themselves ever blinked upon hearing it. I mean, just to show what I'm talking about, one of the nicest old ladies I've ever run into, not only on the res but in Bozeman and Billings and all the other little dippy places I've visited in my limited experience, answered to the name of Martha Cut Nose. She never got a second look from anybody when she said her name, as long as she stayed home, and my being called Kills His Horses never mattered to a single soul on the res or in the elementary school the Feds ran for us young ones below the age of twelve.

The only time I had to think my name was a burden was when Miller Blue Light had his sole bit of imaginative insight when he came up with the answer to the question he posed about why I was called Kills His Horses. I can still recall the scene in literally chilling detail, that one day at recess, when a bunch of us gathered in a clump together in the face of a brutally cold wind blowing across the playground in January, pellets of frozen mist hammering away at us elementary-school Sioux kids, and Miller looking at me and beginning to grin as a weak little thought worked its way across his brainpan and out of his slack mouth.

"Hey, you know why Billy's last name is Kills His Horses? You know why his horses got killed?"

"Why?" somebody said. "I don't know. Why?"

"Because," Miller Blue Light said, his mouth hanging open wide enough to let me see his tongue working as he strove to make words with it, "the reason Billy's horses got killed is because Billy's so fat he mashes them to death every time he gets on them."

They all got a good laugh at that, their shoulders shaking as they guffawed and forgot about how cold the wind was for a few seconds. I couldn't think of anything to say back to Miller to counter the way he'd stung me, and as usual it never crossed my mind to hit him in the face with my fist, right in the middle of that hole which was his mouth where the hurtful words had come from. I never had the will to go up against anybody physically, big and strong looking though I was, and I knew as I stood there listening to all of them laughing away at the smidgen of wit that Miller Blue Light had just displayed that I'd never have the will or the courage or the gumption or whatever it took to stand up for myself like a big Indian should.

So I did my usual thing on such occasions of humiliation. I slunk off, headed for the indoors where the grown-ups were holed up, trying to think as I sought the door to the shelter inside something I could have said in response to the insult Miller had made to my name. I came up with nothing, as usual, and it wasn't until late that night after I'd gone to bed in the house where I lived with my parents and brothers and sisters that I thought of something apt to say about Miller's last name. That did me no good. Too late, as always, no matter how clever my comeback might have been.

So when I showed up in early May on audition day for a role in the reenactment of General George A. Custer's Last Stand and waited in line outside a huge RV for over an hour before I got called in to meet Alec Murray, the director, who had the godly power of yea or nay over all us aspirants, I thought of my name and considered ways to respond to any questions put to me about it. White people always notice Indian names more than the bearers of them do, a fact I'd discovered a long time ago, and it would be incumbent upon me to have something appropriate to say when this particular white man made public his particular insight into indigenous labels.

I thought I was ready for what he might send at me. Why'd you kill your horses? That was a usual one they'd put to you. How'd you do it? That took second place. Was that a good thing or a bad thing, killing your horses? That got asked by a few, now and then. What a unique name! It must have a fascinating history. That compliment, or a variant of it, often came from women. That gender is more vicious, thus their need to be polite.

So when I finally got called in by an assistant to meet Alec Murray and make my pitch for a part in the pageant, I was surprised to hear a different take on the usual first question put to me about the label I'd had to bear all my days so far. "Kills His Horses," Alec Murray had said, looking up from a sheaf of papers attached to a clipboard. "What did your steeds do to deserve killing?"

"They questioned my authority," I heard myself saying, and before I'd had time to go over in my mind what I'd just uttered, Alec Murray was sticking out his hand toward me for a white man's shake. I gave him that, putting enough force into the clasp to make him realize I'd been to some places off the reservation and knew how to stand up straight, look a man in the eye, and white tooth him with a big grin.

"You may be Kills His Horses at home, but here on Custer's Hill, you're Gall," he said. "Physically perfect. You're him. All you've got to do is learn to project the necessary power to convince an audience."

"I've spent a lifetime learning how to project inner power," I said, giving him my best Clint Eastwood and seeing his eyes widen as I did. "My heart is bad."

If that doesn't work, I told myself as I watched Alec Murray look me up and down, I don't know a thing about white folks. I do believe that bad-heart claim hit home, and thanks be to Mrs. Hazel Chambliss for drilling into my head in senior English class at Bozeman High the need to do a little research before I subjected myself to any interview for a job. I'd done that. I had read about Gall, and I knew that the white historians loved to write about what the Hunkpapa war chief had said about his state of mind after learning two of his wives and several of his children had been done in by a bunch of Crow scouts the Seventh Cavalry was using to guide them on the right path.

Did Gall actually utter that wonderful truth about his emotional state at the time he was suiting up for the big game? Did he really say he was so ferocious in battle because his heart was bad? Who knows? Probably not so succinctly, but he knew what to tell the white men who interviewed him years after the last act of that drama had occurred and the curtain had gone down. There's nothing a white scholar or social worker or government administrator loves better than hearing an Indian deliver a mythic statement like the one Gall had supposedly said, especially one that included the mention of a heart. They love that shit. I had learned along the way, growing up on the res and going to the federally funded elementary school and then to the public high in Bozeman, that whites who considered themselves sympathetic to the red man love to hear one of us reveal emotional depth and motivation. It gets them all hot and squirmy.

If you're an Indian dealing with the man, don't try to get intellectual, now, or truculent, and whatever you do, don't launch into a logical argument about some point of disagreement. White folks don't want to hear that kind of garbage from an Indian. But say something that smacks of the mystical or uses the concept of the heart as representative of a knowledge not subject to intellectual inquiry, and baby, you're no longer an Indian whining about rights and dispossession, you're a Native American in touch with the immeasurable.

So my name did me good with Alec Murray, and my quoting the supposed statement by Gall about his feelings after learning his wives and children had been killed sealed the deal. I was to be Gall, war chief of the Sioux, and my body girth and my less than chiseled facial features would not work against me and bring me down, but do me good for a change. Who knows, I thought to myself as I left Alec Murray's oversized RV, I might be noticed by Steven Spielberg himself as I swing my foam-rubber club and my plastic ax against the blue-clad bodies of the guys playing the role of troopers in the Seventh Cavalry. He might be taken by my display of ferocity and elemental selfhood enough to cast me in the movie. Then I'd have my chance. Then I'd be gone for good from bleaksville Montana and the nowhere reservation where I'd spent most of my days so far.

And here's the good part, I told myself, as I skipped lightly across the plain outside the headquarters RV—if an Indian weighing more than 240 pounds and looking like a down lineman for the Washington Redskins can be said to skip at all—as Gall, I won't be simply one of the subsidiary bunch who chased Reno's boys across the river and into the trees and up the hill. No, I'll be in at the final kill. I'll be part of that swarm of guys who offs Custer and his brothers and brother-in-law and all the rest of his battalion on Last Stand Hill. Maybe I'll be picked out to brain Tom Custer or Myles Keogh or even be in at the taking down of the man himself. Could I possibly be able to count coup on the Son of the Morning Star, even if I wouldn't be allowed by the director to pull trigger on him?

I hope, I hope, I was telling myself as I sat on my pony and listened to Alec address the bunch of us who'd soon be charging up the hill toward the summit where the full orgasm of the Last Stand would take place. Here I've been living my life wandering between two worlds, one dead and the other powerless to be born, and now maybe I'll bring them both together and unify my consciousness at long last. And yes, I knew what poet's words I was appropriating, and I used them because they were perfect for the moment. I'm not an insane purist, locked into one culture's mode of apprehending reality, and that only. I may be called Kills His

Horses, and I may have snatches of poetry stolen from white men floating around in my head, but I know where I am and I'm happy and at ease with ambiguity. My heart may be bad, and I knew my pony was groaning at the weight he was having to bear, but so what? I'm Kills His Horses, and I knew if things went just a little bit right for a change, I might be able to portray the killing of a white man so important he'll always be known and studied. His death could be my life. God, I do relish paradox!

Hoka hey, baby, hoka hey. Watch me, Mr. Spielberg. I'm Gall, war chief of the Hunkpapas, and I am your huckleberry.

Patrick Bruce
COMPANY F, SEVENTH CAVALRY, ON LAST STAND HILL

June 25, 1876

*T*HEY CALLED OUR BUNCH THE LEFT WING, US IN COMPANY F along with them in Company E, but I wasn't worried about the name they'd slapped on us. We knew who we were, and that was the main body of General Custer's battalion, the ones he'd kept to be with him after he'd sent Major Reno and Captain Benteen way off across that little river with their companies, way out of sight. They might do some clearing of the way for us, Reno's and Benteen's troopers, as the commanding officer of Company F said to us boys in his bunch, as they put pressure on that big village full of Indians, but the real hammer was going to be us. Otherwise, why was the general saving us to go with him? We knew why, and that was from several reasons, the main one being that General Custer's favorite scout was right along with us. Where he ended up was always where the general wanted to be.

That fellow was a Crow Indian they called White Man Runs Him, a name that when I first heard it made me laugh and think it was an insult to him. "No," one of the older privates told me, "it don't mean what you think, Patrick Bruce. It means something different, they tell me."

"Well," I said, "back in County Cork we ain't so delicate in understanding what a thing you call a man might mean. Every Irishman knows when he's being called out for insult, and he knows what he ought to do about it when he hears something equivalent to White Man Runs Him. That'd be like saying in Ireland the name Englishman Runs Him when you're talking of some native lad there. It'd mean somebody's head has become a candidate for to get whipped on."

"All you micks want to do is fight among yourselves," Captain Yates had said to me, me letting him get away with voicing that label because of his rank, but filing it away in my head for use later if I got the chance. "You'll be getting the chance to do all the fighting you can stand a little later on now," he went on to say. "Just wait a bit, and every Irishman here'll find that out." And you know what? He proved to be right.

I'd not been in the Seventh Cavalry but a little over two months, soon turning to the soldier's life after arriving in the Black Hills to fill my pockets with gold and discovering naught but rocks and thorns and little to eat and naught to drink. But I'd already learned when the officers and the sergeants told us to cinch our saddles tight, see to our weapons, and mount up that we'd be moving down off that hill toward the Little Bighorn down below us and fetching up against some Indians here directly. That was after they'd starting dividing us up into different parts and when they started calling our bunch the Left Wing, the one the general was riding with, and the other one, the one a fellow Irishman named Myles Keogh was captaining, was called the Right Wing.

Nobody bothered to tell us why that bunch was staying higher up on the hills than we was, but that wasn't unusual. Nobody ever told us what any collection of soldiers was having to do anyway. Just tend to what we tell you to do, and do it. That was the habit they urged on us. You don't never need to know more than what we tell you to know. Keep your mouth shut and start moving. Don't think, lads, it'll just confuse you.

I would have liked it a little if I'd been in the Right Wing commanded by Keogh, him being of the old country, but that was only on principle. He'd never said a word to me, nor me to him, and that had nothing to do from the both of us being Irish but from where in the order of things in Ireland he had come. He was in no way of my ilk, and I knew it, and so did he. He was high placed, and I wasn't. That didn't bother me, not the Boyo. I'd worked at and made a solid place for myself in this land of America, and I was never the one to look back or regret a damn thing. Let's go on from here, I'd always told myself, whatever happened to me in Cork in the old country, or in New Orleans or Memphis or St. Louis or the Black Hills amongst the Indians. What's new, and how can I handle it? I'm your man to take hold of the here and now.

Besides, being in the bunch with General Custer himself, that was compliment enough to me to satisfy. There'd be fighting where he was, and he'd always had the luck wherever he landed, as I'd been told by many a one who ought to know. And an Irish lad has to depend on luck more than most folks, not having a thing else but that and his fists to back him up. I'd settle for that, I thought to myself as we began to work our way down toward the river, moving careful as we went because of all the draws and hillocks that lay in our way. Luck and hard knocks, that's served me before and it'll do me now.

On the way down to the bottom, you couldn't see much of a thing other than the fellow in front of you and the ones beside and the one following if you turned in your saddle to look over your shoulder. That was because of the way the land lay with all them draws and ravines running off to the sides and front and every direction, making you have to pick your way and hiding the next thing that lay in front of you. I was thinking to myself as I moved on my good gray horse down that decline about how wrong an idea I'd had before of what a prairie in the West would look like. It would be like a tabletop, I'd figured from what I'd heard, that land would be, flat and one color like the surface of a billiard table in one of the sporting houses in New Orleans or St. Louis, and you'd be able to see on all sides to the end of the world once you'd entered that country.

But it's not that way, I was considering, not at all like I'd expected. Trying to see ahead of yourself here is more like being in some dark wood down in a river valley in Ireland and night coming on with the shadows creeping out from the trees and bushes, the light fading and birds beginning to call one to the other as they got ready to bed down, and not a soul in sight but yourself. I might keep that picture in mind to mention to some of the other lads in that Left Wing of the Seventh Cavalry once we'd got the job done of whipping these red men. I'd see how much argument I could stir up with that topic later on by the cook fires once our job of work here was done. Somebody would challenge my notion, thinking they had a better way to put it, and that'd give us all a chance to argue the point. Fight, dig, drink, and argue. Always the Irishman's way.

In the middle of dwelling on that, I thought I heard something like a noise made by one of them birds back in Ireland in that dark thicket of green woods by a river. It was a rustling sound that came to me, making me look up toward the fellow riding ahead of me on his gray, and I did that because he had made a quick jerk of his head and shoulders just at the time my ears picked up on that rustling noise. Something was sticking up a foot or so above his right shoulder off to the side, and it had feathers on the end of it, making me wonder just for the blink of an eye if it truly was a bird that had made the racket that got my attention. Then the fellow groaned a little and cussed and started trying to pull the feathers away from his shoulder like they was bothering him. He was from Italy, this lad was, and he didn't talk good English, though I'd got to know him a little bit despite that. Bruno, he was called, Bruno Alberti, and he had long eyelashes like a woman would have if she was lucky. He was a friendly lad, as little as I had got to know him.

It was an arrow that was stuck in Bruno's shoulder, I was coming to see, wiggling back and forth as he jerked at it, just as that sound came again, this time a lot louder and a lot more of it, with the arrows that was causing the noise now hitting all around me and the boys in that Left Wing bunch moving down toward the river at the bottom of that long hill. "Dismount," was the order all us troopers was hearing, that order coming from the sergeants and lieutenants, and we began piling off to the ground and the horse holders started grabbing at the reins of the troopers whose first job was to get off a volley at the ones shooting them arrows. By this time, you could hear gunfire, too, aimed at us, and I could tell by how fast it was coming that some of the bullets was shot from repeating rifles, not from single shots like the Springfields we was issued to carry in the Seventh.

It was a strange thing I was thinking, that though the arrows was still coming down like big rain drops from overhead, most of them missing everything and just hitting the ground all around the troopers, but some sticking into horses and making them squeal and buck and fight against the men holding them, and bullets from rifles and shotguns was flying now, I'd yet to see an Indian. It was like we was under attack by ghosts or men invisible to sight, there at first, when the whole thing started up.

Where was I going to shoot my first round from my rifle, I was wondering, and how do I aim at nothing or something that ain't there, with all this smoke starting to get in the way of seeing anything farther than three feet from me and not a single one of the hostiles in sight? Then it seemed to me like I was standing in a theater building, or in a music hall back home in Cork, and all of a sudden the sounds of horns and whistles being blown got louder with more of them joining in, and a big set of curtains opened and you could see all the folks who'd been hidden from your sight up until then. Only it wasn't a bunch of fellows playing music on horns and drums and fiddles or a line of women with their legs showing and them kicking and dancing and grinning and singing and everybody clapping their hands and shouting at who they was seeing.

No, it wasn't that kind of show you could now see behind the curtains being pulled back, that being a thing you'd been relishing getting the first sight of, your eyes all popped open and you leaning forward in your seat or where you was standing in the aisle waiting for the great surprise you was all ready to enjoy. It wasn't a show up on stage. Instead, it was a scene of hell you might picture in a terrible nightmare, complete with knives and clubs and axes and every kind of demon Satan himself could imagine. One of the imps in particular caught my eye from all the ones to choose from to study, one close to where I was standing, and I began to draw a bead on him with the Springfield rifle that they had provided me to use back at Fort Lincoln.

This one's black hair was long and hanging loose except for right in the middle of his head where a hank of it was tied up by a string so he looked like an oversized bird, his face all painted yellow with a streak starting on his forehead and the color reaching all the way down his throat to where it ran into what he was wearing. It looked like a lady's blouse she might choose if she was stepping out of her house in St. Louis to visit some establishment that sold goods to folks with lots of money to buy them. The lady's dress was too little for the man wearing it, if you could call him a man all done up the way he was, and the cloth bodice of it was busted open just below his neck, making it look like the lady wearing it in St. Louis had all of a sudden grown too large for the finery she was used to donning before going out on Locust Street or Olive or Broadway to do her buying.

This yellow-faced Indian fellow was looking straight at me and was fumbling with an old musket that appeared not to be functioning like he wanted, him being one of the unfortunate few who possessed a firearm older and worse than the ones me and the rest of the lads of the Left Wing of General Custer's Seventh Cavalry had been issued to use against the red devils of the Black Hills. So before this Indian fellow dressed in the bodice of a lady from back east out for a morning stroll in St. Louis could get his weapon to do what he calculated it ought to do, send a ball of lead into the chest or belly of the Dogtown Boyo before him, I was able to get my Springfield rifle to fire first. The fellow didn't look surprised or even bothered much when my single shot weapon sent its load into him, but he did what a man ought to when hit mid-body. He just fell straight down, like a bunch of strings that had been holding him up had been cut all of a sudden, him not knocked back off his feet but settling onto them, like the ground beneath was putting a pull so strong and hard and sudden that he didn't have time to deal with it in any way but to stop being a man and turn into a stuffed doll with no backbone to hold him up.

The relief I felt from seeing I'd had the advantage over that yellow-faced Indian wearing a white lady's blouse didn't last me long, though, since right behind him was another one of the devilish-looking fellows, this one a lot less got up in his dress and coloration, though, and not holding a firearm ready to discharge in my direction, but swinging what looked like a club, one made from a length of wood with a good-sized gray-colored stone mounted and tied to it somehow. He wasn't close enough to me to do any harm with his instrument yet, but he appeared to be determined to work his way into range just as soon as he could arrange to do that. I could club my rifle, I considered, and get ready to swing that at him, but that wasn't a thing I'd practiced before, and it seemed to me that the Indian fellow with his stone club was well accustomed to putting that tool to work. He would have the advantage on me.

I swung around, grabbed at the reins of my gray behind me, hearing as I did the order from a sergeant to mount up and prepare to withdraw, and I put foot to stirrup and was following the order from the sergeant almost before the words was fully out of his mouth. Most of the rest of the troopers right around me were matching my actions, though I could see two or three fellows to my right and one to my left all caught up in grappling with more Indians than it seemed possible could be there, given the fact that just a couple of minutes ago you couldn't see a one, covered up as they was in the bushes growing in them ravines and gullies and draws. Some of the lads were trying to fight off the ones swinging clubs and thrusting knives at them, yelling as they fought back and scrambling as best they could to find their horses and try to climb on them, while in the meantime struggling to keep from being brained and stabbed and shot. Some others looked to have been paralyzed by what was happening to them, standing still and holding their weapons without trying to use them, some of that bunch, and others letting their rifles and pistols slip out of their grasps and fall to the ground without seeming to notice they was giving up any means of defense they had been holding onto up until then.

Here's a thing I saw, there near the bottom of that long hill that runs down to the bank of the Little Bighorn, and I swear to its truth, as outlandish as it seems. A trooper from Company E, a lad I'd never talked to much at all, but one I'd seen with others in that bunch and him acting like the rest always—quiet sometimes, loud others, talking a blue streak himself now and then, listening to others jabber other times, being in other words like most lads, in different moods at different times, but doing his job and obeying orders and appearing to know he was a soldier and acting like that fact meant something that could be dead serious on down the road—I saw him standing in front of an Indian who was reaching up with a butcher blade to cut his throat and the lad doing nothing to stop it. Not knocking away the red devil's hand wielding the knife, not pushing back, not trying to run away, not trying to fight off what was happening to him in any fashion, not seeming to care that he was being killed while he stood there quiet, watching it happen, and looking to all the world like he was just waiting for nature to take its course and was hoping it would be soon now.

He had done quit living, though he wasn't dead yet. But his mind was gone already. All he was waiting for was to fall down to the ground and have it all over with. Not me, I yelled out loud. Not yet. I ain't ready to lay down and die. And I turned my gray horse, along with the lads who'd managed to get mounted, and we began our retreat back up the hill, the Indians not following close on us for some reason, though as I was looking back down that slope toward the river, it seemed to me that the very ground was growing Indians as fast as you can see ants swarming out of a nest after you stir it up hard with a stick. They was piling out of them draws and ravines and gullies like they had been stacked up in there on top of each other and now had to have some air and light, slowing down as soon as they hit the open, but promising to move in a great clot after us as soon as they decided to take the notion.

I never looked back at the lad standing still as he waited to have his throat cut, remembering as I leaned forward on my horse to give him as much encouragement to run uphill as hard as he was able, a time when I, a boy back in Ireland, saw a hog getting butchered at killing time in early winter. A skinny old fellow named Joe Baxley had leaned forward as the hog was eating some slops they had put down in a great pan to get the beast's attention, and the old boy had stuck a long thin blade into the animal's throat, hitting that big artery that'll let all the blood out quick. The hog never looked up or gave any sign it knew what had just happened to it, keeping on eating the slops off the ground until it finally keeled over and kicked a couple of times and died. I swear it was still chewing at a mouthful of slops until its heart quit.

To get that thought and the way it touched on that lad from Company E standing there waiting for the Indian to finish killing him out of my head, I leaned way low forward on my horse's neck and then looked back over my shoulder to see if I was in danger of anything catching up to me. That's when I caught sight of General Custer himself in the middle of three or four officers pounding up the hill on horseback, all of them closed in around him while he sat straight up, looking about him at the bunch of men from the two companies making up that Left Wing of that battalion of the Seventh like he was doing a survey. To keep his hat from blowing away, he was holding it and the reins of his horse in his right hand bunched up in a wad, and he had his left hand lifted up toward his face the way a man will do when he's thinking hard about something that's bothering him and is using the touch of his hand to his cheek to help him concentrate. Now that sounds a little strange, I know, but that's the way it struck me as I watched General Custer and his officers heading up the hill toward a flat place close to the top where they figured to set up a defense against all that bunch of painted devils swarming below and working to keep close to all of us still able to keep moving.

The look on his face, General George A. Custer I'm talking about now, wasn't what I would have predicted. He appeared to be thinking of what he'd tell the officers to do in getting us turned around and settled into a defensive posture that might discourage the Sioux and Cheyennes from trying to run right over us before we could get ready for them, but judging from what little glimpse I had of his face as I hung onto my mount and offered as small a target for the Indians to shoot at as I could told me he appeared to be having a good time. I don't mean to say he was smiling or laughing as he loped along on that big roan of his, but he was surely looking satisfied to be where he was. He knew right where he was located and where he was headed and he was glad to be there. By that look, he was showing he knew what he would be doing when he got to that location he planned to reach. In the meantime, he was content to be heading where he intended and was well pleased with the course events were taking.

I didn't have long to study on whether what I was thinking when I saw General Custer directing our withdrawal from where he had sent us just a little while ago made any sense or not, because in less time than it takes to tell about it we'd reached the flat area at the top of that hill and was following orders to get in position to defend ourselves. The count of how many troopers was left at that point wasn't on my mind, neither, but I did notice that several of the lads from Company F didn't seem to be anywhere around me like they had been earlier. The number of men holding the horses was a lot fewer than one to four like it ordinarily was, more like one horse holder to six or eight now.

I had just got good turned around and had reloaded my rifle and laid out a handful of rounds beside me like I remembered regulations saying we was supposed to do when preparing to shoot from a prone position when Sergeant Rooney put his face in mine and started telling me what he wanted. "Patrick, lad," he said, which surprised me a little since he'd never called me by my first name before when I was on duty of any sort. And I was on duty at the top of that hill overlooking the Little Bighorn, the Lord knows. "You and these seven or eight others I want to see conduct a charge toward that draw yonder," he went on, pointing a little ways down the hill off to the right where a great clump of brown bushes was choking the mouth of a ravine which reached near to where what remained of the Left Wing was settling into a circle of men and rifles pointing out. "The hostiles are filling that depression up with themselves, and we've got to drive them back before they get enough warriors in there to come boiling out of that cover at us."

"Charge them?" I said, not challenging what the sergeant was saying exactly, but letting him know he was giving us a task to undertake that didn't look promising. "There at the mouth of that draw?"

"That's the order, Patrick. And do what you can, lad, along with the rest of them. I'll be going along with you. Never fear."

So the eight of us, nine including Sergeant Rooney, counted off one by one, and when that was done, we all rose together when the sergeant said, "Do it now," and we ran yelling toward the mouth of that draw filled with waist-high bushes and grasses, all of us holding our rifles out in front, ready to fire. The brush in that draw started shaking well before we got there, and as soon as it did that, I was able to see the figures of men beginning to take shape, no two looking the same in the brush, but all rising at about the same time, a lot more of them than there was of us. A strange thing, though, and one I wouldn't have predicted back before I got into the Seventh Cavalry and was of no experience in organized fighting, not like times when I was all by myself in a boxing match against just one man and his fists and him knowing I was as alone as he was with no other man to depend on.

They ran from us, that lot of Indians did, that's what surprised me, many more of them than us eight or nine from Company F. They just turned tail and vanished back into the bushes and down the draw toward the other end of it. We didn't have to fire a shot for them to do that, neither, and not a single cartridge was busted in our direction, nor did one nasty iron-tipped arrow come flying, neither. All of us recruits had been told when they was instructing us back at the fort about what we might do in a combat situation that just a few determined men can make a much larger number quail and run if they can throw the right scare into them.

It didn't seem sensible to me at the time that sergeant training us said that, I got to say. I figured that was just a way to get new soldiers to put themselves at hazard when a reasonable way of acting would have called for just the opposite manner of behaving. Running like hell is just a step away. But I'll be damned, I told myself, as I saw the backside of that bunch of Indians lighting out before us as we was hollering and carrying on behind them, if that sergeant wasn't telling the truth. "The thing of it is, boys, that no matter how big a number of men a fellow has around him, when he sees somebody coming at him and the rest of his bunch looking like he's wanting to put a killing on somebody, that fellow taking the charge says to himself one thing. Let the rest of them stay around and contest that fellow who's ready to put out the lamps for me. I'll just ease on off here, and there won't nobody notice nor give a damn."

So even red Indians with bows and arrows and repeating rifles and clubs and knives will act like men, I considered, and run away when death and destruction seem to be coming on them. That ought to've made me think things ain't looking nearly so bad for the Seventh Cavalry as I thought when I was coming up that hill horseback and them red devils right behind me yelling like wolves after a deer. It didn't, though, once me and that bunch of troopers got back from clearing out that big wad of Indians from the mouth of that draw. Sergeant Rooney looked satisfied with what we'd done, and he gave us a nod to show his feelings, but I could see that his face was as gray and lifeless as a shovelful of wood ashes from a dead fire, and that let me know more than I wanted to. He didn't have a bit of color left in him.

"See to your weapons," some officer was saying. "Fire in volleys as long as you can. Maintain a steady fire and a constant reload. Don't bang away until you see something to aim at and hit."

"This goddamn shell casing . . . " some trooper was saying, but he didn't get to finish what he'd started, since something hit him in the throat and blood flew everywhere like water does when one of the fountains gets turned on in that big park in St. Louis, but it was spewing out not clear water but red. I could have finished what that trooper was saying for him, though, since I was having the same problem with my Springfield he was having with his right before he took that load in his face and throat, letting him not have to worry about a thing in this world ever again. The barrel of the Springfield gets hot after you'd shot it off a few times, like any rifle will do, but that caused the brass shell casing to swell up and get stuck and not eject in that particular make of firearm. So you couldn't load and shoot again until you'd prised that casing loose, if you could get that done at all.

And you know what? An Indian will not wait for you to do that while he stands around for you to get ready to fire again. No, he'll just kill you while you fumble around and use a knife to work at that stuck shell casing, and he'll do that killing with a club or an ax or an arrow or worst of all, with a shot from a repeating rifle which he has laid his hands on, and which a trooper in the Seventh Cavalry of the United States has not been issued and can't get ahold of.

Our little run at the mouth of that ravine had scared off a good number of that bunch, but that rest it gave us didn't last long enough for me to tell about it. They were coming at us from all sides now, and though we had laid down in a prone defense position at first, in a big circle to provide fire in all directions, that couldn't last long. Pretty soon though, after some of the troopers had shot their horses and tried to lay down behind the carcasses as protection from the arrows coming from the front along with the lead from rifles and pistols, the officers that was still up and fighting started ordering us to stand up, and I knew what that meant. It's a lot easier to fight a man hand-to-hand if you're on your feet like he is, rather than lying down in front of him while he leans over you to do the damage he intends. That's true if you're in a boxing match in a ring against one other fellow or if you're on a hill in the Montana land with so many Indians around you with clubs and knives and axes and guns that it doesn't make a bit of difference that you're alongside and under the command of General George A. Custer.

I had looked around and seen the general and one of his brothers and his nephew, I think it was, all standing together, them all armed with handguns like officers will generally be, pointing and discharging them now one direction and then another and hollering a word or two to each other now and then. I didn't look long at that bunch of fellows in the same family together in the Seventh Cavalry since I had to pay attention to what was happening in front of me and what was coming toward me bit by bit and in fits and starts, but sure as the sun rising in the morning and going down at night. I did want to take another look at the commanding officer of the outfit and situation I had let myself get ended up in, though. I figured I owed that much to myself after my time back in Cork and then the days on that stinking boat from Liverpool and then in New Orleans and Memphis and St. Louis and then walking all that way west and poking at the ground for sign of gold in Dakota and now here in the Montana on the top of a hill full of Indians who'd be killing me soon and putting a stop to all I'd been up to.

He was a famous man, the general, and he was the only one of that kind I had met so far, not counting that Italian boxer from Chicago I could have whipped in St. Louis but didn't for money's sake, and I knew I'd never see another one like Custer. Or no other man or woman, neither, after a little while here. So I took one more look over my shoulder, and just as I did a big spot of red blossomed on the left side of that white deerskin shirt General Custer was wearing, and he staggered a little and put his hand up to the place where all that white was turning red now, looking down at it like he was interested to see what was soiling his clothes. His legs seemed to be giving way about then, and he sank down all the way to his knees, his brother reaching down and holding him around his body like he was helping him sit down without falling over. His brother looked down and then back up before him, since he'd heard somebody approaching the two of them, and he appeared concerned not to be noticing who was coming up and ought to be tended to. The look he gave the one coming toward him and his brother now sitting on the ground and pushing his hand against his breast to hold in as much of what was forcing its way out as well as he could, was like Tom Custer was being polite. It was as though he was indicating he would get to the new one as soon as he could, but that man would have to wait his turn like anybody else.

It was an Indian warrior, toting a little ax in his hand which he was drawing back to get ready to swing at one or the other of the Custer brothers and still hadn't made up his mind which one to address first. He had his hair up in a topknot, and there was a dead bird tied to that, looking almost alive as it sat there on top of the man's head. Just as he drew back his arm to get his ax ready to do its work on one or other of the Custer brothers, Tom stuck the muzzle of his pistol right into the center of the Indian's chest, pulling trigger as he did, and the man seemed to lift off the ground a little bit as the bullet went about its business. The bird fastened to the top knot still looked as alive as it did when I first noticed it sitting up there, but the man supporting it seemed like he had all of a sudden lost half his body weight, folding into himself like his chest had been a musical squeeze box and all the air had gone out of it.

Watching all that go on with the Custer brothers, Tom and George, and studying the Indian trying to do his part to kill the two of them just about cost me more than I had counted on, though. Coming up right in front of me, and me with my Springfield's single shot just used and not a new cartridge yet put in the breech, was a great big Indian looking wide as a house as he stepped in my direction. I had been trained, though not very well, to be ready at all times to club my rifle in just such a situation, holding it so as to be able to swing the butt of it up and against the upper body and head of an enemy closing on me, and that's what I should have been doing without even thinking about it. The sergeant instructing us in hand–to–hand combat back at the fort them few weeks ago kept talking about us having to practice doing a thing until we didn't have to think about it.

"The last thing a soldier should be asked to do is think," he'd said to us time and time again, thinking it was funny when he said it but meaning every word, I could tell. "Your soldier, and especially your cavalry soldier, ain't equipped to think about nothing but what's for supper and where can I lay down and rest. He constitutionally can't think, else he wouldn't be in the cavalry, now would he?" Oh, he thought himself a wit, Sergeant Overstreet did.

But as the Indian came at me, instead of using my left hand as a fulcrum, as they called it, and swinging the butt of my rifle from right to left as I tried to knock the brains out of the man come up to kill me, I dropped my Springfield and went into the stance which had served me so well as the Dogtown Boyo back in St. Louis when I was king of pugilists in that place. I lifted my left fist before me, shifted my weight to my back foot—the right one, now, understand—and I shook my left fist in the face of that big Indian with the great stone club in his hand. He gave it all of his attention, as a poor boxer will do when shown the left fist of a right-handed man, leaned toward my left hand as though to push it aside, thinking that paw was the one which would give him trouble, and that gave me the opportunity such an opening provides. I crossed with the right fist, getting all of my weight shifted and behind and into that blow and I caught that amateur just on the point of the jaw where the lower bone connects to the skull. He dropped like a great sack of potatoes, the poor sad excuse for a boxer did, and the Dogtown Boyo had knocked out another heavyweight clumsy galoot with one stinging blow. And best of all, it was not a cheat as it had been back in St. Louis when I lost for money and not for truth, and I felt as good as a man can feel when he sees a great number of red Indians now descending on him, knives and clubs and repeating rifles in hand, set to take him out of this world.

But you know what? They are coming in force and they're about to prevail, but they're having to step over their great sleeping champion, nosed into the dust as he is, jaw all bruised and dislocated, and all due to the skill and strength and Irish hardheadedness of the Dogtown Boyo. Come on, you great red bastards, and get your taste of what you deserve. The Boyo is serving up just what you must needs savor. Come here in range and let me show you a little footwork and a hard stiff right. Hurrah for Cork, hurrah for Ireland, and hurrah for Dogtown in St. Louis.

Mark Kellogg

JOURNALIST AND REPORTER FOR THE *BISMARCK TRIBUNE*, ON ASSIGNMENT WITH THE SEVENTH CAVALRY

JUNE 25, 1876

*T*HE RUSH OF COMPANY F, TO WHICH I WAS ATTACHED, THAT DASH up the hill from the Little Bighorn came both suddenly and slowly, and I remarked to myself the strangeness of that contradiction as I clung to the pommel of my saddle as part and parcel of that cavalcade of horsemen in flight before the swarm of red men driving us before them. It seemed a simple enough explanation to apply to the sense of slowness which possessed me and I presume the rest of the Company in which I found myself enlisted. When one is fleeing from a would-be assailant, the sense of speed or lack of it which possesses one must strike with a vengeance. Am I running with hobbles about my feet, one feels. Am I moving in molasses? Can I not put on an extra burst of speed to enable a greater distance between myself and that which hounds me with intent to do great bodily harm? Is there no way to achieve a gain in effort and effect as I flee before the pursuer?

All that sense of fear and a definite belief that little if any degree of success in leaving behind the enemy are completely understandable in terms of a sense of a dreadful slowness at work against one's attempt to put danger farther out of range. So one of the pair of contradictory sensations is explainable. What of the other, the feeling that an enormous speed of movement and event is hard at work? So sudden as to bewilder and appall.

Easily understood and explained, I told myself, as I leaned forward over the horse I rode, urging the animal on with all concentration of mind and a continual drumming of my feet against the sides and belly of the animal. What strikes me as so speedy is the sense of a lack of control and the sensations surrounding me personally. Behind me and gaining comes a horde of men clad in raiment which might have been designed by Satan himself. Animal hides and dead fowl and hideous designs in red and yellow and green and black festoon the bodies of these creatures. Their faces are distorted fiendishly by bits of bone and rocks and feathers hanging from their hair and ears and noses; knives and bows are carried by hand and arrows are held in their teeth; shrieks of anger and lust pour from their throats; high-pitched whistles issue from bone instruments held in their teeth so as to force each breath to create a sound heard only by doomed souls in urgent progress toward death and dissolution.

The sense of speed, therefore, of all things rushing by with such force as to make it impossible to seize upon one thought and follow it through to successful completion—all these sensations create an overfullness of mental and emotional involvement so intense as to paralyze any productive endeavor.

Do I direct my mount straight up this hill toward the crowd of troopers from Company F gathering in a formation with General Custer at the center of their position? Or do I allow the animal I ride to veer off to the right as it seems continually to be attempting to do, taking the mouth of that draw as a possible escape from the shrieking band of blood-crazed savages pounding behind me? Is there more safety in numbers at the top of the hill, exposed though it is? Or is it best to join the few who avoid becoming part of that concentration of men steadily becoming more outnumbered as the Indians converge? Do I attempt to mentally record all details in order to have pertinent material for later fodder for writing? Can I afford not to pay attention to the realm of the word?

There is no time to think, to reason out a logical solution more likely of successful completion. No time to look at all sides of an issue, in the roar of gunfire and the shrieks of savages and the pounding of hooves and the screams of men in agony as they die. All this discord and hellish roar joins in one sensation of a bloody conclusion coming to an unavoidable close.

Yet the word resplendent, the adjective I've seized upon as most appropriate in characterizing George A. Custer, comes to mind even as I flee for my life. That word fixes itself like a fire in my mind because of what I see before me, and that is the figure of the Commanding Officer of the Seventh Cavalry. Wherever he stands, he establishes, as all great men do, the center of action and meaning. I can see him clearly now at the apex of the hill. Poised, pistol at ready, surrounded by his brother Tom, his nephew, and a few other troopers. His expression speaks of acceptance, attention to the task of leadership before him, and a commitment to struggle until all strength vanishes.

I know I should make for that circle of dedicated soldiers, and I begin to tug at the reins of my mount to keep him true to the path that will lead me as journalist in that direction. But as I do so I see what seems to be a puff of air tug at the buckskin uniform of General Custer, turning itself into a widening design of red, draining from that dauntless figure at the center of all action above the Little Bighorn.

I ease up on the reins of my horse, allowing him to set the course he desires, and the mouth of the draw leading down into a green thicket is irresistible. Only a few yards lie between us and what looks like safety, and my mount takes me toward that dark green tunnel down into shadow. Maybe the red devils will continue on a straight course toward the troopers surrounding Custer as he lies dying, and if they do that, a chance remains that none will pursue me.

I'm a journalist, an interpreter of event, not a shaper of reality. I should not cause events to take place. That's not my task. My function is well understood and appreciated by human beings like myself. In the recent Civil War, my fellow journalists and I could record the details of a great war between thousands of men from all over this nation. We did so at some danger, but never with intentional hatred directed our way. No civilized soldier would harm a writer. Here, though, in the Montana Territory, pursued by savage heathen animals who deck themselves in bone and fur and paint and shoot Christians with arrows and club them with stone axes, any chance of survival because of my being a journalist has no status. Savages exist beyond reason.

But oh, dear God. My daughters in Minnesota. My editor at the *Tri-bune*. My chance at attracting a national audience by reporting General Custer's mission against the Sioux and Cheyennes. Gone, all gone, unless the ravine into which I've plunged will offer protection. Let me hide myself in the rocks. May they be my refuge. Let me live. Let me survive to write my story. Let me report what I witness today. Where will my notes end up? What of my unfinished work? What will go unreported and unwritten?

I'm not part of this battle. I've not come to be here with Custer. I've not.

Waymon Needler
AS GENERAL GEORGE A. CUSTER, ON THE LITTLE BIGHORN

JUNE 25, 2001

"WHEN YOU'RE TRYING TO CHANNEL THE GENERAL," ALEC MURRAY was saying, his gaze fixed somewhere above in the RV he called his headquarters tin tent, "you're taking on a responsibility akin to his attempt in June of 1876. The consequences of failure are not so dire for you, of course."

I thought to say no, in order to express agreement with what the longtime director of the Reenactment of the Last Stand had just said, but then imagining how George Armstrong Custer himself would have responded to the statement of such a self-evident truth, I merely widened my eyes a bit and tried to look quizzical. Not curious, you understand, or challenged by what Alec Murray had just said, but a bit nonplussed at the obviousness of it. As my reading and study of George Custer over the years indicate, the general did not suffer fools lightly. It was not in my nature to be less than polite to anyone addressing me, but it was now my duty to reflect as accurately as possible the true personality of the Son of the Morning Star. So I'd do that or perish in the attempt. He was never polite simply to be polite. His manners served his purposes. So would mine.

Just realizing I was thinking that way was heartening, and I stretched out my legs beyond the "safe" zone of personal body containment in tribute to what I was perceiving about my ongoing growth into the Custer selfhood. Don't misunderstand that statement. I know I'm not George A. Custer, unlike some previous reenactors who shall go nameless, but I can be him just as a devoted actor can immerse himself in the character of Hamlet, Prince of Denmark.

"I'm not much concerned about keeping that in mind, Alec," I said in what I intended to be a bemused tone. It got there, I think, the subtext of my message. "I think I've absorbed that truth and can live with it."

"Oh," he said, letting his stargazing posture relax enough for his eyes to fall on me rather than on the metal ceiling. "You think you've got a good grasp on the essential nature of the General that quickly, eh? Do you?"

"No, I'm not being overly confident about that, Alec," I said, keeping my gaze fastened on the high shine I'd put on the knee-high cavalry boots ordinarily worn by my predecessor in the role of the general. Both my leather-clad calves seemed to be glowing with an inner fire in the fine footwear encasing them. "I know better than to think any man can capture fully the essence of GAC. So I'm concentrating not on the problems of reflecting the inner Custer psyche, but on a simpler thing. How good a job am I doing at looking physically a bit like the general? That's what's got me challenged."

"Understandable, logical, to be expected," Alec Murray said in a mollified tone. I had calmed him a bit now, and he'd not have to feel more uncertain about the wisdom of his choosing me as substitute general. For the time being, at least. "But not to fret, Waymon. No man can resemble the boy general in all respects, not even Lance. No, not even the man who's been channeling GAC for donkey years. But you know what?"

Again, I refused to give voice to the clichéd answer, that being no I don't know what. What? Instead I went quizzical again, this time with Alec witnessing my facial expression in full, and I made myself wait for him to go on, unencouraged by any eager cheering on from me. I would not be overly modest, in tribute to the man I sought to represent, always one who appreciated his own worth.

"But for a few pounds there in the midsection, I think your physical resemblance to General Custer, particularly in that photo of the picnic, you know the image I'm thinking of, I think the similarity borders on the remarkable."

"You mean the photograph, that one outdoors with Libbie in the chair and Myles Keogh leaning over her shoulder while GAC looks off to his left as though he can't wait to have it all over? That one? The one where the general appears to be a little miffed? "

"Precisely, but more than a little miffed," Alec said. "That's the photo I mean, and your facial expression and the great makeup job with the 'stache and the hair that Clarence has done, that works together really well. I swear once we get that buckskin uniform let out a few inches and your hair cut the way GAC had it on June 25, I'm just going to say it, now. Once we get all that done, you'll be the spitting image of the man himself."

"I wasn't able to lose enough weight in a day to get my midsection right," I said, my voice going up in an excited tone, which I immediately moderated as soon as I realized I was showing too much self-satisfaction and excitement. GAC was never innocent about his effect on others. "But I've been wearing a kind of corset deal which helps the look, I've been told. I'm wearing it now."

"Did Clarence say that?" Alec said in a sharper tone. "That the girdle helps?"

"He did."

"Believe it, then, Waymon. Clarence will make no statement just to cheer someone up. He's too devoted to truth and beauty for that."

I'd been called all my life various names meant to point out my tendency toward a little too much avoirdupois at intervals too frequent to think about, and one of these popped into my mind in my conversation with Alec Murray about the perils of stepping into the role of GAC on the occasion of the 125th anniversary. The hurtful word I remembered was Pillsbury, and the rest of the damn phrase was Doughboy. I had been called that too many times to allow myself to estimate a count. The Pillsbury Doughboy. Though intended by those who applied that scornful label to me to be hurtful, like most things, that phrase was a two-edged one.

It was like the one used to describe the event I was now to play a main role in re-creating. The Last Stand. That's the label. But why was that event way back in 1876 so meaningful still? And why will it continue to be? I'll tell you. Think about the phrase *last stand*. It was contradictory.

Last means something is over, gone, vanished, never to be seen again. Stand means unbeaten, brave, bold, indomitable, all those wonderful concepts that bring tears to the eye and energy to the step. So we love that which robs us, and it's because we've lost something that we love it. We want to lose it so that we can love it all the more. We want contradiction. We need tension. We crave a balance of opposed energies, each striving against the other.

Pillsbury in itself, that word, means little or nothing. But add to it dough, and especially to the heart and mind of a teacher of home economics, that yeasty and tasty word sings of the delicious, the nourishing, and the good. But say *boy* after you've said *dough*, and all you see is a fat little pale giggling creature who everyone feels entitled to poke in the belly. He invites it, the way he's presented, the little creep.

Let me put it this way. I finally have my chance, for which I've worked and waited all these years. I will strive to become the soul and self of brevet General George A. Custer of the Seventh Cavalry, heroic and indomitable, the leader who perishes without taint in character or behavior on a hillside in Montana in 1876, the man who inspires us still each year to pay tribute to his spirit. But I'll be doing it while wearing a girdle beneath my buckskin uniform. And if a band of Indian women were to strip my body after death, they would remark not on how white my skin but on how chubby my tummy-tum. There is your contradiction, and there is the tension the reenactor must suffer and endure. That sums it up neatly.

"Do you think," I said to Alec, hoping to cleanse my mind of the image of the Pillsbury Doughboy stripped bare, his eyes rolled back in his head, and gunshots to his chest and left temple, blood staining his pure white-flour corpse, his little three-fingered hands all splayed out, "that Myles Keogh had a thing going with Libbie Custer? That photo of the picnic does raise doubts, eh? The body language, the posture, the lean and slope of shoulders, averting of eyes, positioning of hands, and crossings or non-crossing of lower extremities, the overly careful way Libbie holds herself together in an image of closed body containment, all that kind of evidence in photographs is now food for thought to the experts."

Food, I said to myself as I waited for Alec Murray to weigh in with his opinion about one of the most fought-over issues arising from the extensive scholarly study of Custer photographs, the Libbie-Myles Keogh relationship. I had just said the word food out loud, I repeated to myself.

Next I'll be hearing my voice refer unintentionally to a girdle while I'm in the middle of issuing an order to the Left Wing of the Seventh Cavalry. My mouth will betray me once again, and the truth will pop out no matter how hard I try to put the best face on it.

As my ignorant old dad would have said, here I am, flapping my jaw and watching what comes out just as surprised as if I wasn't the one saying it. Ask Alec about Myles Keogh and Libbie again. Push that subject to the forefront and keep it there, and drive my unconscious use of food imagery out of his head. Make him defend Libbie and forget about the chubby little Doughboy he's entrusted with the responsibility of channeling the greatest American hero of the last quarter of the nineteenth century. Don't let him think about how I'll look on a horse, not to mention at the middle of a band of troopers full of arrows and me with a pistol in hand and the famous death smile of Custer pasted on my face.

"Keogh had that Irish charm, and all the historians remark upon his success with the ladies," I said, giving Alec an earnest and yet inquisitive look as I spoke in my own voice now, not the one of GAC. "Didn't Libbie mention him in a letter or two to GAC somewhere along the way? I seem to remember that. She did in her book *Boots and Saddles.*"

"Yes, of course she did. He was one of the general's most trusted and experienced officers," Alec said, his tone letting me know he was focused now upon defending a lady, not upon my little tummy held in constraint by a girdle. "Why shouldn't she have? And why shouldn't Libbie have flirted with Myles Keogh now and then in a social setting and occasion? That was considered most civilized behavior in the society they moved in back in the day, she and the general and Keogh, as well. He was from a fine landed family in Ireland. He knew how to be charming and socially graceful and complimentary. So did Libbie, and so did the general. That's the way they entertained themselves."

Well done, I told myself, and after a little more back and forth of minutiae in defense of Libbie, moving from that to an assessment of the horse I'd be riding in the withdrawal up the hill with as many Native Americans in pursuit as we could muster—not nearly enough, as always, and this year even fewer, given that the 125th anniversary was being commemorated—Alec Murray and I concluded our session and I left to find Clarence D'Arcy for a last-minute costume and cosmetic touch-up before the magic hour.

"I wish there was a way to keep the overweight Native Americans out of the pageant altogether," Alec was saying, showing by his choice of labels that he was trying not to offend. "I mean the pot bellies you see on way too many of these supposed Sioux and Cheyenne warriors have become in some cases just simply laughable. We're filming this shit, for God's sake. Spielberg's people are looking us over. Dohlan may actually be here disguised as a tourist. Too many of these red men reenactors hardly look the part of hardened and well-conditioned warriors."

"Didn't the reservation head guy, what's his name, Afraid of His Horses, say he'd make the worst-looking ones wear shirts this year? The ones most out of shape, I mean."

"Sure, Afraid of His Horses said that, but what I expect is that most of them will say it's too hot to wear an authentic-looking upper garment, thick as that fabric or skin or whatever it is they use, and they'll go shirtless, and the ones that agree to put something on to hide their bellies will likely choose to pull T-shirts over their heads. I just pray they don't wear Tee's with commercial messages on them like some did last year, or worse yet, slogans like "I'm With Stupid" or "What Stays in Vegas." God, the things I have to think about."

"The burdens of leadership," I said. "Can't we buy shirts that'll be appropriate for close-up shots?" I went on, knowing what the answer would be, but hoping to get Alec's mind well off the topic of chubby tummies.

"It's budgetary, as always, Waymon, and if I were to be speaking to you in your role as GAC, I'd be saying the same thing. It's budget, budget, budget. All the damn day long."

"Tell me about it," I said, easing down the steps to Alec's RV on my way out, careful not to scuff my highly shined cavalry boots in the process. "Why do you think the troopers of the Seventh had to carry single-shot Springfield rifles? Why were Sitting Bull's warriors better equipped overall than the US Cavalry? Why did the shell casings swell up and stick in the Springfield chambers?"

"Budget," Alec said back. "Budget, that's why. You know the drill. But anyway, break a leg, General."

"Budget," I repeated. "Whatever it costs, I'll give it my best shot."

★ ☆

The sun was high in the June sky, a little breeze was blowing up from the valley, and I could hear a bugler practicing retreat calls, a bright silver sound coming from down by the Little Bighorn. The crowd of onlookers and history buffs was still gathering, a lot more of them it seemed than some I'd witnessed in past reenactments. Walking past a bunch of spectators as I set my course for the horse corral, I slapped my straw hat against my right leg, a broadbrim like Custer had worn on that last day, and a gaggle of visitors near the Battlefield Center and Museum saw me and began to applaud, a few even calling out my name. Custer, Custer, General Custer. Look, it's him. It's the man. Go get them, General. Being silly, a lot of them, but doing that because they'd been taken by the sight of me in full dress. They had to find a way to handle the emotion that welled up in response to what they were witnessing, always the way of the crowds that gather for historical reenactments.

They want to believe it's really happening right before their eyes, but they're embarrassed to admit it. So they poke fun at what they're seeing and the way the entire experience is making them feel, and they think that'll show the world they're not being made fools of against their will. It's not against their will, naturally, their being fooled, but they can't bear enduring the power of the moment's reenactment and their need to lose their everyday self in a vital time not their own. It's hard to admit that the life you're living now is dull, bland, and meaningless. You can't bear to say that or anything like it out loud, so you make fun of your present empty emotional state in this dull drab world before somebody else beats you to it.

Let me do what I have to do, I said to whatever was listening inside my head as I walked away from the headquarters tent, dressed as the general and wanting beyond all things to do him the way he deserved to be done. Let me come through it with the right side up. I waved my hat, and a bunch of Last Stand fans started yelling loud enough for people a good distance off to begin looking in my direction, some beginning to move toward where I was walking.

I spoke again to whatever presences, whatever ghosts, whatever lives alone in my head, a little request. Please, I said inside where only I and the unseen could hear. On this day, I said, let me die right. Please.

Crazy Horse
WAR CHIEF OF THE OGLALA, ON THE GREASY GRASS

JUNE 25, 1876

I AWOKE EARLY, WELL BEFORE THE DOGS BEGAN TO STOP THEIR speaking to the moon. Not until the truly deep darkness comes just before the light begins to gather in the sky where the sun sleeps at night do the dogs begin to know it is time to hush. What will kill has killed. What will be killed has been killed, and now the time to rest from dealing out death and having death dealt has come. Sleep will take all killers to bed, for a time in the Black Hills.

He had wakened me while my wife and her sister and her children slept in the lodge, and I had come awake as soon as he spoke. The women and children still slept, and their breathing was easy. When he woke me, I returned all the way back from the dream in which I had been tasting and listening to silence and seeking about me for a thing I knew I must have but still not yet having knowledge of the thing I sought. What was it? I could not tell.

The word he said to wake me was one of my old names. Light Skin, his voice said it once, that name, and I answered with one word, Father, as I sat up from where I lay.

"You call me Father," he said, his face hidden in the darkness, lit now only by embers in a fire so low they cast too little light to see another creature by. "But you see I am not truly that man."

200

"Not of the blood of the man who sired me, no," I said, not trying to see his face, since I had no need to have that sight granted me. I knew him. "You are not that man, that father. That man gave me my new name, his old one, when I became a man. He made himself become no longer Crazy Horse, but Worm instead. And I am that name he carried until he gave it up as a gift to me."

"Surely," the man speaking in darkness said, "that is the true thing, but you see who I am. And that is true, and I am your father."

"As it must be for every man who becomes the man he should be, you are my father."

"Do you know how that can be? If so, tell me."

"I know that truth. You can be my father though you did not sire me, for you are me as I must become, if my true self is to be. You are me, if I act in the way to earn that self."

"You know yourself when you hear your voice in your ears and within your head where none but you can detect that sound and know it means Crazy Horse. You are satisfied with that name."

"You told me that those years ago," I said, "when I went into the Black Hills alone. I did not eat, nor drink, nor sleep for all those days. And I was able then to see you and know you were who I would be if I lived the life I should. If I learned it and did not stray."

"Yes, that is true. I am your father, and I am you, and you are your own father and your own self."

"Why do you come to tell me this truth I already know? I learned it alone those years ago in the Black Hills, when you came to me while I was nothing yet."

"I answer you this way, for I am you speaking to you. Do you have your stone selected, the one to place behind your ear? Do you have the paint to put upon your face in the shape of lightning? Do you have the paint to trace hailstones on your body and that of your horse? Do you have the paint of the color red to make a handprint upon the body of your horse? Do you have your bow and your arrows? Do you have an ax? Do you have a white man's rifle?"

"I have all these things that will prepare me for that long and hard day when it comes."

"I come to tell you it comes when the sun rises next. It will be here, that day, and Long Hair will once more be riding upon the People with his blue soldiers. The Greasy Grass will turn red and flow that way for a time not counted. You will listen to yourself, and you will lead your warriors, those that want to ride with Crazy Horse."

"I will prepare and ask if others will go with me. And if they will, they may. But I will not wait upon others. I will do what I must do, and I will be you, and you will be me."

"Truly, this is so. For I am Crazy Horse."

"I am you, and I am Crazy Horse," I said. "And none may touch me."

Mirabeau B. Lamar Sylestine
AS CRAZY HORSE, ON THE GREASY GRASS

<small>JUNE 25, 2001</small>

AFTER ALEC MURRAY HAD CALLED ME INTO THE HEADQUARTERS RV, I passed Waymon on the way. I literally walked right by him, looked him full in the face, and almost spoke his name, but didn't take that step, waiting instead to see if he'd acknowledge me first. He didn't, as usual, and I didn't expect him to and took no offense, knowing if we were back home in Annette, Texas, he'd probably be mulling over some recipe he'd devised to challenge that gang of young ladies in his senior home ec class. He'd be deep into nutritional matters, hoping for a bit of fun and special tastiness to accompany the truth he was trying to impart. He'd have seen me walk by, but it wouldn't have registered yet in that clot of synapses in his head all jangled up with measurements of flour and baking powder and anise and God knows what all that occupies most of Waymon's waking hours. His dreaming ones, too, probably.

At any rate he didn't speak, and his eyes swept right over me as though I was a small jar of pimentos not in the current recipe, and for a second or two I wondered what was up with my favorite home ec teacher until I realized the true reason Waymon Needler was so preoccupied. It was who he was at present. He was in full regalia as General George A. Custer, white buckskin gloves matching his trousers stuffed down into his cavalry boots so shiny it was hard to look at them for more than a few seconds at a time—sunlike they truly were—and a proper mustache covering his upper lip, pasted on though it was, and to top it off, the pearly pale deerskin blouse with the insignia of the Seventh sewn just where uniform regulations would have it be.

So he was deeply sunk into Custer and not into thoughts about the chemical changes occurring to cake dough in a 350-degree oven in the laboratory kitchens of Annette High School. Thinking about how I'd misjudged Waymon's mindset as I passed him coming out of Alec Murray's RV center of operations, I think I must have had the remnant of a smile on my face when I stepped into the sanctum sanctorum of our Fearless Leader. Not that I'd have called Alec Murray that to his face. When you've acted in New York City, even as just one of the boys in the chorus line of a show that lasted only a week way back in the early seventies, you don't take to jollification from underlings on the banks of the Greasy Grass during yet another reenactment of Custer's last dance with the Sioux and Cheyennes.

"Eagle Beak," Alec called out as I nodded, adding as I did so to my facial expression a good touch of red man reticence and what I hoped would be perceived as mythic unreadability, "it's great to see you smiling in the midst of all that's going on today. My God, it's reassuring to see a look of confidence on a player's face on this 125th anniversary."

"You mean," I said, "I assume, the fact that we've got a brand-new GAC on our hands. Not to worry, I'll declare here and now. I know Waymon Needler from way back, and he'll give it his best shot and all will be fine. I really think so."

"You do? It's great to hear that assessment from you, Eagle Beak, but I wasn't referring to Waymon as Custer when I just said what I said. Nope, I'm not worried about that one just now."

"You're not? Well, that's good," I said, allowing myself a quick look around Alec's RV. I hadn't been actually inside that think tank on wheels up to that moment. But I will say that lack of an invitation to me to visit didn't bother me, never had, and doesn't up to now. I know myself, and small slights do not register on my consciousness. I have too many other things to think about to let some small discourtesy register with me. I'm bigger than that.

"No, not the reenactor of GAC, that doesn't concern me now. We got it covered, I do believe. Got that little situation grabbed up tight by the short and curlies. No, what's of moment now, Eagle Beak, is another defection or perhaps I should call it a mishap. An accident, even. A blow of fate. A failure of attention to crucial matters. A letting down of the side. That's what I'm talking about."

"Do tell," I said, feeling my heart leap a bit at Alec's words. "What can you mean, oh Exalted One?" Why did I say that, I instantly asked myself. Why did I call Alec Murray such a dumb thing? How silly my tongue can be at times. Nothing to do now but brazen it out, make a joke of it. "I mean, pardon my tone," I went on, "but what you just said sounds so dire I can't keep my mind focused. Please excuse my outburst."

"It's the same old sad story, Eagle Beak," Alec said, obviously taking no offense from my characterization, letting me know the matter was a serious one in its own right. "Firewater, to use a pejorative term which I would never voice in public. That's at the heart of it. The red man's poison, the white man's elixir, when rightfully used. But genetically deadly dangerous to Native Americans, a fact I don't have to prove to you. Not to say you let yourself be affected by that drug, but you know better than most the sad result of alcohol consumption by your people."

"Too true," I said. "The stories I could tell you from personal observation would break your heart. Who is it, and what's the upshot? Who's fallen prey? If you're willing to tell me."

That's when Alec Murray said the magic words I'd been wanting to hear for donkey years of the Last Stand Reenactment, though never imagining it would arise as it did. Douglas Snake Finder, a Santee Sioux and a man usually as reliable as the prairie wind blowing in summer, had gone on a bender in Bozeman, drinking untold amounts of vodka and getting into altercations not only with a couple of Crow scout impersonators, whom he took as enemies in his delirium, but slugging a sheriff's deputy who'd come to calm things down. Bad enough, certainly, but to top it off, Snake Finder had bitten, yes bitten, the sheriff deputy's left thumb, and that led to what the situation now was on the morning of June 25, 2001, the big day of the 125th anniversary.

"We have no Crazy Horse," Alec Murray said, looking directly at me as he finished the tale of Douglas Snake Finder, now a guest of the county for at least thirty days, and non-bail eligible until a week forward. Our impersonator of Crazy Horse was in the white man's lockup. "We have no war chief of the Sioux, and events are scheduled to begin in less than three hours, as you know. There is no postponement possible."

"What about Tommy Gene Afraid of the Water?" I said, knowing the answer to that even as I spoke. "Didn't he do Crazy Horse four or five times a few years back?"

"He did, and he wasn't worth a damn at it, and besides that, he's in the hospital in Bozeman and not likely to come out."

"What? An accident?"

"Diabetes, amputation, the whole schmear, so no accident and no fallback on him. You know what it means, Mirabeau."

"Please call me Eagle Beak," I said. "While I'm here on the Greasy Grass."

"Point taken," Alec said. "But what I really need to call you and for damn good reason is another name altogether."

"No," I said, my voice crawling up in my throat out of control. "I can't. I'm not ready yet. I've not prepared emotionally."

"You're the most learned scholar of any man here, Eagle Beak. You have studied the history of these events from A to Z and back again. You know the Native American side of things in your bones, even better than any of these so-called historians. You know that. Assuming the self of Crazy Horse will be second nature to you. No one else can do it with the authority you'll be able to bring to it."

"But that's all intellectual and scholarly and learned. What I know is books and Internet and conference discussions. It's not emotionally earned by me. Not now, not yet. I'm not ready."

"Let me tell you something," Alec Murray said, "a true thing. You know it in your bones. As soon as you get that magic stone fastened behind your ear, as soon as you've painted hailstone markings on your body and a lightning bolt on your face, as soon as you mount that pony marked with the red hand, you'll be the man. You'll be Crazy Horse of the Oglala Sioux, not Eagle Beak of the Alabama-Coushatta, and for sure not Mirabeau Lamar Sylestine, code writer in a tech firm in East Texas."

"Please," I said, feeling what I imagined Julius Caesar must have experienced when he put aside the offer of the crown three times, "I'm not worthy to be Crazy Horse. I can't take a bite that big yet. I can't do it, Alec."

"Do it, and you'll become it. Accept your destiny in this reenactment, Eagle Beak. Be the man you've worked to be."

"Could I see the stone?" I said. "Can I touch the bow and arrows? Can I come into contact with the artifacts themselves before I say anything final?"

"It's here, in the RV," Alec Murray said, rising from his chair with the grace and power of a dancer, which he had once been. "All of it that you'll need. I knew what you'd have to do and what you'd have to see. I got it ready for you. Come. Step into the sleeping room and see the things you'll need to work with. Come, Pale One. Come, Crazy Horse. Step up, War Chief. It's time."

☆　☆

Something happened then in that little compartment of Alec Murray's RV, that space too small to be a bedroom but big enough to hold the mind and magic of a war chief long dead in fact, but living forever in meaning. That's what I believe, at least, and I don't expect others to be able to dispute that assertion. That's their problem. I don't care what they may think. Here's what I know. After I had fastened the smooth river stone, one shaped by water for eons and by that process made ready for its role in the retelling of the leadership of Crazy Horse, securely behind my left ear, I could immediately feel a growing warmth coming from the cold rock. It was palpable, and it was real. I couldn't help but exclaim that fact out loud to Alec who chuckled in response as if he were hearing yet again a tale he had heard others tell countless times before.

"You're not going to believe this, Eagle Beak," he said as he picked a stone ax from the collection of objects on a small table, "but it's true. I've had the opportunity to fix this stone behind the left ear of at least three Crazy Horse impersonators, and every last one of them, including our current guy now in the Bozeman calaboose, has said the same thing you just did. They swear they can feel a heat coming off that stone as soon it touches them, and yet the rock itself held in your hand is as cool as spring water."

"Could this rock be the original one which Crazy Horse used?" I said, touching the rock again to see if it felt cool to my fingers, yet warm against my head. It did. "That's not what you're claiming, is it?"

"That's impossible. I picked this thing up over fifteen years ago right on the edge of the Little Bighorn River, and that choice of rocks I made from the thousands there was completely random. Couldn't have been what Crazy Horse actually used. You know what I think? I think it's the place that blesses the ear stone, the place and the purpose the stone serves. The magic doesn't come from the thing itself, but from what we do with it."

"You're sounding mighty mythic, Alec," I said, a giddy feeling welling up in my throat as I touched the stone and hefted the weight of the war club in my other hand. "You sound like you're fixing to go Indian on me."

"That's the best compliment you could ever have paid me, Eagle Beak. The closer I can get to that place where the Indian begins and the white man leaves off, the better job I can do with directing the reenactment."

"But you're a white man," I said. "Not Indian. No offense intended."

"None taken, Eagle Beak. Here's what I believe happened 125 years ago and what we bring back with every reenactment. Back then, when that historical moment happened, the Sioux and the Cheyennes on one side and the soldiers and officers and General Custer himself on the opposing side weren't really battling each other and trying to destroy every last man as they did. No, nuh-unh."

"No? What were they doing then when all that killing was going on?"

"They were playing their parts in a great dramatic production. They were fulfilling their roles and contributing their necessary obligation to the director of the piece and to the writer and the crew putting it all together. It was all fated and therefore—and here's the kicker, Eagle Beak—it was meant to be from the foundation of time. That's why it meant something then and means something today. Do you see what I'm saying?"

"Maybe a little. Is that why we do it every year, try to bring it back to life the way it was those years ago?"

"Of course," Alec Murray said to that, his eyes bright and glistening with tears, "and that's why the stone behind your ear and the one behind the ear of Crazy Horse that first time on the Little Bighorn is both warm and cold. Warm because it yet lives, and cool because it cannot die."

"Alec," I began to say, "I don't know what to think of that, but . . ."

He broke in as I stuttered. "Don't worry about why, Crazy Horse. Worry about what and when and where. You've got work to do this day. You haven't got time for why."

"Yes," I said, feeling the sensation of something like water lifting me off my feet in a deep pool. All I had to do was stand there. The lifting up would take place on its own. "You're right, Alec. I've got to lead my warriors and break through that extended line of General Custer's Company L to keep it from joining up with Company E. I can't let that happen if we're going to succeed, and as long as I take no scalps and claim no coup, nothing can touch me."

"Why's that?" Alec asked, extending a pot of red face paint toward me, holding it in both hands as though it were too heavy to support in one.

"Because," I said. "Here's why. It's because I am the war chief of the Oglalas. I must go before the warriors and let them know I am not afraid to die. I am Crazy Horse."

"That's what I'm talking about," Alec Murray said, almost screaming the words. "Sit down, Crazy Horse, and let me get you made up."

Johann Vetter
LIEUTENANT, COMPANY L,
SEVENTH CAVALRY

JUNE 25, 1876

I OBEY ORDERS FROM MY SUPERIORS, WHETHER THAT MAN BE A HERR
Doktor Professor at the University of Heidelberg, an officer in the
Prussian Guard, or a brevet general of the American Seventh Cavalry.
Yet I reserve the right to consider within myself that the consequences of
some orders, no matter how efficiently executed, may lead in directions
not finally desirable. That former major in General Robert E. Lee's Army
of Northern Virginia, now a mere sergeant in the Seventh Cavalry of
the United States, made to me only yesterday a statement which haunts,
given what I see before me now.

What Henry Harrison Davis said about the military strategy of the
savage tribes which the Seventh Cavalry would be facing on the Little
Bighorn was that they would swarm like a nest of yellow jackets disturbed by a boy poking these insects with a stick. These yellow jackets,
known as wasps in the world outside the Virginia of Sergeant Henry
Harrison Davis, would come in clouds with no organizing principle to
guide them. The foe they attacked would be overcome by sheer numbers
and mass. And their stinging would be massive and fatal.

I tried to reassure him that a well-regulated body of trained troops
under good command would swat such a swarm aside and render it help-
less and bleeding through the exercise of sheer discipline alone, if nothing

210

else. In the fashion of the Americans from the Southern part of the nation I have encountered, he smiled and laughed as though I were making a joke for his entertainment and left me shortly thereafter, shaking his head and whistling as he went. What is so funny, I wanted to ask him. Do I talk simply to be humorous?

If anything I pride myself upon, it is my commitment to recognize and face truth when I see it, no matter how such revelation may conflict with opinions I've held prior. I confess therefore my assessment of the reliability of the comparison of Sergeant Davis, onetime major in the Rebel army, has been proven wrong, and that handily done in less than two hours. When Company L proceeded down the slope of hills leading to the river on the other side of which the vast village of hostiles is located, not more than a few Indians showed their presence to us as we progressed.

Some savages, those mounted saddleless on the ponies they ride, came toward us, emitting yelps and shaking feather-covered clubs and bows and a few rifles in our direction. The troopers in my charge showed good poise at that point, dismounting on command and proceeding to ready themselves for firing, and all troopers of the company seemed in good tone and readiness. Yet when not more than a quarter of an hour had passed, it was clear that few of those mounted savages had been affected by the fire of the troopers' Springfield rifles. In addition to that fact a more alarming truth soon arose.

Suddenly as at a single signal, up from the ravines and draws leading down to the river and covered thickly with low bushes and grasses, scores of Indians popped up like dolls one might see in shops selling toys in Munich, those made so that when the handle is wound a hidden latch releases the figures. As these warriors rose, they began to shoot great clouds of arrows which arched up into the clear sky and came rattling down, each with the sound of an exhaled breath. None of the soldiers in Company L seemed seriously wounded in that barrage—nor did their horses—badly enough to be considered near death or total disablement. Those affected, though, soon proved to be of no aid in repulsing the swarm of savages which grew with enough speed to deserve the description of yellow jacket wasps in an angry cloud.

A general order to retreat back up the hill came from all officers, announced by the bugles in every company of the Right Wing, our part of the division into which General Custer had divided his force. Staying back to bring up the rear of our company as was my duty in retreat, I could see every draw and ravine vomiting forth savages painted and be-feathered, many half-dressed, some wearing a variety of animal skins and others in cloth rags, firing rifles and launching arrows and racing their ponies to get as near as possible to the retreating soldiers so as to be able to assault them with clubs and knives. I knew that if we were to avoid a rout a good number of troopers had to dismount and get off a volley or two to slow the progress of the Indians in pursuit behind us.

"Dismount, Company L," I called out to the sergeants near me, who relayed the order, though a few noncommissioned sergeants said noth-ing, feigning having been deafened by the reports of rifles, the screams of horses hit by arrows, the shrieks of Indians sounding whoops and cries and grunts, and the high-pitched wails of bone whistles which the aborigines blew as they plunged into battle. Despite this noise which seemed to be arising from Hell itself, enough troopers obeyed the orders to dismount and let loose a volley of shots from rifles and pistols. That barrage slowed the advance of the Indians enough to allow the bulk of the rest of the troopers to put some distance between themselves and the pursuing warriors.

By the time that bunch reached the top of a ridge near the crest of the small hills, they were able to dismount and deliver covering fire for the men of Company L who had been holding off the line of savages still appearing in great numbers from the ravines and depressions and gullies. All of us able to do so left that exposed position with as much speed as we could muster, heading for the ridge which was promising a possible linking of all companies of the Right Wing into a defensive line to give protection necessary for us to hold off the pack of savages boiling up from farther down the hill.

"Swing out a squad to the right and anchor us to Company E and Company F," Captain Myles Keogh was shouting to his lieutenants, his Irish-accented English sounding more welcome to me than it ever had before. "Seal off that gap, and close it tight. Give them a strong volley, lads, and prepare to drop and reload to let another come from the com-pany behind you."

That looked promising. To me, reassuring would be a better word, and I knew if we got that jointure made, we'd be able to strengthen the security of the line all along the crest of the ridge. We'd have a great chance of swatting away that swarm of yellow jacket wasps trying its best to sting us all to death. Let us heed the Irishman who wears the medal of the Agnus Dei. That was my first hopeful thought since the swarm of yelling hostiles had come at us.

"With a will, Company L," I shouted, "pivot and fire and drop and reload." In a manner that amazed me, given my experience trying to train these troopers, many of them so new that they still had problems understanding orders issued in the English language, the men in my command rose as one, stepped off on the right foot, and began to swing their line like a pendulum, headed for a joining with the company scattered not fifty yards to the right. The phrase "the beauty and use of discipline" sprang to my mind as though it were a lesson I'd learned in school, as I watched the line of troopers becoming not a mere collection of individuals but a single thing made up of parts joined into one with a single goal. To close a gap in a defensive line.

It was then, as I leaned my own body to the right in sympathy with the line of troopers, hoping to witness the joining of the end of that body of my men with the left end of the company to our right, that the event transpired which cut off the success of our maneuver. A single horseman, a savage dressed only in a species of animal skin about his loins, bearing a great number of spots of white paint all over his body, along with a great smear of red and yellow coloring his face itself, suddenly burst into view just at the flank of the company which my men had been straining ranks toward. He leaned over, this apparition with long light-colored hair streaming unconstrained down his back, and began swinging a long-handled club at the head of the trooper just at the end of the company which my men were struggling to reach.

The impact of the stone at the end of the club knocked the trooper off his feet, and I could see that the effect of that single action resulted in setting off a quailing movement in the entire line of men. Unity of purpose vanished at once. Each trooper gave signs of thinking only of his own fate, and not a man made a motion toward assaulting the warrior who'd stopped all progress toward the joining of our two separate bodies of men into a stronger force of one. "Kill him," I shouted to any trooper who would hear. "Shoot that man. Knock him off that horse. Stop him."

It wasn't until after I'd started in the direction of the warrior still laying about him at any trooper he could reach, now having dropped his club and beginning to use a steel ax which shone in the bright sunlight as though afire, that I realized my order to kill the man I had spoken not in English but in my native tongue. No matter, I told myself, those closest to that one man with the ax would not have responded to orders in any language. They had fallen into separate pieces, one by one, and they were no longer functioning as a unit but as single men, each thinking only of his safety. Such a state is truly the habit of mind most dreaded by leaders of men in combat. Soldiers must never think of themselves as anything but a part of something not them. To lose that sense of selflessness is the situation all military training is designed to prevent, and now it lay in shambles on this blazing hill in the Montana Territory.

As I ceased to try to inspire obedience from my men, and began to run in the direction of the single warrior working his way from one to another, his weapon chopping away as though he was preparing firewood for burning, I could see that other Indians were now pouring through the gap which our two companies had been rendered unable to close by the actions of that one warrior. We could do nothing now as a unit, I knew, and each man was on his own. And a man on his own in a battle is doomed, unless some unreasonable fate saves him, as it had done for this warrior on horseback with a bloody ax in his hand.

Let me kill him, at least, I prayed to whatever god there might be who watches over soldiers in war. Hear me in Valhalla. Let me take that warrior with me, that single man who has killed us all on this hill with no name, this place so far from Heidelberg. Let me see his blood. Show me his guts. I deserve that allowance. Look at my face. See my scars. Regard the great one across my left cheek, the deep gash going into my eyebrow. It was put there by the best swordsman in Heidelberg in my time at university, and I did not flinch nor show sign of pain when I suffered it. I will not quail now before a painted and naked savage. I will not show the white feather now. I will not.

Captain Myles Keogh
I COMPANY, SEVENTH CAVALRY, RIGHT WING

JUNE 25, 1876

So ALMOST TO THE RIDGETOP ITSELF WE'D GOTTEN, MYSELF AND the troopers of I Company, my collection of Italians and Germans and a great clot of Irish potato chompers and some Americans, too, and for the most part in good array and in a controlled and disciplined retreat. And when I ordered that stiff-necked young officer from Heidelberg, Germany, as he's always saying to any man who'll listen, to have his company dismount and lay down a couple of volleys to throw a little scare into the heathen devils swarming after us, he never wavered nor blinked. And by God, when he gave the order to the sergeants and the bugler relayed it to the lads who'd be carrying it out, they did just what they were supposed to do. Miracle of miracles, they did. And what that little display of discipline accomplished was to give the rest of us, I Company and stragglers from E and F, wherewithal to reach the top of the ridge and prepare to receive a charge. And all in some decent order and with no more panic than was warranted in a full-scale, pell-mell run-out and retreat before a superior force.

A force shooting arrows with rusty steel points on the buggers, too, let me add to that. The one that punched through my second-best uniform coat proved that to me, sticking up in the flesh of my upper arm as though it were a signal identifying me as the man who would be an official target for all bowmen who wanted to better the first red devil who'd stuck me. It didn't hurt me much when I yanked it out, and that was due to two things. Nothing hurts when it first hits you in a fight, no matter how hard it lands, whether it's an arrow with a rusty point or a man's fist upside your jaw or a hunk of lead that slams you in the midriff. I don't mean to claim that such will not harm you, now, or maybe even kill you in the next few minutes or right then or on down the road a way. What I'm saying is that when you're in a fight, whether alone or with other poor bastards in the same fix as yourself, your blood is up and your mind's not working right and you're scared to the point where you can't even remember to draw a full breath to live, and all that combines to make you not feel a great hurt come upon you. God's letting you continue to function for a bit more time.

Now if you were sitting at night at home with no one around to bother you or to draw your attention, and let's say you're drowsy and about to drop off to sleep, if a mosquito bit you you'd feel that, for sure. Not so in battle. And the other reason I didn't feel that arrow hit me until well after I noticed I had it sticking in my arm, and not from feeling the pain of that rusty point in my flesh, but from noticing there was a length of wood with feathers attached interfering with my pointing out to a sergeant a particular red man I'd like to see killed, was this. I was wearing that nice, thick uniform coat, hot though it was in the Montana country, and why so, then, one may ask, in such a climate and such a time? From habit is all the reason, and because I like the way it hangs on me, finishing off the whole image of a Seventh Cavalry officer in its robing of me. You may ask the opinion of any number of young ladies at the forts and other locations where I've spent time, whether unattached or married, as the case may be, and they'll likely tell you the same thing. They've always testified so to me, at least, the darlings, always ready to flirt and have a good time.

But to the point of discipline. That German officer, the ramrod-straight officer from Heidelberg and its university, he had so impressed and ingrained discipline in the troopers in his company that they obeyed his order to dismount, stop running for their lives, shoot back, and not leave their assigned spot until told to do so. They did that, and that let the rest of us reach the pinnacle of the ridge, see to our weapons, and assume a defensive position which I hoped would teach the red devils a lesson about the effect of massed fire and alternating volleys of the same at mid and close range. I'll remember what Lieutenant Johann Vetter had done, I told myself as I saw to the distribution of the soldiers in my command, and when and if we get this assignment brought to a successful conclusion, I'll cite the man in my report and recommend him for notice and decoration. For what all that's worth, naturally. No man thinks about reward and meritorious service in the middle of earning it, if it can be said to be earnable. Such attention to one's career and reputation can come only when you're safely at home and not a bow and arrow or a stone club or a bullet presently in good range.

That was not the case now on that hill in Montana, but if we could get the complete command joined so as to close that gap at the top of the ridge we'd gained due to the good disciplined work of that tight-assed German officer, we'd be in condition and readiness to throw enough lead at Mr. Sitting Bull's boyos to make them want to go home and eat buffalo meat and prairie turnip roots and wallow around with their old ladies. That was the plan and the hope.

And bless Pat, my little martinet of a line officer had got his troops stepping off to their right, arms at ready and eyes all fixed on the target toward which they were working, the as-yet-unanchored end of the defensive formation of Companies I and E and remnants of F, and in fewer than fifty yards, we'd have jointure, provided Vetter's troopers reached the place in question. I was just being able to rub a bit at the cut place on my left arm, left by the arrow I'd jerked out a bit earlier, as soon as I recognized it to be what was causing me to look awkward in my dress coat. I'd shed the coat, having to cut one arm of it to pieces in the process, and regretting that sorely, and I was having the luxury to see to the place where I was hurting. I was both looking down at the wound, not a bad one, and straining to see the two segments of our divided line of defense become whole, doing first one thing and the other, when I sensed something pounding toward the gap still left in the line.

It was but one red man on a pony making all the commotion, I could see, as I looked up to find out where all the racket was coming from, and him looking like a booger bear, long hair all streaming down and whipping in the wind and him naked as an animal save for a piece of what looked like deerskin around his midpart. He was painted up like most of that bunch of savages was wont to be when they were of a mind to kill somebody, his face a bright red and yellow in color and even his horse all smeared up to look like some beast I couldn't figure out. I was thinking it was a kindness to the creature that it wasn't able to know how unnatural it was tricked out to be.

The one Indian by himself shouldn't have been a real worry to the two squads of troopers about to join up into one line here directly, should somebody of that bunch of Seventh Cavalry soldiers have done what he ought to do in such a situation, that being to deliver a chunk of lead into that Indian or a rifle butt up against his head, but something was going wrong with the way the troopers he was bashing with a club were acting. Rather than closing ranks around that single horseman, putting the muzzle of a firearm up to the murdering bastard and shooting the heart and liver and lungs out of him, what they were doing was cringing down under his blows, the ones closest to him, them being who he was swinging a club at and then an ax following. The others farther away and out of range and so out of any real danger from the painted-up man, the ones who should have coolly taken good aim and blasted the red devil to Hell, these lads were turning away and scrambling off in opposite directions. What they were thinking of was themselves, the last thing you want a soldier to be doing in battle.

What a soldier ought to be up to, and what he's trained to do, is think he's just one part of something so big that he can't be hurt, much less killed, and his job is to pay attention to killing the enemy, the creatures who have no place in what he's that small portion of, the side he's serving. But to do that, naturally, a soldier has to have been trained well and at some good length by experienced men who know what they're doing. This cadre, for the most part, was so new to the military that they hadn't had time in service enough to have come to believe themselves invincible. They still knew they could die, and this group which had got themselves so close to joining together into one unit and acting like real brainless creatures, was scattering to save itself, man by man, one by one, and the Indian on the horse swinging his ax had them all whipped and believing they were whipped and that by him all by himself.

He wouldn't be that way long, I knew, alone, and I could tell by the yipping and whistling and yelling behind him that a whole mob of the red men following him would be on us in no time unless something was done quick to bring him down. I could hear the German lieutenant from

Heidelberg yelling at the men in his command, and I knew by his doing that that he understood what was happening now and would happen worse than ever in a minute or two. Vetter was trying to have done what should be done. He was speaking in German, though, and I figured that not three men in that bunch would know what he was saying, even if they could be persuaded to act like soldiers rather than men wanting to keep on living, and I knew I had to take matters into my own hands if anything was going to be done to give us a chance to live through the day.

So I began to run toward the spot in the line where the naked painted-up savage was chopping the life out of yet another young recruit all huddled up with his back turned toward the fury that was on him, hoping beyond reason that all this hell happening to him would stop by itself. As I ran, I lifted the revolver I carried, checking with my left hand to see if it was primed to be able to fire, given what I'd done with it while charging up that hill in retreat to reach a spot where we could make a stand, and in the middle of that business, I felt a great push or shove come against my left knee, causing it to give way and let me tumble into a skidding fall well before I got in range of the Indian on the pony, the one with the ax and the hair flying every direction with every blow he delivered.

I looked at what had happened to the knee and could see bone with a great chunk of meat barely hanging onto what was left of that joint, and I was surprised at how yellow the bones beneath my skin looked, not white at all like you'd expect they would be. Like I said before about wounds taken in battle, it wasn't hurting yet, though that leg was not going to give me any help with moving around now, and the thought came to my mind that by the time the pain rose up and took charge of me, I was going to be dead anyway. So that's the last bit of comfort and good luck I'm going to have in this world, I do believe and accept. Apart from the comfort of knowing that I did write to my sister back in Ireland before I left Fort Lincoln with the Seventh Cavalry searching for the great body of Sioux and Cheyennes that Georgie would catch and whip. All people great and small and kin and even just folks friendly to me, all that needed to have last words from Myles Keogh would have them. Good on you, I told myself, for thinking ahead.

We've caught them all right with a vengeance, that great gang Custer was bound and determined to fasten upon, and our share of the red devils are pouring through that hole on this ridge we never did get closed. The one man who kept us from bringing those separate parts together into a solid line, why he's ridden right on through us now and is looking for more little rabbits hiding their faces in the weeds. That painted heathen's got more mischief to do and him untouched by any sign of harm. By the time the great clot of the rest of them gets here and says hello, I've got to get up on my feet, whether that left knee wants to contribute to the effort or not, and I've got to prepare myself.

I intend to leave here standing up and acting like a soldier. It's not my part, nor my plan nor inclination, to lie down and hide my face under the covers and hope the booger man will go away. I'll look the bastard in the eye, give him a great big grin, and try to slap the living hell out of him one more time. Come on, you ill-clad and unkempt creatures. Let me show you what Myles Keogh has learned to do and what thunder he's got left to dish out to you.

Mirabeau Lamar Sylestine
AS CRAZY HORSE, ON THE GREASY GRASS

JUNE 25, 2001

I WAS IN COMPLETE COSTUME, FACE AND BODY PAINT, WIG IN PLACE
and securely positioned, and all appropriate weapons (fake ones)
at hand, fully prepared to impersonate the war chief of the Oglala Sioux.
At that moment, he would have had on his person a stone club, a small
ax, and perhaps a repeating rifle, though there's disagreement among
scholars about that matter. All agree he wouldn't have been carrying a
revolver. He might have had a bow and some arrows, not over eight or
ten. Personally I don't think he'd have had that entire equipage at hand,
judging from accounts of his actions on Calhoun Hill that afternoon.
How could he have managed all that material and been able to do what
he did? It boggles the mind.

The time was just after midday on the twenty-fifth of June, and Alec
Murray had given me a long hard look, pulling at his nose with his right
hand as though he had just discovered it was too short for some reason
and he was having to get that lack remedied before another minute had
passed. I knew what he was pondering. He was thinking I was too small
to look right as Crazy Horse, war chief of the Sioux, sitting up on a horse
way too big to look like the pony Crazy Horse would have been riding
when he led the breakthrough of that line of troopers on Calhoun Hill
back on the afternoon of the day.

221

That was not my fault, as I delicately informed Alec, modulating my voice and my manner of address so as not to appear the least bit nervous, not even to hint hysteric. The mounts that Crazy Horse and all the rest of the warriors rode in action that day on the Greasy Grass would have been ponies, I'd said to Alec, not great big lumbering American geldings or stallions or mares even. He knew I was right about that, and that to argue against the logic of my statement was fruitless. There was no way he could prevail against that reality. So what does the director of the Custer's Last Stand Reenactment on the 125th anniversary of the event do? You get three guesses, and the first two don't count.

He threw logic to the winds and he went all show-business dramatic. "It doesn't make a dime's worth of difference, Mirabeau," he said, raising the volume and intensity of his voice a good deal beyond where it should have been, given the context. "Not a bit will the audience and the viewers and the participants and the film crew care about what really occurred back on that day in history. We're creating a look now, giving life to a moment today which will convince all those experiencing it that it's really happening. At least for a moment or two. The time is not then. It's this day, in its heat and dust and light and feel. The moment is now. Get what I mean?"

"Of course, I do, Alec," I said. "Please don't misunderstand me. I know that logic and literal truth must go out the window when we're working to create a meaningful moment. I'm just, you know, remarking something about background, and I'm in no sense saying there's any justification in defending our work on the grounds of historical fact. Puh-lease believe me."

"Oh, gosh, I do," Alec said, satisfied that I've kowtowed and cringed and deferred enough to let him know I recognized his authority. He was the big dog, and I was the little yapper on the sideline making noise and meaning little by it. I can play along. I can say yessir. I've spent a lifetime doing it.

"What if I cheat up on the back of this great beast by sitting farther forward on him?" I said, scooting up so that I was sitting almost on top of where the nag's front legs joined its body. It did feel to me as though it was adding a couple of inches to my seated height when I made that move.

"You know," Alec had said, letting go of his nose, "I think, Mirabeau, you may be onto something. It does look better when you sit where you are right now on the horse. And if you could sit just the tiniest bit straighter, that might help too. Just imagine you've got a steel rod all the way up your spine and it's pushing you up, up, up."

"Like this?" I'd said, straining to make all parts of my actually quite compact body loom as large as possible.

"That's it. I love it. It's a thousand percent better, and nobody will have to convince themselves that you're a big-enough physical specimen to mimic Crazy Horse."

"Wonderful," I'd said, thinking to myself that all contemporary accounts of the historical Crazy Horse emphasize an overall impression of a much slighter, slimmer-built man than one would assume a war chief to be. After all, though, wasn't Napoleon a little fellow himself, all the way from his foot to his head, including his phallus, which is preserved somewhere in Europe today as I seem to remember reading in some publication? His penis was quite small, but he seemed to have been able to satisfy Josephine with it. He had a big head, though, physically, and that made up for any overall impression of slightness that someone might have had of the conqueror of Europe. I myself have a quite large noggin, too, though taken as a whole I am what many would consider on the short and light side. Who cares? I get my work back at home done, and I receive compliments all the time about that and about my personal intensity, and I'll take that any day in place of a great hulk of an overweight body fed on a commercially produced diet.

But that quibbling with Alec Murray about my appearance on the back of a big American horse was behind me, and I was now positioned down the hill a little way from the ridge line where Crazy Horse had made his famous dash and breakthrough of the gap between the wings of Custer's last three intact companies. Here is the moment on which turned the battle on the Greasy Grass, and I was here to be of that moment. I was ready to do my thing and to convince all viewers that the thing I was doing had been Crazy Horse's thing those 125 years ago. This would be my thing, my time, my moment to shine in that deep western sun so unlike the shady pine forests of the East, and I would make the most of it or die trying. Hoka hey, it's a good day to die, as many a Native American before me had chanted before entering upon that never-ending task of showing the white man what a red brother could do.

"All right," Alec Murray was saying into a handheld shortwave radio jammed against his head, "we're ready up here on Calhoun Hill, location point B-eleven. Let's hear some guns going off, cue the buglers and the war cries, and let's see what we've got. We're as ready as we're going to get."

Alec was sounding like a man announcing the commencement of his own death scene, and he was having to speak very loudly into the radio set, making his directions much more publicly audible than I knew he'd like. But in 2001 there wasn't a good cell tower within twenty miles of the Last Stand Battlefield, and so it was shortwave handsets or waving colored flags at each other or yelling into the open air. A hundred years earlier, they had no means of communication save direct conversation and messages carried by hand. Oh, well. Here we are. Here we go. Whatever.

In a minute or so, the sounds of blanks being fired and troopers and Indians yelling and screaming began to drift up the hill, and I touched my heels to my big old American horse and started him back down the crest of the ridge toward the draw from which Crazy Horse burst upon his pony that day when he kept the companies at the top of the hill from consolidating and from where I'd come boiling forth in about three minutes. Some of the guys impersonating troopers of the E and F and I companies looked up at me from where they were kneeling at the crest of the ridge, giving thumbs-up and mouthing the old show biz adage about breaking a leg. All of those troopers in every company were keeping themselves apart from each others' units, even before the action marking the reenactment of the big spasm of 1876 started up.

That was Alec's idea, the continuing separation from other military units, the notion of never letting the actors from those separate companies join forces even before official reenactment action kicked off. That sort of integrity on Alec's part I really have always respected, no matter how some persons I will not name smirk and make belittling comments at Alec's insistence on maintaining an ongoing attempt at historical accuracy. He does that for a great dramatic reason, I'd argue most strongly. And to honor the past, I might add, if anyone dare push me.

"They never joined forces in that last action before all came to grief," Alec would say to anyone who raised questions about whether it was truly necessary for actors to observe some condition that took place well over a hundred years ago. "And they desperately wanted and needed to join forces. It was a matter of life or death to them. And I want that hint of separation and incompleteness and looming disaster to permeate the mindsets of every actor in this pageant. That awareness will add an immeasurable soupçon of anxiety to the entire production. If you can't abide that principle, the highway to the real and the mundane is right there, and it's open to all those wanting to travel it."

Hoka hey, I say to that, not out loud, naturally, but within my own mind, the private dwelling place I maintain for ghosts and glory and the glamor of the past. Let me not dwell too much on that, or I'll surely tear up and maybe even snivel a little, here on this great horse someone's given the stupid name of Tommy, for God's sake. His mythic name, though, is Wind Rider, at least to me and Crazy Horse, who will be here with me when I charge that line of blue soldiers. As I do so, I will not subject the spirit of the war chief of the Oglalas to the inane attempts at humor which some impersonators of historical characters cannot stop themselves from revealing. I've heard some of the snickering that goes on about his name, but that was before I was given the honor of chan-neling the spirit of Crazy Horse. I will brook no such nonsense now, and there will be no breaking of the illusion of reality surrounding any part of my performance.

Thinking of that gift and responsibility makes me almost wish my stone club was real and not just molded rubber foam, but enough of that play of the Western mind which inhabits my Native American conscious-ness way too much and too deeply at times. Let me, as I wait upon this hill for the signal to charge that line of troopers with death in my hands, let me lose my white man mind. Let me leave my Alabama-Coushatta woods-Indian self behind, and let me be the warrior I'm portraying and am meant to be. Let me be a Native American of the Great Plains and the Black Hills. Let me be him.

Crazy Horse, be here, be here now.

As I felt that identity, that great selfhood welling up in my chest like a rising tide pulled by the moon in a starless sky, I could hear a whisper of a voice deep within my head begin to speak. The language was one I did not know, its roots not those which informed and shaped the tongue of the Creek Confederation in the dark wooded lands on the eastern side of the Mississippi River, the speech which formed the oral communications of the Alabama and Coushatta tribes. It was the voice of the Sioux I was hearing, not that of my home people, and yet I understood it without knowing it, I felt it without touching it, and I became *of* it without ever having been within it.

Talk about your mythic sense of joining another self. I was getting there without even trying, and I knew that was the key. To will oneself to be another is self-defeating. Instead, gi ve yourself up to the other, open your heart to whatever will enter and possess it, and strain not at the ant but instead swallow the elephant.

At that point, just when I felt my own soul slipping from me in a great swoon of letting go and acceptance, my horse reared a bit at some internal signal from within, its name no longer Tommy but fully and certainly Wind Rider, and I knew my time had come to act in complete fulfillment as the war chief of the Oglala Sioux. I said two words, words I'd never heard before and words whose meaning had never existed for me in the past and did not now, since they were not my tongue, neither Alabama which I'd learned in my father's house on the reservation, nor the English I'd learned from television and radio and the schools of Annette, Texas. Yet I understood what these strange sounds echoing in my mind told me. And I acted in accordance, drumming my heels into the ribs of Wind Rider and emerging with a great rush from the mouth of the draw where Crazy Horse waited for the moment to charge the line of blue soldiers, those killers brought to the Greasy Grass by Long Hair on a mission of death and enslavement.

As I reached the summit of the ridge and guided Wind Rider toward the line of soldiers kneeling before me, their rifles in hand and all in the process of being turned to aim at me, I could feel the hawk which I'd fastened to the clump of hair at the crown of my head begin to stir. Alec Murray had not wanted me to fix that stuffed creature in place, citing the fact that no contemporary commentator on Crazy Horse's appearance during the battle on the Greasy Grass had ever mentioned a stuffed hawk as making up any part of the war chief's adornment for combat. "Trust me on this, Alec," I had said to the director of the reenactment, "I feel I must do this, since something tells me I should."

"Mirabeau," he had said, using my white man's name quite purposely for argumentative effect, which I recognized immediately and resented, "what need do you have to tie a stuffed hawk to your head in creating a representation of Crazy Horse? With him, more is less, and less is more. That's the power of the way he dressed himself. You know. Simple. Clean.

Elegant. One rock behind one ear. Clearly random hail stone paintings on his body. A symbolic lightning bolt in only two colors across his face. Not a feather fastened anywhere, no upper body garment, hair flowing unbound and wild and free. He was not just a simple warrior. He was an artist.

"He was always playing against type, quite consciously, and just imagine how he must have studied and thought to come up with that notion, considering the context in which he dwelled. The Sioux warriors typically went way over the top in bodily adornment. I don't have to tell you that. Crazy Horse had the fashion sense to go against that and to gain great effect by so doing. He understood down to the bone the power of the simple and the direct. What need do you have to fasten a dead hawk with wire to your head? What's the need, Mirabeau?"

"Reason not the need, Alec," I'd flung back at him, and that little shard of theater history and psychology stopped him in his tracks. I let him know he wasn't talking to an unlettered primitive. So I got my way costumewise, and in so doing I discovered that what I was wearing and how I was adorned ceased being a costume in any real sense. By following the dictates of myth and emotion, I had broken free of mere imitation, and I had become the thing itself. I wasn't imitating the war chief of the Oglala Sioux. I was becoming him.

So I was wearing my stuffed hawk on top of my head, finishing off the look I wanted and needed to give Crazy Horse in my channeling of him, and as I've said earlier, as soon as I hit the level ground which the draw led to, not only was I speaking in a language I had no prior experience or knowledge of, and understanding what I was saying in an unaccountable fashion, I could feel the dead stuffed hawk atop my head begin to shift its talons, open its wings to full extension, and begin to issue a great attack cry, a sound I instantly understood as the call a raptor would use as it closed with its prey.

I joined my voice with that of the hawk atop the head of Crazy Horse, and I headed for the blue soldier first on the end of the line on the left, lifting my stone ax in full extension as I made ready to scatter the brains of Long Hair's trooper on the sacred ground of the valley of the Greasy Grass. That blue-clad trooper before me was not a high school English teacher from Dickson, Tennessee, all dressed up in an authentic-appearing pair of wool pants which fastened by buttons and had never been sullied by a metal zipper, his replica of a single-shot Springfield rifle hugged up close to his overfed belly and a wooden-sided canteen hanging from his belt by a steel hook. As I charged toward him on my pony blessed by the Great Spirit and imprinted in red with the true image of the hand of Crazy Horse, the expression on the face of that Seventh Cavalry trooper didn't reveal a reenactor satisfied with his historically accurate appearance, but instead the look of terror of a man in the wrong place at the right time about to get his brains scattered by a warrior of the Sioux nation. He was feeling what he should have felt, and he had earned the right to die, that right purchased by fear, the truest of all feelings.

The hawk riding upon my head as talisman of my commitment to victory over the blue soldiers of Long Hair screamed its single-minded note of terror, and I smashed my long-handled stone ax against the head of the first soldier I would attack. He fell to one side, and I moved to my next target, the hawk's scream sounding above the sounds of battle around me and the hoofs of my pony flinging great clots of earth behind it as my mount carried me on my mission of vengeance.

"See me," I spoke thunder in a language I had never known. "Know you are paying the debt of blood you owe the People. Feel the justice of your death as you fall."

"Woo," someone was shouting in a white man's voice, "look at Crazy Horse. He has got his game face on. Go get them, Chief. Swing that mallet."

"Him," the hawk was speaking to me now, not in a hunting cry but in that language of the People I had not known before. "He is the next one to die." I went the way of the hawk then, making no outcry and showing no anger as I worked my way through the line of soldiers who dared to challenge me, Crazy Horse, war chief of the Oglala Sioux. Many lifted weapons, but no one touched Crazy Horse as he killed them, all dead before they had the chance to know they were no more. He had broken the blue line of soldiers, and the warriors of the Sioux could now pour through the fractured defense toward Long Hair himself.

Crazy Horse
WAR CHIEF OF THE OGLALA SIOUX, ON THE GREASY GRASS

June 25, 1876

As I prepared in my lodge after I had heard the gunfire and the horses running and the women and children crying, I made no hurry. The battle would be there when I joined it, and I would not seek it until I had done the things necessary to make me what I must become. I was wearing the deerskin, and I had all the colors of clay and oil in pots ready to hand, and I would not need to touch the hair of my head to arrange it. I knew where to begin the painting, and I put my fingers first to my face, where would be the lightning bolt and then my chest and arms and legs upon which would fall the hailstones, and in the final application I reached over my shoulders on each side, sure to put the white markings of hail high upon my back.

Outside the lodge would be my pony, one caught and brought for me to mount by the son of Hears the Rain, a young boy known still by his birth name, Little Strong Arms. He could go today with the men of the Oglalas if he wished, though his mother would claim he was not ready for war. "I see you have my horse waiting," I said to Little Strong Arms. "Now to give him the painting he wants."

"He is ready for you to do that," Little Strong Arms said. "That he has told me."

"Did my horse speak aloud to you?"

"No, he spoke no words, but he looked at me and lifted his head high and held it there."

"That told you the horse felt ready?"

"It did," Little Strong Arms said. "He will not lower his head to feed again until you paint the red hand on his neck. He is hungry enough to feed, but he will not until you prepare him for battle. He knows what comes first."

"Soon you may decide to go against the enemies of the People," I told him as I began to place the mark of the red hand on my pony's neck. "You will know when that time comes."

"I would go now, but my mother weeps too much."

"You are not ready yet," I said. "For you still hear your mother's voice and notice her tears. When such no longer happens, you will not notice anyone telling you how to behave and act. Then you will leave without knowing you have left, and that leaving will tell you how to behave without making a sound."

"Who goes with you today against the soldiers of Long Hair?" Little Strong Arms asked, placing the bridle in my hand. "How many warriors will you take?"

"I take no one now, and I never have done so. Some warriors will go, and some have gone with me before, but I take none. It is not proper to ask another man to come with you against an enemy. Each man goes where and when he will. And when the battle is decided and each man left alive returns to his lodge and his family, only then can the true counting begin."

"I would that I could go with you now."

"When the true time comes, you will ask no one, and you will travel alone," I told the son of Hears the Rain, a boy bearing his birth name and not yet grown enough to become his own father, but soon to be that.

As I crossed toward the stream of the Greasy Grass, I could see many big horses carrying soldiers through the water, all of them with their backs turned toward our village as they rode to cross the river and flee up the hill. Warriors of the Sioux and the Cheyennes surrounded most of the blue soldiers with many others hurrying on ponies to join those already there, the ones swinging stone clubs and shooting arrows and pulling the triggers of the rifles. The sounds of their cries and songs were loud and becoming louder as I leaned forward on my horse to urge him on.

I would go where I was told to go by the voice in my head that started from outside but grew within, like the seed inside the seed, the one so small it is thought to be nothing. But then it comes on its own, and by that you know it started from a place where it was not. That place cannot be found, but it calls you to come to where it is and if you get there, it is there no longer. If you seek it, you may not find it. It is like the stone I wear behind my ear that speaks to me in words that none can hear but me. Yet I was told to wear that stone in battle, and to harken to its voice, though none other might hear it.

That is how I rode into the water to pursue the blue soldiers Sitting Bull had seen in his vision as they fell upside down into our village. In his dream, they were marked with blood, and their hands and arms were cut, and their weapons fell beside and around them and were of no use. There was no holding by them of rifles and pistols and knives any longer, and the blue soldiers no longer had eyes to see, nor ears to hear, and they lay quiet where they fell, upside down with their feet no longer upon the earth. No longer could they walk, and nothing inside them told them to move again. That Sitting Bull dreamed, and that dream was coming alive now.

After I had pulled many soldiers off their horses, using my stone club first to hit them and cause them to cease their moving to escape, they fell into the water of the Greasy Grass, and the stream began its work of carrying their blood away from that place of killing. Soon the water would be pure again and clear, and a man could drink it without fear of its taste and the blood and death it carried.

I gained the shore then on the other side of the river, my pony strong in its motion, and I entered the dark draw that led to the top of the hill where Long Hair and his other blue soldiers waited. What I would have to do when I came up out of that deep passage in the earth, I already knew. I had been shown that, and I had been told in that dream I entered long ago that if I took no trophies, nor sought to keep any belonging that was not mine, I would not be harmed by any man's weapons. Bullets from the white man's rifles, arrows from the Crow and Ree scouts who rode with the soldiers, long knives and small ones, any hurtful thing that could be used to harm or kill me or any other man—none of these could prevail against me. They would not touch my body, and if by chance a thing did come against me, it would have no strength but would bounce away as the small pellets of ice from the sky will do in an early winter storm in the Black Hills. Such things of ice and of death will convey a true coldness, but they have no power to harm one who wears the covering a wise man uses.

My pony carried me through the heart of the deep draw to the top of the hill, and though along my way blue soldiers pointed their rifles and pistols at me, discharging smoke and lead as I rode among and past them, no harm touched me. At the top of the hill, I could see the two unmet lines of blue soldiers yearn toward each other, just as a man and a woman who want each other will lean in a direction promising a coming together, but I would not let that joining of lovers take place. Instead I moved upon men at each end of those two lines, and I would allow no touching and no final joining together. I sought nothing to keep for my own benefit, and the Great Spirit saw that refusal working in me as a warrior, and he allowed me to attack my enemy with no harm coming upon me as I did the thing I had dreamed and now saw become real.

Those warriors behind me, seeing what good ends came from good behavior in living a dream so that it is real, pursued my way as well. And the two lines of blue soldiers never married, and then we came upon the last bunch on the crest of the hill, standing there, some of them, and lying down still alive some others, and sleeping forever now, others of them, with no dreams ever to come to them again. Some held weapons and fired at us, some threw their rifles and pistols down to the earth unused, some trembled and wept, some fought like bull buffalos pursued by wolves, all knew what was to come.

It was time now to complete all of what the dream of Sitting Bull told us had come to him in the Sun Dance, and we felt ourselves being moved around to finish the fight. We had no need to tell our hands what to do now. A great wind led us one and all to where we were, each man separate in himself, and at the same time, together in one thing and that joining together was of the People. The wind blew us before it, and we came upon the blue soldiers on the hill just as leaves driven before a storm in the cold time of year will fly up in a man's face, do what he can to prevent them. No one can stop the wind from blowing. No one can catch every leaf the wind blows. They will come, and one by one and all together they will strike.

And that we knew we would do this day, leaf by leaf, man by man, blood by blood.

Billy Kills His Horses
AS GALL, HUNKPAPA WAR CHIEF, ON THE GREASY GRASS

June 25, 2001

ERE I WAS, ALL DRESSED UP AND SOME PLACE TO GO, AND LET me tell you I had my game face well on and firmly in place. The makeup guys, both of the men and one of the women, had come together to get me looking right and lusting for big-time conflict in the crucial moment of the drama to come. I was to be in for the kill, the moment when George Armstrong Custer and the remnants of his boys got their final comeuppance, and as Gall I was one of the main players and a centerpiece in the denouement of the big production.

I was stoked, though I might not have looked it, my facial expression tending as always toward the saturnine, big Sioux Indian that I am and getting into my role as Gall, to boot, but I was prepared to emote whenever I got the ghost of a chance. I had all the materials for it, and I had the motivation as Gall for showing deep feelings from a great range of possibilities. I had lost two wives—count them, two. I had had three children killed by Custer's Crow scouts, suck-up scum as that bunch always were to the white man, and as Gall I was by nature truculent and not nice to be around. To top that, professionally as a war chief of the People, I had a responsibility to lead, set examples, and get my share of payback on the blue soldiers who had done us Indians such harm, including me personally.

I had the stage now, the setting to show what I could do as actor and as big old burly Indian present-day guy, and according to reliable gossip, scouts for an impending Spielberg production would be out in force to find likely lads and lasses among the local red men and women to play parts in the movie rumored to be made of the annual pageant of the Last Stand of General Custer and his boys. I had the ticket to ride in my hand, and all I had to do was find a way to cash it in.

One drawback, though, loomed large in my squirming little Native American mind, and like most problems, it presented simultaneously the twin faces of possible disaster and triumph. Here's the up side. Gall had delivered one of *the* best, and possibility the best, lines of the whole historic doings on the Greasy Grass. It was a statement's statement. I love to say what he had said, and I had about worn it out on Alec Murray by the time us warriors had been given the orders to charge the final group on the top of what's called Calhoun Hill now, but not back in the day, of course. I'm talking about the Custer brothers and nephew, and the final officers left in the Right Wing of the companies, and the rest of the little people, the privates and noncoms and so on. I'm talking a huge boffo Hollywood finish to the whole thing. I would be there, and looming large.

So the big line that Gall had to deliver? What was it? Everyone who's the least bit knowledgeable about the Last Stand knows it. "My heart was bad," Gall had said in justification of his savagery in the last scene of the drama back when it first took place. And I so wanted to be able to deliver that line, to look deep into some important camera lens while I'm doing my best evil red man-heathen-savage-brute-killer imitation, and growl it out. "My heart is bad." Present tense, please notice.

That is certainly arguably the best line in the whole production, but here's the downside of the opportunity as impersonator of Gall. When I asked Alec Murray at what point would I deliver the immortal words of my predecessor, he had looked at me dismissively and said, "Oh, Gall delivered that opinion well after all was over, months, maybe years later, when he was being interviewed by some reporter for an Eastern newspaper. It was an afterthought, and probably an invention of the reporter who was doing the story at that point. That claim's unsubstantiated, and no big deal."

"Excuse me?" I said. "Pardon me all to Hell. How do you know that, and why in heaven's name would you pass up a chance to take advantage of that bit of wonderfully effective savagery? It was the perfect sound bite then, and it still is. Better now, in fact, than when Gall first came up with it."

"Billy, Billy, Billy," Alec had said. "This production is not about Gall as war chief, and it's certainly not about a present-day impersonator of the old boy. Sorry, my talented young friend. But it's not on."

I stumbled away, heartsick at that point, stunned, disappointed, brought down so low I almost wept in frustration. I mean, it's one thing to play the big burly massive savage swinging a club and braining guys in blue uniforms and straw hats, and that's certainly worth doing and all that. Don't get me wrong. I might even get noticed in that action by a Spielberg underling or two, given my size, my look, my makeup, and my natural acting ability. But not to have the chance to speak those wonderfully immortal words first voiced by Gall lo these many years ago? That is agony.

As I wandered up to my horse, a big beast especially assigned to me because of my weight and presence, I must state that something which I can only describe as mythic and mysterious took place. It happened, though, no doubt about it, and I was wide awake to witness it. I was just reaching out for the reins of the beast when it turned its head and looked deep into my eyes. I kid you not. I swear it did. And here's the strangest part of all. I did not hallucinate in my state of deep emotional distress, and the horse didn't speak words of encouragement and comfort to me, either in Sioux or in English, but I swear it conveyed in that long stare from its deep brown eyes something I could read. Be assured that I am not a horse whisperer, and I don't believe that Native Americans have a special relationship with the animal kingdom. I've never before looked at four-footed creatures as anything but meat walking around until somebody kills it, rips off its hide, and eats it.

So what was the deal? It's this. The horse let me know with that look that it sympathized deeply, it felt my pain, and it knew I would find a way to seek a camera lens somewhere focused on me in the last scenes of the massacre of Custer and the boys on Calhoun Hill. In due time, I'd be able to speak those celebrated words of Gall directly into a hot mike. That would be the door that would open for me, not for Gall, who had already achieved a limited sort of immortality, but for Billy Kills His Horses, he who has spent a life buried on the res. Up until now, that is. Up until now, let me repeat. My heart has been bad. But friend, it's not only about to get better, it's about to get well. Billy Kills His Horses will speak, and he will be heard. You just listen.

Hoka hey, hoss. Hoka hey.

Gall
HUNKPAPA WAR CHIEF, ON THE GREASY GRASS

June 25, 1876

At first, they thought we were coming a few at a time, the blue soldiers, since they couldn't see that all the gullies and draws were already full of the young warriors, the ones crawling up toward the top of the hill with the bushes hiding them. Now and then, a few would rise up and shoot a rifle or a pistol if they had one, but mainly at first the young men of the Sioux and Cheyennes were using arrows, sending them high up and letting them come down like they'd started in the sky somewhere. That wasn't doing as much damage to the blue soldiers as guns would do, but it was all adding up. Their horses were pitching around and fighting against the men holding their reins. Nothing was staying quiet.

I was on a pony, like most of the warriors who were older, and by the time all the soldiers who'd been with Long Hair reached the top of the hill, then turned around, and started making ready to stop and make us come at them head-on, I'd dropped back behind where all the young men were crawling toward the crest of the ridge. It wasn't until a little time after some of the blue soldiers had stood up and come running together in a bunch toward us, shooting their rifles in a volley, making the young warriors in front of them start to back up and turn tail a little, that something happened to make the last part of the fight between the

Sioux and Cheyennes and Long Hair's troopers start up. Once that last part started, you could tell nothing would last much longer. The end was showing itself.

It was Crazy Horse that started it, that last part, and I knew it would be him, not because I'd dreamed it or saw it in a vision, but because I knew how he fought from watching him do it. He never talked about what he'd done and how other folks might do like him, too, if they paid attention. He just did things. Here's how it worked with him, facing an enemy. When Crazy Horse would start up going into a fight, he'd be slow at first, even getting off his pony to stand by it to shoot his rifle, if that was what he was carrying, or use his bow to shoot arrows if that's all he had as a weapon. I didn't need to ask him why he did that, though, because it was easy to figure out. He could aim better and make his shots count more, whether from a white man's rifle or an Indian bow. He couldn't see no percentage in just pulling the trigger or shooting as many arrows as fast as he could, hoping that something good would happen. He liked to plan all he did. His horses always knew what he was doing, and they would stand and wait until he'd finished the job before they showed signs of wanting to leave.

Now I got to say that sometimes when Crazy Horse got his blood up, it was hard to see his plan, but that wasn't because he didn't have one. You just didn't understand his plan while it was going on, and what was happening when he got all hot and busy doing something was not that Crazy Horse hadn't bothered to plan. The planning was over. He was just carrying it out now, and he could afford to let his heart pump hard and his sweat and blood fly off into the air and his breathing come quicker and deeper. He could allow himself to get worked up and wild acting, just as though he was a regular man, if doing that didn't get in the way of his plan.

So when the young warriors let that little bunch of blue soldiers chase them backwards for a spell and get them running away from the crest of the hill, that's when Crazy Horse started putting his plan to work. I had seen it before, what he would do all on his own without asking a single other warrior to join him, and I was not surprised to witness it again. I mean his going ahead all on his own to take on a job you'd figure would need a lot more than one man to finish it.

I'd decided a long time before that fight on the Greasy Grass that when Crazy Horse was acting like he was going to do something dangerous on his own, not looking back to see if anybody else was coming, it was all part of what he expected to take place. You can't ask a Sioux to do something that you want him to do, no matter how much sense it makes. You have to start doing it yourself, and maybe if he gets interested and starts to believe it would gratify him somehow to be part of that, why then he might take on the same job you've started.

He doesn't consider that you're leading him, though, or that you thought of a thing to do that needed doing when he hadn't and you were showing him just the right way to act. If he thought that was going on, he was more likely than not to just sit back and watch you get killed, or see you count coup and then back off if that's all there was to it. He did what he considered was his to do all on his own, the Sioux or the Cheyenne fighting man, and if he came to believe somebody was expecting him to undertake an assignment, he'd just ride off in the opposite direction or sit still where he was and make judgments. He would be glad to explain to you where you were going wrong.

The way it was in that hot part of the day on the Greasy Grass proved out to be different from the usual behavior of each Indian by himself, though. As soon as Crazy Horse took himself right into the middle of those two lines of blue soldiers trying to join up with each other, every bit of that part of the hill began looking different, and not just different because there was a running battle going on. No, it was strange because new things I'd never seen before started showing themselves. First, what began to settle in the air all over the hill was different. It was all the smoke from the rifles and pistols starting to roil up and get mixed up with the dust and dirt being kicked up by the big American horses of the blue soldiers and the ponies of the Sioux and Cheyennes.

It got so dark all of a sudden, as soon as that mix of gunsmoke and dirt began being one thing, that the sky turned almost black as night when the moon is down and the stars are covered up. In front of me where I was standing with my pony hobbled, a great wall of that dust and smoke mix settled down like a buffalo-hide robe brought down between you and all you'd been seeing. Other people, their faces and hands, the clothes they were wearing, what they were holding, the world around you—all the things that weren't just the buffalo robe slipped out of sight and went away, all hid somewhere.

I stood watching that big robe of dust and smoke fill up the air where all the fighting was going on, wondering what it meant, and then I noticed another thing I hadn't kept track of. The sound. And that sound was sharp and sudden, and it was so much mixed up with the dust and smoke that I could see the sound as well as hear it. It came from gunshots and hooves of ponies and the American horses, and it was made up of those gunshots and the cries of men killing and being killed and yelling and singing battle songs and grunting and calling out words you couldn't understand. Above all of it was the same sound going higher and higher. And that sound which stitched all the other sounds together came from the eagle bone whistles which the warriors blew as they shot rifles and arrows and swung clubs and slashed with knives and hacked with axes. Now and then one of the calls from the bugles that the blue soldiers used to talk to each other would ring out and lay on top of the eagle-bone whistle sounds, and then that would break off in the middle and that bugle would not be sounded again.

Then a thing announced itself near me, and I knew it was a new cry which I'd never heard before in this battle, though I knew what it was. I had heard it many times before, but not here. It was the cry of a raven, a bird all black with a song as dark as its feathers and its heart. Where that cry came from, though, that was the surprise. The stuffed raven which I had fastened to my head with a leather string cut from the hide of a deer was moving its claws as it opened its bill to tell all who could hear that it was in battle, as well, dead though it had been since two winters ago. "You are speaking now," I said to the dead raven, alive again as Crazy Horse fought the blue soldiers by himself, and as warriors came up behind him and poured into the gap he made in that blue line, in the dark cloud of dust and smoke. "I didn't know you could do that," I said to the black bird riding on my head.

My raven spoke again, and I moved to leave the sunlight and clear air outside the place where the killing was going on and to put myself into the dirt and smoke and blood and become part of the sound of dead ravens and dying blue soldiers before me. A voice came from beside me as I lifted my stone club in one hand and leaned forward. "Gall," the voice sounded, deep like thunder and sharp like lightning. "War Chief, father and husband, go to where you belong."

When I looked to see who had spoken so directly to me just before I would seek my share of the blood which must be shed, I did not know who it was at first. Then I saw the blackness of the horse he rode, the total shade from hoof to head and from nose to tail, and I knew I could name who he was. It was the Great Spirit mounted on a black horse, so dark it pulled the light into it.

The Great Spirit rode with us that day against Long Hair and his blue soldiers and his Crow and Ree scouts, and his horse was of the starless night and his voice that of the deepest river in the Black Hills. "You have come to be with the People," I said, knowing that any words I uttered could not heard by the Great Spirit, but offering all I could.

He rode forward into the great cloud of dust and smoke, his garments black yet shining as he left the world of light and clear air, and he fought beside the warriors of the People on the Greasy Grass. And many saw him, as busy as he was, yet during that whole time he spoke to none but me, Gall, war chief of the Hunkpapa Sioux. I alone received that gift, and I would possess it from that time forward, on the day we killed Long Hair and his blue soldiers.

Thomas Custer

CAPTAIN, AIDE-DE-CAMP, SEVENTH CAVALRY, ON CALHOUN HILL

JUNE 25, 1876

George didn't use words to tell me to move away from the squad of men I'd been urging to spread out in a fan-shaped formation to achieve a better coverage in face of the enemy swarming up the hill, coming not simply in a frontal attack but from all sides of the 180-degree arc before us. But he didn't need to speak for me to know what he wanted. Growing up next to him, as second oldest of the sons of the family, I had come to learn what my brother wanted me to do in all assignments, large and small. He could simply look at me, catch my eye with those blazing blue orbs, and there was no doubt about what he demanded that I do.

It took a good long time for me to learn how to oppose him successfully, whether the matter involved my stealing a sweet from the kitchen for him or getting the attention of some young lady he wanted to have admire him or standing united beside my big brother as he questioned some command promulgated by our father. I was his to order about, and I obeyed for the most part all he laid down for me. I complied, since I had learned that was the easiest way to get along with the brother in command.

All that was true until the war came, and by volunteering, I was able to get out from under the authority of George Armstrong Custer for a good long spell. I did my part away from him, while he became the youngest brevet general in the history of the US Army, staying ahead of me as usual. But I got my innings in, as well, and did it in a way that Georgie couldn't catch up to, this time. I'm not overly proud of what I did to earn the two Congressional Medals of Honor, leading a couple of charges and by luck seizing the standards of a couple of Reb companies. It didn't mean much. It was all accidental, largely, and I never bragged about it, knowing I'd make myself a target for justified sarcasm if I sought attention. I'd just been seen by chance carrying out an action that a superior officer deemed worthy of note, knowing that my being decorated would redound upon his command and to his credit. So he put me up for the citation. Twice.

All of that understood by anyone knowledgeable about military matters and battlefield heroics, nevertheless my older brother was never able to get over the fact of my two medals and his zero. Oh, he was cited for merit, and he defeated Jeb Stuart's cavalry at a crucial time at Gettysburg, but Tom had gotten the congressional medals, and George hadn't.

Of course that's why he hectored me after the war ended, urging me to stay attached to the army and to seek assignment to the Seventh Cavalry where I'd be where I was supposed to be, at least in his mind. Under the direction of and subordinate to my big brother once again. So I did it. Why not? I was ruined by the war, and I knew how to conduct myself in a military setting. Thus my post as aide-de-camp to the commanding officer of the Seventh Cavalry, with members of my family around me, and a military mission to carry out, one that promised to be difficult and at the same time rewarding and instrumental in ending a threat to the country, just as the suppression of the Southern rebellion had been. Pacifying the red man. Making the West safe for settlement by the white man.

Yet when George caught my eye on that hill in the middle of all that dust and heat of battle and by so doing let me know I was to hie myself to his side, I realized once again, this for the last time, that my brother had need of my presence and my carrying out of assignment. And I was being made aware of that, and I must obey and show up for duty.

"Tom, old fellow," George said to me after I'd repeated twice to my lieutenant what I wanted the troopers to do in reforming a defensive line and had trotted up to my brother's side, "what we must do is hold off this bunch for an hour or two. At least that period, and I fully expect that

Benteen's battalion will appear in the rear of this horde. Then we'll pinch them between us, and they will not have the stomach to stay in place. They'll scatter like they always do when a determined push hits them. What say you, Little Bub?"

"Georgie, I hope you're right and that Benteen will be crossing the river here shortly and coming up. That's our only hope."

"A strange word to hear from you, Captain Custer. Hope. Hope? What does hope have to do with anything, especially military strategy? What you want to say is not hope, but will. Will and maybe another word. Determination. That's what I like to hear bruited about. Eh? Agreed?"

"All those are good words, Georgie," I said. "I won't quarrel with that. But what I really wish is that the damned cartridge casings wouldn't swell from the rifles being fired and get stuck in the chambers of the Springfields. If that were remedied, I'd feel a lot more comfortable talking about abstractions such as will and determination."

He gave me that long look I'd seen all my days, ever since I first remember running after my big brother, begging him to wait for me as he coursed at full tilt across the ground of some field or wood, steadily gaining on me with his legs so much longer than mine. "Well," he said, beginning to formulate a reply to put me in the position which he considered appropriate for a brother —speechless and thoroughly defeated in a verbal contest—and that's when a sudden blow to his chest knocked my brother back as though he'd been run into by an invisible man who'd lowered his shoulder and collided with him full force. I knew instantly what had happened. How many times had I witnessed the effects of a chunk of lead slamming into human flesh? How many soldiers had I seen suddenly begin to shrink like they were so many dolls filled with sawdust now leaking from a huge hole in the fabric supposed to be holding them together and upright? How often had I marveled at the change that comes upon the face of a mortally wounded man?

Then came the blossoming of the flower of blood, growing so rapidly on George's deerskin shirt that in less time that it takes to say the word *blood* the red gouts had reached near his waist. "Georgie," I said, and before I could speak another word, Boston was there, the truly young son, his arm around George as he eased our big brother down into a sitting position.

"Will he die?" Boston said. "Take a deep breath, Georgie, and hold your hand on the wound. It's not that bad, is it, Tom? Is it?"

The firing from our circle of troopers seemed to be diminishing as I helped prop George up, the sound more sporadic, and when I looked away from George's face, rapidly graying now as his head seemed to sink deeper into the neck of his deerskin shirt, I could see that the arc of the defensive circle I'd worked to establish was now vanished. Individual soldiers were still working away at the firing chambers of their Springfields, and those whose rifles were still functioning were aiming and firing at the swarm of Indians now rising up within a few yards of the three of us Custers.

Dust and smoke hung in the air like a shroud, the sounds of Indian whistles were deafening, and the fight on the ridge where we thought we'd be able to consolidate forces had become now hand-to-hand, some troopers battling away with two or three enemies, some sinking to their knees in supplication as they threw away their weapons and tried to surrender, and all men, red and white, screaming and groaning as they struggled and died.

I pulled my revolver from the belt where I'd stuck it when George had signaled me to come to him, looked at Boston whose eyes were popped so wide I could see a line of blood outlining each, and I turned to George.

"Georgie," I said. "You're my big brother and my general. I love you. Good bye."

I shot him in the left temple. Since he had cut his hair some few days earlier, the hole the bullet made was instantly visible, and it did not bleed on that side of his skull, and that gave me comfort. I would not have to see the damage of the exit wound. I turned my brother's body to the side so that he lay straight on the earth, I patted him on his cheek, and then I rose up with the pistol in hand. Boston remained crouched beside the body, and I made a rising motion with my free hand.

"Boston, get up," I said. "Get up from there. Let's look them in the eye. Give them a taste of old Michigan. Come on, you wolverine."

"That's what George said at Gettysburg," Boston said. "He told me he said that."

"He told everybody everything he ever said and did," I said. "Here they come, Boston. Make them kill you while you're standing up."

Kate Big Head
A WOMAN OF THE CHEYENNES, ON THE GREASY GRASS

JUNE 25, 1876

HE FIRST TIME I SAW LONG HAIR, HE WASN'T YET CALLED THAT by the people he kept following around to catch and fight. I first saw him after what had happened on the Washita when all the old men and women and children were killed that morning when we heard the music start up, coming before the horses running and the blue soldiers shooting. I didn't see him there, though.

No, when I saw him first, it was later, the time he came to the People to say he wouldn't fight any more with us. He smoked the pipe with the council in the big lodge, and when one of the chiefs knocked out the ashes so they fell on the great boots of Custer, he didn't know what that meant. It was just an accident, I guess he thought, but every chief who saw it knew what it said. If he tried to fight the People again, the ashes on his boots said, it would end up with him and his soldiers lying dead somewhere on rocky ground where nothing but weeds would grow.

I was young then, not married, and when I first saw the man that we named Long Hair he was wearing white clothes and a big hat and those boots that reached all the way from his feet to above the bend of his knees. His hair was reddish yellow, and it fell in long curls all down around his head to his neck and below his chin. His eyes were light, bluer than the sky, and when he looked at a woman, he showed his teeth as white men

will do when they want to start something. He was handsome, and all
the young women and some old ones, too, said he looked just right, like
a white man would look if you had to imagine what would be good to see
in one of them. None of the women thought he would ever pay mind to
them, though, since we all knew my cousin Monahsetah had become his
woman already and he belonged to her. That happened after the killing
at Washita, when the blue soldiers got all the young women rounded up
together and picked out the ones they wanted. Being the big chief, Long
Hair got first pick, and as soon as he saw her, he wanted Monahsetah.

Long Hair got Monahsetah, and she did not want that at first, and
she tried not to want him because of what had happened on the Washita.
It didn't do her no good, she told me. Her mind said not to let herself
want Long Hair, but the other part of her did not listen to reason like
she wanted it to do. It never does. Women know that. So off and on
Monahsetah was his for many seasons, and the child he got with her had
light hair, and his skin color was not as dark as the shade of a Cheyenne.
So the name she gave that child was Yellow Bird. I don't know where he
is this day. Nobody does. Is he alive? Or is he like his father now on the
hill above the far side of the Greasy Grass?

When the soldiers came upon Sitting Bull's village, we knew what
it was as soon as we heard the horses and gunfire, and then our men
began to dress themselves for war. They had to take the time for that,
so things would turn out right. They put the paint on face and body
that suited what they were about to do. Some painted figures on their
horses, some put charmed rocks and stuffed birds or special headgear or
bracelets on themselves, and all gathered the weapons they would use
on the blue soldiers. "This time," my oldest brother told me when he
saw me running away from the sound of gunfire, "we will teach them a
lesson. They have got to learn to listen to the good advice we give them.
If they don't, we'll take away their ears to hear and pull out their tongues
so they can't speak."

"I will cross the river to watch this lesson," I said. "And I will see where
Noisy Walking will be fighting. I will sing him a strong heart song."

I said that to my brother to make certain that he wouldn't tell me not to
watch the fighting the People would do. Since I would be going across the
river to sing strong heart songs to his son, my nephew Noisy Walking, as
he fought, my brother couldn't forbid me. He did not speak, but looked

at me as a brother looks at his sister, shook his head, and then he left to add his part to the lesson-giving that would take place.

All that happened on the other side of the Greasy Grass after the blue soldiers turned and ran away after seeing how many warriors were in Sitting Bull's village, afraid and dying as they ran through the water and tried to get away from the Cheyennes and Sioux who were killing them. All of it happened fast. By the time the sun had moved only a little way in the sky, causing the shadows to get not much longer than they were before the fighting began, the sound of the guns and horses and the eagle whistles and the strong-heart singing and the warriors shouting and chanting began to fade. By the time the warriors had told the women they could come to the places where all the blue soldiers were lying down, most of them dead now but a few yet alive, the time was still in the hottest part of the day.

You could hear the white men crying out from the wounds they had suffered when they were being given the lessons, some moaning softly and some crying out in loud voices, and some asking for water, though they didn't know the right word for that. When a man is shot with arrows or bullets or he is cut or hit with a club, if he's still alive, he becomes very thirsty and cries out for water. It is strange that he would want that more than any other thing. Yet what I say is true. I have witnessed such behavior in every place where men have tried to kill each other. Water is what they want when they're hurt and dying.

I did not take part in what most of the women were doing to the bodies of the dead blue soldiers and to the ones still alive when they all got there, bringing with them their pounding stones and blades and wires and sharp pieces of rock. Many of them at some time had lost husbands, sons, nephews, brothers, and some had lost daughters and granddaughters and sisters, all these killed or taken away by the blue soldiers. So they were doing their part to teach a strong lesson, and they were doing that not with weapons that warriors would use, but with the tools for cooking and cutting hides from buffalo and deer and with the stones for pounding corn and beans and nuts and the awls for digging marrow out of bones.

I didn't like to see warriors scalping and cutting enemies after a fight was over. Particularly, I never liked to see the women at work on the bodies and especially on those not yet dead, so I walked past all that without looking down at what was going on. But I couldn't keep from hearing the white men screaming and groaning as the work commenced and all that noise that went on until the men were not able to make sounds anymore. The soldiers already dead were the lucky ones.

What I wanted to find was the husband of my cousin. I wanted to see what had become of Long Hair during the fight on this hot day, and I went up the hill looking from place to place, trying not to see what the women were doing with their tools, but keeping my eyes open for a man with long red and yellow hair. He would be dressed in white buckskins, I'd decided, since that was the outfit he wore to war, just as my nephew Noisy Walking always wore his hair in two long braids worked with beads and dressed himself in some long britches he had found in the white man's Fort Lincoln.

I thought also that Monahsetah's husband would be wearing a big hat, maybe a black one or it could be white like the rest of his clothing. He would have pieces of silver fastened on the shoulders of his upper garment, and he would have on his legs long boots, which would be shiny from being rubbed with grease. Finally, I knew that since he was always the chief of the soldiers, he would be in the middle of the place where the hardest fighting had taken place. He would be at the center with other men gathered around him. They would have tried to save him as their chief as long as they could. I hoped I would find him before the other women got there, and I hoped he would be already dead. My kinswoman, Monahsetah, would want that, too, no matter how much her head told her different.

She had told me once how she felt broken in half when she thought about Long Hair. "I am a woman of the Cheyennes, and my head speaks to me clearly. Yet when I consider this white man, something inside my belly seems to turn against me. I feel sick, as though I would lie down to rest and hope to sleep forever, but a thing inside my body craves to move. I understand nothing when I feel that way, except I am sorry I am a woman."

I'd almost reached the top of the hill, where several of the women were gathered around two or three blue soldiers, only one of them still alive, when I thought I saw what I was looking for. It was a man flat on the earth in a white buckskin shirt, the front of it covered with blood. The man was lying with his arms flung out to each side looking up at the sky with his eyes wide open like he was trying to see what kind of bird was flying above him. Or maybe he was trying to figure out what the clouds over him meant, whether it would be clear weather coming soon or a rainstorm with bad winds.

When I leaned closer to get a better view of the dead man's face, I knew this had to be what was left of Long Hair after the spirit had left him. But he didn't look right somehow, no matter that his eyes were the color that Monahsetah always mentioned when she talked about the white man who had become her husband, and no matter the long shiny boots like he always wore. The women hadn't got to him yet to take off all that he had covering him. With his clothes still on, he didn't seem fully dead yet.

No, though the clothes and boots were right and his eyes were light enough to be less blue than the sky in summer in the Black Hills, what was missing was the long hair that gave the man the name the People called him. He had not been scalped, since I could see no signs of the skull that always shows through when the skin of a man's head is cut and ripped off, but something else accounted for what was missing. All his hair had been cut off, maybe with a sharp knife or a razor, and his head looked almost like that of a man so old and close to death that all his hair has fallen out and been rubbed away. His long curls had not been removed by an Indian. He had done the cutting himself.

He wasn't Long Hair any more, and to call him that would be to say a name that was a lie. Though he had a hole in both sides of his head, one big and full of bloody matter and the other small and burned on the edges as though a red-hot piece of metal had been pushed against it, the way he was looking at the sky with his empty eyes didn't show him to be hurt or afraid or worried at the time he was killed. His lip didn't look like a white man's does when he is showing you he means no harm by lifting it and letting you see his teeth, but it looked like he was about to do that. He wasn't smiling yet, but he seemed ready to.

"Is that him?" someone was saying to me. "Is that Long Hair?" She was Long Robe Moving, a woman of the Cheyennes I had known for a time, but had never spoken with much.

"He is gone," I said. "Long Hair is. And this is what is left behind of him now. Not much still here."

"Look at his ears," Long Robe Moving said. "They seem large enough to let talk get inside them and take messages to his heart. But I don't think they worked well when he was able to walk about and lie with women."

"Maybe the holes inside his ears are not sufficient to let enough words pass through," I said. "The outside entries may look of good size, but the passage inside where you can't see might be too small for all words to get through to his heart."

"Something was wrong with his ears. Of that there's no doubt," said another woman who had just joined us to look at the man dead, the man who was Long Hair in life and now only the husk of him. "He was told what would come of him and his blue soldiers if he did not heed what the council said to him. He didn't hear them, though. He didn't listen." She was Moon Woman in the Dark, this one who spoke. She had an awl in her hand she had been using to reach inside a blue soldier's belly to see what she could find there. Whatever it was she found had contained much blood and some white sinew in it.

"I would like to open up this Long Hair," Moon Women in the Dark said. "I believe it would be interesting to inspect his heart. Do you suppose there is such a thing inside this dead chief?"

"There would be a heart," I said, "as there is in any man or woman. That I am sure of. Look at all the blood which came out through the hole in his chest. He had to have a heart to do that. Did it do other things, too, that heart? Did it only beat? That is what I would want to know. But to open him up would not reveal that answer."

"That is true," Long Robe Moving said. "But this man when he was alive was the husband of a Cheyenne woman. We should not cut him up like the others, just to look."

"But he needed to hear," Moon Woman in the Dark said. "Husband to a Cheyenne woman or not, he did not listen well."

"Let me have your awl," I said to her. "I will work it through his ear holes, and see if we can open up his hearing so that he will hear well in the other world where he lives now."

"Let me do it myself," Moon Woman in the Dark said. "It's my awl we have to use here. I can use it. And if I can't look inside his chest for his heart, I should be able to open up his ears for him."

"Yes," Long Robe Moving said. "You should do that now, and after then there is a thing I would do to the body of this Long Hair, a thing that has long needed doing."

"He was the husband of Monahsetah," I said, "who told me many times that she loved him, despite all she could do not to do that. And she had a child which he made in her. Yellow Bird he is named."

"That's what I want to do is intended to remedy," Long Moving Robe said. "I would recognize the misuse of Monahsetah which Long Hair made when he took her to his bed all those times. When he put a child in her and she grew it so it could come out and live. Yet when Long Hair acted not as a good husband should, he made himself deserving of being punished."

"You do not mean to cut his body or to pound a corn stone against his head, do you?" I said. "For I think such treatment of the body of her husband, white man and chief of the blue soldiers though he was, Monahsetah would not approve."

"No, she is a woman of the Cheyennes, and her wishes must be observed and carried out. All I would do is place a long thin cottonwood stick in the part of him which he placed in the body of Monahsetah, and I would push that stick far enough up his seed planter that he would never be able to put it in a woman again, in this world or in the one where Long Hair dwells now."

"Monahsetah would approve of that action," I said. "I know she would."

"Let me get to work on his ears and get that done," Moon Woman in the Dark said. "Then I want to tend to that blue soldier lying beside the bush yonder. I think he's still alive a little and is playing dead. I'll find out what's the truth about that situation as soon as I can get to it."

I left them, then, those two and the rest of the women working away on top of the hill where Long Hair and his little chiefs were wiped out like toy dolls on that hot day. That was the time when the dust and smoke mixed up so well with the sound of the eagle bone whistles and the gunshots and the cries of men fighting and dying that all things became one. And that one thing I saw grow like a green tree, and I knew it would stay. From then on that place where we killed Long Hair and the blue soldiers we would call the Greasy Grass. That would be its true name, no matter what the white men might say about it.

Waymon Needler

AS GENERAL GEORGE ARMSTRONG CUSTER, AT THE LAST STAND ON CALHOUN HILL

JUNE 25, 2001

IN PAST REENACTMENTS, AN ATTEMPT HAD BEEN MADE TO REPRESENT in real time the entire last couple of hours of the popularly named "Last Stand." What that meant to the actors playing the role of the companies with the general was that they had to come all the way up from the Little Bighorn on foot and horseback, pursued by the mob doing the Sioux and Cheyenne roles, reach the top of the hill where they'd cluster around GAC and the officers and men left to defend at that point, witness the charge of Crazy Horse, and endure being killed, manhandled and tortured by the tribal women, and then rise up resurrected to take their bows. All this activity would involve nervous horses and running on foot, and blanks going off, and rubber foam arrows being launched to bounce off and maybe hit somebody in the eye. And all this in the midst of whatever the weather would bring in any given year. Hot sun, blistering winds, storm clouds, rain at times, even numbing cold one year, and the whole production being viewed by an audience which had to move along with the players, red and white, Indian and trooper, as they rode and ran hither and yon for up to two hours, come what may.

It had gotten to be too much, for the reenactors, certainly, but especially for the spectators, those who paid good money for the show and who expected a modicum of comfort to be provided to enable them to enjoy the spectacle. Picture, if you will, a whole herd of older people, women and men, and some children as well, being expected to charge up a steep incline with uneven ground dotted with thorns and brush, and finally at the top, required to stand around huffing and puffing and overheated to watch the general and the Seventh Cavalry be slaughtered at end of day.

It proved to be problematic and increasingly unattractive, and consequently we were all coming to our wits' end. Everything seemed to be shrinking and dwindling. Though the white reenactors who'd traveled hundreds of miles to get there could be depended upon to continue doing their parts—they were historical enthusiasts, after all, if not fanatics—the local Native Americans had become increasingly reluctant. They began demanding exorbitant subsidies to participate. They claimed to be getting tired of the whole charade, as one of the current chiefs once remarked in a famously contentious public meeting. Let his name not be forgotten. It was Larry Waits on the Badger.

Faced with all this, who stepped in and saved the day and made the reenactment possible, not to say profitable, once more? Alec Murray, that's who. Say what you will, he has an eye for what makes a dramatic production go and stay the course. And he came through like a champ.

I was considering all this past history with its problems and the solution found to them as I sat on my horse, a nice quiet mare that would not jump suddenly at the sound of gunfire and screams and shouts and bugle calls. I was waiting at the location Alec called the final venue, and that very name is a tip-off as to what shape the reenactment now took. Here's what Alec came up with to address the increasingly serious problems we were having with staging. Break it up into parts, he said. Just that. Forget attempts to reproduce real-time production. Have a beginning act, an intermediate act, and the final one, that scene of the Last Stand itself.

"Learn from Shakespeare," Alec had said. "Learn from the Greeks. Give your audiences seats to sit on, for Pete's sake. Don't try to show each and every step. Cut to the chase. This is not history, after all. It's a gesture at history, which is all folks can bear to watch. Learn from a movie as early as *Birth of a Nation*. Move from one dramatic moment to the next without all the stuff in between. It's show business we're talking about. Not the recreation of the world minute by minute. Only God can do that. And even he makes mistakes at times. We can't afford to."

We took his advice, and as Alec says whenever the box office results are counted up at the end of each fiscal year, "Good God, how the money rolls in."

So I was beginning my moment as GAC at the point when the general was backed up on the hill, surrounded, hostiles swarming all around, Crazy Horse having done his thing, and the end truly in sight. All this is to say, my time as the Son of the Morning Star was occurring in the middle of things, and I was the central actor of this unfolding drama about to appear to the spectators perched on the portable stands and milling about the other side of the cordoned-off area marked by yellow police tape. I was expected to be instantly convincing as Custer. I had to be. It was my first time in the role, but that could be no excuse. The show works or it flops. I couldn't work up to it or into it. I had to perform as though I had been transported by space ship from some other planet, dropped down into an entirely new environment, and required to start emoting.

Talk about pressure, talk about dramatic urgency, talk about method acting, I don't want to even think about it. What'll I do to prepare, I had asked Alec. It's all so sudden and so demanding emotionally. What did he say? You guessed it. "Just do it," he said. "You're an actor. Act."

At the sound of a single bugle call, one which was not actually in the repertoire of a cavalry bugler in the nineteenth century, the action on the crest of Last Stand Hill was to start. I sat on my horse, Suzanne, who had dropped her head to graze at something growing on the ground before her, and I was thinking two things simultaneously, one thought inevitable and the other just plain silly, the way my mind always works in moments of stress. First, I was telling myself, be the man, be Custer, look the part, sit up straight, be prepared, don't look at the audience, channel what you're attempting to reproduce faithfully and well, and don't fall off this fucking horse. That was the series of inevitable and logical thoughts I was having while I waited for the bugle to sound the beginning of the next thirty minutes of dramatic action. The silly thought, the one occurring simultaneously? What is my horsie eating and what if it upsets her tummy and makes her throw up?

See what I mean about the way a divided mind will bedevil you? That you don't need as an actor. In fact, you need no mind at all as an actor. If you're thinking, you're not acting. And if you're not acting, you're a dead man. All this was roiling in my head like an overactive washing machine, and then it came, two silver notes from the bugle being blown to launch the last venue. I involuntarily shivered as though suddenly cut by a chill wind from northern Canada. This is it. The big time.

I looked up, lifting my head slowly as I had planned to begin my opening moment as GAC, swiveling my view from right to left and back again as General Custer would have done as he surveyed the Sioux and Cheyennes closing in on the remnants of his Seventh Calvary companies at bay on that fateful crest. As I did so, I caught the eye of one of the Indian reenactors from the Pine Ridge reservation. He was kneeling in the circle of warriors waiting for the signal to commence his performance, a vintage rifle in his hand and a really well-done headdress in place—he was wearing running shoes, though!–and he mouthed words at me, a message which proved instrumental in getting me started on the right foot.

"I'm going to kill you, Custer," he said, and I could have kissed him as I read his lips. Whether he truly meant what he said didn't matter. He had presented me with that magic gift. The cue.

"Bring it on, buster," I mouthed back, and the last act began. All thoughts of who I was and what I was attempting to do simply vanished. In their place came calmness, a settled sense that I was now about to meet my fate on that isolated and barren hill in the western wilderness. I would not survive this day physically, I knew, but if I performed my duty and accepted what the gods of battle had chosen, I would not truly die, but would live in the mystic annals of history forever.

They came then, the Sioux and Cheyennes, all rising as one, no longer at long range with their attacks confined to arrows and rifle shots, but in close battle between troopers and savages one by one, hand-to-hand, club and knife and fist meeting flesh and blood and bone. My brothers, Tom and Boston, stood beside me, joined as one, the encouraging cries of the spectators in the bleachers sounding all around us as we awaited the inevitable. Poor Boston, I thought, as a thought relevant only to a big brother raced through my fully disengaged, therefore perfectly attuned, mind. He's so young to have to die on this hill in front of all these strangers.

Tom was saying something to me, leaning close to speak into my ear as the roar of battle consumed the very air around us, "General," he was saying, "your revolver, your revolver."

"What, Tom," I said, looking not at him but at an Indian warrior moving toward me with his rifle ready to fire. "What about my revolver?"

"Pull it, Waymon," he said, "get it out of the holster, and start banging away. Custer wouldn't have been just standing there like a duck hit in the head."

"That's insubordinate talk," I said, pulling the revolver and getting off a shot at the Indian before me as he surprisingly stood stock still as though waiting to die. "In the midst of battle, you dare to criticize your commanding officer. What sort of brother are you?"

"That's a good one," Tom said and pointed to the Indian with the rifle, now toppling to the earth with a lot of spinning action and kicked-up dust added to his descent. "Did you hear what he just said? He said the word *finally* when you pulled trigger at last. Tired of waiting around to be shot, I guess."

"Stop talking crazy, Tom," I said. "You're sounding addled. Straighten up, and help me make these savages pay dearly."

"You are a riot, Waymon," Tom said. "Please stop, or I won't be able to keep from laughing."

"If you weren't my brother and we weren't in the middle of fighting against impossible odds, I'd have you court martialed for expressing such cowardly sentiments," I told Tom. "Be a man. Be a soldier."

"Puh-lease," said my brother, the winner of two Congressional Medals of Honor for valor on the battlefield, now obviously driven into hysterical madness by the destruction of the Seventh Cavalry taking place before us. "I'm begging you to let up. I can't hold back. I'm about to start giggling."

"For that I'd shoot you myself," I said to him, "but for the filial bond and the situation in which we find ourselves. Straighten up. Go down fighting."

"You can't shoot me. I'm supposed to be the one who shoots you," he said, "not the other way around. And isn't it past time to punch the blood pack on your chest? I can't shoot you until you do that and fall over for your big finish."

"The blood pack?" I said, tapping my chest toward which Tom had gestured and feeling an instant impact as I did so. A bullet must have hit me in the middle of my breast, just below the pendant I wore beneath my clothing, at the very moment I had lifted my hand to touch the spot Tom had indicated. A fountain of red sprang from beneath my buckskin garment, unaccompanied by any pain, telling me by that lack of sensation that the wound was serious and probably fatal.

A swimming in my head just behind my eyes began to make itself evident, my legs felt as though they no longer existed, and I found myself sinking to my knees, though I sensed no loss of perspective as I saw before me a Sioux warrior moving deliberately in my direction, his steps unaccountably slow and plodding as he came nearer. I was able to discharge my revolver into his body, and he carefully sat down as though he had been served a plate of food to eat which he must take while at rest. He took a deep breath, mumbled something, and lay down.

My eyes felt heavy, and I could not keep their lids open, slumping toward Tom who had knelt beside me as I sank more deeply toward the dusty ground beneath me. "That was a hell of a bit of business you did with the blood," Tom was saying. "And just in time, too. You saved me from busting wide open in front of all these people."

"People?" I said. "What people?"

"Mom and Pop and Billy and Sue from Akron and all their kinfolks, I mean. The ones in the paying seats. Are you ready?" Tom said. "I think now's the time. The Indians are starting to have to slow up. They're getting pissed. Things are beginning to look like the pace is off. What I'll do with my gun is I'll hold it away from your ear, so it won't be too loud. It's got a light load, anyway. No more than a cap pistol."

"Tell Libbie," I said to Tom as he lifted his revolver and began to aim it at my head. Why was he doing that? Had he become truly maddened by the battle? "Tell Libbie I always loved her, no matter what. . . ."

"Great last words, Waymon," Tom said. "But you're ad-libbing now, and you're still trying to break me up. Please stop, you funny man. Here's the bang bang, and then you can lie quiet until it's all over. I've got some hand-to-hand and then a big death scene to do. You were great, man. You were great. You knocked them dead."

And then the pistol shot sounded in my ear, and that somehow made me see a cliff with a deep drop into a valley far below it, and it was quiet in the Black Hills, with nobody with me, only two of my dogs, Grip and a dark gray one I'd never given a name to. I would name him now as a cool breeze comes up from the valley below, but I'll wait to do that until I've slept a bit first. I've grown tired, and I'll rest. Maybe I'll name him Montana after I wake from my nap. Maybe Thunder Boy. I'll think about that later, when I've rested and my eyes are open and I can see.

BREVET GENERAL

George Armstrong Custer

COMMANDING OFFICER OF THE SEVENTH CAVALRY, ON CALHOUN HILL, ABOVE THE LITTLE BIGHORN

June 25, 1876

W HERE IS BENTEEN?

That is the question that consumes me, the answer to which will determine the fate of the Seventh Cavalry. Even if he didn't get the message delivered in writing by that Italian trooper, DeRudio, or some name like that, he'll have heard the sounds of guns and battle from across the river. He'd know to come. His battalion's not that far away. I could see his colors earlier with the unaided eye from where we were stopped at the far end of the village, waiting for him for over half an hour. He did not come, then. When enough hostiles gathered to force us to turn back, during the whole pursuit up the hill, our gunfire along with that of the Sioux and Cheyennes was constant and audible.

He knows to ride to the sound of the guns, just as the cavalry always behaved in the war. It was the heart of true strategy then and is now. That principle never needs stating. Benteen's heard me recite that slogan in every staff meeting as though it was one of the Ten Commandments. Why isn't he here yet? It's clear that Reno's battalion is cornered for a while, so there's no immediate help for me there. But there's no excuse for Benteen's bunch.

The look in his damned eyes themselves puts me in mind of the countenance of Lawrence Barrett as he played Cassius in those wonderful performances in New York back in the winter. His eyes are empty and gray, and they glint like shards of flint in the sun, flat sharp pieces sheared off to make arrowheads in the way the Sioux used to employ when I first knew them. There is no bottom to them, no depth, not in Benteen's eyes and not in the traitor's in Shakespeare's play. Lawrence would make that stunning revelation of his evil intent evident early on in the drama, speaking as Cassius, and then he would turn his face halfway toward the audience so that the lanterns threw light and shadow in such depth that he looked positively malevolent. His eyes were naught but surface, as are Benteen's.

What was the phrase, the character analysis given? "He hath a lean and hungry look," some player said of Cassius. "Such men are dangerous." I can't remember the character or the actor who delivered that line, as fixed as I was upon studying the features of Lawrence Barrett, to the exclusion of all others. Each time I attended a performance, I sensed something new and different from the time before. I knew that Lawrence was not consciously changing his interpretation of Cassius and his deception from one performance to the next. But I soon realized that his understanding of the truly treacherous nature of that creature was so profound that to view Lawrence's presentation again and again did not simply confirm for me the nature of man in his least loyal state. It revealed layers upon layers of the complexity of evil. That portrait of betrayal spoke volumes to me.

When Lawrence protested to me at one point, I think it must have been after the twenty-fifth straight performance of his Cassius in the production of *Julius Caesar* I'd attended, that I had to be getting quite bored by sitting through so many nights at the same place in New York, he was duly impressed by my response. "Lawrence," I told him, "I go each night to watch you perform not because you are my dearest and best friend, but for a quite different reason, one not tied to affection."

"Oh," said he, with that humorous and droll expression so characteristic of his wit. "Should I be disappointed or downcast by this admission?"

"Hardly," I said. "I go for professional reasons. I go to understand more fully the true nature of what I must face each day in my military profession. And that is jealousy, envy, rapacious greed, vaulting ambition, character assassination, malignity of the first order, and determined resistance to all things devoted to the successful carrying out of duty."

"Oh, my," Lawrence Barrett had said in response to that revelation, "I am humbled to be of such service to my dearest friend, and I grieve for what you must endure daily in your attempts to serve our nation."

Were Lawrence here at this moment, with an overwhelming number of warriors rising up to send arrows and lead into the defenders on this hill, I would remind him of his portrayal of Cassius and what it meant to me, and I would point to Benteen as proof of the accuracy of my interpretation of what I had learned in viewing forty performances of Julius Caesar in New York. Here is your betrayer. Here is your derelict from duty. Here is the man who dooms my command and my mission. And though he is called Captain Benteen of the Seventh Cavalry, his real name is Cassius. I will miss Lawrence particularly, among some others. But the one blessing that I can wholeheartedly appreciate is that my friend Lawrence is not here on this hill in Montana, surrounded by howling warriors thirsty for blood.

Not many men or officers are left to defend. The number of our horses has steadily been dwindling, and we'll soon be reduced to shooting the ones left to use as shields against the bullets and arrows. My heart aches when I think of my brothers and my nephew and my brother-in-law, all the Custer chicks in one basket, a circumstance I had worked to create to let us be together as a family. Now it's one I regret to the depths of my being.

Tom is a soldier, his relationship to me of no real consequence in behavior. First and foremost, he's a soldier. He might well have been on this hill, fighting as long as he's able, no matter who might have been his commanding officer. He's the Congressional Medal of Honor winner, not me, and that I do not regard with envy but with joy and pride. He will die as a soldier, in the role he has chosen for himself. So be it. It's the others I cannot bear to think of. The young ones, the unprofessionals, the skylarkers.

I think of Libbie, back at Fort Lincoln, and as she was in Michigan as Libbie Bacon, a desirable young woman far above me, as her father explained in no uncertain terms. I was not of her class and never would be, he announced. But I got her, and she was wild to be with me, and what earned her for me was not my rank at the time, but what I could do for her as a man. I will not let myself specify details. But let it suffice that though we cannot have children, we have been good to each other as husband and wife. And I have so far by now outranked her small-town father that I've not needed even to speak to him for years, much less show deference and drop my head in his presence.

That I never did with him, drop my head and speak in soft tones, on any occasion I ever spoke at all to the old bastard. And quite soon after I'd taught his treasured daughter what she really should appreciate and relish in a man—and she did, she did love what I was to her as a man—he learned to drop his eyes before his son-in-law, the youngest brevet general ever in the United States Army, and to brag to others about what a catch his sweet daughter Libbie had made.

Not like his first comment to me, the fact that he'd learned I ranked last in my class at the Point when they released us for service against the rebels. I mumbled something apologetic, not saying what I wanted to express, that I might have failed a course in natural philosophy but that I'd ranked first, not only in my class but at the entire Point, in horseman-ship. My revenge has been that for years now I've not needed to mealy-mouth any man, least of all my small-town father-in-law in Michigan.

And all that's ever concerned me domestically since those early days has been the notice taken by some and remarked by many that the reason George and Elizabeth Custer have no offspring is due to a shortage in maleness on my part. Having no way to answer that charge, one way or the other, and not knowing the truth about the matter and how to obtain it, I made no challenge to such suppositions. We had not a child. Was it due to a flaw in me? Perhaps so. If so, I will not complain. Neither will I explain.

Ah, yes, but then. But then, indeed, did occur an event which relieved me of all worries and doubts pertaining to such a topic. From then on, I had naught to plague me or to cause me to doubt my virility as man and possible father, though I could not announce such nor make it public. I could tell myself, however, the good news, and the best audience for me has always been myself. And the source of my new assurance was a woman whose name I could not acknowledge and whose relationship to me I could never admit.

And this woman proved to be both much easier and much more dif-ficult to conquer than Libbie Bacon had been. She was Monahsetah, a woman of the Cheyennes, one whose beauty and grace I had noted at the Washita when I routed Black Kettle's warriors and destroyed his enormous herd of ponies, thereby rendering him and his warriors of no threat to order for the foreseeable years to come. Lieutenant Samuel Springer had brought her and two other young women to my headquarters tent after the battle itself had ended successfully, a few of the several women he had chosen from the lot the men had rounded up and held in a group.

Sam had proven to be a good judge of horseflesh and woman flesh over the years I've known him, and I'd come to depend on his powers of observation. As soon as I saw the creature I grew to know as Monahsetah, I had eyes for no other in that collection and so informed my expert procurer of a supply of females. "Lieutenant Springer," I'd said, "you may remove these other two, comely as they are, and allow the other officers to take a look at them. This one here will suit me just fine."

"As soon as I took note of this one, I concluded that she would meet your requirements, General," he said. "You might want to have her lift that garment up a bit so as to furnish you a glimpse of calves the likes of which are seldom seen on an Indian woman. They tend to be a bit skinny for my taste, their legs do, ordinarily. I guess that comes from the squaws having to do all the carrying of loads in a village, as lazy as the bucks usually are."

"I won't need to have you indicate the fine points of any woman, Lieutenant," I'd said. "But thank you for doing such a fine job of recognizing my taste. I can take over from here."

"Yes sir," Springer said. "She's been thoroughly searched, and she's not carrying a single weapon of any sort now. She did have a knife in her belt, but she's unarmed as she stands. I hope you can get her to look at you. Nobody else can."

Monahasetah was not armed with a physical weapon, as the lieutenant had said, but her mental defenses were formidable. Far be it from me to specify the details of the interactions between a man and a woman getting to know each other, but suffice it to say that a prize won too cheaply is seldom worth the getting of it. This prize was precious, its obtaining was hard fought, and its enjoyment was deeply relished.

I had intended the relation between me and this dusky beauty to be brief like others of its sort, perhaps remembered for a time, possibly fondly regarded in idle moments, but it proved to be lasting in a manner which has not been true of any other meeting of the heart and body I've enjoyed over the years. Save that of Libbie, I must hasten to declare. The result of my coming into possession of Monahsetah was not only an excitement that could never be forgotten, but it informed me practically that the physical flaw which prevented my wife and me from conceiving a child was not mine but Libbie's. My perfect wife was proved to be hampered by a lack after all.

Monahsetah in due time gave birth to a child, a male of distinctive skin and hair color which has given rise to great supposition among officers, men, members of the Cheyenne and Sioux nations, and other gossips of many descriptions. Not to be counted among these eager news sharers, however, is my good and dear Libbie, a loyal and trusting wife. She has never voiced a suspicion to me, and I have not brought up that topic ever. I have myself never seen this child, one named Yellow Bird, as I've heard, and I've never intended to do so. There are countless Indian children I've never met or felt an impulse to see. Such is true of this one. Why should he be different? He is but one of countless many of his breed, as far as I'm concerned. And I've not yet seen him.

I'll never have the opportunity to do so after this day, but I'm certain that gossip will echo down the ages. Let that be. A great man attracts hordes of small creatures following in his wake, eager to consume the crumbs he scatters.

What I must attend now is the need to counter a great number of enemy warriors creeping, crawling, and dancing nearer each moment toward our last line of defense. That cannot last much longer unless Benteen, he of the cold flat affectless gray eyes, arrives in support and relief. Our packs of ammunition are near depletion, our soldiers capable of continuing to return fire steadily shrinking in number, the horses left to us few and that few crazed with arrow wounds. All appears dark and impossible and final.

Would that I had a battalion of Jeb Stuart's rebel cavalry with Major John Pelham's horse artillery on its way to relieve us, Stuart with his glistening blue eyes so expressive of his character and intent, traitor to his nation though he was. He would not agree with that description of himself and his cause, and he would argue the point with energy. You would have no doubt ever where he stood, and if he heard the sound of guns he would ride to it, as hard and as fast as his steed would take him. And

Pelham, my old classmate at the Point, would that he were here with his cannons loaded with grape shot.

Stuart's long dead now, though, killed at Yellow Tavern, on the charge when he was hit by a single bullet. John Pelham killed on the bank of the Rappahannock by a bit of shrapnel no bigger than a finger, and I find myself on a hilltop in Montana indulging in a dream instead of facing the truth before me. No Benteen will arrive. My troopers will be killed to a man. My poor brothers and nephew will die here, and I'll never get back across the Mississippi River to the East again. I'll never see my dear Lawrence acting Shakespeare on a New York stage again. I'll not see Libbie ever in life again, and I'll never lay eyes on my lightsome maiden, Monahsetah, here on the Great Plains or in any world other than this one. Where do the Cheyennes go when they die? Is there a special purgatory for them? Are they capable of sin? Do they comprehend as we do?

The sound has reached a new level. The dust and smoke are dark as night. Now it's coming, the final push by the Sioux and Cheyennes all around us, and I would stand to face them with my revolver if I were able, but something in my chest won't let me draw the breath I need to lift me from the ground tugging at me. Tom is saying something to me, close enough to my ear that I can feel his breath, but I can't hear what that is. I want to tell him to pay attention to what's going on in front, not to me, and to tell him that good byes are not wanted nor timely, but he's patting me on the shoulder and I can feel that touch, my brother's hand against me, like a caress. I want to lean on my little brother since I can't seem to stay upright on my own. It's always good to have a brother or a wife to touch you and to help keep you standing—you need that—even when you're the youngest brevet general ever commissioned in the grand Army of the Republic, back when you first rode to the sound of the guns.

Libbie Custer
WIFE OF GENERAL GEORGE ARMSTRONG CUSTER, FORT LINCOLN

JULY 6, 1876

I HEARD THE WHISTLE OF THE STEAMBOAT, THE *FAR WEST*, EARLY enough in the morning that light was not yet fully come to Fort Lincoln. The sound of the whistle, three long notes and then two short blasts, did not wake me, since I had slept but little the night before and the nights before that, unable to lie still in the bed Autie and I shared in the house of the Commanding Officer of the Seventh Cavalry. In that bed, I could scarcely close my eyes, much less find slumber, as I lay alone in the darkness and silence.

So when the whistle of the *Far West* sounded, its tone so like a wail or an extended sob one might hear at a funeral or at a wake for the dead, I gave a sudden start in the chair where I'd been sitting for most of the night, and for all the nights before, ever since Autie led the Seventh Cavalry out of the gates of Fort Lincoln, the band playing lilting tunes at first and then as the last horseman passed into the world outside the walls, sequencing its sound of martial music into the piece Autie had grown to love so. "Garry Owen," it was, now become the regimental anthem of the Seventh with its vaunting and exuberant tune of good cheer and vitality, yet touched in every note with a dark tone of loss.

I always felt tears rise up unbidden whenever the bandmaster struck up the sound of "Garry Owen," and Autie would smile as he saw me begin to show that sign of dread and sorrow. "Why, little girl," he asked once, "do you always take the playing of the Seventh's regimental ditty as a signal to weep? Shouldn't it make you happy? It does me; it does the men."

"Oh, Autie," I said, holding back a sob, "when I hear the notes played and of the words that go along with the tune, I fear for your safety and I dread that I may never see you again, as I watch you trot away. You look so brave and beautiful that I fear for what harm may come to you when that song is played somewhere in a place of danger."

Upon hearing that, he had simply, I remember, taken his pipe from his mouth, and pointed it playfully in my direction. "The only ones who should dread hearing the tune of 'Garry Owen' are those enemies to our nation," he said. "They have reason to fear that tune, and we look to nothing but a victory to celebrate and satisfaction for a job well done. That's what 'Garry Owen' says to me and the Seventh."

That was my Autie. And when I started at hearing the long wail of the steam whistle announcing the arrival of the *Far West,* I knew in my heart of hearts that my life had changed forever now. That sound told me that my Autie, my cavalier and my love, was gone from me forever.

The wives and families of the Crow and Ree scouts had already heard news of which the white people in Fort Lincoln had no knowledge. The Indians always knew what we did not, and I wondered how such could be possible. Myles Keogh, with his wonderful Irish wit, joked about the Indians being able to get their news from birds and prairie dogs. We had the telegraph, we had newspapers in most cities, and we had a written language that could be transmitted among us. Yet the Indians always seemed to know what had happened before we did. That was not always true in every case, I must admit. But it was always so when the news was bad. They knew bad news to the core.

Here's how I learned what the wives of the Crow and Ree scouts had already heard about the expedition of the Seventh to the valley of the Little Bighorn. One of the women that I'd taught the rudiments of how to work in a white woman's home, a good-natured squaw who had an unpronounceable name in her own language and a quite rude one in translation, I called Molly. She'd come into the back door of my house, not the front, as I'd taught her with much effort to do, three mornings earlier, refusing to meet my gaze and rubbing her hands together as though to wash them of some lasting stain.

"What's troubling you, Molly?" I said, and then repeated in a simpler term. "You hurt, Molly. How hurt?"

"A great battle," she said. "Many Sioux and Cheyennes. Many blue soldiers fight."

I attempted to question her further, as far as her vocabulary would allow me to do, but she had nothing but those few words to say. She was adamant about not identifying the source of her information, refusing even to acknowledge she understood what I was asking. Several other wives of officers and troopers came to me with the same story, gleaned from other family members of Indian scouts, but with no more detail than I had.

I knew then all I feared to know, and far more than I could stand to contemplate. So when the whistle of the *Far West* sounded on the dawn of that day, letting all hearing it know the full news was soon to be shared, I'd already been unable to convince myself that events could be positive, try though I had in the dark of midnight and beyond in the days prior. I will not yet dress fully for the day's work to come, I told myself. Instead I'll only don the apparel appropriate for my morning duties as a wife with a household to maintain. If I address the day as though it were ordinary and nonthreatening, perhaps that will hold events at bay. If I do not give in to presentiments of disaster and death, those horrors might not be able to take hold and prevail.

I will refuse to borrow trouble before it arrives, and unborrowed trouble might not be able to demand payment. If I have no debt owed to sorrow, perhaps sorrow will not arrive at the door of Mrs. General George Armstrong Custer. It will have no place here, no right to presume, and it will be forced to find lodging in some other woman's home. I would not wish sorrow to exist anywhere, but I will be selfish enough to deny it entrance to my dwelling. Do not knock upon my front door. You are not welcome. You may not enter the place where my husband and I live. Go elsewhere.

The knock when it came was not on the front door of the house. It was at the rear of the dwelling, that door which opens from the outside into the kitchen. Molly already at work, silent in her chores, was the person who opened my house to the sorrow that would enter it now, take up quarters, and never again depart to stay elsewhere.

She came to the front room where I was sitting in the chair by the window, the seat that allowed a full review of the parade ground in the center of the compound of Fort Lincoln, the location I often occupied in the part of the working day when Autie was not in the house, not there to be reading or writing, or taking a meal and talking to me. Molly said nothing, and she did not need to speak to let me know that three or four men had entered the rear of the house and were now waiting in the kitchen for me to admit them. It would be the captain of the *Far West*, I knew, and it would be some officers of the Seventh Cavalry, perhaps a Crow scout if he had something to add to what the white officials knew. One person would not be there, however, I knew, ever again, for something deep in the bones of my legs and chest and arms told them that.

They felt a way I'd never experienced before, my very bones did, the skeleton beneath the flesh, and I knew what that feeling meant. They were empty now to the center. They held nothing. They did not ache. There was no pain. There was simply no life in the bones of my body. They were as empty of feeling and sensation as a desert with nothing but the wind blowing across it and touching no living thing in its progress. No flower. No tree. No weeds. Only dust and rock and sand.

"Officers," I said, as I entered the door leading into the rear of the house where they were standing in full uniform, hats and gloves in hand, three of them. "Tell me what the boat whistle has been saying. Let me hear you translate that into words I can comprehend."

"Oh, Mrs. Custer," the man standing nearest me began to say, an officer whose face I recognized but whose name would not come. Perhaps if I can remember it before he goes on to speak those dark words I cannot bear to hear, what he has to say will change. If I can come up with the proper name and title for this man dressed in the blue uniform of the army of the United States, if I can say it aloud to him before he speaks further, I can by will change what he intends to tell me. I can control what he wants to say has happened, and by controlling it, make it not be.

Stop thinking such madness, I told myself as I searched frantically for the name and rank of the man before me, an officer to whom I'd spoken many times before; stop inventing ways to torment yourself. Let his message come. Be the wife of a soldier, as Autie would have you be. Conduct yourself as duty requires. You may mourn, but you may not whine nor whimper nor cry aloud.

"When did it occur?" I heard myself asking, and as I did, I felt gratitude for having come up with a maneuver to avoid having to hear this bearer deliver in words the worst message I would ever hear in my life. Act as though what he will tell you is news already known and is being dealt with. Let him know you will not conduct yourself in such a manner that the subject becomes your state, your condition, in the current moment. Give Autie and the Seventh the stage they've earned and will populate for all time. This moment is not yours to taste and spit out. Hold yourself in control. "Was it about a week ago?"

"Yes, ma'am," the officer said, a captain I suddenly knew, a Captain Abner Fitzpatrick. "Around that time. The bulk of the battle was on June 25TH, the best we can figure it. Almost two weeks ago."

"Was all the Seventh Cavalry lost?" I said. "All officers and all men?"

"Mrs. Custer," one of the other men in the group spoke up, a young lieutenant, lifting a sheaf of papers as though to prove his words, "we do have a preliminary listing of all those identified on the field, those still reporting, and a list of names of those not yet known as perished or present."

"How many names of persons who have family here at Fort Lincoln?" I said, congratulating myself on asking that question which I had not thought of previously, but which came to me unbidden. It is like my bones, I thought, as I waited for an answer. My bones are now empty and dead within, beneath my flesh which is of no further use in this world without Autie here with me, yet they function to hold me up. And my breath comes and goes, and my heart sends blood throughout my arteries and veins to keep me conscious and capable of asking questions and comprehending answers. I would not have believed I could die and yet still walk about and converse with others. Is it a miracle? Or am I truly dead and don't yet know it? The news from all regions of the country which is Libbie Bacon Custer has not yet reached the capital city. The streets are quiet and appear undisturbed.

"I count there to be twenty-six women who reside at Fort Lincoln, who have husbands that perished."

"That would be twenty-seven counting me, right?" I said. "Twenty-seven widows of the Seventh Cavalry here at Fort Lincoln. I have all but one of those to notify this morning of their loss."

"Mrs. Custer," Captain Fitzpatrick said, "That matter need not be yours. We are prepared to handle that obligation. We will relieve you of that task."

"Oh, no," I said. "After I have suitably prepared myself, I will speak to each woman who must be informed about her husband. That is my duty as the wife of the commanding officer of the Seventh Cavalry, and I will fulfill it in a timely fashion."

"You needn't, ma'am," the captain said.

"Oh, yes, I must. There can be no misunderstanding about that. My husband would expect it of me, and in his absence I will not go counter to what I know to be my duty to him and to the wives of those who served with him in the Seventh Cavalry. Just give me a few minutes to don proper attire. Who will accompany me with the list of those women?"

"I will do so, Mrs. Custer," the captain said, "as will any other of us you will require."

"Choose two more men, please," I said. "To go with me to take care of eventualities, if need be. I will meet you outside the front door of this house in ten minutes."

There, I said to myself as I left the room, I was able to get that business addressed and taken care of without having to hear any person say to me that Autie is dead. No one has yet uttered those words, and I will find ways to delay hearing them spoken as long as I can manage. I can say them within my own mind, but I need not utter those syllables aloud to any soul. I need not allow anyone to say such to me. Not yet. Not just yet.

There will be tears and wailing cries of anguish from some of the women I will visit, and some will have already heard and some will have not. The worst will be those who already know he's dead, whoever he is, because when they hear from me what they already know, the numbness will have faded to a degree. And the pain will have begun to announce itself, and it will do that as a lack of something, not a presence. And the worst thing a woman can endure is not a presence, but the lack of a presence. That is what tortures and sears. It is the not-ness that appalls, not the here-ness.

I must prepare myself as best I can for not-ness and lack of presence. It is a long road I must travel, and it will be dry and solitary and filled with dust. But Autie would require me to take up my duty and perform it. And I will do that. I will take that first step and let the others follow. I will not faint or falter on the way.

Here is what I will say always, and it's what I have said before to him. I would not be prideful in offering my own meager stock of words in homage to my marriage to George Armstrong Custer those years ago in Michigan, a marriage which will continue in life until I leave this world and beyond that, if such can be granted.

Here is what I told him on our wedding day. I repeat it, and then I must go to the widows with my news of not-ness and lack of presence. "Autie," I said to him, "I would be, as a wife should be, part of her husband, a life within a life."

And if loving with one's whole soul is insanity, I am ripe for an insane asylum. With that quotation of my own words, I go to the widows of the Seventh Cavalry, those bestilled and residing now in not-ness in the emptiness of Fort Lincoln. Here is where you are, I will tell each and every one. You know where you were, and no one can finally know where she will be. You must walk that road alone, in heat, in cold, in dust, and in rain.

Waymon Needler
ON I-29 NEAR SIOUX FALLS, SOUTH DAKOTA

June 30, 2001

*M*IRABEAU HAD DOZED OFF AND ON EVER SINCE WE PACKED THE last bit of our belongings in the Highlander, and I had taken the first shift in the driving we would be doing from the southeastern corner of Montana all the way home to East Texas. He seemed to be sunk deeper than ever into sleep at the point on the interstate where the exits to Sioux Falls start coming up, three for this town. There'd be more and more ways to exit for each place we came to from now on, as we moved out of the lightly populated West and worked our way back to where there was plenty of water to use in farming and industry.

I was considering whether to take the first exit to make a gas stop, looking down at the gas gauge and estimating how much longer we could go without having to fill up, when I noticed that Mirabeau had opened his eyes and was looking at me straight on. That was unusual, he being the kind of guy who hardly ever looked directly at another human being, even when deep in conversation. I'd never been able to tell if that habitual way of avoiding connection was a personal quirk or just ethnic tribal behavior.

Put another way, was Mirabeau consciously conveying a little insult every time he talked to another person or was he acting out another instance of Native American contempt for the whites he had to deal with?

273

Was he meaning something? No big deal, my thinking that, just a way to try to fill the time in my mind when I was not fully occupied with matters of work or play. I've always wanted to understand why folks keep finding ways to let me know they hold my existence to be a lot less serious matter than I do.

"Well, what did you think of this year's debriefing, Waymon?" Mirabeau said, using a tone a lot less weighty than any I was accustomed to hearing from him, though I was having to note that from an angle. I was driving at the interstate speed limit, after all, and that required close attention to what was going on in front of the vehicle. That was a lot more important than good eye contact. "How do you think it compared to other ones? Was it the same, different, worse? What?"

"Better, a lot better," I said. "A lot more relaxed and a lot less drinking of the white man's firewater than usual. Nobody argued or threatened anybody else. None of the females screamed at each other or started crying."

"You know what caused that, don't you? You could tell what was going on, couldn't you?"

"Not as many people? More new ones than before in previous debriefs? Less big speechifying by Alec and the old-timers? Is that what you mean?"

"All that's results, Waymon," Mirabeau said, sitting up straight behind his tightly buckled seat belt and still looking at me, a real first and a sustained one. "What's the cause? And before you give me your opinion, let me tell you mine."

"Do it. Lay it out there. I'm ready for instruction."

"It's because we've done it, you and me, and it's a completed action. And that means it's really over with, and it can't be repeated. That's why we see the last debriefing that way."

"What do you mean, Mirabeau?" I said. "Everything we do out in Montana is repeat stuff every year. That's the name of the game for a reenactor. Isn't it? The more the same, the better, right? And by the way, do you want to stop for a break up here at this next exit?"

"If we don't need gas, let's keep percolating. Keep those big wheels turning. But let me tell you what I've figured out. Here it is. Why have we kept coming out here every June for years?"

"You know why. Do I have to tell you that? We talk about it all the time."

"Wrong," Mirabeau said. "We lie about it all the time. We don't talk about it. We really come out here so you can finally become the Son of the Morning Star, the man himself, George Armstrong Custer. And I come out here so I can get to be Crazy Horse, and wear a magic stone behind my ear and paint a lightning bolt on my face and put hailstone marks all over my chest. That's why we come out here, and it's been a long damn road."

"But we've done that now. We made it. Is that what you're saying?"

"That's precisely what I'm saying, Waymon. You became Custer, and for the time you commanded the Seventh Cavalry, you were him and him alone. And you died as Custer, and you know as well as I do that there ain't no coming back from the dead."

"You didn't die as Crazy Horse, though. He survived the Little Bighorn."

"The Greasy Grass, Waymon. The Greasy Grass, and yes I survived that, but Crazy Horse was dead in less than a year, killed by his own people. He was a walking dead man as soon as he left that battlefield. Hoss, it is over with. It was for him back then, and it is now. All the posturing. All of it, every bit, from little detail to big picture and back again. "

"Well, this year's reenactment's over with, sure," I said. "But you know that the month of June rolls around every year, and it's coming again, just like a freight train. It always does, every twelve months. Right?"

"All right," Mirabeau said, still fixing his eyes on me. I felt like I was starting to sweat under their weight, even as cool as the AC always stays in the Highlander. I'm talking Japanese quality in the manufacture of automobiles. You can't beat it. The heater's as good as the AC, too. "Let me put it this way, Waymon. I'll ask you face-on, and stop hinting around. Are you coming back again? Will you get into this SUV in a little less than twelve months from now and head west again to put on a costume and ride around on an official national battlefield site? Will you, Waymon?"

"No," I said, the word bursting from my throat as though I was coughing up something that had stuck in my esophagus and was about to choke me to death. I had to get it out or quit breathing oxygen. "No, I won't, Mirabeau. I won't."

"Why not?"

"Been there, done that," I said, falling back upon a cliché but knowing it was perfectly responsive to Mirabeau's question.

"Me neither," he said. "And I'll tell you why, just to add to what you said. You can't die twice, and still live with yourself. That's why."

"That sounds completely crazy, but it's right," I said. "When Tom Custer blew my brains out, he did all he could do for George Armstrong Custer. He was dead, then, and he wasn't coming back. And you know what?"

"What?" Mirabeau Lamar Sylestine said. "Tell it on out, Waymon."

"I want to think about other things now, not just Custer's Last Stand, things like a whole new way of preparing my students at Annette High to look at kitchen chores and cooking responsibilities. Suppose I set up a brand new series of practical experiences allied with artistic and cultural layers of meaning? Suppose I lead the girls to think of what they do in the kitchen to be not simply the practice of homemaking but a chance to express their individual artistic and creative impulses? What if I install a new philosophy of home economic management? Just throughout all the curriculum? What if I rethink everything I've been doing for as long as I've been teaching the economy of the home in American culture? What would be wrong in starting from the ground up?"

"You've been thinking about something like that for a while, haven't you, Waymon? But not saying a word until now, because you were afraid to. Now that you've been in the shoes of the Son of the Morning Star and found you could wear them just fine, you're ready to try on a new set of footwear."

"Something like that," I said, "but I'm not able to say it as well as you just did."

"You know, what you just said about taking a new road, that's what I'm thinking for myself," Mirabeau said. "In my own realm, of course, but just like you in principle. You know what? I'm leaving Annette, Texas, and I'm not going to try to stay near the reservation for a spell. I am taking a job in Houston, one they keep offering me at TechTonics, Incorporated, and I'm going to live in my own apartment and spend some money and dress up and meet some new folks and get a girlfriend and have myself a time."

"You're not going back to the res? I can't believe that."

"Maybe at times I will. Who knows? I've not fastened there, and I'm not doomed to wander off looking for the magic white buffalo any more. I don't have to do that, if I don't feel like it. I can take a break from myth."

"Hoka hey," I said. "It's a good day to die."

"Bullshit," Mirabeau said, starting to laugh. "I know something better than that to say. Sing it with me, Waymon. Come on, you Son of the Morning Star."

Then he began to hum, and after he'd found the tune he wanted, he started off with the words. After the first ones floated out into the cool air of my Japanese SUV, I was able to join right in, the lines of the song coming without my having to strain a bit.

Please, Mr. Custer, I don't wanna go.
Hey, Mr. Custer, please don't make me go.
I had a dream last night
About the coming fight.
Somebody yelled attack
And there I was with an arrow in my back!

Mirabeau Lamar Sylestine and I sang that whole song from 1960 by Larry Verne, all the verses and the chorus over and over, that seriously unserious one-hit wonder I'd first heard on the radio when I was a kid, every silly word repeated again and again, until we saw the exit sign ahead. We carried that tune together, looking back and forth from each other to the road, shouting that lyric at full voice like the truly converted in a gospel tent revival as the song transported us all the way into Sioux City, South Dakota, the last stop on the interstate before you cross the Missouri River, that marker that leads toward the Mississippi, the stream that tells you where the East ends and where the true West begins.

It all depends on how you're turned and the final direction you decide to head.

ACKNOWLEDGMENTS

Playing Custer is a novel and makes no claim of allegiance to literal truth. It is, however, based upon a defining event in America's past that occurred in June of 1876 and continues to fascinate historians and commentators, professional and amateur, to this day. Three books on the battle between the Seventh Cavalry and the Sioux and Cheyenne warriors of Sitting Bull's great encampment on the Little Bighorn (or the Greasy Grass— take your pick) have been most helpful to me: Evan S. Connell's *Son of the Morning Star: Custer and the Little Bighorn* (1984); Larry McMurtry's *Crazy Horse: A Life* (2005); and Nathaniel Philbrick's *Custer, Sitting Bull, and the Battle of the Little Bighorn: The Last Stand* (2010). For matters of fact and historic interpretation, I've gratefully depended on these works. All else in this work of fiction can be blamed only on me.

ABOUT THE AUTHOR

GERALD DUFF is a winner of the Cohen Award for Fiction, the Philosophical Society of Texas Literary Award, and the Silver Medal for Fiction from the Independent Publishers Association. A member of the Texas Institute of Letters, he has published nineteen books. He published *Home Truths: A Deep East Texas Memory* with TCU Press in 2011. He resides in Lebanon, Illinois.